LAMORNA
Susanna Lambert

Text Copyright ©2015 Susanna Lambert

Cover illustration ©2015 Elisa Rose Cunningham

http://elisacunningham.com
http://www.facebook.com/elisacunninghamillustration

All Rights Reserved

This book is a work of fiction. Names, characters and incidents are a product of the author's imagination, other than those events clearly in the public domain. Any resemblance to actual persons, living or dead is entirely coincidental.

With thanks to Beth, Amy and Joe

Donations from the sale of this book will be given to various charities. Please check out my Facebook page for updates.

https://www.facebook.com/susannalambertauthor

PROLOGUE

July 4th 1968

'I didn't know my Dad was going to die. I didn't know we'd never come down here again. Nothing's been the same since. Nothing's gone right.'

Lamorna was lost in her childhood, remembering the last time she'd made this journey. The last time she'd crossed the Tamar. Her Dad had told her all about Brunel. How he'd built this bridge. He was always sharing stories about the world with her. And then he was gone. And her life had changed forever.

She'd been hanging out of the window then, trying to see the river far below. Soot had blown into her eyes and the wind had tangled her hair so that her mum had been cross with her at bedtime, dragging a hairbrush roughly through the knots.

Wiping away tears she looked down through the girders. The tide was out and the river was a slow coil between banks of shining wet mud. The train curved around the track into Cornwall, another world, almost another country. She recited the names in her head as she'd always done, anticipating each station, Par for Newquay, St. Erth for St Ives. And suddenly the sea appeared. The familiar sweep of Mount's Bay, and her destination, Penzance, huddled around the shore.

Stepping down onto the platform she looked out across the bay. The turrets of St. Michael's Mount stood out against the blue sky. A flash of sunlight caught a window pane. 'I wonder if that princess is still up there, waiting for her prince to come from over the sea.'

She smiled, and turning felt the warm breeze brush her face, caught a faint scent of sea and salt. A clamour of gulls flew up over the station roof. It was as though the world was new and fresh, and a wave of joy swept through her.

'This is it. My new life starts today.'

Chapter 1

July 5th 1968

Spotting a newsagent shop she ventured in to see if the weekly 'Cornishman' had arrived. Fumbling for her purse, she half listened to the man in front of her.

'A week for starters. Might have more luck getting someone this way.'
He paid, and left the shop. She watched the newsagent pinning a card to a window board.

'Getting someone?' she said to herself, and rushed out to read the advert:
Odd Job Man wanted as soon as possible for busy Hotel. Must be willing to work shifts as required. Some heavy lifting.

The man was walking briskly away now. She ran after him.
'Excuse me. I'm looking for work.'
He turned, looked her up and down, his gaze lingering on her sandaled feet.
'You're just a slip of a girl. Couldn't lift barrels. Wouldn't want to clean the chicken shed'
'Please, wait. I'm stronger than I look, I'm willing to try. I can start now.'
'You haven't asked how much the wage is.'
'How much would you pay me please?'
'Reckon it'd be three pounds a week, with board and lodging.'
'I'll take it.'
'Haven't offered you the job yet.'
She looked hopefully at him, noticing that despite his serious gaze there was a smile in the corners of his mouth.
'And who might you be?'
'Lamorna, Lamorna West.'
He looked surprised. But people always did.
'How did you come by that name?'
'Lamorna Cove was my Mum's favourite place. We used to come down here every summer.'
She watched anxiously as he scrutinised her for a moment before speaking again.
'Don't know what the wife'll say. You can give it a try for a week. But if I get a bloke interested then that's it.'
'Thank you,' she said, smiling.
'Where are you staying? We'd best pick up your things.'
'These are all I have.'
'Well come along then.'

He picked up her rucksack and strode off down the street. She grabbed her other things and hurried after him. He crossed to a small blue van. Painted on its side were the words *'Penlee Hotel.'* He opened the door for her, and she piled her stuff in the back, amongst some wooden boxes and crates. There was a strong fishy smell. She clambered into the seat beside him, negotiating various packages in the foot-well. They drove west along the coast.

'Sorry about the clutter. Been on a few errands. I'm Sam Tremayne. What are you doing down here then?'

'I'm a student. I'm learning photography. I want to get pictures of the standing stones for the course.'

'My son knows all those stones and places. Did a project at school.'

'Oh, that's helpful. He could give me some advice.'

They passed the rest of the journey in silence, Lamorna watching out for glimpses of sea along the route. They turned at last into a driveway bordered by bright red and purple fuchsia.

'Bring your stuff. I'll show you where you'll sleep.'

A dark haired young man came out of a nearby door and crossed towards them.

'Come and help this young lady carry her bags. This is my son, Michael,' he said.

'Oh, I thought he was a schoolboy.'

His blue eyes met hers in a steady gaze that was unsettling.

'Who is she?'

'She's our new odd job man.'

'She's only a girl.'

'Well I can't find a man, and she's willing to give it a go.'

'She could carry her own bags then.'

But he picked them up and took them across to a small brick cottage before turning and disappearing back indoors without another word.

'Sorry he was so rude. He's a bit down at the moment. I'll talk to him.'

'Please don't. It really doesn't matter.'

He led her across to the building. Behind a blue painted door was a small kitchen- come- living area. She saw a stone sink, cooker and a scrubbed wooden table. Across the room was a settee covered in a colourful patchwork and crochet cushions, and a table with a TV set. A couple of wool rugs warmed the stone-flagged floor.

'This'll be your place. You can pick up some stuff from the hotel kitchen, tea, milk. Here's the bedroom.'

He opened a door. There were two single beds separated by a small table and lamp, and a white painted chest of drawers. One corner propped up by a book. Just off this room was a toilet and wash basin.

'It's lovely, but who will I be sharing it with?'

'The other girls and Alec who runs the Bar live in the village, so it's empty right now. Will you be alright on your own?'

'I'll be fine. When do you want me to start?

"Get settled in, and then come across to the door over there. You can eat with us and meet Aileen, my wife. She'll see you have everything you need. You can start tomorrow at six. We've a delivery to unload.'

She gulped at the thought of six o'clock, but managed a smile. She unpacked her bags, folding her clothes into the drawers, and arranging her few belongings on top. She had two pairs of shoes: the sandals and flip flops. 'Might need some stronger shoes for work,' she thought, worrying. She only had a few pounds. She changed into a wraparound skirt which floated around her ankles, and a cheesecloth shirt. And then she went on an exploration of her new home. There was everything she needed. A jumble of crockery all higgledy-piggledy on a wooden dresser. Some blue and white Cornish ware, rose- patterned china, and a bright blue teapot. Someone had left a few old magazines; a couple of paperbacks, and a copy of 'The Hobbit.' There was a local entertainment guide, Summer 67, a year old. She browsed through it for hotel advertisements. Sam would be sure to find a man before long.

A movement outside distracted her. She pulled the net curtain aside and saw the moody son walking across the lawn. He was wearing a faded pair of shorts and a turquoise shirt with sleeves rolled up above the elbow. He was stocky in build with dark brown, almost black hair curling into his neck, and his skin was brown, the sort of colour you get from working outdoors all year round. He disappeared behind what looked like a summer house.

The lawn sloped away down towards the sea. There were borders filled with delphiniums, marguerites and lupins. Amongst them were exotic palms flaunting their spiked hair. Old roses rambled over the wall behind them. She thought about the garden she'd loved in her childhood home. The long summers when she'd helped her dad with sowing and planting.

At twenty past twelve she plucked up all her courage and crossed the yard. Tentatively opened the door. To her horror it creaked loudly. A small, dark-haired woman was standing at a wooden table in the centre of the kitchen, patting dough into balls. She looked up smiling, and held out a floury hand.
'You must be Lamorna. Welcome my dear, I'm Aileen.'
She took the proffered hand without hesitation, warming immediately to this friendly, motherly woman.
'Thank you for giving me a chance, Mrs Tremayne. I won't let you down.'
A chair scraped on the stone floor, and turning she saw the son hurriedly get to his feet, pushing an empty plate away.
'I'll be getting back to work,' he said, striding to the door, and letting it bang shut behind him.
'Take no notice of him. He's been like this since his young woman finished with him. And please call me Aileen. We don't stand on ceremony here. Would you like to just help me finish these splits before we eat?'
'Splits?'
'They're a bit like scones. They're traditional with cream teas down here.'
'You're not Cornish?'
'No, bless you. I've lived here twenty five years, but I'll never be Cornish to local folk. I'm from Ireland. I came over to work in the hotels one summer and I've been here ever since.'

They worked peacefully side by side, rolling the risen dough into balls and placing them on a baking tray.

'These are for the afternoon teas. We open at 3 o'clock for the guests and other visitors. I don't know about you, but I'm ready for my lunch.'

'I'm starving. I only had a small breakfast at the Youth Hostel.'

Aileen bent to open a door on the cooker, and lifted out a large pot.

'Rabbit stew, I hope that's alright with you?'

'Mmmmm it smells wonderful.'

She was serving out the food, and then lifting a loaf of warm bread from the oven, just as Sam appeared.

'Smells good my lover. Michael's cooking the crabs and lobster I got this morning.'

'I've never eaten lobster or crab, any of those. We're so far from the sea. My mum cooks cod or smoked haddock, that's about it.'

'You must try some while you're down here. Can't beat it. Get 'em straight off the local boats when they come in.'

They all tucked into their food, breaking off lumps of the fresh crusty bread to soak up the gravy. Afterwards there was fresh fruit.

'I don't tend to cook a pudding at lunch time.'

'It's a good job. I'm not used to eating so much. I'll be putting on weight.'

'Looks like you could do with that. You're all skin and bone.'

'Sam! Young people now are all slim.'

'I prefer a woman with something to get hold of,' he said, giving Aileen a squeeze.

'What will my work involve?'

'As I said, you're a bit of a jack of all trades. You could help Aileen in the kitchen. Michael will show you how to do the crabs. And you'll work in the garden, weeding, and digging up the potatoes and so on. We need someone who'll fit in like one of the family, willing to turn a hand at whatever's wanted. Michael usually manages all the work, but this summer we've bought a cottage down in the harbour. Doing it up for holiday lets. Michael's working on it. I'll get him to show you how to do the chickens.'

Her heart sank at the thought of chickens and Michael at the same time.

'I'd like a hand preparing for the dinners tonight,' Aileen said, 'and then you could take the rest of the evening off. Tomorrow you'll want to go into Penzance and get some shopping maybe. Sam could give you a lift in.'

Lamorna loaded the crockery into the dishwasher.

'The only things it can't wash are the teapots,' Aileen told her. 'We do them by hand after the cream teas. What brought you down to Cornwall?'

'I used to come for holidays with Mum and Dad. Every year until my Dad died. She and Dad had their honeymoon down here. That's how I got my name. I usually get called Lorna back home though.'

'It's so unusual, I wondered if there was a connection to the village. It's very near here.'

'Yes, we always had to go there.'

'Sam said you're doing photography.'

'I thought I could get some good pictures of standing stones.'

'Isn't that grand now. Michael studied them. He could help you.'

'That's what your husband said, but I don't think he'll be keen.'

'Don't you mind him. He knows we need someone, and we've tried to get a man for weeks now. They don't want to know.' She sighed. 'I'm sorry he's so off hand with you. It's not like him. We never even got to meet his young woman. He won't talk about it, just bottles it up and goes about like a bear with a sore head. Let's have a cup of tea now, before the big afternoon rush, and you can tell me some more about yourself.'

They took their mugs outside, and sat on a garden bench. It was a beautiful afternoon. The scent of stocks and lavender filled the air. Somewhere a blackbird was singing.

'I'm sorry to hear about your Dad.'

'It seems a long time ago now. I was only eight. He was a railway engine driver. Shunting engines. He was crossing the lines after work, and somehow he just didn't see the wagons being moved. No-one could understand it.'

'It must have been hard for you and your Mum.'

'It was. I hated it. My Dad was great; he loved to have me helping him in the garden and making things with him. I was horrible to my Mum after he died, always cross and grumpy. But she would never talk about him. And then she got married again. I've got two younger brothers now. I just have the small box room, and it's not big enough for all my books and photography equipment.'

'That is difficult. It was a bit the same for me, I was the oldest of seven. I had to get a job to help support the others. And then I escaped, met Sam. We've got two great children, Michael, and his sister Ellen and that's my life now.'

'It's an escape for me too. I just needed to get away for a while. I'm hoping to find a place to live with some friends next year. It'll make things easier at home. The boys can each have their own room then.'

The door creaked open and Michael appeared.

'Dad says I'm to show you the chickens. You'd better get some decent clothes on.'

She hurriedly put down her mug, and went off to the cottage. Pulled on jeans and a sweatshirt, and changed into flip flops. He was waiting outside for her.

'Haven't you got any boots?'

'I'll be fine with these.'

She followed him up the garden, and waited whilst he pulled a wheelbarrow from a shed, loaded it with straw and a shovel, and then trundled it over to a wire enclosure. The chicken run must have been an old orchard once. There were ancient gnarled trees bearing small apples and plums, their branches bent almost to the ground like wizened old men stooping to pull up their socks.

Chickens were stabbing at the soil. One of them strutted over and pecked at her foot. She tried to shake it off, and was attacked even more ferociously. Michael waved the shovel, and it retreated, squawking.

'I told you to wear boots. Do you want to just watch me clean the shed?'

'I can do it.'

'Okay. There's a couple of broody hens sitting, but they won't bother you. You've got to shovel out all this old straw, dump it in the barrow, and take it down to the compost. It'll take you three or four trips. Then sweep the shed out and lay the new straw.'

'No problem,' she said, more confidently than she felt.

He led her down the garden to see the compost heaps, and then she was on her own. It was hot and smelly in the shed, and it took six journeys to get rid of the dirty straw. Each time she had to run the gauntlet of one or two chickens. On the last trip she misjudged the path, tipped the straw onto the beetroot plot and had to spend the next half hour carefully clearing it away by hand. She was mortified to see Michael watching her. The sweeping was the worst of all. Still cross with herself, she pushed the broom forcefully across the floor, sending a cloud of filthy dust into the air. Coughing and sneezing she turned for the door, and found Michael blocking her way.

'Here, you need this,' he said, handing her a bucket of water
She could see what she thought was an amused look in his eyes. She took the bucket and drank some of the water.

'The water's for laying the dust.'

'I know that.'
She sloshed water over the floor, starting right by his feet. Of course he was wearing boots, so just stood and watched her, as red with anger and mortification she began to sweep again.

'I probably look like a demented old witch,' she muttered to herself.

'Just what I was thinking,' he said, walking out.
She threw the broom after him. It clattered against the door. Two chickens were startled from their roost in the rafters. They flew down, cackling and flapping around her. The noise set off all the others. She fought her way out and closed the door behind her.

'You're not meant to be killing them,' Michael called.

She stamped back into the shed, took a deep breath, and finished the job. The hens had calmed down now. She could see them sitting on their nest boxes. It didn't take too long to finish the job. She returned the barrow to the shed, and stopped at the end of the garden for a few minutes to look out over the sea. There was a small rocky island just off shore, and a fishing boat, a flock of screaming gulls in its wake, was chugging by. Grey rooftops speckled with yellow lichen tumbled down and away towards the village.

Someone was shouting. She turned and saw Michael hurrying across the garden. She'd left the gate open. Several chickens had escaped and were tearing at lettuces.

'Grab one,' Michael called.
Terrified she picked up a bird, but it struggled and pecked her, so that she dropped it again. Michael was holding two by their feet, and dropping them back into the pen. In the time it took her to catch one more bird he had captured the rest.

'I'm sorry.'

'You'll learn maybe,' was all he said.

It was late now. She rushed indoors to get washed and changed ready to help prepare the teas.

'You've caught the sun,' Aileen said as she came into the kitchen. 'Better be careful with that fair skin. What have you done to your arms?'

'The chickens didn't take too kindly to me, and I'm afraid your son thinks even less of me now.'
She told Aileen her sorry story, and was surprised when the response was laughter.

'You'll soon get used to it.'

'I won't have time to, your husband will be glad to employ the next man.'

'Don't you worry, the fellas round here don't want this kind of work. I think you'll do nicely. What man would want to lend a hand in the kitchen? We need you this afternoon, the sunshine's brought everyone out, and they all want teas.' They prepared the splits, spooning the home-made raspberry jam into dishes, and scooping out the clotted cream.

Mary arrived, and was introduced. Lamorna liked her at once, a smiling local girl of around her own age, dark-hair straggling from under a neat cap. She was dressed in a black dress with a crisp white apron. She and Aileen served the visitors, who were all sitting in the garden under brightly coloured sun umbrellas. The third tray load had gone out when Lamorna heard a commotion. Mary came in laughing.

'There's a chicken loose in the garden, one of the guests spotted it. Michael came to catch it and it, it....' She burst into laughter, and the words spluttered away.

'It shit on his head,' Aileen finished for her. 'I've never seen him look so cross for sure.'

Lamorna's heart sank. It was her fault. This was the end of her job.

The two women forced themselves to stop laughing as they heard the latch on the door. Michael came in, his hair dripping with water.

'I don't know what you're laughing at.'

'Aw, come on, where's your sense of humour?' Aileen said.

Mary was in a corner, stuffing a handkerchief into her mouth. Michael looked across at Lamorna. He left the room, slamming the door. Mary, red-faced with stifled laughter released the hanky in a burst of giggles.

'Don't look so worried Lamorna,' Aileen said. 'It was great entertainment for the guests, and Michael has no say in who we employ.'

'No,' she thought, 'but he can make my life hell.'

It was the busiest Friday they'd had. Lamorna cooked a fresh batch of splits, and was winked at by Aileen when Michael unknowingly praised them at the end of the afternoon.

'Lamorna's a good cook,' Aileen told him. 'Those are her first attempt.'

'Women are best kept in the kitchen,' was his surly response, as he strode off without a single glance at her.

In bed at last, Lamorna stretched out her aching legs. She'd been on her feet all day, made a mess of her first day's work and made an enemy of the boss's son. 'What's gone right?' she thought, 'I made some good splits, and I like Mary and the Tremaynes. Except Michael. And that's just as well.'

Chapter 2

In the morning the world was grey, shrouded in mist and drizzle. Lamorna hurriedly washed and dressed.

'Morning Aileen, not such good weather today.'

'Oh the mizzle will clear by eleven, don't you worry.'

'Mizzle?'

'That's what we call a mist down here. Help yourself to some breakfast.' Lamorna sat down and took some toast from the rack. There was more home-made jam, and yellow Cornish butter. She'd just finished a mug of hot tea when Sam appeared.

'No need to come out, Michael will help with the delivery.'

'No, I'll come. You said it was my job when you took me on. Thanks for the breakfast Aileen.'

Michael was already rolling a barrel around from the drive to the cellar door. Lamorna watched his technique, and then got hold of a second barrel. It had looked so easy when Michael did it, but the barrel would not do what she wanted. No matter how she tried it kept on rolling into the flowerbeds, crushing some of the bedding plants. She felt herself getting hot and bothered. Michael re-appeared.

'I'll show you. Like this,' he said. She tried again and the barrel rolled over her foot. She winced in pain. He seemed genuinely concerned.

'Are you hurt?'

'You need proper boots,' Sam told her. 'Watch how we do it, and you can try next week.'

They rolled the barrels skilfully to the hatch, and Michael went to steady them as they tumbled down into the cellar. She was able to carry crates round on a sack truck, but they were heavy to lift, and her arms were trembling as she dropped the last one down with a crash.

'You've not done too badly for a girl,' Sam told her. 'I'll see you in an hour if you want that lift.'

'Thanks.'

She rushed to grab her wash bag and towel, and then find the bathroom. Aileen was in the kitchen with Mary, preparing the breakfasts.

'Sunday is Mary's day off Lamorna, so I'll need you to come in and help with the breakfasts. We give the guests a lie in, so eight o'clock will be fine.'

'Of course, it must be easier than barrels.'

'Don't be so sure, some of the guests can be really grumpy in the morning, fussing about their eggs, forgetting what they ordered.'

She ran a deep bath, pouring in some bath salts she found on the windowsill. She soothed her scratched arms with the sponge and then leaned back, eyes closed. Lamorna had always loved singing in the bath, and she decided she was far enough away from everyone now. She began with Elvis Presley ballads, and moved on to the old songs she'd learned from her grandmother.

'Better get out, before I'm all wrinkled and late for the lift.'

She dried herself quickly, sighing at the scars running down her left leg. She was just emerging when an adjacent door opened and Michael appeared. He nodded briefly at her and then clattered off down the stairs two at a time, whistling a tune. '*My grandfather's clock.*' She realised he must have heard her singing. A momentary embarrassment quickly dissolved as she reached the bottom of the stairs and met Mary with a breakfast tray.

'Everyone seems mighty cheerful this morning. First there's Michael whistling and now you grinning from ear to ear.'

'It's my day off, and I'm going into town. Then I'll go exploring.'

'I could show you around this afternoon when I'm finished.'

'That would be lovely, thank you.'

Sam was just getting into the van. Sliding into the seat beside him she glimpsed Michael in the wing mirror. He stood watching as they drove away.

'Will you be getting yourself some work clothes?'

'Yes, I need boots and some overalls. Can you tell me where I should go?'

'I'll drop you off, there's a place near the quay. Want a lift back?'

'No, that's okay thanks. I'll do a bit of shopping and get the bus.'

'There's one goes every half hour from the station, a blue and cream coach. Can't miss it.'

They drove up the hill and along the coast road. Over to the right was a fence, and beyond, the sea. She glimpsed St Michael's Mount, a grey shadow in the distance. Gulls clamoured as they went on down through the next fishing village, and Lamorna gazed with interest at the boats alongside the quay.

'So many fishing boats. There must be a lot of fish caught around here.'

'Aye, but it's getting harder for them to make a living. Too much competition from the bigger trawlers now. Michael wanted to work on the boats, but we couldn't let him. Needed him in the business.'

'What about your daughter?'

'We wanted a man about the place, and she's got the brains for study. Worked hard for her exams. Michael was set on fishing. He wouldn't stay in school. Here we are.'

She was outside a general store, the sort of place that sells everything you might ever need, hardware, garden equipment, and kitchenware. There was a chandler, with ropes and spars, cases filled with shackles and knives, fishing gear and clothing. She found some overalls to fit and a pair of sturdy boots. Back outside with her bulky brown paper parcel, she set off uphill to the main shopping area. Penzance was just as she remembered from childhood: the grey stone buildings on the high pavement of Market Jew Street, the Aladdin's caves of shops at their feet. She bought a few postcards.

The coffee bar could have been in her home town, with its fifties style décor, Formica topped tables and spluttering Espresso machines. There was a juke box in the corner playing Beatles hits. She sipped her coffee and quickly wrote the cards, saving her friend Jude's until last. She chewed her pen for a moment before writing:

'*Got a great job as odd job girl in the Penlee Hotel, you can just see the roof in this picture. DON'T tell Gary where I am. I've forgotten him already. Write and tell me what's happening up there.*'

She thought about Gary. She re-lived for the hundredth time the moment when he'd emerged from the shop where he worked on Saturdays with Chrissie on his arm. A moment when the world seemed to come crashing around her like pieces of a puzzle toppling from a table. 'Don't know how I'll cope back at College, seeing him around.' She pushed the thoughts away. 'Better get back and meet Mary I suppose.

She sauntered along the street, window-shopping, buying some fruit and a small bunch of Sweet Williams for her room, and then hurried to the bus.

Getting off just before the hotel she walked the last hundred yards. There were a few white sails in the bay, and a couple of fishing boats heading out. She could see the hotel summerhouse. A bank of mauve and pink hydrangeas grew beside it, vivid against the blue of the sea. Michael, shirtsleeves rolled, was toiling in the garden. The air was balmy now, a light breeze lifting her hair, and the cry of gulls from the rooftops drowned out any other sounds.

She unloaded her shopping, and just as she was wondering what to do about lunch there was a tap on the door. The latch was lifted, and Mary stuck her head round.

'Are you coming over to eat with us?'

'It's my day off.'

'Well you still need to eat. Come on.'

So Lamorna found herself back in the kitchen once more. Michael came in from the garden, and she watched as he went over to the sink to wash. There was a strong smell of outdoors and earth about him. There was salad for lunch. It was Lamorna's first taste of crab, and after a slight hesitation she pronounced it delicious. She talked about her shopping trip and the work clothes she'd bought. Michael was noticeably quiet.

'I sent some postcards too. One to my family and one to my friend Jude. She's on the same course as me.'

Michael stood up.

'I'd better get back to work.'

He loaded his plate into the dishwasher and strode purposefully to the door.

'Will you clear up for me Mary, before you go?' Aileen asked. 'I want to get on and do the flowers before the new guests arrive.'

'I'll help,' Lamorna said, jumping to her feet and collecting plates.

The two girls had the kitchen to themselves now.

'Have you worked here long?'

'Since I left school. I'm saving up to get married. Chris works on his Dad's boat, and one day it'll be his. We hope to get one of the houses up the hill.'

'Wouldn't you want to live in one of the cottages round the harbour?'

'Oh no, they're too small and dark, and some of them are let to the emmets.'

'Emmets?'

'Sorry.' She blushed.

'I mean visitors, that's what we call them.'

Lamorna laughed.

'It's a good name, sounds like insects crawling everywhere.'

The kitchen finished, they collected their bags and set off.

'We'll go down along the cliff path,' Mary suggested, 'and miss all the traffic.'

Michael was at the end of the garden, shovelling compost from one bin to another. He ignored them. Beyond the summerhouse a gate led out onto steps leading down to a path above the rocks.

'He seems to have a big chip on his shoulder.'

'He's been like that with everyone since his girl trouble. I heard he had something going with one of the hippy commune lot and she dumped him.'

'Commune? Who are they?'

'I don't know much about them. They're all into love and peace and making jewellery and things. They live together in a big old house. It used to be a flower farm. They've got cats all over the place and the blokes have long hair and beards. Very weird.'

'Sounds interesting,' Lamorna said, wondering what Mary would make of some of the art students on her course.

'Best to keep away from them my Mum says. A bad influence they are.'

'Who was the girl Michael was involved with?'

'I don't know. My sister Tamzin saw her in the pub with him in Penzance. She was wearing a long skirt and beads, and you know what, Tamzin said she had flowers in her hair. Tamzin went out with Michael at one time,' she added.

They'd reached the edge of the harbour now, and Mary was smiling and waving to people as they passed.

'That's my Mum's cousin Fred. He's bringing dahlias down for her,' she told Lamorna, as a grey haired old gentleman drove past in a gleaming Wolseley.

'My mum really hates them. They're full of earwigs. But she hasn't the heart to tell him. They're his pride and joy.'

Lamorna bought them both ice creams and they leaned on the harbour railings to eat them. Gulls soared screaming over their heads as eager young children threw bread crusts for them.

'I wish they wouldn't feed them,' Mary complained. 'It just makes them greedy. They're a real pest.'

'But it's part of a holiday, you have to!'

'Well I wouldn't know, I don't have holidays, we're always here.'

'You're so lucky, all these lovely places, great sandy beaches. I always wanted to come down here to live.'

'Don't ever go on the beach, not since I was little. Don't notice it really. If you lived here like we do you'd be bored just the same. Too much work all season and emmets everywhere, and then it's dead all winter.'

'I can't believe I'd be bored, there's so much to see, and all that wild weather, waves crashing on rocks, amazing skies.'

'That's just romance. The rough sea stops the boats going out, or they get into trouble and the lifeboat's called. Chris and my Dad, and my brother Ian are lifeboat crew. We dread the winter storms.'

'I don't think I could really live somewhere like this for the rest of my life. So far away from everywhere. No bright lights and cinemas.'

'We do have lights for Christmas, all around the harbour, really pretty they are.'

'Well yes, but I mean all the shops and the coffee bars, all night parties, and music.'

'I suppose it's very nice,' Mary said. 'It's all according to what you're used to.'

'Shall we go down to the beach?'

'Okay, but there's nothing to do.'

They clambered down the steps to the small beach. There was a woman there with two young children. They were building a castle, filling bright yellow pails with sand and tipping it out. They had little paper flags to poke into the turrets. Lamorna thought about the castles she'd made with her Dad on this same beach.

'That's my Uncle's pub over there. We go down some nights. Chris and Ian are in the darts team. Why don't you come down? I'll introduce you to the local lads.'

'No way,' Lamorna protested, laughing. 'No men. I'm dedicating my life to work.'

'You're as bad as Michael, a right pair you make.'

At the other end of the beach Lamorna noticed two young women in flowing ankle length skirts, their long hair braided with ribbons. They seemed to be making something; twisting leather strips in their fingers.

'Are those the people from the commune?'

'Yes, that's those hippies. Don't stare at them. Some people down here don't like them. They're planning a big meeting soon to get the council to move them on.'

'Why?'

'Some folks say they're bad for business, annoying the visitors, trying to sell the stuff they make. Wandering about with no shoes on like gypsies or beggars.' She blushed, 'And they're into free love.'

'Oh, they look quite friendly and ordinary to me.'

'I expect you're used to that kind of thing where you come from.'

They sat down together. Lamorna ran the fine sand through her fingers, watching as it trickled softly into a heap.

'I suppose I am used to it a bit, but I don't go along with all the new ideas. I've just finished with my boyfriend. I found out he was seeing other girls all the time we were together. I came down here to get away.'

Mary seemed shocked.

'I never heard anything like it. You're best off without him.'

'I know. You're right. But we got on so well. We planned to go to India next year. I went to surprise him, meet him out of work, and he was with this other girl.'

'The lads down here wouldn't go along with that sort of thing. Well, I suppose some of them do flirt with the visitors. It's because they think they're easy. Sorry, I shouldn't have said that.'

'It's okay. I expect some of them deserve it. I thought Christine and Maggie were my friends, and all the time they were messing about with Gary.'

The two girls on the wall got up and walked away.

'Do you think that blonde one is the girl that Michael got mixed up with?'

'I don't know. I never saw them together. Chris says Michael used to go down to their place. He used to take them into Penzance to sell their stuff. I don't think they do that well. They should be in St Ives or Newquay. That's what my Dad says. There's more queer folk over that way and all the surfing lot. Come on, I'll show you the famous cave next.'

They clambered down the steps from the harbour wall and onto the rocks, scrambling over boulders until they turned a corner. Mary proudly pointed out the Mouse Hole cave that was supposed to give the village its name. They wandered back. Small stones had caught in Lamorna's sandals so that she hobbled uncomfortably. She thought about the story of the little mermaid. The pain she'd felt with every step she took.

'The stupid things women do for love. I seemed to be the one who always had to make concessions. We always did what he wanted to do, and I always went along with it. He expected me to accept Chrissie, but I don't think he'd have done the same if the boot was on the other foot. Well that's it, I'm done with men.' She reached the flatter rocks and shook the stones from her sandal. A sudden booming sound startled her.

'It's the maroon for the lifeboat, come on,' Mary shouted.

They rushed back up to the harbour and climbed up onto the wall for a better view. Some minutes later the lifeboat sped by and disappeared round the headland.

'Aren't you scared for Chris when he goes out on the lifeboat?'

'Of course, but it's no worse than when he's out fishing.'

'I wonder what's happened.'

'It'll probably be some false alarm, or an emmet stuck on a cliff. Come on, we'll go back home, you can meet my family. We'll find out when Ian and Chris get back.'

There was a warm welcome from Mary's mother, who insisted that she stay for tea.

'It's only pie and potatoes my lover, but you're welcome to share it with us.' They'd washed up and were sitting in the garden when the men folk came.

'It was a day tripper,' said Chris. 'Went out in a rubber dinghy at Porthcurno. The coastguard saw him waving. Thought he was in trouble. He reckoned he was only waving at his wife, but we towed him in anyway. Could've been washed out to sea in those currents round there.'

After the men had eaten they all walked together down to the pub. Lamorna made her excuses, and set off for the hotel,

'I've got an early start tomorrow.'

She felt a little lonely on her way back. She thought about Mary's family, the way her Mum had made her feel welcome and how they all seemed at ease with each other. It was very different from her own home where the atmosphere was constrained. Her mother always on edge.

Chapter 3

'It's beginning to get busier,' Aileen told her as they were getting the breakfasts ready. 'We had two new couples arrive yesterday afternoon. We'll get on with the baking when we're done here.'
Michael turned up after lunch.
'There's weeding to be done, and salads to sow,' he told her. 'Can you manage that?'
'I always helped my Dad with the gardening.'

She didn't see him again after he'd given her a tour of the shed. She enjoyed the work, making the long drills and sprinkling the seeds. She loved the feel and damp smell of the soil. Every now and again she found time to stretch her back and admire the view across the hydrangeas to the deeper blue of the sea, feel the warm breeze on her face. And then it was three o'clock, and Aileen called her in for tea and splits.

They sat outside together whilst the village girls finished clearing away.
'How did it feel when you first came down here, did you miss your family and Ireland?'
'Sure, it was hard at first, until I met Sam. His family were cool with me for a while. They wanted him to marry a local girl, not some Irish foreigner. But they warmed to me in time. I helped nurse his Gran when she was dying and I think that was a turning point. But I will always be the girl from Ireland.'
'I tried to get my Mum and Dad to come and live down here, but I'm not sure I'd want to now.'
'That's what I thought. I never meant to stay. I was heading for London. The bright lights. But I can't imagine any other life now. Sam once had this idea of getting a bigger hotel. It was me who persuaded him to stay. The kids didn't want to go. They had their friends, and Michael was set on going to sea. Sometimes I wonder what might have been. Maybe Michael would have studied and got to University like Ellen.'
'I can't imagine him buried in books. He seems such an outdoor sort of person.'
'Yes, he is, but he does love reading. The other boys used to rag him if they saw him with a book. It was always a story about adventure or ships.'
'What's Ellen doing?'
'She's just finished her final year. She studied English, says she wants to be a journalist. I don't think she'll come back to Cornwall. She's in Europe at the moment, travelling around. She'll probably stay in Bristol. Or go down to London.'
'Do you miss her?'
'Of course. I'm outnumbered by men now! But I'm glad she's got a chance I never had. Back in Sligo no-one in my family ever imagined I'd want to go to University. My teachers told me I could get a scholarship, but it was no use. I had to get a job to support the family. I was the oldest. Two of the younger ones managed to go on to college though, and my brothers are working in America now.'

'Do you feel bitter about that?'

'No, what's the point? I'm happy with my life. I love this business. And I think I'd better get back to it now!'

On Monday evening she walked down to the Ship Inn to meet up with Mary. Chris and Ian were there and a couple of Mary's school friends. The group soon split into two, with the men joining others at the bar, and the women sitting and chatting in the window. They talked about Mary's engagement.

'It's been over a year now, and Chris never wants to talk about a date for the wedding.'

'Why don't you suggest one?' Lamorna asked.

'Oh, I couldn't, what would he think?'

'He'd think you wanted to marry him.'

They all laughed. But Lamorna felt they'd considered her idea to be completely bizarre. They talked on about where the wedding might be held, and who would be a bridesmaid.

'My cousin got married in June, and she and the bridesmaids wore mini dresses and carried paper flowers,' Lamorna told them.

'Were you a bridesmaid?' Mary asked.

'No, she had too many sisters.'

Lamorna didn't tell them that she couldn't wear a miniskirt and show her scarred leg.

Michael turned up at around nine o'clock. His jeans were streaked with paint and he looked tired. He went up to join the other men. She looked quickly away when he turned and glanced in their direction. The others were still talking about weddings, but Lamorna's attention was drifting. She wished she could hear what they were discussing at the bar. Whatever it was it was causing a great deal of hilarity.

'Sorry to be boring, but I think I need to get to bed, I'm up early in the morning,' she said, yawning. 'See you tomorrow Mary.'

'Why don't you wait for Michael to walk up with you?'

'Oh, he's staying at the cottage he's working on, so he won't be going my way.'

There was a delivery next morning of soft drinks and provisions, and she was up early to help Sam. She worked in the hotel for the day, making packed lunches, helping with the teas.

'There are only two tables booked for dinner tonight,' Aileen said, 'So take some time off.'

She grabbed her camera and set off down to the harbour to get some photographs. A group of the commune girls and one long haired man were sitting on the slipway below the memorial. A sudden impulse made her take out her camera and take some pictures of them. There was something attractive about the way they were sitting together, a group lost in their own world. As she adjusted the settings to get a second shot, she noticed that another man had joined the group. It was Michael. He was in earnest conversation with one of the women, the attractive girl with long blonde hair threaded with beads that she'd seen on the beach. Not wishing to be noticed she went down a flight of steps onto the sand, and made her way along below the wall, stepping over the ropes that tied the boats to the mooring rings. Risking a furtive glance she saw that Michael had gone.

For the next hour she was completely absorbed, sitting patiently by a rock pool, waiting for the creatures she'd disturbed to venture out of hiding again. She was fascinated by the muted colours in the pools, the grey rock with pink- beige dappling of barnacles, the darker wine colours of bladder-wrack. Each miniature world had its own harmonious colour scheme, into which the little crabs and small fish blended perfectly. She gently touched a feathery plant, and was startled when soft tentacles closed over her finger. And then she was back in her childhood again, remembering these sea anemones and magical pools, where she'd been content to sit for hours and watch life unfold. She'd hated the way other children had dragged their nets through the bigger rock pools, catching fish, stirring up the stones and seaweed like giants trampling the miniature worlds.

The light began to fade, and she packed her camera away and set off, choosing to walk along the street this time. The hippy group had left the harbour now, and their space on the railing was occupied by two teenage girls who seemed to be talking together in an invented language of their own She'd just got back to the cottage and put the kettle on when Aileen knocked on the door.

'Hello Lamorna, I've got your friend Jude on the phone for you. She rang up to book a room for next week. I've not said anything yet, but I thought you'd like her to stay over here with you.'

'Oh, I wonder why she wants to come down. She must have got my postcard. I suppose she could share this room with me if you don't mind.'

'Not at all. It would be company for you when you're not working.'
They walked over to the hotel together.

'I'm putting the kettle on, come and have tea with us when you're done.'
Five minutes later she was back in the kitchen. Aileen and Sam were sat at the table with mugs of tea.

'Jude can come down next Wednesday, if that's okay.'

'Might find her some jobs,' Sam said.
Michael appeared whilst they talked and went to pour tea.

'Get Lamorna a cup,' Aileen said.

'Jude thinks she could get some good photos down here. She's doing a study of markets.'
Michael placed a mug of tea in front of her.

'Thank you.' She felt herself blush.

'Lamorna's friend is coming down for a few days,' Aileen told him.

'She could come with me when I go for the produce,' Sam suggested. 'Isn't she looking for work?'

'She doesn't need to, her parents are wealthy.'

Michael drank his tea down quickly.

'I'm off, early start tomorrow. Got a plumber coming. Thanks for the tea.'

Chapter 4

On Thursday evening Lamorna was in the pub again, with Mary, Chris and Ian. She was trying to explain her project to them.

'They're just a load of grey stones in the middle of fields,' Chris said. 'I suppose you could get them made into postcards, but most people want harbour and beach scenes.'

'Maybe you could sell them,' Mary suggested, 'they have big photos of sunsets and stuff like that in the gallery by the harbour.'

'I don't have to do anything with the photographs yet, it's just a way of getting experience so that I can see what kind of work I want to do in the future. I could go into advertising or journalism, I'm not sure yet.'

'We could take Lamorna to see the Merry Maidens on Saturday Chris.'

'Yeah, we could. I've got to go over that way to do a job for my Aunt Dolly. She could come on to Lamorna with us too.'

'Oh, that would be great; I was thinking I'd have to walk the whole way. Thanks.'

The conversation changed to everyday topics such as the current price of fish and the Cornwall cricket team. She sat back and relaxed, looking around the inn. There were nautical things here and there on the walls, a navigation chart, and old photographs of fishing boats with men unloading catches on the quay. It was a friendly sort of place, a lot of the customers seemed to be local, and they all knew each other.

'I'm glad I came down here,' she thought. 'I'll get some brilliant photos for the course.'

A letter arrived from her friend Jude on Friday morning. There was some interesting news:

'I saw Chrissie in Boccaccio last Saturday night. She was with Alan Cowley and they were all over each other. Dave Springett had an all-night party while his parents were away and some gate crashers smashed a glass cupboard and poured drink in the fish tank. We've all got to pay for the damage. Gary's really mad at you for just going off like that. He had a go at me, as if it's my fault.'

It all seemed suddenly remote to Lamorna, a world she no longer belonged to. Just for a moment she allowed herself to wallow in self-pity, and harbour a hope that Gary might want to contact her. But she pushed him out of her mind. She realised that she hadn't given him a thought all week.

Chris picked up Mary and Lamorna from the hotel on Saturday afternoon. 'There's a bit of a mizzle. Do you still want to come?

'Yes, oh yes, it's perfect for atmospheric pictures, if you two don't mind.'

It was even mistier up at the Merry Maidens, the iron grey sky and streaks of white fog created a mysterious aura, and here and there a stone was lit by a gleam of light. Mary and Chris watched bemused as she moved around, taking pictures from different angles, even kneeling or lying down on the wet grass. Between shots she paused to note the technical details for her college journal.

'Never imagined there'd be so much to it,' Chris commented.

After half an hour or so they were all grateful to pile back into the car to make their way down to Lamorna Cove. Aunt Dolly was pleased to see them, bringing out platefuls of Saffron cake and mugs of hot tea.

'Don't know what you'd be doing out in the fields in this weather, and just look at your knees! What've you been doing scrawming in the wet grass?'
The mist had cleared and sunlight lit up the room as they finished eating.

'If it's okay with you, I'd like to have a look around 'my' village,' she said.

'You do that my ansome. We've got some jobs to do around here,' Dolly said.

She walked down the lane and onto the granite wall that curved around like a protective arm to embrace the tiny harbour. Looking back from the end of the harbour wall she saw the houses almost avalanching down the grey rock- strewn slopes. It was a little desolate, yet also picturesque, with the cottages seeming to have grown out of the rock itself.

Back at Dolly's cottage she found that Chris had been given some extra jobs to do, and after drinking yet more tea she and Mary decided to walk back along the cliff path.

'We'll meet you back at The Ship and we can have dinner there Chris.'
They climbed steeply up out of the cove. The sun's warmth had brought out the butterflies, and the air was sweet with the scent of gorse. They stopped to look back at the village and allow Lamorna to take some photos.

The path wound its way along the cliffs, and St Michael's Mount came into view. Sometimes low trees created an arbour through which they walked, and Lamorna noticed the way they leaned inwards, backs turned to the wind and storms that might blow in from the Atlantic.

'I feel at home here, as though I belong in this wild place,' she thought.
After an hour or so the path began to climb down to Mousehole. The tide was in, and the sea beyond the harbour was a beautiful aquamarine. As they approached the fringes of the village Mary whispered,

'Don't look now, but that's where the hippies live.'
Of course she did look, and saw a large granite house, its windows flung open, a curtain reaching out into the breeze. Music could be heard wafting from the open door. The house was surrounded by an overgrown garden, the grass long and invaded by buttercups and dog daisies. Someone had been digging. She noticed garden tools; a fork and spade lying discarded. A hammock swayed gently between two old apple trees. A young woman was lying in it, reading a book. Across her stomach a baby lay kicking, its little fists reaching up towards the branches. Two kittens were rolling and tumbling in the grass below.

'There's a baby,' Lamorna whispered as they passed on by.

'Yes, there's a rumour going round that it's Michael's. People think it belongs to the girl he was going with, but you can't be sure. You never see the baby with the same girl twice.'

'I wonder if the girl in the hammock is its mother. Wouldn't Michael know if it was his baby? I saw him talking to a girl. She looked like the one in the hammock.'

'Maybe, but he doesn't mention it. He gets cross if anyone dares to ask. Come on, let's hurry, Chris'll be waiting.'

He was already in the pub, propping up the bar and chatting with a couple of fishermen. They chose a seat by the window.

'Dolly had a lot of jobs for you today Chris,' Mary said, when he'd joined them.

'She's on her own, see,' he told Lamorna. 'So I goes down every month to see if she needs help.'

'What happened to her husband?' Lamorna asked.

'Fisherman, Mum's brother. Lost at sea a good many years ago. Brought up three girls on her own, she did.'

'Oh that's terrible; it must have been hard for her.'

'Aye, I daresay, but it happens in the fishing, and folk rally round to help. He was never much of a husband. Some folk reckon she's best off.'

Sam appeared.

'Who's best off?'

'Oh. I was just on about Dolly. What some folks say about Jack.'

'You don't want to be listening to those old gossips.'

He turned to Lamorna,

'Did you get some good pictures?'

'Yes, the weather was perfect, all that mist up there.'

'Michael looks a little like him,' she thought, 'but he has his mother's eyes and hair.'

'I reckon Michael could take you out on Tuesday evening. You could go over to Men an Tol.'

'Thank you, that would be helpful,' she replied, unable to protest in the present company.

'You'll find them interesting. They do say that they're all about healing and fertility.'

She couldn't be sure, but thought that he winked surreptitiously at Chris as he spoke.

'We'll have to try it Chris,' Mary said, laughing.

'Not yet a while my lover, we're not even married yet!'

The alarm woke her early on Sunday morning, and she regretted the late night in the pub. She dragged herself out of bed, her head throbbing, to put the kettle on. There was another mizzle, and she couldn't see beyond the summer house. She was standing by the window, warming her hands on the mug of tea when a shadowy figure appeared, followed by a knock on her door. Michael was on the step.

'Mum says could you come now and help. One of the weekend girls has called in sick.'

A quick wash, and then she hastily dressed and hurried over to the kitchen. She grabbed a piece of toast before getting stuck into the cooking. Everyone wanted a full breakfast, and it was the beginning of a hectic day. She helped Annie, the other local girl to make up the beds and tidy the rooms once the guests were out. There was time for a quick lunch before the afternoon teas were served. Later the dinners had to be prepared and then cleared away. It was an exhausting day's work.

'You've done well Lamorna, thanks for helping out. I wouldn't normally expect you to do such a long shift.'
They were relaxing with coffee in the kitchen. Sam was still busy in the hotel bar, and there was no Michael to be seen.
'I enjoyed being busy, better than a slow sort of day. No time to think or worry.'
'What's a young girl like you got to be worried about?'
'Oh I suppose just my course, hoping I get all the photographs done.'
'Sam says Michael is taking you to see some stones.'
'Yes, he told me, but I can't let him, I don't want him to feel obligated.'
'Michael was the one who suggested it, and I think it will do him good to be in your company.'
'But he doesn't like me. I can't believe it was his idea.'
'Whatever makes you think that? I hope he hasn't been rude to you.'
'No, of course not, it's just that he ignores me, avoids talking to me.'
'I'm sorry to hear that, it may be because he's shy of you. And I think he feels embarrassed that he was a bit scathing when Sam took you on. I'll talk to him.'
'Please don't, I'm probably imagining it anyway.'
'If you're sure. Come on then, we'd best clear up and get to bed, another busy day tomorrow.'

Lamorna spent a good part of Monday outdoors, weeding and hoeing around the vegetable plots. It was a beautiful day, and she was happy in her work. She collected ten beautiful brown speckled eggs.
'Here's all the produce for tonight,' she said, bringing her basket into the kitchen. And was just in time for a cup of tea and a fresh split with Mary and Aileen.
'That was another exhausting afternoon. We had a coach load in, and a group of rowdy children who left most of their cake on the lawn. Thank goodness we're quiet tonight. Most of the guests are eating in Penzance. A couple of pubs do cheap deals on Monday nights. I know I shouldn't wish our custom away, but it's good to have a breather now and again.'
'Why don't you come down and meet us in the pub? There's a folk band playing tonight,' Mary said.
'Isn't that a grand idea now? Wish I had the energy. Summer's such hard work in this business. At my age I just want to fall into bed at ten o'clock.'
'Is Michael coming down tonight?' Mary asked.
'I don't know. He probably will. He usually enjoys a folk night.'

It was still warm when she left her little room to walk down to the pub. A crescent moon was rising as she made her way along the pathway and up onto the quay. The bar was already full and she struggled to squeeze through the mass of bodies to reach their table.

'We bought you a drink, not much chance of getting to the bar again in a hurry.' Lamorna smiled in thanks, and eased herself gratefully onto the end of the seat. A local group was playing, and they were really good. The crowd had stopped chatting and were listening attentively, some joining in when they knew the song. She sat back contentedly, sipping her beer, letting the music wash over her. Ian fought his way to the bar and bought them all another drink just before the interval rush.

'That's my cousin playing guitar,' Mary told her proudly. 'I'll introduce you if you like.'

'That would be great. The band's good. They're playing some music I've not heard before'

'They've got into folk rock now. Trying out some new songs,' Ian told her.

'Not sure how well it'll go down here. The locals are more into traditional stuff. Where's Michael?'

'I don't know. I've not seen him.'

The music started up again, and thankfully there was no more chance to talk about Michael. The room was beginning to feel very hot, and Lamorna struggled out of her shirt. She was wearing a sleeveless tee shirt underneath which was a lot cooler. She found herself listening intently to the words as the singer began a song of lost love and sorrow of parting, and she felt tears prick her eyes. A wave of self-pity swept over her.

'Are you okay?' asked Mary.

'Yes, just very hot, I'm going outside for a few minutes.'
She stumbled to her feet and eased her way back through the crowd to the door and the cooler night air. The harbour was quiet. She walked over to the railings to lean and look across at the boats.

'It's enchanting,' she thought, listening to the music spilling out through the doors and windows and the sound of wavelets lapping languidly on the shore. It was a still, warm evening and the boats were bobbing gently on their moorings. She wondered why she'd allowed herself to get upset.

'It's so lovely here, and I've never felt happier.'
A hand grabbed her arm.

Chapter 5

Someone was pulling her around. She clung to the railings, struggling to resist.

'I knew it was you. Come 'ere.'

Gary. He was dragging her towards him. His breath rank with stale beer. His mouth slurring over her face. She fought him. Tried to push him away. She felt his hand fumbling under her tee shirt. Tried to knee him and stamp on his feet. But he was expecting it, and shifted his body away.

'Get off me. Leave me alone.'

'Let go of her.'

Someone pulling Gary away.

'She's mine, gerroff.'

'I'm not yours, I'm not yours. I hate you.'

The other man's voice again,

'Get away from here and don't come back.'

There was a scuffle and the sound of a fist meeting flesh. She was slumped on the road now, trying to catch her breath, fighting back tears. Then someone was helping her up, and enclosing her in his arms. She realised that it was Michael. He whispered to her,

'Are you alright?'

His breath was warm on her neck as he gently lifted her hair from her face. She felt herself trembling in his arms.

'You're cold, here, have my sweater.'

He pulled it over his head and handed it to her.

'Thank you,' she said, struggling to push her arms into the sleeves, the wool warm against her bare skin. 'I don't know how he got here.'

'Your lip's bleeding. Here.'

She took the handkerchief and wiped her mouth. Tasted the blood.

'He came to the hotel asking for you. Mum told him you were down here. I didn't like the look of him. He'd been drinking. So I followed him. He couldn't get in because of the crowd. I watched him skulking about, peering through the windows. And then you came outside. I thought you'd seen him at first and come out to meet him. I thought you wanted to be with him, and then I heard you telling him to get off.'

'Thank you,' she mumbled into his hanky. 'I never want to see him again. I didn't tell him I was here. How did he find me?'

'I don't know. Maybe your friend told him. Do you want to go back in?'

'No, no, I couldn't, not like this.'

'I'll take you home then.'

'Home?'

'Back to the hotel.'

He walked with her, choosing the shoreline path just in case Gary was lurking in the road. He opened the door to her cottage for her, and checked inside.

'Are you sure you'll be okay? You could stay in the hotel tonight. My room's free.'

'Thank you, but I'll be alright. I'll lock the door.'

There was an awkward moment then as she stepped inside.

'You sure you'll be okay?'

'Yes,' she said. 'Thank you.'

He turned to go.

'I left my bag and shirt in the pub.'

'I'll go and find them. I'll tell them you weren't feeling well shall I?'

'Yes, please. I did tell them I was hot.'

And then he was gone, striding over to the kitchen door.

She went inside, and locked and bolted the door for the first time. She flung herself down on the bed. She thought about the way Michael had held her, his gentleness, and a wave of longing engulfed her.

'No-one ever held me like that before.'

She heard Aileen gently knock on her door and whisper her name. She couldn't let her in. She felt so ashamed. She lay awake, thinking about Gary now. 'He said "you're mine," like I'm some sort of possession, I'm not his, and I never will be, he's nothing to me now. 'She lay and sobbed into her pillow, her thoughts a confusion of anger against Gary, and a realisation that she wanted Michael to hold her again, and that he would want nothing to do with her after tonight.

Chapter 6

"Lamorna, are you okay?'
Clambering out of bed she stumbled over to open the door.
'I've brought you some breakfast over.'
Aileen came into the room carrying a tray covered with a tea cloth, and set it down on the table.
'I'm sorry, I'm sorry, I've got blood on your pillow.'
She felt herself drawn into Aileen's warm embrace, and felt a soothing stroking on her back.
'It's not your fault. Michael told me what happened. Come and sit down and have something to eat. There's hot tea and toast. The important thing is that you're alright. I'm sorry I told that young fellow where to find you last night. I can't have been thinking. Thank heavens Michael had the sense to follow him.'
Lamorna took the mug and gulped down some warm tea.
'He wasn't always like that. I thought I loved him.'
The words came out as a sob.
'I know, I know,' Aileen soothed. 'I think you should get your breakfast and then come over and have a lovely warm bath.'
'I've messed up Michael's sweater. I must have fallen asleep in my clothes.'
'Don't worry about that. It can never be as bad as the state it gets in when he's been messing about in boats.'
Lamorna sat down, and then suddenly realised the time.
'The breakfasts, I should be there .....'
'Don't worry, it's all done. Michael came in to help. He told Mary a little of what happened to you when she arrived this morning. We're all managing.'
'Thank you.'

She sipped some more tea, and Aileen left. She sat, staring blankly, looking at the shrivelled petals of her Sweet Williams. And that was how Aileen found her half an hour later.
'I'm sorry, I've not eaten anything.'
'Well never mind, come along over and get your bath now, I've a towel warming for you. You'll maybe feel better then. Bring your clothes and I'll pop them in the wash.'
She allowed herself to be led like a child up to the bathroom, and watched as Aileen ran a bath for her.
'There now, you get a good soak, and I'll have a proper breakfast ready for you when you come down.'
She stood and stared for a few moments, listening to the bubbles as they popped and fizzed, and then she peeled off her clothes, leaving them abandoned in a heap on the floor, and sank down into comforting foam.

'Lamorna, are you okay?'
Aileen's voice outside the door.
'Yes, yes, I'm sorry, I'm coming.'
'Don't worry, I was just checking.'

The water was cool now. She sponged herself over, and stepped out onto the mat, curling her toes into the tufts. She quickly dried and pulled on her clean clothes. Looked at herself in the mirror. She practised smiling, and decided that she could do it.

'And there's Michael. I don't want him thinking I'm pathetic, or that I care,' she told herself. She cleaned the bath out carefully, dropped her towel into the laundry basket, and gathering her discarded clothing into a bundle skipped down the stairs.

Mary was emerging from a bedroom on the next floor down.

'We thought you'd drowned, you were so long.'

'I must have fallen asleep,' she said, smiling.

She opened the kitchen door carefully. Only Aileen was there.

'How are you now, feeling better?'

'Yes, thank you, the bath was just what I needed. I feel like a new person. Where is everyone?'

'Sam's in the bar, Mary's doing beds, and Michael's down at the cottage now. He'll do the chickens today.'

'No, I have to do it, I need to work to stop me thinking. And I've already missed half a morning. I don't want you giving me the sack.'

She managed a half smile, but felt a sob rising in her throat. Aileen looked at her, but only said,

'If you're sure.'

'I'm sure.'

'Well come on then, But you need to eat something. I'll do you a poached egg.'

'I'll make it.'

'No, just sit down by the range. I'll get us a pot of tea. I could eat a bit of toast myself.'

They were both sitting with their tea when Mary came in and joined them. No-one talked about what had happened the previous night. There was a conversation about the state of one of the rooms.

'It looks like a war zone. There's dirty underwear on the floor, papers, beer and wine bottles, make up all over the table,' Mary complained. 'Never seen anything so bad before. Half her clothes were still in the wardrobe.'

'We'll have to pack them up and put them aside in case she comes back for them, but somehow I don't think we'll see either of them again,' Aileen said. 'And from the way she flounced out I'm not sure he'll see her again either. But he did pay for the whole week. And he left a large tip.'

Lamorna felt herself jump when the door opened. Michael came in. He looked across at her.

'Are you okay?'

'Yes thanks. Thank you for last night.'

'I'll do the chickens.'

'No, I want to do them.'

'Okay, if you're sure. You might like to know the gossip I've just heard.'

Aileen handed him a mug of tea.

'Sounds intriguing.'

'I just went into the newsagents, and they were talking about Mrs Jenkinson up on The Parade. Apparently she found a strange youth asleep in her porch this morning. She was horrified. He'd been sick all over her steps.'

'No. What happened?'

'She called the Police, and they took him away. Rumour is that he got put on a train.'

Lamorna felt the colour drain from her face.

'Sounds like that bloke who came after you,' he said to her. 'You shouldn't have any more trouble. They'll all think he was a stray over from Newquay. They get some bad drunken types over there. I'd better get going. Did Mum give you your things?'

'I'll get them for you,' Aileen said.

And then Michael was gone, and the kitchen seemed an emptier place. She took her stuff back to the little cottage and changed into her work clothes and boots.

'Michael was cool towards me, and that suits me. Who needs men when they can behave so badly?' But she had to stop herself smiling when she remembered again how he had held her. He couldn't hate her that much. Somehow the thought made her feel better. She cleaned out the chickens in half the time, singing to herself and doing her best to put everything behind her. With each shovel full of dirty straw she piled onto the compost heap she imagined that she was burying Gary, and took great pleasure in beating it down forcefully. Even the chickens seemed cowed by her determined air, and not one tried to escape or attack her.

It was a different Lamorna who appeared in the kitchen later for lunch.

'I'm sorry for all the trouble I've caused,' she told Mary and Aileen. 'But this is the new 'me' now. I'm going to concentrate on getting my work done and make a brilliant job of my project. I can really forget Gary now. Men are just a waste of space.'

As she spoke the last words Michael came through the door. They all sat down around the table, and Sam came in and joined them. He nodded at Lamorna.

'I got the chickens done, and none of them got away.'

'Yes, I just checked. You've done a proper job.'

Mary talked about the folk evening in the pub.

'My cousin's band is playing again on Friday in Penzance. Why don't you come with us?'

'I'd love to. My friend Jude will be here tomorrow, she'd enjoy it.'

'What about you Michael?' Mary asked.

'Reckon I will.'

'Are you still taking Lamorna up on the moors to take some photos?' Sam asked.

'I'm not sure she'd want me to.'

'I would like to, if you don't mind. I need to get more work done on my project.'

'Chris could take you if Michael's busy,' Mary suggested.

'It's okay, I can do it. I'll pick you up at eight o'clock.'

'You could leave earlier,' Aileen said. 'I won't need Lamorna this evening, there are only two guests booked for dinner now that the young couple have left, and we don't usually get busy on a Tuesday.'

'That would be great. I might catch the sunset.'
'I'll come for you at 6.30 then.'
Michael pushed back his chair, cleared his plate and was gone.

'What's eating him?' Sam asked.
'Oh you know Michael, full of contradictions,' Aileen said, glancing meaningfully at him.
'Well I don't know as I do know him these days.'

Michael arrived promptly and with barely a word exchanged between them they set off in his van. Lamorna felt that the air between them was charged as if by electricity, like the strange atmosphere before a storm. 'He's trying to send out vibes against me,' she thought.
They parked on the verge by a footpath sign, and Michael led the way across the fields to the mysterious stones that were the Men an Tol. A ring of stone flanked by two upright stone pillars. Michael lay down in the bracken, staring up at the sky. She crawled through the hole nine times.
'You should try it. It feels magical. I've magicked away all my past.'
'I don't believe in all that old stuff.'
The sun was beginning to set, and an indigo sky was streaked with salmon pink and blood red. She was aware of his gaze as she got on with her work. She captured him framed in the centre of the hole as she took a longer range shot.
He took her next to Lanyon Quoit. It was growing yet darker, and the stone shapes seemed sinister against the sky. The last streaks of red sun lay like a bloodied gash across the horizon.

They didn't speak as they drove back to the hotel. Lamorna sat and stared at the passing scenery, all strange and shadowy in the dusk; the high banks and walls topped with turf, and dark hedges pierced by pin prick eyes caught in the headlight's beam. She felt that each of them was resolved against the other in a strange game. As if they were carefully wrapping themselves in a cloak of indifference. Some sort of magic cloak that could resist all impulses and protect against the shock of contact. He dropped her at the hotel.
'Thank you. And thank you for last night too.'
'You're welcome.'
She watched the red tail lights disappear around the curve in the driveway.
***

Jude arrived on Wednesday evening, and Lamorna went to meet her off the bus.
'What have you done to your lip?'
'Come on. I'll tell you later.'
As they opened the door to the cottage Michael turned the corner and went into the kitchen.
'Wow! Who's that?'
'He's Michael, the owner's son. I'll get the kettle on.'
Jude filled her in with news from home. There was not much to tell. Most of their friends were away on holiday and nothing much was going on.
'Now, it's your turn. What's happened to you?'
'It was Gary. He turned up on Monday night.'
She went on to describe what had happened.'

'That's terrible. It must be my fault. I showed him your postcard. I felt he ought to know you were having a great time without him. I'm so sorry. But what about your knight in shining armour? How romantic. I could really go for him, that dark curly hair, blue eyes, tanned skin.'

'Jude! He really hates me. He was against me getting the job.'

'Well you're crazy, but if you don't want him then I'm going to flirt with him while I'm here.'

'He won't want to know, he's nursing a broken heart. He doesn't want anything to do with women.'

'Sounds like you're warning me off him. I don't think you're telling me the truth about this Lorna West.'

'I really don't like him.'

'If you say so.'

'I don't want any complications with men in my life now. I want to concentrate on my project. In a way it was a good thing Gary turned up. He was so horrible, and drunk. I realise that I don't want any more to do with him. I can't believe I ever thought I loved him.'

'What a waste though, you could have a fling with Michael.'

'I don't want a fling. I'm already focussing on my project. I've got some great shots of standing stones, there's this one that's round like a giant Polo mint.'

'I just can't get started. I've been to the market once or twice, but it's not got me excited yet.'

'There's a great market here, Sam said you can go in with him one morning.'

'Sounds good. I'll maybe do that. Shall we go to the pub, I'm starving?'

'To be honest I don't want to go out while my lip's swollen. And Aileen has invited us over for dinner in the hotel.'

'Yeah, let's do that. Might see that gorgeous Michael again.'

'Jude!'

'Okay, okay. I get the message, he's yours, keep off.'

'That is not the message! You're impossible, but you've cheered me up already. We'll have a great week. I'll be working, but you'll find plenty to do. And I'll have the whole day off on Saturday.'

There was no sign of Michael. Jude got on well with Sam and Aileen, and he told her about the market.

'You won't find a better one in the country.'

Later when they'd finished chatting in bed, and the lights were off, Lamorna examined her feelings. 'Was I relieved that Michael wasn't around just in case he did fall for Jude? She can charm anyone, and I'm so clumsy and awkward.' She thought about how the kids at school had laughed at her leg and called her 'alligator', always taunting her, chanting the rhyme 'see ya later alligator...' when they saw her. No boys from school had ever asked her out. 'Even if I wanted to, there's no point in me thinking about Michael. He'd be just like the others.'

Chapter 7

Lamorna was up early, ready for a busy day at work. The hotel was almost full, and she knew they'd be rushed all day, with breakfasts, afternoon teas and dinners to be done. There was gardening to fit in too. In the afternoon Sam asked her to fix the gate down to the shore, and she surprised herself by finishing the task competently, and winning his approval.

'Good as a man could've done it,' he told her. 'Proper job.'

'Thanks Dad, all your instruction came in useful,' she whispered.

Jude had spent the day exploring the village, browsing in the gift shops, and eating ice creams.

'Guess what, I met these hippies, and we're both invited over to their place on Saturday. They've been down here for ages. Rosa showed me how to make these bands. I got one for you, look; it's got beads woven in and bells on the strap. It's just made from bootlaces. It's amazing.'

Lamorna fastened it around her wrist.

'Thanks, it's lovely.'

'They make them to sell, but hardly anyone buys them round here. I said they could sell loads up our way. I might take some to sell at college next term.'

'They're not popular with some of the locals. People think they put the tourists off with their bare feet and strange clothes.'

'I think they're great. You'll see on Saturday, they're really friendly.'

'But how do they get money to live?'

'I suppose they must be on the dole.'

'That's what the locals think. They see them as scroungers. They think they should all get jobs like everyone else.'

'It'll be interesting to meet them,' Lamorna thought. 'I might find out more about what happened with Michael. And the baby.'

'Come on; let's go. I said we'll meet Mary in the pub. And we're invited to join them for a folk night in Penzance on Friday.'

'I'm up for that.'

The bar was crowded, but Mary had saved them seats in their usual corner. Lamorna was relieved that no-one mentioned her lip. The swelling had gone down a little, but it still looked bruised. Jude was a great hit with everyone, with her irrepressible humour and enthusiasm for life. By the end of the evening she was sitting on Ian's knee. Her mood and confidence affected the others too. Chris even kissed Mary in front of his mates.

Lamorna and Jude walked back together around the harbour and up to the hotel at the end of the evening.

'Ian's taking me out in his boat tomorrow. We're going fishing. I thought I'd get some good photos. But I've got to be up at five o'clock.'

'Jude! You hate boats!'

'Where'd you get that idea? I was going to join the Navy remember.'

'Yeah, only because of the sailors! You would never come out when we went rowing.'

'Well, nothing ventured. I have to make sacrifices for my project.'
'You're crazy if you think I'll believe that!'

***

Jude did seem to have had a great time with Ian the next day.

'We caught so many fish, and I got some brilliant pictures. I really liked Ian's Dad. He sang some shanties for me. He said it was bad luck to take a woman on board, but we got the best catch he'd had in ages. I can't wait for a bath. I smell like a fish market.'

'Didn't put Ian off though, did it? I saw you both when he dropped you off.'
'You're just jealous!'
'Jude, please get it into your head, I don't want a man in my life. That's it.'
'Okay, okay.'

Later they were clearing away the dinner pots when Jude reappeared.
'Come on, Ian's calling for us in a few minutes.'
'Do you mind if I don't come? I'm feeling tired.'
'Oh, come on, you'll be fine when we get there.'
'Sorry, just a bit down in the dumps. Wouldn't be good company.'
A car horn blared outside.
'That's my lift. I'll see you then.'
And with the usual rush and door slamming she was gone.

'She's a whirlwind, your friend,' Aileen said. 'Fancy a cup of tea? Keep me company for a bit. Sam's busy in the bar, and I could do with someone to chat to.'
'Thank you, I will.'
They sat together with tea and biscuits around the big kitchen table.
'How are you feeling now?'
'I'm okay. My lip still feels sore. I'm a bit tired. Not getting much sleep with Jude around. We seem to talk late every night. I just felt like a quiet evening. Sometimes Jude can be a bit overwhelming.'
'She doesn't waste time, does she? She's already made a hit with Ian.'
'Yes, I don't know how she does it.'
'I must say I'm glad she's taken up with Ian. I thought she might go for Michael, and I think she'd be too much for him at the moment, the last thing he needs.'
Lamorna felt herself reddening. And just at that moment Michael appeared.
'I'm off to the folk club. Do you want a lift?'
'No, no thank you, I'm not coming.'
'What about your friend?'
'She's gone with Ian already.'
'Oh, well, see you then.'

'You could have gone with him, you don't have to stay and keep me company.'
'No, really, I am tired.'
'Oh no, I've forgotten to give Michael his cards. Have to wait for tomorrow.'
'Cards?'
'Yes, it's his birthday today.'
A feeling of emptiness washed over her, as though she had somehow let him down by not going with him.

'More tea?'

'Jude's right. I'm dull and boring,' she thought. 'Sitting here drinking tea, pretending I don't want to be with him when I do. Torturing myself.'

'Do you want to talk about what happened?' Aileen asked.

'I think I've got over it, and in a way I'm glad it happened. I can forget about Gary now. But I still don't understand why he came here.'

'It must be because he's fond of you.'

'I don't think so. I think it was just a whim. He wanted to satisfy himself that I still cared about him. When Michael rescued me he shouted 'she's mine' as if he owns me. Well he doesn't own me, and I know now that I don't care for him at all.'

'How did you meet him?'

'He's on the same course. He'd already tried Jude, and she didn't want him. He wanted me to pose for his project. He's doing a study based on pre-Raphaelite paintings, and he decided I look a bit like Lizzie Siddal. She was Rossetti's muse. So he took some pictures of me in settings like the paintings. And then he wanted me to pose for the scene with Ophelia drowning. He wanted to do a variation with me naked. I said I wouldn't, but he talked me into wearing just my underwear. That's when things went wrong.'

'Why did that make things go wrong?'

'Because of my leg. He saw my leg.'

She unwrapped her skirt to show Aileen the scars.

'Oh, what happened?'

'It was when I was nearly eight. I got too near the bonfire on firework's night. My friend had a jumping jack go down her welly boot, and everyone was busy helping her. They didn't notice me playing, poking a stick into the flames. And my coat caught fire.'

'That must have been terrible for you.'

'Yes, the worst thing was being in hospital.'

'If this Gary went off you because of your leg, then he's not worth knowing anyway.'

'I suppose so. I let it get to me. It's hard when you know what the reaction's going to be. My leg is horrible. I never let anyone see it. And I don't have the confidence, not like Jude.'

'Well, it must be difficult, but not everyone will feel like that. The right person will come along for you.'

'I'm not going to wait around. I'm determined to do well on my course. I want to get a good job and be independent. It won't matter then. But I don't know how I'll feel when I see Gary back at College.'

'I should think he'll be too embarrassed to cause any problem for you.'

'You're probably right. Thanks for listening Aileen. I think I'll get to bed and read for a while.'

'Will you be okay walking over on your own?'

'Yes, I'll be fine.'

'Well, goodnight then. You know where we are if you need us. Thanks for the company.'

She lay in bed later, thinking. 'I wish I could talk to my Mum like I can with Aileen. I've never even told her about Gary. Maybe if I could have talked to her it would all have been alright. But then I wouldn't be here, I wouldn't have come to Cornwall.'

It was late when she heard voices outside the door. Jude crept quietly into the bedroom.

'I'm awake, how was it?'

'You should have come. It was brilliant. The band was fantastic. And Michael got up and sang too. He did some Paul Simon stuff. He was really good. And we all sang happy birthday to him. And guess what!'

'What?'

'Ian's going to row me over to that little island on Sunday why don't you come?'

'I'll be working remember.'

'I think I'm getting to like boats.'

'Jude, was Michael with anyone?'

'Aha, why would you want to know?'

There was no reply.

'Well, he wasn't as it happens. He hung about with a group of lads and the people from the folk group, and us, of course.'

Lamorna turned to face the wall. Her eyes were wet with tears. 'Maybe he's not with anyone because all he wants is the girl in the commune, and he'll get back with her again.' Wallowing in self-imposed misery she eventually drifted into a restless sleep.

Chapter 8

A shaft of sunlight woke her early. Leaving Jude to sleep on she washed and dressed, and went over to the kitchen for breakfast. The hotel was busy, and Mary was late after her night out, so there was no time to eat. There was still no sign of Jude or Mary when they finally got through, and were loading up the dish washer. Mary arrived first, flushed and breathless as they sat down for a welcome cup of tea.

'I'm so sorry. I overslept. Mum thought I'd already gone out, and only found me when she came to change the bed.'

'Don't worry, Lamorna was here to help. How about some breakfast with us, I don't suppose you had any?'

'No, I was too rushed. Thank you.'

They were tucking into their bacon sandwiches when Michael appeared.

'Great night Michael. Haven't heard you sing in ages. You should have come with us Lamorna, it was fantastic.'

'So Jude tells me. Happy Birthday for yesterday Michael.'

'Thank you.' He seemed surprised.

'Reminds me, there's something for you here.'

Aileen rummaged behind the clock and found his cards.

'Thanks.' He stuffed them into a pocket.

'I just came to pick up a few things. I'm working on the cottage today unless you need me.'

'No, we should be fine.'

'Okay, I'll be off then.'

'I'll go over and see if Jude's awake.'

Jude was just stirring. She was persuaded to have something to eat before they set off. It was quieter round the harbour, hardly anyone about.

'Change over day,' Lamorna explained. 'One lot of emmets gone and a calm before the new ones invade.'

They walked on up the hill and were soon turning into the communal house garden. Lamorna saw that the hammock was empty, but there was a young woman playing with a baby on a rug thrown down under the trees. She had long blonde hair, and Lamorna was sure she was the girl she'd seen talking to Michael in the harbour.

'Hi Rosa,' called Jude, 'This is Lamorna.'

'Hello. Thank you for inviting us. Lovely baby.'

She stooped to touch his hand, and smiled when she felt his fingers curl around hers. He gurgled and kicked his legs in delight.

'Say hello to Lamorna, Dylan, come on, smile for us. He's three months old now,' she added.

'Is he named after Dylan Thomas?'

'No, Bob Dylan.'

'Is he your baby?' asked Jude.

'Well yes, I gave birth to him, but I don't think I own him. He's not my baby in that sense. I think of him as a free spirit. We can all share in the joy he brings.'

'That's great. I love your ideas about sharing and not being possessive,' Jude said.

A dark haired girl came out carrying a tray loaded with mugs of coffee and biscuits.

'Meet Laura,' said Rosa, she started this commune, and she makes all the biscuits!'

She introduced Jude and Lamorna, and then had to repeat it all when two others joined them. They were a tall slim young man with dark hair tied in a ponytail, Paul, and Jean, a small quiet woman with round glasses and reddish hair.

'There are six of us most of the time,' Rosa explained. 'Martyn and Heather have gone to meet some people off the train.'

'Some friends are coming up from London for a couple of nights,' Laura added. Dylan began to grizzle.

'He needs a nappy change,' Rosa said, starting to raise herself up from the rug.

'My turn, come on baby,' Jean said, jumping quickly to her feet, and lifting up Dylan into her arms.

'It's lovely the way you all help. Not just leaving it to Rosa,' Lamorna said.

'It's what the commune's all about. I breast feed him of course, but everyone wants to join in and help with him. It's like he has lots of parents, one big family. He was born here too. A friend of mine from Bristol is a midwife, and she came down to help bring him into the world. He was conceived this time last year, so we're all gathering this weekend to celebrate.'

'We love celebrations,' Laura said. 'There are so many bad things happening now, Martin Luther King assassinated, Vietnam, nuclear weapons, all that stuff. We're trying to break away from it and create a more peaceful, fairer society.'

'We celebrated the Summer Solstice up at the Merry Maidens,' Paul said. 'And we had a May Day Party. We wanna be in touch with the earth, with lost traditions.'

'I wish I'd been here. I could have taken some photographs for my project. I'm doing a study of the stones.'

'The locals don't like it,' Paul went on. 'They think it's weird, even though they still do all the Furry Dance stuff down here. They don't like outsiders joining in.'

'Sam thinks you'll drive away the tourists.'

'Who's Sam?'

'My boss up at the hotel.'

'Oh him. He's our arch enemy. He's campaigning against us. Have you seen the posters?'

'No.' She felt uncomfortable under his gaze.

'They're planning a meeting at the Hotel. They're getting together to discuss the threat to their livelihoods. That's us,' Laura said.

'I didn't know. I could talk to him. He seems reasonable.'

'Too late for that, but I don't suppose it will come to anything. I can't see what they can do. We pay our rent. We're not breaking the law.'

'They'll stop us selling stuff round the harbour,' Paul said.

'Well, we'll rent a stall in the market then.'

Jean came back out with Dylan, plonking him in Paul's arms.

'Here you are Daddy.'

'I'm not Daddy,' he said, scowling at her, as he lifted the baby up to his face, 'Hello Dylan, I'm Paul.'

Dylan began to cry, and he passed him to Rosa, who unbuttoned her blouse and began to feed him. They all spent the next hour or so relaxing in the sunshine, listening to music drifting through the windows. Lamorna recognised Fairport Convention. She noticed clean nappies blowing gently on a line, and the patch of dug earth where a few salad vegetables were growing. The plot was bigger than when she and Mary had walked by the other day, and sticks marked the ends of rows where seeds had recently been planted. There were a few flowers around too, marigolds and nasturtiums, petunias and sweet peas. She got up and walked over to the hammock just as Paul turned his attentions to Jude, moving over to sit beside her and engage her in conversation. She clambered in, and lay contentedly gazing up at the clouds as the hammock swayed gently.

There was a sudden lurch as Paul climbed in beside her, straight away bending to try and kiss her. She winced, and he looked at her bruised, sore lip.

'How did you do that?'

'I had an accident with a doorpost,' she replied curtly, shifting to extricate herself. He got the message and climbed back out, slouching back to where Jude was sitting.

'I'll get this baby to bed,' Rosa said.

'Can I hold him?' Lamorna asked. And she was handed the tiny bundle, warm and smelling sweetly of milk. They rocked together and talked baby talk. Rosa and Jean carried the pots away to be washed up. Laura was sleeping on the cushions. Paul was seriously attempting to seduce Jude, but Lamorna was pleased to see that he was not succeeding. Jude shrugged him off and went over to the house. He looked over at the hammock, and she closed her eyes, feigning sleep. Soon she was sleeping, Dylan grunting gently on her breast.

She was woken when Dylan stirred, and heard voices. A group of people were coming through the gateway. Struggling a little she managed to slither from the hammock, and carrying the waking baby she crossed to join in the welcoming. Rosa took Dylan, who had started to grizzle, as the newcomers were introduced by Laura.

'This is Nick, an old school friend, he works at the Arts Hub now, this is Suki, she's in a band, and this is Rog and Marianne, and this is Heather and Martyn, who live here too.'

'Hi ' they said, almost in unison.

Lamorna noticed that Marianne was pregnant. They were all long haired, wearing cheesecloth and tie dyed clothing, beads strung around their necks.

'How do you all know each other?' she asked. 'And what's the Arts Hub?'

'So many questions,' laughed Nick, a blonde, slim man with glasses and the longest beard. 'We all live together in a squat, and we know Laura because of me and school. Martyn was at college with me too. Small world. The Arts Hub is a great place; we have exhibitions, radical music and performances, happenings. You should come and visit some time, it's groovy.'

'We could go down at half term, it sounds fantastic,' Jude said.

They talked together for a while and then Heather took the guests indoors to show them their sleeping places, and Rosa carefully laid a sleeping Dylan back in the hammock.

'Listen out for him Paul,' she called over.

Laura, Jean, Jude and Lamorna went into the kitchen with her to begin cooking. They all worked together to prepare a large pot of vegetable chilli and brown rice.

'Someone pick some fruit before it gets dark,' called Laura, and Heather and Suki went off out to the strawberry patch beside the house.

'We're all vegetarians,' Laura explained, 'we don't eat anything with eyes. We think killing animals is cruel.'

'What about potatoes?' Jude said, laughing.

They were listening to Leonard Cohen as they worked. Lamorna had never heard him before. She loved the songs, their poetry of love and longing.

Suki appeared with a bowl full of strawberries. She looked stunning with her long brown curling hair, lips smudged with strawberry juice, and ankle- sweeping dress in muted shades of plum and blue.

'Where did you get that amazing dress?' Jude asked.

'Oh, it's from Biba. It's my favourite boutique.'

It was time to eat, and they all sat around on the rugs, each with a large bowl into which Martyn served rice and chilli. Jean turned the music up, and they caught up with each other's news as Jefferson Airplane played. Dylan stirred again, and Jean carried him over to Rosa, who fed him whilst spooning food into her mouth with one hand. The strawberries were wonderful, and they all felt content after the meal was finished. Lamorna and Jude gathered the dishes to wash up.

'We'll do the dishes in the morning. You're at work tomorrow Lamorna, just relax,' Jean said.

So they sat together and listened as Nick, Suki and Martyn played guitar together. Dylan was taken to bed, and Lamorna felt relieved when Rosa returned and sat with Paul. Some people joined in with spoons or tapping on a saucepan lid, and everyone sang along with the most well-known songs. Overhead the moon was a golden crescent in a sky dizzying with stars. Nick rolled up a joint and passed it round. Lamorna watched as everyone inhaled and then passed it on. It came round to her, but she was afraid to try, and no-one noticed as she handed it on to Jude, who did take a long draw. Twice more it was passed around, and Lamorna felt strange and apart as she saw everyone relax and seem to drift away into their own worlds. After a while Nick took up his guitar again and strummed quietly. Marianne and Rog crept away into the house, and were followed by Paul and Rosa.

Lamorna broke the spell at last, whispering to Jude,

'I'd better go, I'm working tomorrow morning. But stay if you want to.'

'No, I'll come. Need my beauty sleep.'

They pulled themselves up, and walked around the circle to speak to Laura and Jean.

'Thanks for a wonderful evening,' Lamorna said, bending down to hug them both. 'I have to go. Early start in the morning.'

'Come next weekend,' Jean said.

'I'm going home Wednesday worse luck,' Jude complained.

'Well, come on Tuesday evening then, we'll make a farewell party for you.'

'That's great, thanks.'

'What's that stuff like? Lamorna asked as they walked back.

'You mean pot?'

'Yes.'

'Didn't you try it?'

'No, I don't know how.'

'I can't believe you've never tried. It makes you relaxed. Everything seems so much more intense, colours are more, and everything seems, well, more. Try it.'

'I don't know. I never even tried to smoke.'

'You'll be telling me you're a virgin next.'

There was silence.

'God, Lamorna. Where've you been? This is 1968. You're not living. You should get to know all of them better; it'll be a good experience for you. I could really get into that lifestyle.'

'I don't know, it could get boring, all that sitting about. I want to do more with my life.'

'You sound like a fifty year old. You've got plenty of time to do all that work stuff. Live a bit. Anyway, they don't just sit around talking about peace and love. It's like the hippies in California. They go to anti-war demos, peace marches, all of that stuff. Paul was telling me. I can't wait to go again. I might catch some fish with Ian, we could take them some.'

'They don't eat things with eyes remember.'

They reached the hotel, and Michael came out.

'Goodnight,' Jude shouted over.

'Goodnight,' he replied, and turned the corner.

'There, he's all alone; I reckon he really fancies you. You should make an effort.'

'Jude!'

'Okay, I know: "I don't want any men in my life, I'm dedicated to my work." It's going to be so much fun living with you next year.'

Lamorna lay awake, listening to Jude's gentle snores.

'She's right, I am boring. But I don't know how to change. I can't be like her. She's so confident and good looking. She can do what she wants, and everyone likes her.'

Chapter 9

There were crowds in for afternoon teas next day, and Lamorna baked three batches of splits. Later she was working in the garden, enjoying the last sunshine when she saw Michael arrive, and he was still in the kitchen when she carried in the harvest of salads and vegetables.

'Tea Lamorna? Michael's just been enjoying the splits,' Aileen said.
She glanced across, and he actually smiled at her.

'They're good.' he said. Then washing up his mug and plate, he kissed Aileen and was gone.

'He could have kissed me. If I was Jude I would have said "Hey, what about me, where's my kiss." What am I thinking? Do I want him to kiss me?'

'What are you smiling about?' Aileen asked.

'Oh nothing really. What can I do next?'

'Can you help me prepare dinner later? Will Jude join us?'

'I'm not sure. She's out with Ian on his boat today.'

'She's a fast worker, that one. I'm glad I'm not her Mother, I'd never stop worrying.'

'She can look after herself.'

'Maybe. She'll be alright with Ian though. He's a decent lad.'

Lamorna was surprised when Michael turned up for dinner with the family. Jude and Ian appeared as they'd just sat down to eat.

'We've had a great time,' Jude enthused. 'We went to see the Merry Maidens and Ian rowed me out to the island. A hermit used to live there.'

'Don't know why she wanted to go over to a pile of rocks,' Ian said, laughing.

'Would you like some dinner Ian, there's plenty?' Aileen asked him.

'No, thank you, I'm expected at home. Are you coming down to the pub tomorrow night?'

'We'll be there, won't we Lamorna? Are you coming Michael?'

'Yes, I reckon I might.' He grinned at her.
And much to Lamorna's embarrassment Jude got up, her chair scraping loudly on the floor, and kissed Ian in front of everyone. Astonishingly no-one seemed shocked at all, and conversation went on as normal after Ian had gone. Jude chattered away about the island and the standing stones. Michael talked to her about the origin of the stones, and then turned to Lamorna.

'Lamorna took some photos of the stones and Men an Tol for her project.'
It was the first time she'd heard him use her name, and she felt a jolt in her heart.

'Yes,' she croaked awkwardly, her throat suddenly dry. There was an amazing sunset. You should try and see it Jude.'

'Michael could take you,' Sam suggested.

'I don't know,' he replied, I'm a bit busy at the cottage this week.'
Lamorna allowed herself to breathe again.

'Maybe another time,' Jude said. 'I'm sure I'll come down again.'

***

A coach load of tourists arrived on Monday afternoon and they all turned up at once for cream teas. Jude had just come down from her bath, having spent most of the day in bed, and she was drawn in to help. She volunteered to help serve in the garden, while Lamorna worked in the kitchen. Jude was a great hit with the old men, who pinched her bottom and laughed at her awful saucy comments.

Michael called in for tea, and Lamorna felt a pang of jealousy when she saw him joking and laughing with Jude.

'She finds it so easy; men just seem to swarm around her in droves.'
But there was no time to brood, with another batch of splits to be made. By five o'clock they were all exhausted. Even Michael had helped for a while, loading the dishwasher and washing some teapots. He tucked a stray hair behind Lamorna's ear as he left, and her heart lurched.

'You're all floury,' he said.
Aileen made them tea, but none of them could face eating a single split. Mary rooted around in the pantry and found a pack of fig rolls, slightly stale, but they munched them gratefully.

And then Lamorna was outside again, raking over the lawns, clearing up the discarded serviettes, spoons and other debris left by the crowds, whilst the others blitzed the dining room. She and Jude finished washing all the teapots and trooped wearily over to the cottage to change for the evening out. Jude had brought a suitcase full of clothes with her, but Lamorna once again wrapped around her flowered skirt and pulled on her cheesecloth shirt.

'You wore that last night!'
'It's all I've got. I didn't come here for the social life, it's a work trip.'
'Well, you ought to treat yourself to something new. There's a fantastic boutique in Penzance. One of the girls told me about it at the folk club. Why don't you come with me on Wednesday when I go, we could have a browse and buy you something?'
'I might do that. But come on, we should get going. I wonder if Michael might turn up.'
'Ah, Michael,' Jude teased.

It was quiet in the pub, no sign of Mary or Chris yet, or any other young people. They chose seats by the window, and watched the world go by.

'There are the Londoners,' Jude pointed out.
Nick, Suki and Marianne were wandering by with Martyn. Suki had her guitar slung across her back. Some lads on bikes swept by and made some rude gestures at the group.

'They do look out of place here,' Lamorna thought, 'with their long hair, beards and beads.'
The door swung open, and Mary and Chris came in, closely followed by Ian. Jude went over to the bar to buy them all drinks. There was some discussion about the hippies.

'They all look so weird,' Mary said.
'Well we hung out with them on Saturday, and they were great fun.' Jude said.
'They're all into drugs, aren't they?' Chris said.
Lamorna gave Jude a warning look.

'They're just normal young people. They invited us for dinner and we sat around the bonfire and sang,' she told them.' I wished I'd taken my camera with me.'

'How's your project going Lamorna?' Mary asked.

'Michael took me to Men an Tol and Lanyon Quoit, but I've not done any since Jude came.'

'She's a bad influence,' joked Ian, who received a dig in the ribs for his effort.

'I've hardly done a thing,' Jude said. 'I was going to get some photos in the market, but I haven't got around to it.'

'Why don't you wander round the village and take some pictures of the little stalls people set up, you know, just by their gates, with a few vegetables or eggs to sell,' Mary suggested.

'And there's the fishermen's stalls round the harbour. They sell shells and urchins they find in their nets,' Ian added.

'That's a brilliant idea,' Jude said. 'I'll do it tomorrow.'

'Come on,' he said, pulling her to her feet, 'I'll show you where to find them.' They left arm in arm.

'You'll miss her when she's gone,' Mary said.

'I will. But then I'll have peace and quiet again. She can be exhausting in large doses.'

Chris went up to the bar to buy a second round of drinks.

'Ian seems very taken with her. Do you think anything will come of it?'

'I don't know, you never know with Jude. But she does seem keen on him. I think he's good for her; he's got his feet firmly on the ground. She normally goes for all the wrong types. Her last big flame was keen on pot holing, and she spent every weekend in dark wet caves with him. She realised in the end that she didn't really know what he looked like!'

They both laughed.

At that moment Michael walked in and came over to their table. Lamorna felt her heart miss a beat. Chris came back with the drinks, and then went to get one for Michael. There was some general chat about issues around the village, rumours of a shop closing, someone from London buying a cottage.

'Where's Jude?' Michael asked after a while.

'She's gone out with Ian,' Lamorna told him. 'He's showing her little stalls around the village where she can get some good photos.'

'If you believe that you'll believe anything. I hope she can look after herself.'

'Are you being rude about my brother Michael?'

'Sorry Mary, but you know he's a bit of a lad.'

'It takes one to know one.'

'Jude can look after herself,' Lamorna said, blushing.

'You coming bowling with us tomorrow night Mike?' Chris asked.

'I reckon I will, I've not been for ages. It's Graham's birthday isn't it?'

'Yeah, the gang will all be there.'

'Would you and Jude like to come up for tea tomorrow,' Mary asked, 'seeing as all the men are going out?'

'I would have loved to, but Jude's got us invited to the Hippy place again.'

'I'm not sure I'd want to go.'

'They've got some friends from London staying with them. One of them's in a rock group.'

'You know one of the girls up there don't you Michael?' Mary asked mischievously.

'I did for a while. I'm off now, thanks for the beer Chris. See you tomorrow night.'

He pushed his chair back, swallowed the last of his beer and went out.

'You've upset him now Mary, you know he's still brooding about that maid.'

'Which girl was he involved with?' Lamorna asked.

'A blonde one, think she was called Rose, something like that. She seemed nice enough, but she led him on. She was seeing some other bloke up there. Had a baby. They're into all that free love, I've heard about it.'

'They're not like that. They're all really friendly, and they all help with the baby.'

'It don't seem right to me,' Chris said. 'Babies need to know their Mum and Dad, and they should be married.'

'That's the first time I've heard you say a good word about marriage,' Mary teased, cuffing him.

'Aye, well.'

'I don't know,' Lamorna went on, 'doesn't marriage make people get possessive and jealous? That can't be a good thing. We can't own other people.'

'It's not about owning,' Mary said. 'It's about commitment and loyalty, not hurting each other, working together for the children, whatever happens.'

'Yeah, it's too easy for a bloke just to walk away if there's no piece of paper,' Chris added.

'But it works both ways. What if there's a baby and the woman pushes the father away?' Lamorna said.

'He'd be glad to go,' Chris said. 'Ow.'

Mary had cuffed him again.

'Well I wouldn't want to live like that,' Mary said firmly, holding Chris's arm as if he might try to escape.

'I don't know. It would be nice to have all that help with a baby, not just dependent on a husband, or stuck on your own with it all day every day. It seemed like a lovely atmosphere up there to me, and the baby, Dylan loved being with all of us. He was happy to go with anyone.'

'Yeah. All those different girls. Sounds good to me.'

This time he'd gone too far. Mary picked up his glass and poured the last dregs of beer over his head

'I was only joking,' he protested.

'Many a true word,' she said, as she pulled her engagement ring off her finger and tossed it onto the table before stamping out.

'I'm sorry. It's my fault for talking about the hippies.'

'She'll come round. She always does. She gives me the ring back every month.'

'Maybe she's trying to tell you something.'

'Yeah well, maybe I should get round to naming a date, but I was waiting 'til I'd saved up a bit.'

'But if you want to marry her why wait, you'll find a way?'

'Maybe you're right. Mary's the one for me, always has been. Michael says we could rent that cottage he's doing up come autumn. It's not what Mary wants, she's hankering for one of those new places near her Mum's, but it'll do us for a bit.'

'Well there you are then.'

'I'd best go find her and make the peace. Shall you be okay walking home alone?'

'Yes, of course. Good luck!'

Lamorna finished her drink. 'May as well go,' she thought, 'no sign of Jude coming back. Where could they have got to?'

She walked out onto the harbour. It was quiet now, only the creak and bump of the boats jostling together in the tide. The little cottage was dark, silent apart from a steady drip, drip from the bathroom tap. She washed, cleaned her teeth and snuggled down into bed. 'Another night with the hippies, and then a morning free on Wednesday. I'll see Jude off and then I'll go to the boutique and buy something new. I'll miss her but I'll enjoy having this place to myself again.'

She woke sometime later to the sound of mattress springs.

'That you Jude?'

'Yeah, sorry I woke you.'

'Are you alright?'

'Yeah, I had a great time. I was on the beach with Ian.'

'The beach! In the dark!'

'Oh Lorna, you're so naïve sometimes. We were having sex. It was great.'

After a pause Lamorna spoke again.

'Jude you're crazy. You'll probably never see him again.'

'I don't care, it was the best ever.'

'Michael was right then, he's got a reputation.'

'Well he deserves it, he knows what to do, no fumbling about. Anyway, Michael can't talk. Ian told me lots of the lads used to try and seduce girls. They always went after the girls down here on holiday.'

There was another long pause.

'What if...'

Jude threw her pillow at Lamorna.

'You're sounding like my mother now. I'm not stupid. I've been on the Pill for ages.'

'You never told me.'

'I've never told my mother either. This is the sixties. You should try it sometime.'

'How did you get the Pill? Thought you had to be married.'

'Easy. Just wore my Gran's ring. They asked me if my husband approved. As if it's a man's decision. Honestly. What about Michael? I reckon he's keen on you. You keep denying it, but I think you fancy him. Even Ian thinks so.'

'Well you're all wrong.'

'Have it your own way. But if I were you I wouldn't waste your life. Take the chances when you can. Can I have my pillow back? And by the way, I told Ian you didn't want anything to do with Michael, you're right off men, so you don't need to worry.'

Lamorna tossed the pillow onto Jude's head. There was no sound from her friend. 'Could it be true, does Michael like me? Do I want him to like me? No use thinking about it. Jude's told him I don't want to know. I suppose it's for the best. He still seems to be wanting Rosa. What Mary said upset him.'

Chapter 10

Jude spent the whole of Tuesday with Ian. Lamorna was working hard again. There were the chickens to clean out, an afternoon of baking and a non-stop stream of folk wanting teas. She was tired when she met up with Jude at six o'clock to get ready for their evening out.

'I had a great day. Ian took me swimming on a beach somewhere and then we had a picnic in the sand dunes.'

'Picnic. That's a new word for it.'

A sock whizzed across the room, just missing Lamorna's head.

'I don't know what to wear, I'm bored of these three tops,' Lamorna said, sighing.

'Have this one,' Jude said, handing her a jade green top. 'It will suit you. I don't really like it.'

'Oh thanks, it's lovely.'

She slipped the soft velvety top over her head, before brushing the tangles from her hair.

'Do you want to lend me your hair too?'

She had always loved Jude's sleek dark hair.

'Why do we always want different hair? My Mum spends hours getting her hair permed, and I'd give anything for her hair.'

They set off to walk through the village and up to the old house. The sun was low in the sky, and the last few stragglers were leaving the beach. A small child was crying, and they saw him look back at an ice cream cornet on the ground as he was dragged away.

'I remember dropping an ice cream once,' Jude said. 'I got bought another one, and after I'd eaten half of it I decided it would be a good idea to drop it again and get another. It didn't work. I got smacked for being clumsy.'

The commune garden was lit with candles in jars, and lanterns hung here and there in the trees. Music was playing, and the sound of voices greeted them as they walked up to the house. Martyn and Heather were tending a bonfire, and Lamorna couldn't resist joining them. She was still fascinated by fire, despite her scars. Jude took their gifts of wine and chocolates to the kitchen. Paul sauntered over and tried to get into conversation with her. She was polite but cool towards him. Soon everyone was outside. Baked potatoes were rescued from the embers.

There was yet more unfamiliar music, Country Joe and the Fish, which Nick had brought up with him from London. It prompted a discussion about the war in Vietnam. Rog, Nick and Marianne talked about an anti-war demo they'd been involved in back in March.

'Over a hundred people were arrested, and loads got beaten up by the Police,' Nick said.

It all seemed a different world to Lamorna. She had only been dimly aware of these events back home, and she wished now she'd joined the students from her college who'd gone down to London for the demo.

'I was so bound up with Gary, and struggling to get my course work done. It all seems so selfish now,' she thought.

Suki played for them. She and her band were working on an album, and she was trying out some of the songs. A joint was passed around and again Lamorna let it go by. Laura was blowing bubbles and she watched as Dylan reached up as if to try and catch them. It seemed a magical evening. She lay back and gazed at the sky. No falling stars tonight. She thought she could see the Plough, and maybe Orion. After a time Dylan was taken to bed, and Rosa climbed into the hammock with Paul. Suki stopped playing, and Lamorna listened to the distant sound of the sea on the rocks below the cliff, a tranquil lulling sound. It was the sort of evening she wanted to last forever.

'But there is something missing, someone to love,' she thought. And then she remembered her resolve and spoke crossly to herself. 'That was the old me, I'm Lamorna the photographer now. No time for dalliance.'

'What did you say?' Jude asked.

'Oh, just talking to myself. Jude,' she said. Then after a pause, 'Did you get any photographs of the stalls around the village?'

'Here's my conscience again. Ian and I walked around the village before we went off for our picnic. I got some good pictures of sea urchins and shells on a little stall down by the harbour, and there were two tables with stuff like tomatoes and eggs for sale. One turned out to be Ian's cousin's place, and she made us come in for tea. We ended up being given eggs for me to take home. Don't know how I'll carry them.'

'People here are so friendly aren't they? It's hard to believe they can't accept the commune.'

'Fear of the strange, the unknown,' I suppose. 'Do you think we should get going? I've got a train to catch tomorrow worse luck.'

'Yeah, okay.'

They made their farewells, and Lamorna promised to come and see them again.

'A peaceful evening,' she remarked as they stopped for a few moments to look at the tide running into the harbour.

'Yeah, they're great, aren't they? We could do something like that, set up a creative commune with artists and photographers.'

'But how do you know you're going to like everyone?'

'You don't, that's the challenge.'

'I don't know if it's possible. They all seem to get on though.'

'You should spend more time with them, escape the hotel more often.'

Chapter 11

They both overslept, and it was a mad rush to get to the station in time for Jude's train.

'I'm right about you and Michael,' Jude shouted from the window. You'll see.' Lamorna spent the rest of the day in town. She found the little boutique in Chapel Street and bought a tie-dyed skirt and floaty top, and then couldn't resist a beautiful long dress in the sale. It was a pale silky material with a pattern of faded blue flowers, and smocking around the neckline. She treated herself to some lunch in the coffee bar, and sat gazing out of the window, thinking about the last few days.

'I can't be like Jude, but maybe it's just as well. I've got to make my own way in the world, no parents to bail me out all the time. And I want to be successful. I want to be a good photographer and get an exciting job someday.'

It began to rain. She watched the droplets running down the pane, joining together in never ending patterns. Martyn and Suki were hurrying by. She wondered if she would meet up with them again. They'd told her she was welcome any time, but there was no specific invitation. 'Maybe I'll go on Friday evening. I need to get some more photos done on Saturday. Should have brought the films with me to get some contact prints done. Wonder if there's a photography place here.'

She just scrambled onto the bus in time, and shivering, sat down as it rattled onto the road, wind screen wipers scratching the glass like chalk on a school blackboard. Sam was just emerging from the garage when she splashed up the hotel drive.

'You look wet through. Go in and have a warm bath won't you?'

'Thanks, I'd love to. Jude caught the train alright. Typical of her to miss the rain.'

'That's good. Thought you were pushing it.'

She dumped her bags in the cottage, and grabbing a towel and some clean clothes made a run for it across to the hotel kitchen.

Later, feeling warmer again she sat by the range, drinking tea with Aileen and Mary.

'You're wearing your ring again Mary!'

'Chris asked if we could be married in October, on my birthday. Aileen says we can have the reception here, and we can stay in the new cottage until we get our own place.'

'They may as well; we won't get any holiday lettings until next spring or summer.'

'And I want you to be a bridesmaid, with my sisters, will you Lamorna, could you come? It was Chris's idea.'

'I'd love to,' Lamorna said, giving her a hug.

'Chris asked Michael to be his best man.'

'You'll have to catch the bouquet, and you'll be the next bride,' Aileen said.

'I won't. I've got two more years on this course, and then I want to travel the world.'

'Ian's keen on Jude, do you think she'd come down for the wedding? He's been moping about all day since she left.'

'What happened to that local girl he was seeing?' Aileen asked.

'Oh you mean Maureen. They're always on and off. I reckon they'll get round to marrying someday, depending on Jude.'

'Are you coming out this evening?' Mary asked as she got up to leave the kitchen.

'No, I won't thanks, I think I'll stay in and get my stuff sorted. I've not done anything all week.'

***

Lamorna was asked to prepare a buffet lunch in the morning. The hotel lounge was rearranged with the tables in the centre, and soon almost all the chairs around them were occupied. She was serving them all with coffee, weaving her way through the tables with a tray, when she caught a few words of the discussion.

'We should ask them to leave altogether.'

'They don't spend any money in the village. They're all scroungers. All they do is sit around with no shoes on trying to sell knick knacks like gypsies.'

'It must be the meeting Laura mentioned, the thing about the hippies,' she thought. She made her way slowly around the room, pouring coffee, smiling politely, and all the while listening with increasing anger.

'Yes, the emmets will get fed up of it and stop coming back down.'

'They won't, they're wrong,' she thought.

'We need a proper plan of action,' Sam said.

'They give the place a bad reputation,' chipped in the solitary woman.

'Aye, a chap came in the shop last week, worrying they might try selling drugs to his kids.'

Lamorna dropped a spoon and bent to pick it up. 'What do they mean? They wouldn't do that. They're talking rubbish.'

'We should move them on to Newquay or St Ives, there's all sorts there.'

'No, they don't want them over there; my sister reckons the locals are fed up with them.'

'They're just layabouts.'

A murmur of agreement rippled through the room. Lamorna plonked the tray down on the table. The empty cups jumped and rattled.

'They're not layabouts. I've met them. They're just normal young people trying to live a better life, trying to escape the horrible world of greed you've created with all the wars and fighting...'

'That'll be enough Lamorna,' Sam interrupted. 'Get on with your work.'

'But you're all wrong. They're nice people, they...'

'Lamorna, please take your tray away. Leave the meeting.'

'They buy things in the village.' She picked up the tray, pink with anger and embarrassment. It was then that she noticed Michael sitting at the edge of the room, seemingly taking notes.

'I should have said something about Michael. About him knowing them.'

She reached the kitchen. No-one was there. She started to load the dishwasher, banging plates in so fiercely that two shattered. Aileen came back in with Mary, and she hid her face as she worked so that they wouldn't see her tears. Sam appeared later.

'We're going to try and ban the group from selling their stuff around the harbour and village. It's probably illegal anyway, we'll get the Police to check and then move them on.'

'Don't know why they have to wander about like that with no shoes,' Aileen said. 'They're mothers would die of shame. A bad influence on the village youngsters.'

Sam turned to Lamorna

'I can't have you, an employee, standing up for them.'

'Well then, I'll go, I can't work for you any longer if you're not prepared to listen.'

'There's no need for that.'

She untied her apron and hung it over a chair. Tears spilled down her cheeks.

'Michael was friends with them, you ask him. They're not like what everyone was saying, just because of the way they dress. You don't understand.'

'That's enough. It's what folk believe. It's what the visitors think.'

'Well they're all wrong. I'm a visitor. I don't think like that.'

'Lamorna, calm down,' Aileen soothed. 'I need you here, this will all blow over, and where will you go?'

'I don't know what I'll do. I'm sorry, I can't stay. They're my friends.

She walked out.

Chapter 12

Back in the cottage she packed up her belongings, then cleaned and tidied ferociously. 'Why did I do that?' she asked herself. 'What am I going to do now?' Only Mary was in the kitchen when she returned the key.

'I wish you'd stay, I'll miss you. Will you still be my bridesmaid?'

'Of course,' she said, hugging her. 'I'll come and see you in the pub one night. I'll try and get a job in Penzance. Will you save any post that comes for me? Jude may write.'

'Yes, but how will I get it to you?'

'Don't worry, I'll see you and pick it up sometime. I'm bound to get a day off. I suppose I might not get a job, and then I'll have to go home. Here, I'll write my home address just in case. I'll try and let you know.'

She tore a page from her notebook and quickly scribbled her address down.

'I'll stay in the hostel tonight and see what turns up.'

'Michael will have to come back and work here now, and the cottage won't get finished.'

'I'm sorry Mary, but you do understand, don't you?'

'Not really. But I can't see as they do any harm myself.'

'Oh Mary, you really are the kindest person. I'd better go.'

Aileen came back into the kitchen just as she was opening the door.

'I wish you'd change your mind. Sam will calm down. He doesn't want you to go.'

'I can't, it's a principle. They don't understand. They don't even know them.'

'Well, I'm so sorry Lamorna. Here are the wages we owe you. Please come back if you need help, won't you. If you change your mind.'

'Thank you. I loved my time here. Say cheerio to the chickens for me. Here's some money for the two plates I just broke.'

Stuffing five shillings into Aileen's hand she turned and ran before they could see the tears running down her face.

She struggled to the bus stop. Her bags seemed much heavier than when she'd arrived. She regretted buying the new clothes, and she'd had to bundle the overalls and boots into a big carrier bag. There were ten minutes still to wait. She sat forlornly on the harbour rails. The bus came along. Jean and Heather got off.

'Hi Lamorna, what are you doing?'

'I was waiting for the bus. I've just left my job.'

'Oh no, what happened?'

Lamorna explained.

'That was really brave of you to speak up for us,' Jean said. 'You must come and stay. Don't go to the hostel. We'll go into Penzance with you tomorrow and show you how to sign on, and then it won't matter if you don't get a job. It'll be great to have you.'

'Thank you that would be lovely. I've just been paid the wages I was owed, so I can give you some rent right now.' She fumbled in her pocket.

'Don't worry now,' Heather said. 'We'll explain when we get home.'

Taking her bags they walked together through the village to the house

'First some coffee,' Jean said, and then we'll get everyone together to welcome you.'

They went into the big kitchen, leaving Lamorna's bags piled by the door. Heather put the kettle on, and Jean went to round everyone up. Martyn was at work, and it seemed that the London visitors had gone.

'We'd just been to see them off when we found you,' Heather told her.

Lamorna sat at the table and looked around while the kettle was boiling. She'd been in the kitchen before, but never really noticed her surroundings. It was a large room, with the huge cooking range where they'd made the chilli that first Saturday. Bunches of drying lavender and herbs hung from the beams, and a rail above a row of cupboards was hung with shiny pans of all sizes.

Jean reappeared with Rosa, Laura and Paul just as the coffee was made. So they all sat around the table and listened as Lamorna told her story again. They unanimously declared that she was truly courageous, and agreed that she must stay as long as she wanted.

'Was Michael in the meeting?' Rosa asked.

'I didn't see him at first, but then I noticed he was taking notes. He didn't say anything.'

'Huh, coward. He was happy to get what he could from us.'

'Paul, you're not being fair. Michael never exploited us, and I think it must have been hard for him when his Dad had called the meeting,' Laura said.

'He should have stuck up for us.'

'I suppose it's family loyalty,' Lamorna said bleakly, realising that she would probably never see him again.

'Well their loss is our gain. It'll be great having you here.'

'We don't have many rules here. Everyone is expected to help. There's no formal rota. We usually do our own washing, but we help each other out too. We keep the house clean and tidy, but in your own room you can do as you please as long as it doesn't affect anyone else. If there are any problems we have a house meeting, but it doesn't happen often.'

'There are no crazy rules here about having sex and all of that which we've heard some communes have. We just expect everyone to respect each other,' Heather added.

'Where can I sleep?' Lamorna asked.

'Come on, let's show you round.'

Laura led her out into the hallway again.

'This big room is our main living area.'

It was a spacious room, flooded with light from two large windows. There were views over the garden and across to the sea. The wooden floors were covered with patterned rugs.

'Jean and I brought the rugs and spreads in India and Morocco,' Laura told her. Two comfy old sofas were supplemented by colourful floor cushions, and there were baskets of fruit and a wooden bowl full of shells and stones. She stared in amazement at the shelves piled with books.

'We were lucky these shelves were here,' Laura said. 'Jean and I have far too many books. Feel free to browse and borrow them.'

She walked over to a record player and put an album on the turntable. Bob Dylan's voice filled the room.

'It's lovely. Who made all the pictures?'

'The paintings are Jean's, and Suki did the textiles. Maybe you could leave us a souvenir when you go back to college, a photograph would be nice.'

'I'm not sure I'm up to this standard, these paintings are fantastic.'

They were abstract landscapes, she thought, in colours of the Cornish countryside. She noticed jam jars filled with beads and buttons on the window sills, and there were pieces of driftwood and large smooth stones. In the central wall was a huge open fireplace, a hearth piled with logs, and the fire ready laid.

'Come on, let's go upstairs now.'

They went up the wide old staircase, and onto a galleried landing.

'This room is mine and Jeans.'

It was a tranquil space; a large bed covered in a mirror work throw, an old wardrobe, its doors carved with oak leaves, and a chest of drawers piled with bead necklaces and jars of various potions.

'Jean and I are together, we're lovers. I hope you're okay with that.'

'Oh yes, but I haven't, well, I haven't met any, any lesbians before.'

'How would you know? People usually don't tell anyone, not even friends.'

'I suppose not. I hadn't thought about that.'

Laura smiled.

'It's getting easier since the Act made us legal last year.'

'I don't know about that.'

'Most people don't. We don't flaunt it in public, especially down here. It's just about possible to hold hands in some places in London. These are some of our favourite little pictures. They're postcards and prints of Hockney's work. He's homosexual, and he's not afraid to show it in his art.'

She pointed to a collection of small prints on one wall.

'I love Hockney. I saw some of his work. I did a project about him at school.'

'I bet you didn't realise he was homosexual.'

'No, it was never mentioned, but it's obvious when you really look at these isn't it? I've got that poster of Elvis too.'

'We think he's beautiful.'

Paul was sprawled on the bed in his room

'You can shack up with me. Plenty of space.'

'You must be joking,' Laura said. 'No woman would ever want to set foot in this hovel.'

Clothes were strewn on the floor and books tottered in piles amongst discarded sweet wrappers. The windows were firmly closed and the air felt stale. It smelt of sweaty socks. The bed was covered with clothes and odds and ends. Lamorna noticed a dirty plate and three used mugs amongst the clutter on the floor. There was a mantelpiece on which were arranged small cardboard boxes each containing butterflies pinned to cork.

Rosa had one of the front rooms, with a small side room where Dylan slept in a cot. There were baskets of baby toys and a pile of clean terry nappies on a chest of drawers. Martyn and Heather shared another front room, and in between this and Rosa's domain was a small room which Lamorna learned was to be hers. There was a double bed covered with a cotton throw, and a chest of drawers. A small chair occupied a corner, and the wall was decorated with posters for art exhibitions and music events.

'This is the Hobbit Hole,' Laura said, 'We use it for guests. Suki and Nick had this room. We've already washed their sheets, so I'll find you some clean ones. I'm sorry it's so small.'

'It's perfect, and about twice the size of my room back home.'

Lamorna carried her things upstairs and made herself at home. Jean came in with a jar full of wild flowers for her.

'I can't believe how lucky I am. A new home, and tomorrow I may find a job. Something is bound to turn up.'

After a while she joined everyone again downstairs. They were all in the kitchen still, planning what to make for dinner.

'Hi Lamorna, have you settled in?' Heather asked.

'Yes thanks, it's lovely. What can I do to help?'

'We've just decided to make a pasta meal, so we'd love some help chopping vegetables.'

'Okay. Where do I put my rent money?'

'Here's the kitty.' Jean reached down a red pottery teapot from the shelf. We all put about one pound ten shillings in each week, and it covers most things. We eat frugally, mainly vegetables, beans and rice and we grow some of our food. A woman up the hill sells us eggs. We always send Martyn, she's taken a bit of a fancy to him and he gets them cheaper.'

Lamorna dropped her money into the pot.

'I saw you had fruit trees too.'

'Yes, and we've got the strawberries and raspberries now.'

'We make our own bread, and Heather loves baking cakes.'

'My Mum and Dad are in business down here, so they give me an allowance,' Heather said.

'And she's far too generous.'

'Well what else would I spend it on?'

'What happens when you cater for guests like me and Jude?'

'Oh we just make extra food and it seems to go round. Our friends from London put money in the kitty, and they brought us some wine, beer and cheeses. We don't drink much alcohol usually.'

Dinner was soon ready, and they all sat around the big table.

'Do you always have candles and flowers?'

'Yes,' Heather replied. 'We always try and eat together and make it a special occasion. It's an important part of the day.'

'What made you decide to set this up Laura?'

'I finished university and decided to do some travelling. I ended up in California, and met some flower people. I stayed a few weeks in a commune. I was hooked. It seemed the ideal way to live. When I came back over here I came down to stay with Heather for a few days. We were at College together.'

'Yeah, I was down here with my parents, looking for a job. I thought the commune idea sounded great, and we decided Cornwall was where it's at. My Dad knew about this place up for rent, and he used his influence to get it for us.'

'Everyone else just appeared as if by magic,' Laura went on. 'I met Jean on the bus from Penzance.'

'It was amazing,' Jean said. 'I was looking for something new. I'd just lost my job, and I thought I'd come down here and paint, and there was Laura, we got on well straight away.'

'But why Cornwall?'

'In a way it was just expedient. Heather was here, this place was waiting. But I think it's more than that. There is something special. Maybe it's the magnetic fields, or energy lines, but it is magical. It seems to be the right area for communal living. There were a lot of people down here last year for the summer of love.'

'I thought that at Men an Tol,' Lamorna told them. 'I crawled through the stone, and it felt different, like an electric charge, like the feeling before a thunderstorm.'

"That's exactly it. What were you doing there?'
Lamorna talked about her project, and then felt safe enough to mention Gary.

'He sounds bad,' Paul said. 'We don't believe in all that possessive stuff here. People can be free to fuck without owning each other, without all those ties that cause hassle.'
Lamorna felt a blush creeping over her face. It was a good thing there was candlelight.

'It's free love,' Rosa added. She had been preoccupied feeding Dylan. 'It's liberating for women. We can choose partners. We're not tied to the old fashioned rules of marriage.'

'Yeah,' Paul went on. 'It's good for men too. I was in a commune in London which had some extreme rules. Like you couldn't have sex with the same person more than three nights in a row. We don't have rules like that.'

'Paul and I were together for a while, but we decided it wasn't going anywhere, and that was okay,' Rosa said.

'Yeah, that's because you had that fling with the enemy, until you found out he was only after one thing.'

'That's not true Paul. Michael wouldn't have sex with me because I was pregnant. He was kind. But he was too serious, he wanted to look after me, he didn't understand the ideas of freedom and he couldn't live here, so it was pointless.'

'Too right. He's just like his Dad, he don't want no truck with us hippies.'

'Let's move on,' Jean said. 'We'll wash up and play some music.'

Paul left to get his guitar. The women cleared away.

'Washing up seems like fun when everyone's helping,' Lamorna remarked.

'We just take it for granted now, but you're right. Everyone joins in and it's a sociable thing. We often have our best conversations and make good decisions while we wash up together.'

'We try to do all the chores as an act of love and caring,' Jean added.

Rosa came back into the room.

'Dylan was tired, he's asleep already.'

'You didn't say how you came to be here Rosa.'

'Not a very interesting story. Laura put an advert in Oz, asking people to come and join. My parents were just splitting up, and there was a terrible atmosphere at home, so I thought, why not?'

'And what about Paul?'

'He was a real waif and stray. We just found him in the street in Penzance one day. He'd been living with some people in London, and they kicked him out for no reason. He got a train, ended up down here with a few pounds and his guitar.'

'Martyn's a surfer. He was in Newquay with friends on holiday. I was over there, visiting the folks, and met him in the pub, and the rest is history,' Heather told her.

'You mean you were over there scrounging from your rich toffs,' Paul said, sneering as he came back into the room.

'Paul! We can't be blamed for what our parents are, and I don't hear you complaining when Heather buys us all special treats.' said Jean.

'You don't know my parents Paul. They were bohemians in their youth. That's why they accept us. My Mum had to come down and take on the family estate and business when my grandparents were killed in an accident. There were employees to consider. You can't just make assumptions.'

'Oh you know me. I'm a communist. I grew up in the slums, watching the rich get richer. I want to change all that. We should be revolting here, demonstrating like the Paris students, get rid of the monarchy.'

'Nothing is that simple Paul. Communities depend on each other. It's a complex web, and you can't just change it all overnight,' Heather argued. 'One day I will have to take on my parent's responsibilities, and then we'll see what we can change.'

'Paul is our real radical; he was at that demo in Grosvenor Square that Nick went on. He was arrested, weren't you Paul?'

'Yeah. One of two hundred. The fuzz beat a lot of us up. Did someone mention coffee?'

'It's made,' Laura said. 'Come on, let's go through and make a fire.'

The fire soon caught. Laura lit some candles, and they sat listening to Paul strumming his guitar. After a while he put it down and stretched out beside Rosa. Heather went over and put an LP on the turntable. It was a woman singing some beautiful quiet songs.

'This is new; someone called Joni Mitchell. My friend Ced sent it over from the US. He's coming down here on Monday I think. He's travelling in Europe, escaping the draft,' Laura said.

'Ah, Rosa, here's a song about Michael,' Paul said, reading the album sleeve. 'You'll like this.'

'Shut up Paul, we're fed up with your jibes,' Laura told him.

Lamorna listened to the words.

'Mermaids in colonies. That could be you, living here in this commune.'

'Well you could pass for a mermaid with that hair,' Paul said.

'I'd make a terrible mermaid; my singing would drive the sailors away.'

'Well I'm outta here. Feel free to come and share my room tonight Lamorna.'

'Thank you, but I'm very tired, and I have to be up early to go job hunting.'

'Why bother? Some other time then.' And with that he slunk away.

'You need to be firm with him, don't let him bully you.'

'I won't Jean,' she said, more confidently than she felt. 'He seems to have a chip on his shoulder.'

'Yes, we think it's to do with his childhood from comments he's made. He was brought up by an aunt. We don't know why,' Rosa said. 'Tell us more about you.'

'There's not much to tell. Just a normal childhood until my Dad died. I came down here to get away, and I'm hoping to find somewhere to share next term.'

'What about Jude, could you share with her?'

'Well maybe, but she has a pretty good situation. Her parents run a business and they've got loads of money. She has an entire attic to herself and does what she wants. She is talking about finding us a house though. I'm not sure about it. Don't get me wrong, we're best friends, but she can distract me too much. She doesn't work hard on the course. I want to do well; it's my best chance of making my own future.'

'I'd never have guessed you were so ambitious,' Jean said.

'Well it's harder for women to get on, isn't it? I want to be independent. And I love photography, it's my passion. I was wondering if I could take some photos here, it's such a great atmosphere. And I could make you an album for the house.'

'That would be lovely, I don't think anyone would mind,' Laura said.

'You could try and get a positive message across, get people to understand that we're just normal, not high on LSD all the time'

'Well, I don't know if anyone would be interested, but I'll try. Can I start now?'

She rushed upstairs to get her camera. There were some good pictures to take: Jean curled up on the sofa making patchwork, Rosa immersed in a novel, and then feeding Dylan who'd woken hungry again, Heather busy with her macramé. The fire was beginning to die down, and a burning log fell onto the hearth. Heather put her work down and lifted it back onto the fire with the tongs. Lamorna took her photograph with the fire's glow illuminating her face, her ear rings sparkling in the light.

'Fire's nearly dead, it's probably time we all went to bed,' she said. 'Martyn's late tonight.'

'It's only just gone 10.30. I'll stay up a little longer and wait for Dylan to settle. Put another log on for me.'

'I'll stay for a while too,' Lamorna said, 'I'm too wide awake now. I'll find a book to read if you don't mind.'

'Help yourself,' Laura said, 'Goodnight.'

Lamorna browsed the shelves, found a book of poetry and curled up on the sofa to read. She found it hard to concentrate. The log shifted on the fire, sending red sparks up the chimney. She imagined a family of fairies living in the cave of fire, sending the young ones up the chimney to make their own way in the world. She remembered the stories she and her Dad had made up about them. He'd told her that the fairies would look for smoke from chimneys and find a new home that way. After he'd died she liked to imagine that he'd become like a spark fairy, leaving the crematorium and finding a new fireside somewhere. He had blamed himself for her burns, thinking he'd encouraged her to become too fascinated by fire, and she knew her Mum thought that too. But it wasn't true. She'd just always loved fire. A new sound broke into her thoughts.

'Hi, anyone home?'

Martyn came into the room.

'Just we two goddesses of the hearth,' Rosa laughed. 'How was the pub tonight?'

'Busy. Hi Lamorna, didn't know you were here.'

'I lost my job, so I'm your newest refugee.'

'She lost her job because she stuck up for us at that village meeting,' Rosa told him. 'She was so brave.'

'Good for you, nice to know someone supports us. Where's Heather?'

'They're all in bed. There's food keeping warm for you in the kitchen.'

'Great, I'm starving.'

'I'd better get to bed. I'll take the book with me.'

'I'll come into town with you tomorrow if you want,' Rosa said. 'Dylan loves the bus.'

'I'd like that. Will you wake me if I'm not up?'

She crept quietly upstairs and into her room, turning on the small lamp by her bed. Someone had made the bed up for her, and it looked so inviting, with a plump feather filled pillow, the blankets turned over and a beautiful embroidered throw in shades of burgundy and peacock blue. There was a piece of paper on her pillow and a small box. One of the boxes she'd noticed in Paul's room. She opened it, and found a small blue butterfly.

'No need for a lid. It can't fly away now.'

She examined it carefully, touching the soft wings with her fingertip.

'Poor thing. Who would want to do this to you?'

She picked up the note. *'For you Lamorna. Come over and join me sometime soon. Paul'*

She scrunched up the note and tossed it into the bin. Placed the box carefully on her cupboard.

She lay awake for a while, thinking about the conversations they'd had, thinking about what Rosa had said about Michael. 'He must have really cared about her. I don't understand why he didn't speak up in that meeting. Maybe he wants them all gone too, after what happened with Rosa. He really couldn't be interested in me. Not after Rosa. She's so beautiful.'

Chapter 13

'I wasn't sure if I should wake you, but it's a glorious day,' Rosa said, drawing back the curtains. 'Dylan's been awake two hours already.'

'Oh thank you, what time is it?' She rubbed her eyes sleepily.

'Only eight thirty. We're making breakfast. How do scrambled eggs sound?'

'I must come and help.'

'No need, we're all up except the men. There'll be plenty of opportunities to help.'

Twenty minutes later she was washed and dressed and enjoying toast at the kitchen table. Martyn was up now too.

'I want to get out in the garden for a few hours before my next shift,' he said. There was a clattering in the hallway.

'Post,' said Laura, coming into the room with a handful of mail.

'Postcard for you Martyn, electricity bill, rubbish, rubbish,' she said, dropping some papers into the bin. Letter for Rosa.

'It's from my sister Marie. She wants to come and stay. She says Mum's decorating the kitchen and it's a nightmare. She's really bored.'

'Of course she must come,' Laura said. 'What do you think everyone? Can she share your room? How old is she? Will your Mum let her come?'

'She'll be glad to see the back of her I think. She's only fourteen, so she can't help much.'

Everyone agreed that she should come.

'We'll all be on our best behaviour.'

'Thanks. I'll phone her when I get to Penzance.'

Dylan was gurgling in a basket at Rosa's feet.

'Yes Dylan, you've got an Aunty Marie and she's coming to see you.'

'Does she know about Dylan?' Lamorna asked.

'Yes, I told my Mum. As you can imagine she was not thrilled. I was taking a year out before medical school, and she and my Dad think I've thrown my life away. Well, come on Dylan, let's get ready. Shall we try for the ten o'clock bus?'

Dylan was fascinated by the bus, alert in Rosa's arms, and smiling as everyone who climbed on board stopped to speak to him. They got off on Market Jew Street and strolled around the shops, looking at notices, hoping to spot a suitable vacancy for Lamorna. They grew more and more despondent. The postcard announcing the post of *'Odd Job Man'* was still in the window where Sam had placed it, and she wondered if he would ever get anyone.

'If I don't find anything I'll have to go home.'

'You can always sign on like we do.'

'I'm not sure; don't you have to be a permanent resident?'

'Oh, there's a phone box, will you hold Dylan while I phone Marie?'

Lamorna held him, rocking him gently and watching the passers-by. A van went past, and she saw that it was Michael at the wheel. 'If I have to go home I'll never see him again,' she thought. Five minutes later Rosa was back.

'She's already packed her case, and she's coming down tomorrow. She says it's impossible at home. They're living on sandwiches and fish and chips whilst the kitchen's stripped. Mum was threatening to send her to my Aunt's farm, and she couldn't bear that. Come on, let's buy the local paper and get a coffee, there's sure to be something for you.'

They only just managed to find a seat by the window. The very table where Lamorna had sat on her first day in the town. The room was noisy with the chatter of customers, the hiss of coffee machines and clatter of cups. Someone put money in the jukebox, and the sounds of 'Heartbreak Hotel' filled the room.

'That's got to be my theme tune,' she thought.

'There's Michael,' Rosa whispered. He was striding past the window, made as if to open the door and then just as swiftly turned, and was gone from view.

'I wonder if he saw us.'

'He would be embarrassed to see me after what happened,' Lamorna said. 'I don't know why he couldn't speak out for you, after all, he knew you.'

'It may be me he's avoiding. He finally told me when we met in the harbour one day that he wouldn't be coming round again. He kept calling to see if I needed anything even when I'd told him I didn't want to be involved. It's strange how we don't get what we want, isn't it? Dylan is Paul's baby but he's not really interested. I was crazy about him, but he just doesn't want commitment. And then there's Michael, swearing devotion.'

'Breaking up with you really upset him. He was horrid to me when I started the job, and his Mum said it was connected to the situation with you.'

'I'm sorry he gave you a hard time, but I had to send him away, I didn't feel that way about him. I didn't want to hurt him.'

'The weird thing is I can't get Michael out of my head now. When he rescued me from Gary he hugged me, and it was like an electric shock. I don't think I like him, but he's always in my thoughts.'

'It's like a chemical reaction. That's how I was with Paul. But now I don't know. We still have sex but it's different since Dylan was born. I think he only bothers because there are no other available women. Now you're here he'll be turning his attention to you.'

'I don't want him to. I've decided not to get involved. I just want to get my project done. And I don't like his little boxes of butterflies. Why does he want them, poor dead things?'

'I don't know. He's a needy sort of person. He can be possessive. I think he's jealous of Dylan because of the time I give him. He's always telling me I'm a slave to him.'

Dylan must have known they were talking about him, because he suddenly began to cry.

'I need to feed him. Will you get us another coffee so we can stay sitting here a bit longer?'

'Yes, I need to look through the job section in the paper too.'

She brought their coffee over and turned to the vacancies. There was a washing up job in Perranporth, too far away, a chambermaid job in Newquay. Nothing in the right area at all.

'Why don't you put a card up in the employment place and some of the shop windows? Someone might see it. We're thinking of going to a beach and having a barbecue tomorrow. Come with us.'

'That sounds fun. Let's go. I'll pop into the post office and buy some postcards.'

She stood at the post office desk, chewing her pen, and then wrote;

GIRL FRIDAY SEEKS JOB.

ANYTHING CONSIDERED

PENZANCE AREA

And then she realised she had no phone number for anyone to ring.

'Oh no,' Rosa said. 'I never thought of that. We'll have to think of another plan. Maybe you could just come here and knock on every hotel door. They might not realise they need you until you ask. Could you get a reference from Sam Tremayne?'

'I wouldn't dare ask.'

It was late afternoon when they arrived home. An orange camper van decorated with psychedelic swirls was pulled up in the yard.

'It must be Laura's American friend. I thought he wasn't coming until Monday.'

Rosa went upstairs with Dylan. Lamorna unpacked the shopping, and put the kettle on, then went through into the living room. Laura, Jean, Martyn and Heather were there with a tall fair haired stranger.

'Come in and meet Ced.'

'Hi Lamorna, what a cute name. Good to meet you. Laura says you're a photographer.'

'Yes, I'm trying to do a project about the standing stones around here.'

'We could go in search of some then, but hey, where's that tea and cake you promised Laura?'

'I put the kettle on,' Lamorna said. 'We brought loads of shopping.'

'Where's Rosa?'

'She's gone upstairs to put Dylan down for a nap.'

Laura and Lamorna went into the kitchen to make the tea.

'Paul made us a cake.'

'Where is Paul?'

'Up in his room, he'll be down for the tea.'

He did appear as soon as tea was made, and ceremonially cut the cake he'd made that afternoon.

'Smells good,' Ced remarked.

'It's one of my specials.'

'Tell us about your travels Ced,' Jean asked.

Lamorna had never met an American before and she was fascinated by his drawling speech and stories of the world that she had never experienced. After a while though she began to feel peculiar.

'I feel funny all of a sudden, like Alice when she grew big in the Wonderland room. I feel as though the walls are crowding towards me. It's weird.'

'It's the cake,' Jean said. 'It's dope cake.'

'Dope cake?' her voice seemed to be coming from some other part of the room.

'We should have warned her,' Rosa said. 'Have you tried it before?'

'What is it?'

'It's made with cannabis,' Paul told her, 'that's why it's special.'

Rosa went over and sat with her.

'You'll be okay, it's just a bit strange the first time, especially when you're not expecting it'

Lamorna felt calmer with Rosa sitting beside her. She was vaguely aware of everyone talking, of laughter, and music being played. Everything seemed more intense, the colours, the sounds, and the room still appeared to be moving. She felt giddy, as though she'd just stepped off a merry go-round. She lost all sense of time, and was surprised when she suddenly felt herself being shaken.

'Come on Lamorna, everyone's gone outside. Ced's cooking over the fire for us tonight.'

She felt strange still and drowsy.

'You fell asleep, it was the effect of the cake, but you'll be alright when you've eaten something,' Rosa said, helping her to her feet.

They went outside to join the others, and Rosa was right, she began to feel more like her normal self again. They sat around talking for hours. Ced was still describing his adventures.

'I can't believe how friendly folks are,' he said. 'Never had to wait long for a lift, got offered places to sleep. Invited for meals. The only bad thing was in Greece. Hired a scooter, should've known better. Took this English girl for a ride across the island. The road just turned into a dirt track, potholes and boulders all the way. Hit a dirty great rock and came off. And these little old ladies came from nowhere. Faces like wrinkled old leather. Took us in and cleaned our scratches. Painted us with some purple stuff. Stung like hell. Wouldn't take any money.'

'When did you get over here?' Jean asked.

'Only at the beginning of the month. Just managed to get to the Woburn Festival. It was something else. You shoulda heard Hendrix.'

'You saw Jimi Hendrix?' Paul said.

'Yeah, on the Saturday evening. He sure can play that guitar. It was all pretty good. Fleetwood Mac cancelled on the Sunday. Big disappointment. But I met loads of real friendly folk, got invites all over the country. But what are we gonna do tomorrow?'

Most people had plans for the morning. Rosa had to go into Penzance again to meet her sister off a train. Lamorna said she'd go with her and try for a job in the hotels. Laura had a dentist appointment in town.

'Guess I could take you all into town in the van, I'd like to look around, only passed through today.'

Chapter 14

The three women and Dylan piled into the camper van next morning. There were a few stares as they drove through the village. Lamorna looked over at the hotel as they went past, but there was no sign of anyone around. They split up in Penzance, arranging to meet up for coffee later. Ced went to explore the shops.

'I don't know how Marie managed to get such an early train,' Rosa said. 'She hates getting out of bed in the morning.'
She headed off to find a chemist.

Lamorna bought a paper, and sat down on a bench to search through the adverts yet again. Someone sat down next to her. She looked up. It was Michael. Her heart skipped a beat.

'Are you searching for work again?'

'Yes,' she said, sighing, 'but there's nothing around here. I'll have to go over to the north coast I think.'

'I'm sorry about your job. Mum's really angry with Dad. We keep trying to tell him, argue with him that he's in the wrong, but he won't have any of it. The more I talk to him the worse he gets. I'm up there all the time now.'

'I'm sorry, but I don't see how I can help.'

'I'm sorry I didn't stick up for you. It was brave of you to do that.'

'It's okay. You couldn't go against family.'

'I know about a job you could do.'

'How do you?'

'My friend Phil. He runs a photography studio here. His assistant has just left, and he urgently needs help. He's got lots of weddings booked. It's his busiest time.'

'Why would he give me the job just like that? There must be better qualified people.'

'He's desperate. He's putting an advert in the paper, but he doesn't think anyone will be able to start straight away. I told him you'd be good. Here's his card. Go and see him. I'm glad I saw you. I didn't know where to find you. I was going to try the hostel.'

'Thank you, that's fantastic. I'm staying at the commune. They found me at the bus stop and took me in.'

'That's good. I'd better be off then.'

He walked away, and Rosa suddenly appeared.

'What did he want?'

'I can't believe it, he's told me about a job, look.'

'I've got to go and see this man now.'

'Shall I come with you?'

'No, it's nearly time for us all to meet up. I won't be long, wait for me though!'

She scrutinised the card and then set off up the road. The studio was in a side street just a few minutes' walk away. Causeway Head. There was a shop front with a display of photographs. She counted to ten, opened the door and went in. A man who seemed a bit older than Michael appeared from a back room.

'Hello, I'm Lamorna West. Michael Tremayne gave me this card and told me you need help.'

'Oh great, you're a life saver. My assistant just upped and went and it's my busiest summer ever. Luckily there are no weddings today or I'd be in a right mess. Can you do developing and printing?'

'Yes, I've just finished my first year of a photography course.'

'Can you start on Monday? I'll give you a trial, and if you like it you can have the job.'

'I won't let you down.'

'Michael said that. How did he manage to tell you so quickly? I only saw him twenty minutes ago.'

'I was in town job hunting, and he spotted me.'

'Can't believe my luck, good looking girl like you will be an asset in the shop too.'

'What else will I be doing?'

'I'll need you to cover the shop while I'm out doing weddings, I've got a fête and two kid's birthday parties this week, and I'd like a hand with the portrait sessions. Are you good with kids?'

'Yes, I've got two young brothers.'

'That's brilliant. I'll see you Monday then.'

'Thank you, I'll be here.'

She walked back down to the coffee bar.

'The drinks are on me! I got the job, I start Monday.'

'Well done, how much will he pay you?' Rosa asked.

'I never thought to ask, but I want the job, it'll be a good experience. It depends on how well I do on Monday, but he's desperate, so I think I should be alright.'

'What's all this jollity?' Laura asked, coming through the door.

'Lamorna's gotten a job,' Ced told her. 'How was the dentist?'

'Just a small filling, but I need that coffee now.'

'We'd better make the most of the weekend. We've gotta take you to find those stones.'

'I must get to the station,' Rosa said. 'Marie's train arrives in fifteen minutes.'

'I'll come too,' Lamorna said.

The train was just five minutes late, and an excited Marie appeared and flung herself at her sister.

'He's lovely, he's lovely,' she raved at Dylan, who rewarded her with his best smile.

'Can I hold him?'

'When we get home.'

'I couldn't wait to get here. It's awful at home. It smells horrid and Mum moans all the time.'

They bundled into the camper van. Marie was even more excited by this unexpected surprise. Half an hour later they were back in the village. Lamorna spotted Michael coming out of the newsagents.

'Can you drop me off here? I need to tell Michael I got the job.'

Ced pulled over, and she jumped out.

'Will you get some milk?' Laura called after her.

She crossed the road and caught up with Michael.

'I just wanted to say thanks. I saw Phil, and he's giving me a try at the job on Monday.'

'That's good. I hope it works out.'

She walked back along the harbour, stopping at a small store for a bottle of milk. On an impulse she went down to the beach and lingered for a while, watching a group of children playing together, digging a big hole and burying their Dad. Just like she used to do.

Everyone was outside in the garden when she got back, sitting around a cloth spread with a picnic.

'About time,' Laura said. 'We were just about to send out a search party.'

'Sorry, I got distracted watching some children on the beach.'

'Did you speak to Michael? Any news of the campaign,' Rosa asked.

'Yes, but no news. I'll get this milk in the fridge.'

She hurried inside, and rushed upstairs to get her camera. There was another note on her bed, with a posy of flowers. The note said simply, *'Tonight?'*

'I'll have to tell him I'm not interested. He doesn't give up easily. I'm not ready for any new romance, and if I was, it wouldn't involve him.'

She skirted the group, taking photographs. Marie was making a daisy chain, and she proudly placed it in her sister's hair. Rosa was feeding Dylan, and she smiled down at Marie. Lamorna photographed the three of them. 'Madonna and child with an angel,' she thought.

Ced and Laura were deep in conversation, and Lamorna zoomed in on them. She photographed Jean lost in her own private world, and then Martyn and Heather, who were feeding each other slices of apple. Paul was sprawled on the grass, eyes closed.

'Sit with me, sit with me,' Marie called to her, and she went around and sat beside her.

'I'll make you a flower chain too; it would be beautiful in your hair.'

'Thank you Marie that would be lovely.'

'Wakey wakey Paul,' Jean shook him. 'You're missing your breakfast.'

'Okay Grandma,' he muttered grumpily, sitting up and taking a plate.

'He's only just got up,' Heather said to Lamorna.

'This is getting a bit like being at home,' he complained.

Martyn passed around a bowl of grapes, and Ced produced a huge chocolate cake.

'Sit still Lamorna, I want to crown you now.' Marie placed the daisy chain on her head, and received a kiss in return.

'You look just like that girl in the painting, the one in the water,' Martyn said.

'You mean Millais' painting. Ophelia in the stream.' Jean said.

'Yeah, it's the flowers and her hair.'

'Not too much, I hope,' Lamorna said, laughing, 'she was drowning.'

A few clouds were gathering over to the west.

'We should get going if we're gonna do this photo expedition.' Ced stood up, gathering the plates together.

'Where are you thinking of going?' Paul asked.

'We could go over to Morvah and Chun Castle and Lamorna could photograph the stones. It may be less cloudy over there,' Heather suggested.

'That sounds perfect,' Lamorna said, helping Ced to clear away.

'I'll wash up,' Rosa said. 'I won't come, I want Dylan to get a good sleep, he missed a nap this morning, and I'd like to spend some time with Marie.'

'But I want to go, why can't I go?' Marie protested.

'Another day, I want you all to myself. When Dylan wakes we'll take him to the beach, phone Mum to say you arrived, and we'll have ice creams. I thought you'd like to help me with the dinner, or play with Dylan while I cook.'

Ten minutes later they were climbing into the camper. They drove up the narrow lane and left onto the minor road, passing the site where Lamorna had photographed the Merry Maidens what seemed now a lifetime ago.

'I'll go and see Mary tomorrow,' she thought.

'There are some stones around here, the Maidens and the Pipers,' Heather called over to her.

'I've seen the Merry Maidens, but I don't know the Pipers.'

'They're quite close, maybe another time. Merry Maid means Mermaid in Cornwall.'

'I didn't know that. They never seem merry to me,' Lamorna remarked.

'They're dangerous seductive sirens luring men to their doom,' Paul said.

They drove inland, heading north -west through St Buryan, and then pulled over in a small village.

'This is as close as we can get,' Heather told them. 'It's a short walk from here.'

'You're right about the weather, it's fine here. That's what I like about England; you can be someplace else in half an hour.'

'Never let anyone hear you refer to Cornwall as England,' Heather said, grinning. 'As far as locals are concerned this is a different country.'
They reached the stones, and after exploring for a while, Lamorna started her work, skirting the site, and taking pictures from various angles. The others were sprawled on the turf, chatting, and she included them in some of the shots. The sun was low in the sky when they finally got back to the van. Lamorna was busy entering information into her journal as they left.

'Why don't we go down to Sennen? Catch the sunset and go for a swim,' Paul suggested.

'I didn't bring any swimming stuff,' Lamorna said.

'None of us did, but there's no-one around on beaches here at this time,' Heather said.

She was right, the beautiful beach was deserted, the curving sweep of sand pink in the fading glow of sunset. They all stripped off and ran down to the sea. Except for Lamorna, who pulled out her camera and took photographs, content to paddle at the sea's edge. She felt the waves wash over her feet, the sand curling away from between her toes as it was sucked back into the depths.

'Come on in, the water's lovely,' Ced called.

'Too busy taking photos.'

They were all completely unselfconscious about their nakedness, running up to pose and splash for her in the breakers. There were some great images of bodies glowing in the sun, or silhouetted against the sky. They all set off to swim out to a buoy, and she walked back up the beach to get some shots of the bay. After a few minutes she sat down in the warm dry sand of the dunes, burying her toes.

Suddenly Paul appeared from nowhere. He grabbed hold of her. She tumbled back onto the sand. She fought to release herself. He laughed.

'I've got my mermaid at last.'

He pulled open her shirt. She felt his cold, wet body pressing against her skin like some wild sea monster.

'You're hurting me.' She twisted her head to free her mouth from his. Struggling to get away from him.

'Stop it Paul, I want you to stop.'

His damp hands snaked over her breasts. Fastened onto her, squeezing and pressing. She knew she should shout, but she couldn't. She felt him hard against her. Opening her eyes she saw a round full moon staring coldly down on her. 'Please make him stop; make him stop,' she cried in her head. His hand was sliding lower now. She clenched herself against his touch. He forced her legs apart. His fingers probing.

'What's this?'

She felt a tug. The string of her tampon.

'Shit. Is that why you didn't swim?'

His hand crawled back over her body, stretching tentacle like over her breast again. She couldn't shout out. She was paralysed by shame and fear.

'You'll have to help me.'

He grabbed her hand and pressed it onto him, making her move her fingers over him, making her feel the smooth, cold snakiness of him. She heard his gasps as he pushed against her. At last she heard him groan. He rolled off her. She stood up, pulled her skirt around herself, fastened her buttons and walked away. Walked down to the edge of the water, holding her sticky hand away from her. She paddled out until she was knee deep, and then plunged her hand into the waves. She scooped up water and washed his traces from her face and neck, splashing water over her skin where he'd smeared her.

The others came running back along the beach, breathless from exertion. They retrieved their clothes from a haphazard bundle, and began to dress. Someone noticed Paul's clothes in a heap.

'Where's Paul? Hope he's not decided to end it all and disappear into the waves. A Merry Maiden has captured him.'

'He's up by the dunes.' Lamorna said.

In the dusk no-one seemed to notice that she was strangely quiet.

'You should have joined us,' Heather said, 'it was so exhilarating.'

'The sunset was too beautiful to miss, I had to capture it, and I got some good pictures. Especially the ones of you all.'

'We need to spread the word that we shouldn't be ashamed of our bodies,' said Laura.

'Too right,' she heard Paul add as he approached. 'Maybe Lamorna is a little scared to go naked.

"No, I'm just too obsessed with this project. I want to do well. Why do you collect those butterflies,' she asked him, changing the subject.

'I got them in Looe, there's a guy who catches them on the cliffs and then mounts them.'

'Aren't they lovelier when they're alive and free?'

'But you can't see them properly, they move too fast. I can see all their colours and patterns now. Did you like the little blue one I gave you?'

'It's pretty, but I'd rather it was alive.'

'I couldn't give you a live one.'

'I didn't ask you to give me one.'

There was a dinner waiting for them at home.

'We made a giant macaroni cheese,' Marie said, 'And an apple pie for pudding. Your daisy crown is all squashed and sandy Lamorna. I'll make you a new one tomorrow. Don't be sad.'

Chapter 15

Rain spattered the window and the wind chime clanged and jangled out in the garden. She burrowed back under the blankets and thought about the horrible experience with Paul. 'Why did he do that? He knew I didn't want to. He must know he's in the wrong. I don't know if I should tell the others.' A faint sound. Someone was opening her door. A voice. Paul's.

'Are you awake?'

She held her breath, clenching her fists and tensing her whole body against him. It was several minutes before she allowed herself to relax again. When she was absolutely sure he'd gone. She lay listening to the sounds of the house stirring. A floorboard creaking, someone running lightly downstairs, whistling. A knocking in the pipes. Dylan woke in the room next door; she heard his muffled crying, and Rosa, hushing him so that he wouldn't disturb Marie.

'I'll get up; I can't lie here forever dreading seeing him.'

She tiptoed to the door, opened it a crack, and peered across the landing. The coast was clear. The bathroom door was open. Grabbing a towel and wash bag she padded over. There was a bolt on the door, and for the first time she drew it across. She ran a bath, and lay back in the warm water, washing away all last traces. She washed her hair, and untangled the crown of daisies, reluctantly dropping them into the bin. She unwrapped a fresh tampon.

'Saved by a tampon, that could be a new advertising strategy. Wear a tampon and protect yourself against rape.'

It was the first time she'd used that word.

'But that's what it could have been. He forced me. I have the upper hand now. He can't touch me again. I won't let him. If he dares to try again I'll make sure everyone knows about him.' She returned to her bedroom and quickly dressed.

Her heart raced when she heard the door open, but it was just a smiling Marie.

'Are you coming down?'

'Yes, let's go together and help with breakfast, shall we?'

Hand in hand they ran down the stairs. Ced was alone in the kitchen, pouring tea into a mug.

'Want one? You could take a cup for Rosa, Marie.'

He filled two mugs for them, and Marie set off to carry one up for her sister.

'Looks like we're the only ones out and about. Can't say I blame them in this weather.'

Baggins and Gandalf, the two commune kittens skittered over, squeaking for food. Marie came back, and Lamorna showed her how to open the can and spoon food out for them. They left her with them and went through into the living room with their tea.

'Can't believe how much tea I've drunk since I came over. Never touched it back home.'

They curled up on the sofa together.

'Do you miss home?'

'I guess I do sometimes. I miss my Mom and sisters most. My Dad walked out on us years ago. Don't have a lot of respect for the country right now with this war.'

'It must be terrible, all those people getting killed. I don't understand what it's all for.'

'Sure, but it's not gonna end some whiles yet, that's why I'm over here. I'm enjoying this little country of yours. I don't figure on going home yet.'

'Ced. What do you think of 'free love'?'

'Is that a leading question?' he said, grinning.

'No, but I thought you'd have some views. It started over there in California, didn't it?'

'Well, I guess it's all about anarchy, getting away from the repressive rules of society. Moving on from marriage as a kind of bondage.'

'What do you mean?'

'It's about freedom. People can choose to have sex with someone freely, it doesn't have to be part of a dependant, legally binding contract. Some women back home are saying that marriage is a licence for men to rape women. Women can be more liberated now we have the Pill.'

'So people have to agree to have sex with each other, one person can't make demands on another? Force them.'

'Yeah, sure, you have to have respect, no pressure, no force.'

She sat sipping her tea, thinking.

'Trouble is,' Ced went on, 'people aren't too good at respect. So many of these anarchists are just kids. They've gotten no experience of life and relationships, and they generally make a mess of living together. I was in California, squatted with a bunch of flower people. They called me Grandad, and I'm only thirty five! There was a lot of tension there. Some of the group seemed to think they should be having sex five times a day, and I had a hunch most of the women just went along with it even if they didn't want to.'

'That's worse than marriage, all those random men.'

He laughed.

'What do you think Lamorna?'

'I don't know. I'm really confused. I know that possessiveness and jealousy is a really destructive thing, but what if someone really loves someone else, and then that person is disloyal and dishonest, and really hurts them? It's easy to be objective if you don't feel that way about someone. But if you're really in love with someone I can't see how you can share them.'

'Sounds like we're getting into personal territory now.'

'I suppose so. Well, I was thinking about me. How can you live with others and be into free love when you really love someone? Don't we have that need to be together?'

'That's a tough one. Do we only think we need someone because that's what we've grown up with, it's what's expected? And what's love anyway? I'm sure I don't know. If you really love someone can't you accept what they want too?'

'I don't know. I know I was wrong, I didn't really love him. I never want to see him again.'

'That's a bit extreme. Live and let live, I say. Maybe love is just a chemical reaction, something nature developed to make sure we breed. Maybe it's just lust.'

'Well why do people get married and stay together?'

"Never tried, so I don't know. But as far as I can see most marriages don't work out. Not where I come from. But hey, this is kinda serious stuff. Why don't we get breakfast?'

He pulled her to her feet and led her into the kitchen. Marie was breaking eggs into a bowl.

'I'm going to make scrambled eggs.'

'Great plan, what if I fry up some mushrooms?' Ced suggested.

They found tomatoes too, and Lamorna made some fried eggy bread. They worked peacefully together, and soon the table was laid, a plate was piled with toast, and the hot food was sizzling on the range. Rosa and Dylan were first to appear.

'I fed the kittens and I made scrambled eggs,' Marie shouted.

Soon everyone appeared, drawn by the smell of cooking.

'What are we all going to do today, it's pouring down,' Jean said gloomily.

'I might take a trip to Land's End in the van, anyone else want to come?'

'Me, me, can I come Ced, I've never been?' said an excited Marie.

'Well I'll come too with Dylan.'

Jean decided she would stay and curl up with her book and the kittens.

'Me too,' said Laura, 'I'll get some jewellery made, we're nearly out of stuff to sell.'

'I've got to go and see my parents, my sister's there today,' Heather said. 'And Martyn's working.'

'What about you Lamorna?' Paul asked.

'I'm going to visit my friend Mary. She's at home on Sundays.'

'Come with us Paul,' Rosa urged.

'Maybe.'

Jean and Laura started the washing up and the Land's End group went to get ready. Lamorna went up to change. She was just pulling a sweater over her head when the door opened. It was Paul.

'Have you still got your period?'

'I don't see what it's got to do with you.'

'I thought maybe we could get it on today if you were finished.'

'I don't think so. You practically raped me yesterday.'

'Come on, this is the sixties. You need to get into the groove.'

'You have no idea what you're talking about. Please leave my room.'

The door opened again. Ced this time.

'Everything okay? Sure you won't come Lamorna?'

'Thanks, but no, I need to see Mary.'

'What about you Paul? We're off now.'

'Think I'll stay here. Got stuff to do man.'

'See you then.'

He was gone.

'You were just leaving.'

'I see what your game is; you're going after Ced now.'

'It really has nothing to do with you, does it?'

He stamped out of the room, and she heard a door slam. 'I can't believe I did that.'

She brushed her hair, grabbed her bag and camera and went downstairs with a new spring in her step. The rain was beginning to slacken, and there was a chink of golden sun glimmering through the clouds in the west. She splashed across the yard and down the lane, skipping through the rivulets running along the tarmac. She took a detour onto the deserted beach, and made the first footprints across the sand to the water's edge so that she could paddle and wash her feet before heading off to Mary's house. A few birds had been before her, leaving a pattern of spiky claw marks meandering along the shore line. She couldn't resist taking a photograph. She kicked off the flip flops for a moment, and added her own foot prints before turning back up to the road.

The village was busy now, as tourists emerged from shelter and wandered from shop to gallery. 'I'm not an emmet now. I live here and work here.' she thought. She set off up the hill. Everything looked new and fresh, and she breathed in the scents of wet leaves from window boxes and baskets. A shopkeeper was setting out his display, and she chose a bunch of gloriously scented stocks to take for Mary's Mum. 'I hope they're all in,' she thought, as the white painted house came into view.

She paddled round to the back door, and found it ajar. She heard a murmur of voices, and the smell of cooking wafted invitingly through. She tapped on the door, before popping her head round.

'Hello, anyone at home?'

'Lamorna' cried Mary, coming over to welcome her, 'come in out of the wet.' She let herself be swallowed up by the welcoming warmth of the kitchen and the smiles of Mary and her Mum, Kate.

'You'll stop and have dinner with us, won't you?' said Kate, as she popped a tray of Yorkshire puddings into the oven.'

'That's very kind, but I didn't expect you to feed me. I've brought you these.' She held out the stocks.

'Thank you, they're lovely. You're very welcome to stay for dinner my lover. It's nice to have a bit of lively company. Ian and Chris are down at the lifeboat house tinkering, and I don't reckon they'll be back dreckly.'

'I said I'd meet Chris at the lifeboat a bit later,' Mary said, so I'll send Ian back for his dinner, shall I?

"Yes, you could. Shall you lay the table for me now my lover?'

Mary led Lamorna into a small dining room, and they set the table together. There were place mats with pictures of birds, a seersucker tablecloth, and a glass cruet, just like the one at Lamorna's home.

'Come on then, what's it like down there with those hippies? Michael told me you were there.'

Lamorna tried to paint the best picture she could, omitting any mention of dope cakes, and Paul.

'Everyone is so friendly, and it's really interesting. There's an American visiting at the moment. We eat outside in the garden a lot, and people play guitars. And guess what! I've got a new job. Michael found it for me. I met him in Penzance yesterday, and he told me about this friend of his who needed help in his photo studio. I start tomorrow. He's giving me a trial and if I do okay I've got the job.'

'That'll be old Alf Matthews's place I reckon,' Kate said, coming in with plates. 'Think he retired and his son took over.'

'It'll be a useful job, because I can maybe print some of my photos. But I miss the hotel.'

'We miss you too. They've still not found anyone. I've been doing extra shifts in the kitchen.'

'Has any post come for me?'

'Not that I know of, I'll check tomorrow though.'

They sat down to eat, and Mary's Dad appeared. He nodded and said a gruff 'hello' to Lamorna. Despite eating a big breakfast, Lamorna was hungry.

'I really miss Sunday dinners,' she said.

'What do you eat down there?'

'Lots of things I've never tried before. Vegetable bakes and rice, macaroni, and things like baked potatoes and beans. They're thinking of getting some chickens.'

'I'm going down to the cottage with Chris this afternoon. Do you want to come? We're going to measure up for curtains.'

'I'd love to see it.'

'It's nearly finished now, Michael's been working more at the hotel since you left, but he's down there most evenings. He told Chris he's just got the decorating to do, and we can help choose the colours and the curtains, carpets and stuff. You could help us, you're artistic. There's a little courtyard at the back where we can hang the washing.'

'It sounds lovely.'

'You youngsters don't know your luck,' said Kate. 'When your Dad and I married we had to live with his Mum for six months, and then another five with mine, all crowded in with a new baby, until this house came up.'

'Don't know you're born,' her Dad chipped in. 'Do you know, we've found some bits and bobs for them, but Mary don't want them, it's all got to be new.'

'Sorry Dad. It's just that we want it to be our own. We don't want old fashioned things.'

'I know you do, my lover, and your Mum and I have got a bit put by, so I daresay we'll help you out.'

'Thanks Dad, you do understand, don't you?' She leaned over and hugged him.

'Aye, your mother felt the same when we got wed, but there wasn't the money then in the war. And you couldn't get the things.'

There was lemon meringue pie for pudding.

'How did you know, it's my favourite!' Lamorna said.

Afterwards she and Mary washed up the pots. Mary's Dad went up for a snooze, and her Mum settled with her knitting and a cup of tea.

'Let's get going,' Mary said. 'I'll have to drag Chris away. Once he gets started down there it's impossible to stop him.'

'I've never seen the lifeboat properly. Do you think they'll let me have a close look? I could take some photos.'

'Yes if you want to. We're a bit early. Shall we sit by the harbour for a while?'

Chapter 16

It was still quiet, despite the watery sun emerging from the cloud.

'No Hippies,' Mary remarked.

'They've gone to Land's End with Ced. He's the American. How are your wedding plans going?'

'We've sorted out the reception with Aileen, but we need to plan the details, what we'll eat and all of that. And we've been to see the vicar. I don't know what to wear. I've got to think about my dress and the bridesmaids. Mum says we could go up to Plymouth and have a look.'

'What do you think about marriage? Do you think it's a kind of ownership, all that stuff in the service about honour and obey? It's like you have to give up your freedom, and the man has all the power.'

'What makes you say that? It's a bit old fashioned to think the man's in charge. Mum and Dad are a bit like that, but Chris and I are different. I want to marry him and get our own place.'

'Couldn't you get a place of your own without living with Chris?'

'Why would I? I want to be with him, we want to have children. We have to be married for their sake. We don't want our children born base.'

'What's base?'

'You know, born out of wedlock.'

'But times are changing; people don't say that any more. You could just live with Chris. You don't have to get married.'

'It's different down here maybe from what you're used to. I won't be a slave to Chris. I'm going to carry on working. And look at my Mum and Dad, she does the cooking and cleaning, but she's the boss. She says the secret is to let men think they're in charge.'

'But that doesn't seem honest.'

'The men know. It's the way things are. Everyone stays happy. Living together is just as hard, you'd have to work at it just the same, and you wouldn't get all the wedding presents.'

'How do you know Chris is the right one for you?'

'Because we're good friends, we get on well.'

'What about love?'

'Of course I love him.'

'Have you, you know, made love?'

'Lamorna! We have, but you mustn't tell my Mum.'

'Wouldn't she guess?'

'I don't think so, they've never said anything. What about you, and that boy?'

'No, we never did. I don't suppose we had much chance. I was flattered when he asked me out, but I don't think now that I liked him much really.'

'What about other boys?'

'I've never really had any other boyfriends. How do you know you want to do it with someone?'

'It just happens. You start with kissing and petting, and then it just happens, you can't stop yourselves.'

'What's it like?'

'I can't believe you're asking me. I thought you city girls knew it all.'

'Just goes to show how wrong you can be. Go on then, what does it feel like?'

'Well, it's like a kind of aching all over. You can't stop yourself. It hurts a bit the first time. I don't really know what to say.'

'Were you scared?'

'No, because it was Chris. Come on, we'd better get going.'

They set off to walk up the hill to the lifeboat house. Lamorna noticed a small caravan park.

'That's where we stayed once when I was a child. I loved it. Except for the earwigs. I saw some walking on the walls, and I really thought they got into your ears. I used to put my hat on in bed.'

'What's it like in a caravan?'

'It's like a little house inside, there's gas lamps, and you have to put the bed away in the morning. It's like playing at house.'

'Sounds funny. Here we are.'

There were steps down to the lifeboat house. The door was open. Chris and Ian were both there, hands covered in grease, holding smeary mugs of coffee.

'Mum's got your dinner warming Ian. Have you nearly finished?'

'Yeah, we're just about done. We've had a few emmets looking round to get out of the rain; some of them gave a donation.'

The lifeboat loomed over them, sleek and shining. Lamorna stroked the wood.

'It's lovely.'

'She is right enough. Do you want to look around?' Ian asked.

'Can I?'

'Course, come on.'

He led her up onto the deck. She read the name aloud.

'Solomon Browne. It seems so small when you're up here.'

'Not half so small as when you're out on a big sea. But she's good and strong.'

'You're so brave. Aren't you scared when you have to go out?'

'You don't think about it, you've got a job to do. You trust your mates. We're used to the sea, out on the fishing boats.'

'What made you want to do it?'

'Dunno really, my Dad's on the crew, my Granddad was. It's just summat you do.'

She read the boards on the wall, the lists of lifeboat missions, the tally of lives lost.

'You think the sea is so beautiful, but it's a monster, waiting to catch you and swallow you up.'

'Have you heard from Jude?'

'No, but she's not renowned for keeping in touch.'

'She's a great girl.'

They went back down to join the others.

'We'll get off Ian, can you lock up?'

'Yeah, no problem.'

The three of them walked back into the village.

'I asked Lamorna to come with us Chris, is that okay? I thought she might have some good ideas.'

'Yeah that's fine, but we'd better hurry, we're late now.'

Fifteen minutes later they reached the little cottage, a granite building with freshly painted white windows, and a blue stable-type door, the top section open. Chris opened the door and called out;

'Are you there Mike?'

A distant voice was heard.

'I'm upstairs, come up.'

'You didn't tell me he would be here,' Lamorna whispered to Mary.

They went into the living area. The window here looked out over the narrow street. One wall was natural stone, with an original fireplace in its centre. Other walls had been whitewashed in the past, and looked as though they were in the process of being restored. A flight of stairs led up from this room. Chris and Mary began to climb up, and Lamorna followed. She heard Michael's voice.

'Hi, I'm just getting these windows finished. The frames up here are mostly new, and some of the floorboards too. There was a bit of woodworm.'

He stopped talking as Lamorna walked into the room.

'Lamorna's come to help us choose colours,' Mary told him.

Whilst they talked Lamorna set off exploring. There were two bedrooms and a bathroom on this floor, and she found a wooden staircase which led up to a small attic space. From the windows up here she could see some of the harbour, and a view across rooftops to St Clements Isle. She noticed the hollow in the pillow where Michael's head had rested. Some clothes were slung on a chair, and leaning against a wall was a guitar. Beside the bed a pile of paperbacks. She looked at the books, and saw that one of them was about sea voyages. The others seemed to be thrillers.

'What do you think?' Mary asked when she came back down.

'It's lovely. It could feel a bit dark in the winter though, the windows are small, and most of the walls are stone.'

'That's why we live up in the new houses,' Chris said.

'It would look lovely if you chose natural colours to blend with the stone and wood, plain curtains, it would make it seem lighter and bigger. Then you could have colourful cushions and rugs to add a brighter touch.'

'I'm not sure. Wouldn't plain carpets show the dirt?'

'Don't forget the emmets,' Michael said. 'You can't trust them to look after a place.'

'I think they would if it looked beautiful.'

'I agree,' Chris said unexpectedly. 'But maybe we could have dark carpet, like brown to hide the muck downstairs.'

'Perhaps you could just leave the wooden floors downstairs, and have lovely rugs that could be cleaned, or be cheap enough to change if they get too soiled,' Lamorna suggested.

'I'd like that,' Michael said thoughtfully. 'Bit like being on deck. Somebody get us some tea. There's stuff in the kitchen.'

Of course it was Mary and Lamorna who went off downstairs. The kitchen was beautifully renovated. Michael had put in new cupboards, and there were mugs and a teapot on the window sill. They set about making tea.

'I asked Michael to put the old sink outside the door, so I can grow some herbs in it. He's got to buy furniture. He's given me a catalogue to look at. It's very modern stuff, will you help me?'

'Yes, I'd love to.'

There was a clatter as the men came downstairs. Michael plonked his paint tin in the sink.

'Michael!! You can't do that.'

Mary lifted it out, carried it to the door and put it outside.

'You'd better watch out Chris, she's not even moved in yet,' Michael said, laughing.

There was a bench by the front door and they all took their mugs outside to sit in the sunshine. Mary sat on Chris's knee to leave space for the others. Lamorna found herself sitting next to Michael. She felt intensely aware of his thigh against her own. She slowly shuffled along to leave a space, and then felt guilty when he stood up.

'Thank you again for finding me a job,' she said. 'It'll be great. Philip says if it works out I'll be able to print my own photos.'

'That's good.'

'We'd rather have her back at the hotel though, wouldn't we?' Mary said.

'Yes, we would,' he said, looking straight at Lamorna, who blushed profusely.

'Come in and see us on your way home and tell us how you got on,' Mary went on. 'What was all the fuss yesterday Michael?'

'Oh we had a letter from Ellen. She's my sister,' he added for Lamorna's benefit. 'She's living in a cave with some hippies now. She says they sit around and play guitars at night.'

'Never!' said Mary. 'No wonder your Dad seemed upset.'

'She had her money stolen on the ferry over to Crete. The hippies rescued her. Dad's wired her some funds, but he's going to have to revise his opinion of hippies now. I'd better get going. I've got work to do at the hotel. Just leave the cups in the sink. I'll do them later. See you.'

Mary and Lamorna washed up and tidied. Chris cleaned out the paintbrush that had been forgotten, and then announced that he'd better get home for dinner. They left then, just pulling the door to behind them.

'Don't we need to lock up?' Lamorna asked.

'Whatever for?'

'Don't forget to come and see us. Aileen would love to see you too, she asks after you. She had half a mind to ask if Jude could come back and help out.'

'She's not really the working type, she hasn't got the commitment.'

'Doesn't she need the money?'

'No, her parents are well off. You should see their house. She's an only child and she can have what she wants.'

'She doesn't seem spoiled.'

'No, she's not. Thank your Mum for the lovely dinner for me.'

'Are you coming to the pub this week?'

'I might, but will I be allowed now I live with the hippies?'

'Oh don't mind those old men, they won't even notice.'

And with that she was gone.

Lamorna sat for a while on the bench, and then on a sudden impulse she quietly opened the door of the cottage and tiptoed inside. She wandered through the rooms again. She wasn't in a hurry to get back and possibly have another difficult encounter with Paul. She went upstairs, looked out of the windows and up again into the attic. She felt drawn to the room, picking up the guitar, and strumming a few notes badly. She browsed through the books again and then lay down on the bed, closing her eyes just for a moment. She listened to the sounds coming in through the open window. The gulls' cries. Voices of people wandering through the streets. Someone shouting at a child. A church bell ringing.

She must have dozed off. A noise stirred her suddenly. She sat up, and realised it was someone playing a guitar. There was a space against the wall where she'd seen it earlier. Michael must be back. He must have seen her. She would have to go downstairs and own up. 'Better get it over with.'
She crept quietly down the stairs, and found Michael sitting on the settee, strumming the guitar and singing. He heard her, and turned.

'Goldilocks wakes,' he said, smiling.

'I'm sorry, I don't know what happened. I must have fallen asleep. I, I was.....'Her voiced trailed away.

'Don't worry, I'm not a bear, I won't eat you.'

'I must go.'
She quickly crossed the floor and opened the door.

'Lamorna,' he began.
But she didn't wait to hear more.

Chapter 17

The beach and harbour were quiet. It was too early for holidaymakers to be out and about. There seemed to be some sort of delivery at every shop door, and she had to squeeze past the lorries and vans in the narrow street. A couple of black and white cats stretched languorously on a step, revelling in the sunshine. The newsagent was already open, and she spotted Sam stepping inside to buy papers for the hotel lounge. The bus came down, and she had to run to catch it. Soon it was climbing back out of the village, and she sat gazing out of the window. No-one was about at the hotel. She listened to conversations as locals boarded at various stops. Women were chatting about the weekend, the weather, not getting washing dry. A couple of men were talking cricket.

'We beat Berkshire, but it weren't a match to write home about. Sixteen runs, even with Hosen's seven wickets.'

There were glimpses of the sea, and a good view of the harbour at Newlyn, the quays already bustling. The bus arrived in town, and she walked quickly to the Studio. Philip was just opening up.

'You're bright and early, fancy a coffee?'

She put the kettle on whilst he opened blinds and shuffled through the post waiting on the mat. After coffee he showed her how the till worked, and ran through shop procedures with her. He hovered as she served her first customer.

'You did well. You'd never guess it was your first day.'

'I used to work in a newsagent on Saturdays.'

'I'll show you around.'

He led her through to a second ground floor area.

'This is my studio. I get quite a few portrait jobs, and in this little room is a space for people to change, and a few rails of costumes.'

The studio was spacious, with a camera and lights already set up and all the usual paraphernalia. There were screens against a wall, and various props. In a large trunk were a range of toys for distracting children.

'There's a toilet and wash room here for us and the customers.'

They went upstairs now and through a doorway into the darkroom.

'If I'm here on my own I leave the door at the foot of the stairs open so that I can hear the bell. Sometimes if I'm really busy I close, and put a 'back soon' notice up.'

He showed her albums in preparation, running through how they were mounted, and she was familiar with the process. He left her to finish one, coming back an hour later with a coffee for her. He was pleased with her work. He quizzed her on her knowledge of developing and printing, then, confident that she could work well left her to process a film.

'It's just for me, so it won't be a disaster if something goes wrong.'

She worked methodically. Whilst the negatives were drying she came back downstairs and served in the shop. The morning went by quickly. She took some messages for Philip, who was busy in his office, and advised a customer on the phone about types of film. Phil was pleased, and sent her off for an hour at lunch time.

She strolled down to the coffee bar and munched her way through a sandwich and milk shake. She'd bought a couple of postcards, and wrote a chatty message to her parents, and one to Jude, giving her an update on recent developments. The coffee bar was unusually quiet, but then it was only Monday lunchtime. Back in the darkroom for the afternoon she began to enjoy herself, singing and humming as she steadily processed each negative, and watching as the images slowly emerged. She noticed that they seemed to be pictures of a beach outing. There was a group scene with people in swimming costumes, other shots of a picnic. A final image seemed to show some sort of certificates being presented. And then she recognised Michael in one the picture, laughing, and with his arms around a dark haired girl. She peered closely at it, but didn't recognise his partner.

Phil popped into see how she was getting on.
'I've been meaning to get those done for the last two years. Never seem to get round to doing my own stuff. Hardly ever take any pictures nowadays.'
'What was the occasion?'
He looked at the images.
'Oh, it's older than I thought, must be four years ago. It was a group of us celebrating getting our life saving qualification over in Newquay. Some of us worked as Life Guards in the summer. You probably spotted Michael there somewhere. Never get chance to do that sort of thing now, since Dad retired. Good times. That's how I met Michael, we became good mates, but I hadn't seen him for months when he turned up the other day asking if I had a job for you.'
'He asked you for a job? I didn't know that.'
'Yeah, came in specially. Said his Dad made it impossible for you to carry on at the hotel. It was an amazing co-incidence. I'd just phoned through an advert to the local paper.'
'Why did Michael come job hunting for me?' she wondered. 'Maybe he felt guilty because he didn't support me when I stood up for our friends.'
'Must say I'm glad you were free, I'd have had to close up some days otherwise.'
'Would it be alright if I brought some of my work in to process for college after work? I'll pay for the materials.'
'Of course, you can fit it in when we're not too busy. I won't charge you, costs are negligible. And you've stepped in to help me out in my hour of need, least I can do. I'll be interested to see what you've been doing. Tomorrow I've got some baby snaps to do here, never my favourite job. Would you mind giving me a hand?'
'Of course, I'd love to.'
'We can do them together in the afternoon, and if they work out okay I'll leave you to do some wedding prints. Bring some of your work in, there'll be time, I'm sure.'

On her way home she popped into an off licence and bought a couple of bottles of celebration wine, and on a sudden impulse picked up some chocolates for Mary's Mum.

She walked down through the hotel gardens and then tentatively knocked on the kitchen door. Aileen opened it, and greeted her warmly.

'You must have known. We've just put the kettle on, how was your first day?' She sat at the big table with Mary and Aileen, telling them all about it.

'And the best thing is Phil says I can process my own photographs when we're not busy.'

'Well, that's good, but I'm missing you here, I have to admit I was half hoping it wouldn't work out, and I'd be able to persuade you to come back.'

'I miss being here too; it's not such a sociable job. But I can't let Phil down. He's so busy at the moment. Anyway, I shouldn't think Sam feels the same about me.'

'I'm not so sure, we've just had a bit of a shock. We had a letter from Ellen. She's living in a cave with some hippies now. Apparently they came to her rescue. So Sam has to change his views a little.'

'I'd better get going. I bought these chocolates for your Mum, Mary, to say thank you for Sunday dinner.'

She headed for the door, promising to keep in touch, and bumped straight into Michael, with Chris close behind him.

'Thanks again for helping me, the job is great. I really like Phil. I can't believe how lucky I am.'

'You'd better watch out in that dark room with him around,' Chris said. Michael glared at him.

'Only joking, keep your hair on.'

Everyone was already sitting around the table when she reached the house. Martyn and Heather had cooked a huge vegetable and rice bake, and the wine she contributed was well received. She had to tell her first day story all over again.

'What adventures have you all had today?'

'We went on the beach. We went surfing,' Marie shouted excitedly. 'Ced was so funny.

''Good thing I can swim,' Ced laughed, 'that's all I'm gonna say. It's a great place. Really buzzing. Beach Boys music pumping out in every street.'

'Laura, Paul and I set up our stall, and we sold loads. We've made about ten pounds to put towards the chicken scheme,' Jean told her.

Lamorna dashed upstairs for her camera, and took some photographs as they ate their pudding and discussed plans for the following day.

'I want to stay here and go and see the birds,' Marie piped up.

'There's a bird sanctuary just along the hill,' Rosa explained.

'Guess I'll stick around here and explore the village.'

'We could take you rock-pooling, Ced,' Rosa suggested.

Martyn and Heather decided to make some more crafts to take into Penzance and sell later, and Laura and Jean said they'd join them.

'While we're on a roll. We'll soon have enough for the chickens. Are you with us Paul?'

'Yeah, suppose so.'

'I could meet you for lunch. I have an hour off at 12.30.'

'That would be fun. I'll pack us all a picnic.'

Lamorna took some more pictures as they relaxed later. It was a peaceful scene. Paul strumming guitar, Ced and Rosa sprawled on floor cushions, watching Marie playing with Dylan, who was unusually still wide awake. Jean was sketching. Martyn had the evening off, and he, Heather and Laura were busy making wrist bands. They showed Lamorna the technique, and she managed to produce one passable example before announcing that she was tired, and needed to get some sleep before another day of work in the morning.

Chapter 18

The 'baby shoot' was just as challenging as Phil had suggested, but she discovered she had an unknown talent for amusing babies, persuading the reluctant child to gurgle and laugh by making a Sooty puppet pop up behind Phil's head. The parents were thrilled.

'I wish you could stay here permanently, I could use that skill.'

'Sorry Phil,' squeaked Sooty, 'I've got my course to finish.'

They both fell onto the studio cushions then, laughing, staging a mock fight between Sooty and Sweep.

Laura called for her at lunch time, and they invited Phil to join them for the picnic on the beach. In the afternoon there was time to develop and print some of her own work. Phil was impressed by the photographs she'd taken of the standing stones.

'Could you print up some large ones for the window? The emmets are fascinated by this stuff. I see you've captured Michael too.' He pointed to the Men an Tol shots. 'Don't put him in the window though, he'd put customers off!'

Later he popped in again. She'd finished all the wedding photographs, and he was really pleased. She was just hanging up some of her commune pictures, and he scrutinised them closely.

'The stones are good, but these are much more interesting. Why don't you make this your study? These are really good. Look at this.'

He was poring over a picture of the whole group.

'Who's he?'

'That's Paul, why?'

'Look at his expression. He's really scowling at this bloke here.'

'That's Ced, he's a visitor, he's American.'

'Looks like some jealousy there I'd say.'

He examined the other pictures.

'It's a really good study of this group. You get a real feel about the atmosphere, about relationships. Have these two got something going?'

'Yes, but how can you tell from just one photo?'

'Obvious really. It's their body language. Look how they're leaning in towards each other. And the way she's looking at her. Here's that Paul again. See how he's glowering over at the American.'

'It's strange, when you're in it you just don't see this, it all feels warm and friendly. But you're right. He's a bit of a loner. He seems ill at ease. I've had some issues with him.'

'I'd steer clear of him if I were you. Seriously, I'd make this your special project. They've got real potential. You could try selling them.'

'Do you really think so?'

'I do.'

'It would certainly make things easier; I was wondering how I'd manage to get to see more stones. There's plenty of time at evenings and weekends to do this work.'

'I think you should concentrate on this photo journalism type stuff. You seem to have a real eye for it. It's something I thought about when I was younger.'

'What stopped you?'

'This place was my Dad's business; I grew up in it, spent evenings and weekends in the darkroom. Then he got ill and had to retire early. I put my plans to go to college aside and stepped in to keep the business going. Felt I owed it to him. Don't get me wrong, I do love it.'

'It's never too late, you could do a part time course maybe?'

'I'll give it some thought. If I got the right assistant, someone like you, I could feel confident about leaving the place sometimes. I've got a family coming in for a portrait session in half an hour. Will you come down and help?'

'Of course, sounds fun. I'll clear up here and be down.'

'I love your optimism. Family portrait work is not usually much fun!'

Phil had been right about the family session. It was a challenge to get everyone to agree on positions, and there was almost a major falling out. Then Lamorna had the inspired idea of putting on an LP of calming classical music, and it dispelled all the anger. They were able to get some really good shots. After the family had left they cleared away, and then Phil put on some Tamla Motown and they launched into an impromptu dance with Sooty and Sweep joining in. And that was how Michael found them when he suddenly appeared.

'No need to look like that, I'm not pinching your girlfriend. We were just letting our hair down after a session with a family from hell.'

'Oh, I'm not Michael's girlfriend.' She was blushing.

'Sorry. But hey, Michael, you found me a great assistant. You can go now Lamorna. Thanks for transforming that session. See you Thursday.'

'Thursday?'

'Yeah, sorry, I forgot to tell you, Wednesday's your day off. I close up at lunch time, so I don't really need you in.'

'Oh, thank you, see you Thursday then.' She quickly escaped.

Chapter 19

Lamorna resolved to have a lie in on her day off, but the sun streaming in through the curtains insisted that she was up by eight. Ced and Rosa were already making breakfast. It was nearly the end of Marie's stay and they were planning a trip to Porthcurno.

'Come with us, come with us,' Marie said, hugging her. 'Please please please.'

'I'd love to. Who else is coming?'

'Heather, Laura and Jean. Martyn's working, and Paul wants to hang out here or go into town I think.'

They packed up a picnic, loaded the camper and were ready when Lamorna remembered her camera, and ran upstairs to get it. Then they were off, driving through the narrow high hedged lanes along the winding road that led to Porthcurno. Lamorna couldn't remember visiting this beach before. It was stunningly beautiful, but quite busy. They spread out rugs down near the sea, and she helped Marie to build a huge castle. Then everyone went off for a swim, leaving just Lamorna and Marie on the beach. Rosa and Ced took Dylan for a float about.

'I'll turn you into a mermaid to surprise everyone shall I Marie?'

'Yes please.'

So Marie lay down on the beach whilst Lamorna mounded sand and shaped it for her tail.

'My dad used to make me into a mermaid when I was little.'

'Why didn't Paul come today?' Marie asked.

'I don't know. He likes to be alone sometimes.'

'I think it's because he doesn't like Ced. It's because Ced loves my sister. I don't think I like Paul. He looks at me funny sometimes.'

'Oh, I think he's okay, he's just a bit quiet, not so chatty.'

The others reappeared, and duly admired the mermaid washed up in their midst. Laura and Jean set about getting the picnic ready.

'Come paddling with me Lamorna,' Marie begged.

So they went off down to the edge of the water and dipped their toes. They splashed and jumped the waves, laughing when a huge wave caught them out and soaked Lamorna's skirt.

'Not swimming Lamorna?' Ced queried when they came back up the beach.

'No I can't swim. And I keep covered, my skin burns so easily on days like this.'

It was a fantastic picnic. There were chunks of fresh home-made bread, cheeses, salads and tomatoes from the garden, and boiled eggs. Ced opened some cider. Lamorna took some photographs. Afterwards they all lay back contentedly. Laura and Jean were reading.

'This is the best day of my life,' Marie announced. 'I wish I didn't have to go home.'

'I'm sure Mum will let you come again,' Rosa told her.

Lamorna took some more photographs of the group. They were all dozing now, even the energetic Marie.

'I'm just going to try and get some photos around the beach,' she said, and set off with bag and camera.

She wandered around the headland into a smaller cove, and then beyond the next headland too, finding a deserted bay. At the back of the beach was a large pool of sea water, trapped by a sandy ridge. She paddled in, and the water was so warm. She couldn't resist stripping off and immersing herself in her own private pool. She lay back, feeling the water lapping over her, closing her eyes and listening to the waves curling onto the shore. She could hear the distant sounds of children squealing in the sea on the main beach, and a clamour of feeding gulls. Somewhere above was the drone of a plane. She wondered where it was bound. Maybe America. A voice broke into her thoughts.

'What do we have here, a mermaid washed up on the shore?'
She jumped up, grabbed her skirt and wrapped it around her.

'I'm sorry; I didn't mean to frighten you.'
It was Michael.

'What are you doing here?' Her face flamed with embarrassment.

'I've brought you a letter.'

'How did you know where to find me?'

'I went to the house. That guy Paul was there. He told me where you'd gone. I found the others. They said you were off taking photos. I'm sorry I startled you. I crept up because you were just like a mermaid swimming in a lagoon.'

'Because of my scaly leg?'

'No, because you looked beautiful with your hair floating around you, shining in the sun. Do you mind if I ask what happened to your leg?'

'I had an accident when I was little. I was burned on bonfire night. I didn't see you coming, or I would have covered it up.'

'You shouldn't worry. You shouldn't cover up all the time. It doesn't matter,' he said gently. 'Here's your letter.'
She looked at the envelope.

'It's from Jude.'
She opened it and quickly scanned the three pages.

'She says she's missing Cornwall.'
She didn't tell him the news about Gary. It seemed that he'd disappeared. No-one had seen him for over a week.

'We should get back to the main beach,' Michael said. 'The tide's come in. We'll have to swim around the headland now.'

'I can't swim.'

'It's not far. I'll help you, come on.'

'I can't, I can't, and my camera, I can't get it wet.'

'I'll swim round and get help, call out the lifeboat.'

'No, no, please don't leave me alone. We could climb up there.'
He looked over at the cliff.

'Alright, but we need to go now. Where are your shoes?'

'I've only got flip flops. I can't climb in them.'

'Will you be okay barefoot then? I'll carry your bag. You can't climb in that long skirt. Put it in your bag.'

Holding her skirt up in her teeth she pulled on her knickers, and red with embarrassment, turned away from him to struggle into her tee shirt. Then she took off her skirt, rolled it up, and put it into the bag.

'I'll climb with you on condition that you try and learn to swim.'

'I don't have a choice then.' She managed a smile.

They walked along the foot of the cliff, looking for an easy route.

'This looks the best place, I'll go first and then help you,' Michael said.

He began to clamber up, and she followed him cautiously. The barnacles were sharp and scratchy on her bare feet. They slowly climbed, clinging on to precarious hand holds, feet perching on narrow ledges. She didn't dare look down.

'There's an overhang here,' he said. 'I can't find a way over it. We'll have to go down a bit and back the other way. Can you manage?'

'I'll try.'

They retraced their steps. It was worse going down. She couldn't see where to put her feet. 'Please, please, let us be safe,' she thought. 'Don't let us fall.'

She was leading now, finding a way up over the steep slope. She stopped for breath as Michael climbed beside her, and risked a furtive glance. The waves were already swamping her lagoon. She felt for the next hand hold, and shrank back as her fingers sank into wet slime. She almost lost her balance.

'Are you okay?' He was beside her now, his arm across her back.

'Yes, something nasty. I put my hand in it.'

Somehow they managed to reach the top, and flung themselves into the bracken. Lamorna lay panting, looking up at the blue sky, a scratchy grid of vapour trails. She felt exhilarated now that they were safe. Michael lay still beside her, face down. After a while she broke the silence.

'Thank you,' I couldn't have done that on my own.'

'That goes for me too, I hate heights. I get vertigo.'

'Oh no, I'm sorry, I didn't know, I shouldn't have made you.'

'You didn't make me. But now you know. And you have to keep your word and learn to swim. I don't want to climb a cliff again to rescue you.'

They lay still and quiet again. Lamorna was intensely aware of him lying close to her. She felt the warmth of his body, heard his quiet breathing. She closed her eyes. 'I want him. I want to hold him in my arms. I want to kiss him. Please, make him feel the same. Make him want me too.' She willed the earth below her to listen, to make something happen. She opened her eyes, and watched the clouds piling tumultuously upwards, and moved slightly, spreading her arm out towards him.

'We should go,' he said, 'the others will be worrying about you.'

He stood up and reached out to help her. She couldn't take his hand, fearing to touch him and betray her feelings. She struggled to her feet. He passed her the flip flops. His hand brushed hers, and a wave of shock swept through her so that she trembled.

'Are you okay?'

'Suddenly felt cold. I'd better get dressed,' she said, not daring to look at him. She wrapped her skirt around her.

They picked their way carefully towards the cliff path. She had to take her flip flops off again because the brambles caught at them, ensnared her in their thorns. She trod on a gorse twig, and cried out.
'I could carry you,' he said.
'No, this is my penance for getting us into this mess.'
'You're too hard on yourself.'

At last they reached the path and made their way back and down to the beach. She ran into the sea to wash her scratched and bloody feet. Turning to walk back she saw Michael talking to the others, and then running off up the beach.
'We thought you were drowned,' Marie cried, hugging her.
'We called the coastguard. We were so worried,' Jean said.
'Oh no! They'll send a lifeboat.'
'Don't worry, Michael's gone to ring them and stop the lifeboat coming out. We invited him to come for dinner with us, but he refused. I thought he wanted to, but then he hesitated and said no. Has something happened between you?'
'No, no.'
Laura scrutinised her face.
'There's a different look about you, but I can see you're not going to share it with us, come on, let's get going.'

On the way home she had to tell them all about what had happened.
'Michael's a hero,' Marie said, 'I wish I could have been with you.'
'It was frightening, and I hope nothing like that happens to you. We might easily have fallen from the cliff. Next time I will be more careful and watch the tide.'

Paul was in a foul mood when they arrived back.
'You're all late,' he complained.
Jean explained what had happened.
'Michael to the rescue, it would be him.' He walked out of the room.
'What's got into him,' Laura said, as they busied themselves in the kitchen, making cheese on toast and baked beans. 'I thought he might have made a dinner for us.'
'I've noticed that Paul doesn't seem to do much to help.'
There was a moment's pause.
'You're right Lamorna,' Jean said. 'He doesn't help. I'm sure it was different when he first came. He seems more wrapped up in his own needs now. And I don't know why he seems to hate Michael. I need to talk to him.'
Paul reappeared when they were ready to eat. Rosa looked at him.
'What have you done Paul; you've got a nasty bruise on your temple?'
'Banged it on the kitchen cupboard.'
'There's some arnica in the bathroom,' Laura told him.
'Will you help me to wash up, Paul?' Heather asked.
He followed her meekly into the kitchen.

Chapter 20

'Would you mind posing for a photograph for me?' Phil asked. 'I need a picture of a young woman sitting on a rock, looking alluring. It's for a Holiday Park brochure.'

'Okay, if you're sure.'

'You'll be perfect. You have good bones. You'll be very photogenic. Have a look on the costume rail. I think there's a long blue dress. It should fit. It's just what we need for a mermaid look.'

She hunted around and pulled out a long green dress in a silky fabric. Stripping off her clothes she pulled it over her head, and then went in to show Phil.

'What do you think?'

'Stunning. It's perfect. Let's get it done before the sun decides to disappear again.'

He popped the 'CLOSED' sign on the door, and drove her to Marazion. Luckily the tide was out, and they found the ideal spot. He wanted to photograph her perched on rocks with St Michael's Mount in the background. He was pleased with the way the session went, and bought them ice creams to celebrate. They sat for a while on the beach to eat them, and she told him about her adventure at Porthcurno.

'You were brave to climb up the cliff. You should have called out the lifeboat.'

'I couldn't, it seems such a trivial thing.'

'It was dangerous. It's their job to come out for situations like that.'

She spent the rest of the afternoon processing the portrait photographs they'd taken. At closing time Michael suddenly appeared.

'Don't see you for months, and suddenly you're around here practically every day,' Phil said.

'Dad asked me to call in. He wants to know if you could do a brochure for the hotel. We want a new look for next season, now that we've refurbished the place. And we want to include the holiday cottage too.'

'Yeah, be glad to. Let me know what kind of thing you want, and I'll do you a costing. Come up to the dark room, I'll show you some ideas I've had for a holiday camp brochure. Just been out taking photos for it. Come up with us Lamorna.'

She followed them upstairs. Phil took Michael over to the work table, and showed him the sketches.

'We got a great shot for the front. Lamorna, bring one of those pictures over to show Michael please.'

Blushing, she carried the damp print over. Michael looked at the photograph.

'It's good. I like your ideas. Maybe we should have some guests in our pictures too.'

'You don't want that ugly shower, all those old biddies. Now Lamorna, that's different. A beautiful young woman relaxing in the garden, that would get the clients in.'

Lamorna felt her cheeks burning.

'Aren't you being a bit, sort of exploiting women?' Michael said.

'Well, yeah, but it's good for business. When do you need the work done?'

'As soon as possible, we want to get the brochures out in the autumn.'

'That might be difficult mate. I've got a lot on at the moment. What about Lamorna doing it? She's a good photographer, and she's got a creative way of working. What do you think Lamorna?'

'I'd be willing to try, but I've never done anything like it before.'

'You can use some of my other stuff as a guide, and Sam can show you what he wants.'

'I'm not sure Sam will want me to do the job.'

'He'll be okay; anyway he's put me in charge of it. When could you start?'

'I could get a costing done by Monday, and if you accept it Lamorna could spare some time later in the week.'

'I could do some on Wednesday. It would make it cheaper for you, and I am only a beginner.'

'Okay, if you want to. It would help. We're busy again next week. But I'll pay you.'

'You don't need to. It's good experience for me. If you don't mind I could put a copy in my portfolio. I feel I owe Sam a favour for giving me a chance to work at the hotel. And Michael for finding me this job.'

'You don't owe any favours.' Michael said.

'That would reduce the cost, if you're happy with that Mike.'

'Yes, but don't reduce it too much, or Dad will think he's not getting a good job. He's got a budget put by for it. I'll call in on Monday then. Do you want a lift home Lamorna?'

'Thank you. I'll just print the last couple of pictures.'

'Have a look through these examples of brochures I've done Michael.'

The phone rang and Phil went off downstairs. She was aware of Michael behind her in the room. Heard pages turning as he browsed the albums. And then he was beside her.

'It's a bit like magic,' he said, 'the way the picture slowly appears on the paper.' She was embarrassed, as her own image was revealed. She waited until it was just right, and pegged it up to dry

'All finished.' She went over to a small sink and washed and dried her hands.

'I've just selected one or two brochures to take home,' he said. 'How are you today? Have you recovered from the climbing?'

'Yes, my feet are still a bit scratched and sore though.'

'Come on then, let's go.'

The van was parked on the Esplanade. They clambered in and set off.

'Thank you for yesterday,' she said after a while.

'Have you booked your swimming lessons yet?'

'No, not enough time. It'll have to wait until I get home. You could drop me off at the hotel please, I want to pop in and see Mary.'

'Okay. What time do you want to come on Wednesday?'

'I could do some on Sunday if the weather's good. I haven't any other plans.'

'It would be a good day, I'm free too. Mary's coming in for some extra hours. But what about your project, shouldn't you be taking pictures of stones?'

'Phil suggested I should use my pictures of the commune for my project, and I think he's right. But I do love the stones. Phil's asked me to print some big ones for his window.'

'If you want I could take you out to see some more. I know a place where there are some funny rock markings.'

'I might take you up on that. It sounds interesting.'

They drove into the hotel yard.

'Thanks Michael.'

She skipped over to the kitchen door. Mary was pleased to see her.

'Mum says thank you for the chocolates, and you can come for dinner any time. What about Sunday?'

'I'm not sure, I've got a job on Sunday, guess what it is.'

'That's difficult. A christening?'

'I'm coming here to take photos of the hotel for a new brochure. Sam wants Phil to do the job, and he's really busy, so I'm going to try. And I've got to take some pictures of the cottage.'

'Don't make it look too nice, or it'll get busy before we've found somewhere to live! Do you want to help me get the tables ready for dinner? Aileen's trying to calm a complaining guest.'

They went through to the dining room and that's where Aileen found them.

'I need a cup of tea after that, anyone joining me? I'm glad to see you're back with us Lamorna.'

She had to explain what she was doing, telling Aileen all about the brochure project.

'Will Sam mind?'

'No, and anyway he's given the job to Michael. It's up to him now to decide how it will be done. Why don't you stay and have dinner?'

'I'd love to, but I can't. One of the girl's young sisters has been staying with us, and she goes home tomorrow. We're having a farewell party for her. I must get going.'

'Some of us will be in The Ship tomorrow night, come and join us,' Mary said.

'I'll do that. I had a letter from Jude. Michael brought it for me. Did he tell you about how he rescued me?'

'No, he didn't mention that, whatever happened?' Aileen asked.

'I can't stop now, I'll tell you on Sunday. Ask Michael.'

'Has it got something to do with the lifeboat getting called out and then Michael ringing the coxswain to cancel?' Mary asked.

But Lamorna was already gone.

Chapter 21

They were all waiting for her when she arrived, breathless from running.

'Sorry, sorry, here's some garlands, desperate for the toilet.'

She dropped a package on the table and ran. It was only when she came back into the kitchen that she noticed a tense atmosphere.

'I'm sorry I'm late. Are you okay? Where are Rosa and Marie?'

'Lamorna, something unpleasant happened today, that's why we're all upset,' Laura told her. 'You lot put these up. Let's try and make the evening special. Someone put some music on. Come with me Lamorna.'

She led her into the small front room, and they sat down together on the sofa.

'This afternoon Paul tried to seduce Marie. Luckily Martyn came in and caught him.'

'No. Why would he do that? She's only a child.'

'He said he thought she was sixteen.'

'That's no excuse. How is Marie?'

'She seems fine. I think she thought it was fun, a game. There's more. We found out that Michael hit Paul yesterday while we were out. Paul said it was something to do with you.'

'I don't understand. Michael doesn't know anything.'

'So there was something. Do you want to tell me about it?'

Lamorna's head sank into her hands. Her eyes filled with tears. She told Laura what had happened on the beach.

'But no-one else knows. I haven't told anyone. He shouldn't have hit him.'

'No he shouldn't, but what's done is done. I started this place as a haven of peace and love, and something has gone badly wrong.'

'What a mess. It's all my fault. It's all gone wrong since I got here.'

'It's not your fault. Paul is the one who made things change. He's gone now.'

'Gone?'

'Yes, we asked him to leave. He packed his bags and left at four o'clock. We had a meeting. Ced took Marie into the village, and the rest of us talked with him. We decided that he didn't fit in, that he'd caused a lot of upset.'

'What about Rosa and Dylan?'

'Rosa is upset because she was fond of him. But he's made it clear that he wants no more to do with Dylan. We have to support Rosa through this. It's hard for her. Paul is Dylan's father after all.'

'How terrible.'

'Yes, but it's probably better for Rosa in the long run. We'd all noticed that Paul was not helping around the place. I think you commented on that yesterday. We challenged him with that, and he said *"Why should I have to."* So you see, we decided he had to go. And now that you've told me your story I am even more sure that it was right.'

'I wish I'd said something about what happened, it might have stopped him trying it on with Marie.'

'Perhaps. I don't know. We are all wondering now why he left the previous commune. He obviously has problems, but he won't be helped. His idea of free love and communal living is a selfish, greedy version, all bound up with his own needs. He only wants to take, and we've failed to help him move on.'

'But what could we have done? He never seemed to want to talk.'

'You're right. He kept it all bottled up. I don't know if we could have helped. But that's enough now, let's go and get the party started.'

The streamers had been hung, and candles were lit.

'You bought so many garlands, Martyn and Ced are putting the rest up in the lounge,' Jean said. 'Would you like to go up and find Rosa and Marie?'
Lamorna ran upstairs to Rosa's room and stuck her head round the door.

'Hi, you two, I'm here to tell you the party's started.'
Marie rushed over and hugged her.

'I've been waiting and waiting for you. I've had a horrid day. Everyone's been strange. Paul was cross and shouting.'

'I know, I know, but he's gone now and we're going to have a lovely evening.'
They went downstairs together. There was a fanfare of party blowers as they walked into the kitchen. It was a riotous meal, not the peaceful occasion they usually enjoyed. After the washing up was done, with everyone eager to help, they all went through to the living room. Laura had prepared some games, and the fun continued. Later they drank mugs of cocoa and when Martyn came in he played for them, and they sang Marie's favourite songs. Sometime around eleven o'clock they realised that Marie was fast asleep, so Ced and Rosa carried her up to bed.

'I won't see her in the morning,' she'll be asleep when I leave,' Lamorna said.

'There'll be time before the train; I'll bring her to the studio to see you.'

Rosa kept her promise, arriving with Marie at eleven o'clock.

'Let me take your photographs, if Phil doesn't mind.'
He didn't mind, and came in to help find some interesting costumes in his store.

'I should take some of all three of you, and maybe you'll let me use them in a window display. I don't often get to work with crazy people!'
So they posed for him wearing the most outlandish combinations of clothes, until they all collapsed in a heap, their sides aching with laughter.

'Why don't you take lunch early, as you're going to be working in your own time on the brochure project Lamorna, and you can go with your friends to the station?'

'Thank you, I'd like that.'

'Good. We'll have a stint in the dark room this afternoon, might get these pictures done too.'

The train was on time, and a tearful Marie was persuaded on board. They waited on the platform, waving until it was out of sight.

'Come on, let's get lunch,' Rosa said.
They bought sandwiches and lemonade and took them to the beach.

'How was Marie today?'

'She seems fine. I think I was more upset than she was. I dread to think what might have happened if Martyn hadn't come back when he did. We were all in the garden, clearing an area for the chicken run. Marie went in to play with the kittens. It seems that Paul came downstairs and found her in the living room. He started to come on to her. Marie seems to have been flattered by the attention. She said she couldn't wait to tell her friends. I think I've persuaded her to keep it secret.'

'Will she tell your Mum?'

'I think I've got through to her that if she does then she won't be allowed to come down again. But I feel terrible. I don't want to encourage secrecy. Mum should know. But she already has a dim view of this place. She'd go berserk. Probably call the Police. I said Marie could come for half term, so I think she'll keep quiet.'

'We ought to tell the Police. But I couldn't bear to think of it. Imagine what the locals would say.'

'Yeah. I think it was probably just a one-off moment of stupidity on his part.'

'Let's hope so.'

'Anyway, what happened with you and Paul? Laura mentioned to us that you'd had some sort of problem with him too?'

Lamorna told her about the incident on Whitesand Beach.

'I can't understand it. I really cared for him. How could he do that?'

'I think he really cares about you, and he was jealous, jealous about Ced. That might be the root of the problem.'

'And yet he made it clear to me that he didn't want commitment, even after Dylan was born. I said we could make a go of a relationship. Maybe I scared him.'

'We'll probably never know. I'd better get going, or I'll have to look for another job.'

They bought ice creams to eat on the way back, and then Rosa set off for the market. She was on shopping duty too.

'Damn, I forgot the kitty money in my rush to get Marie moving.'

'How much do you need?'

'A couple of pounds should do thanks. I'll pay you when we get home.'

'No need, I owe this week's anyway.'

The afternoon was busy again. There was a backlog of studio work to process, and no time for the morning's pictures to be done. There was no lift home either, so she hurried to the bus stop, calling at a cake shop on the way.

'Maybe I can persuade everyone to come down to the pub with me tonight.'

The cakes were greeted with great enthusiasm. They all ate one with a cup of tea, and then she rushed upstairs to wash and change. 'I'll try and get some pictures in the kitchen this evening.'

She opened her camera bag. It was empty. She searched her room.

'That's strange, I'm sure I put it away. When did I last use it? I didn't take any pictures during the party. Must have been on Wednesday, maybe I left it in Ced's van.'

No-one else remembered seeing it around. Ced went out to check the camper, but came back empty handed.

'Oh well, let's eat, it'll turn up.'

It was ten thirty before she had time to think about it again. She knew it was pointless, but she opened the camera bag and peered inside. There was a piece of white paper at the bottom. She pulled it out. *'Sorry Lamorna, I needed the money.'*

'No, how could he.'

Rosa came in and found her in floods of tears. She retrieved the crumpled note from Lamorna's hand, opened it and read the smudged words.

'Oh Lamorna,' she cried, hugging her.

'How can I do my course now, I can't afford a new camera. I bought this one with the money my Dad saved for me.'

After a while they went downstairs and shared the news. Laura was particularly distraught.

'We all felt safe here. We never locked doors. We thought we could trust everyone.'

Someone thought about the kitty. Jean reached for the teapot. It was empty.

She couldn't get to sleep that night. 'I was supposed to meet Mary in the pub. And I wanted to talk to Rosa about Michael. Maybe there'll be chance tomorrow.' She lay in the darkness, thoughts tumbling around in her head, her face streaked with tears. 'How am I going to finish the course now?' The quiet of the house was disturbed by sounds from the room next door. Rosa and Ced were making love. She felt very cold and alone. She burrowed down under the blankets to blot out the world.

Chapter 22

'You look terrible,' Phil said.

And straight away she burst into tears. He sat her down and made her coffee.

'Now tell me about it.'

She blurted out the story.

'How can I do my course now?'

'The bastard. Did you call the Police?'

'No,' she sighed. 'What's the point? We don't even know his second name, or where he's from. And he told everyone he'd go to Paris. We'd never find him.'

'You've got some good pictures of him. You could show them to the Police, they could alert the port authorities.'

'It won't bring my camera back. He's bound to have sold it by now.'

'You're probably right. But all is not lost. Come with me.'

He led her upstairs into the darkroom, and over to a tall metal cupboard. Opening the doors he reached up to the top shelf and pulled down a cardboard box.

'You can have this, I don't use it now.'

She opened the box and peered inside. There was a black case. She lifted it out.

'It's a Pentax. A Spotmatic. I can't take that.'

'I want you to have it. It's just gathering dust in here. It's not too old, so it should be okay.'

'You can't just give it to me. It's valuable. You could sell it.'

'I could, but I can't be bothered. Have it. It deserves a good home.'

'Oh thank you, thank you,' she cried, hugging him. 'It's a hundred times better than my camera.'

'Are you okay now? I need to get going. I've left you some films to process. I may call by at lunch time to see if you're alright.'

'Yes, don't worry, I'll be fine.'

'Good, I'll be off then. Don't forget to take a lunch break.'

All day she worked in the dark room, blissfully aware of the amazing camera on the table behind her. At two o'clock Phil stuck his head round the door, and discovered she hadn't stopped. He dragged her out for a quick lunch.

'You'll turn into a mole, stuck in the dark all day.'

She sat opposite him in the coffee bar, grinning at him the whole time, until he could stand it no longer.

'Think of something serious for a while,' he said, 'euphoria can get a bit wearying. Tell me what you're planning for the hotel brochure.'

She explained the arrangements she'd made with Michael.

'You can't work on Sunday.'

'Well, it's not like proper work. It'll be fun.'

'You're a hopeless case. It's may be a good thing you can't take the job permanently; you'd wear me out with your enthusiasm. Will you lock the shop up for me tonight? I want to get straight home after my next job and do the costing for the brochure. I'll drop them off at the hotel in the morning. If he doesn't like the price then you won't need to do the job anyway.'

'Of course, no problem.'

'And Lamorna...'

'Yes?'

'Go home on time tonight. No extra half hour. You look like you need to catch up on sleep.'

'Can I take the camera with me?'

'It's yours now. See you in the morning.'

Lamorna did lock up on time. She was feeling tired and wanted to be home early to talk to Rosa. She thought she should also pop into the hotel and see Mary, apologise for not turning up at the pub last night.

'You must come down on Monday and tell me how you got on. I want to hear all about the photographs of the cottage,' Mary said.

'I will, I promise. Might even get the pictures processed to show you. I think Michael has finished all the work now.'

She was back at the house in time to help Ced and Rosa make dinner. They were all pleased to hear about the new camera.

'It's a miracle, it's so much better than my old one. I'll be able to get brilliant pictures. In fact I'll start right now, I need some kitchen shots.'

Everyone was more relaxed at dinner. Ced and Rosa announced that they were going off travelling together.

'Rosa's going to show me the rest of England. We'll call on her folks, and see Marie, and then we'll maybe go over to Ireland. My ancestors were from somewhere over there.'

'Oh, I'll miss you. When are you going?' Lamorna asked.

'On Monday I think.'

'I'll give you my parent's address so we can keep in touch. I printed the pictures of you and Marie, I nearly forgot.'

She rushed upstairs to get them from her bag.

'They're lovely. Mum will be really pleased.'

'I'm on my own at work all day tomorrow, so I hope there'll be chance to do more of the pictures of this place. A pity Paul is in them.'

'Well he was here, a part of this, and he wasn't always difficult. And I suppose he's made us think about why we're here, and how we make it work in the future,' Laura said.

After dinner Laura and Jean went off to wash up. Ced walked into the village to phone 'the folks back home.' Heather went up for an early night. It was the perfect opportunity to talk to Rosa. They took mugs of coffee into the living room and settled down on cushions.

'I think I'm in love with Michael Rosa.'

'Oh, that's wonderful, I think he's lovely. I wished I could have felt like that about him, but I didn't. Always fall for the wrong men, until Ced, that is. But what about him? Does he feel the same do you think?'

'I don't know. Sometimes I think he likes me, and then I'm not sure again. I'm meeting him on Sunday to take the photos for the hotel brochure. He's offered to take me over to get some more photos of stones afterwards.'

'Will you go?'

'Yes, I want to.'

'Well you'll know how he feels then. I don't think he would have suggested it if he didn't like you. It sounds like he wants to be with you but he's not sure of your feelings either.'

'I have tried to keep him at a distance. I didn't want to get involved with any men. I want to finish my course, and get a brilliant job, and travel around. But right now I can't think of anything but him.'

'You can do all of those things. It's important to live your dreams. You only have one life. If you and Michael are meant to be together it will work out, you'll see.'

The others came through then and they sat peacefully together, listening to music and unwinding after all the tensions of the previous days. Lamorna fell asleep on the sofa and had to be woken up and sent to bed.

Chapter 23

The sea shone as smooth as a satin bedspread tucked into the shore. They were all outside in the garden for breakfast, serenaded by hover flies and bees humming around the flowers. Laura and Jean had dragged an old trestle table out of the shed, spread it with a big mirror work bedspread, and plonked two rickety benches either side. There were hunks of home-made bread, and honey from the village store. Rosa had cooked eggs and made a salad of tomatoes.

Lamorna ate in silence. She was thinking about the day ahead. Just for once she had thought carefully about what to wear, choosing jeans because they were practical, and her new silky shirt, in a shade of aubergine which suited her colouring.

'OW!' Ced's outburst cut through the quietness. 'A cat just pounced on my foot!'

'They got under my blankets the other night,' Lamorna said, 'and each time I twitched they scratched me. I hardly dared to move. But they are cute.'

'Cute is not a word I'm thinking at the moment,' he said, rubbing his foot and fending off another attack.

'You look radiant Lamorna,' Jean commented. 'And you're only going to work.'

'It's such a fabulous day,' she replied. 'And it's Rosa and Ced's last full day here. What will you all do to celebrate?'

'I've never been to St. Ives, how about that?' Ced suggested.

'It's a brilliant idea, I've got to call in and see my parents over there, so we could all meet up on the beach,' Heather said.

'Won't you be over that way later Lamorna? You could join us too,' Rosa said.

'I'm not sure, I think we're going somewhere on the north coast. I can ask Michael to drop me off.'

'He could come too. We'll build a fire on the beach and bake some potatoes.'

She ran upstairs to clean her teeth and quickly plaited a few strands of hair around her face to keep them out of the way whilst she took pictures. She collected her camera and equipment together, and then on an impulse put some silver shell ear rings on. 'For luck,' she thought. She buckled her sandals, and then changed her mind, thinking the flip flops would be better for the beach later on. She wanted to keep the sandals smart for work, and she'd noticed that there was tar on the local beaches. Rosa gave her a farewell hug.

'I'll be thinking of you,' she whispered.

And then she was gone, running lightly down the path and into the lane.

Michael was waiting for her when she reached the hotel. He smiled at her and sent her heart leaping. He made them coffee, and they sat together in the garden to look at some brochures.

'This is the old stuff, and I think it's boring. Can we produce something a bit more modern, up to date?'

'The photographs are very dull, and the layout is old fashioned. Did Phil do this?'

'No, it was an old established firm. They always did the work for the last owner, we just carried on. I'd like us to attract some new people to the hotel, younger couples. And we've refurbished the place now. It has a more modern, stylish feel.'

'I think I could get some more appealing photos, and we could try different layouts.'

They toured the different rooms, and Lamorna made adjustments, placing a vase of flowers here, turning down a bed, moving an ornament, even cheekily putting one into a bin. She asked Michael to find some magazines and books, and she placed them on a bedside table. He fetched a bottle of champagne and glasses and she took a photograph of them in the foreground of a bedroom shot. She took close ups of flowers. In a darker room she turned lamps on.

I'm trying to make it look lived-in, look inviting,' she said. 'I want to make people open the leaflet and think, 'what a lovely room, I could just lie down on that bed.'

'You're right,' he said after a while. Just moving away clutter makes the rooms much nicer. I'll get Mum to chuck the ornaments out.'

'A few natural objects would look lovely, some sea shells, and big pebbles. It would give a seaside feel.'

'That may be a step too far this year, but we could do that at the cottage, that's my project.'

Outside she took some wide shots, and then a few close up details of hydrangeas and fuchsias, before going back indoors to get views of the garden and sea from windows.

Aileen called them for lunch at twelve. Michael enthused about Lamorna's ideas.

'She's so creative. She just sees things I don't even notice.'

'It's good of Phil to give us such a competitive price,' Sam said. 'He said it's thanks to you giving your time for free Lamorna.'

'I'm enjoying it, and it's good experience for my course. I hope you won't mind if I put the brochure in my portfolio. Well, if you like it and want to go ahead.'

'Course not, and by the sound of what Michael is saying it will be very good. Anyhow, the decision is entirely his.'

'We could go down to the cottage next, and you can give me some ideas about final touches, and then maybe we could get the photos done on Wednesday. I've got some furniture coming on Monday, and I'd like it in place before we do the pictures.'

'Yes, sounds like a good idea.'

'How's your project going Lamorna?' Aileen asked.

'I've nearly finished. I've printed everything in Phil's darkroom. He asked me to blow up some of the images for his window too. And I've done a few prints for your cottage. It's a surprise for Mary and Chris.'

'Well, that is a lovely thought. Come by and show us your photographs won't you?'

'Yes, I will. Michael is going to take me to see some little marks on stones later.'

'Would that be the maze markings?'

'Yeah, and I think we should get going. We're going to have a look at Tintagel Castle. And we've been invited to a beach barbecue in St. Ives later, so I won't be in for dinner Mum.'

'Okay, well have a good time.' She and Sam looked at each other.

'You'd best get going then. Thank you Lamorna,' Sam said.

The cottage looked welcoming in the sunshine, with its newly-painted door and white window frames.

'You could put some interesting pebbles and driftwood on the window sills, maybe little model boats too,' Lamorna suggested. 'And we'll need to bring some flowers down from the hotel. We could put some tubs of plants on the front step, and what about some children's windmills and bucket and spades by the door?'

'Wow, slow down, so many ideas. But I love them. We'll buy some stuff this afternoon, and we could go beach combing too.'

'You've done so much since I came down with Mary. I love the rugs and furniture.'

'Yeah, I'll be sorry to move out. But come on, we'd better go.'

They drove through Penzance and onto the A30 through Hayle and Cambourne. Lamorna felt her heart pounding.

'I'm thinking about him all the time. My body feels like a magnet, pulling me towards him.'

She glanced over at his hands on the steering wheel. The sleeves of his shirt were rolled up. It was the shirt she'd seen him wearing when she had first arrived. 'I wish I could just reach over and stroke his arm.' She risked a glance at his face. His gaze was fixed on the road ahead, but she was startled when he suddenly turned to her.

'Are you okay?'

'Yes, I was just looking at the place names on the signs. They're so different: Gwithian, Angarrack, Penhelick. They're so poetic. They're like the names of ancient knights and damsels.'

'You've got a good imagination. They're Cornish, the old language. The words like Pen and Tre at the start of names mean headland and home. Most place names have a meaning. Like where you come from the places are Danish, the ones ending in "by," that kind of thing.'

'How do you know that?'

'Learned about the invaders in school, Vikings, all of that.'

'Does anyone speak Cornish still?'

'No it died out a long time ago. The last speaker was supposedly an old woman back in the village. There's a sign on her house.'

'That's a shame. I always think it's like coming to another country.'

'It is another country. Do you want to see Tintagel first?'

Michael turned off the main road, and they wound their way down to the village.

'Sunday. Not the best day, it'll be packed.'

He was right, it was swarming with visitors. They found a corner in the car park and set off to walk down the narrow stone steps to the castle. She found herself pressed against him as they stood aside to let people pass, and she tried to move so that he couldn't sense the sudden shiver that ran through her.

'Look at that sea down there,' she said, 'it's like a wizard's cauldron, boiling and bubbling.'
She was fascinated by the ruins perched on the rocky promontory, and took a few photographs. But it was too crowded, and they didn't linger long.

'Let's have tea.'

'I've not been near a tea room since I was about eight years old,' he said. 'My mates would have a laugh if they saw me now.'

'We don't have to.'

'It won't kill me, and who's to know? Anyway the pub won't be open yet.'

'I'm going to have a cream tea, and this treat is on me.'

'I'll just have ginger beer thanks.'

'I'm not sure how I can use the pictures of Tintagel in my project. Maybe I'll broaden it to a theme about stone. And I'll print one for the cottage wall.'
The drinks arrived then, and Lamorna persuaded Michael to share her splits.

'They're not as good as the ones you make.'
She blushed as he looked at her, smiling.

A coach party must have arrived because there was a sudden surge of people.

'Let's go, the hordes have arrived,' he said.
The van was hot from standing in the sun. They wound the windows down and set off for the rocky valley.

Chapter 24

A steep path led down from the roadside, through trees and then into the valley itself. They made their way down between the grassy slopes beside a stream. There were rocks and boulders to negotiate, and it was slippery in some places on the steep turfy banks.

'How do you walk in those flip flop things?'

'I'm used to them, although it is a bit tricky going down here.'

They clambered on down until Michael stopped by a group of large boulders with flat surfaces. He pointed out some strange carvings, like spiralling mazes on the rock. She ran her hand over them.

'They're amazing. They're beautiful. Who made them?'

'No-one really knows. People think they're prehistoric. There are others around the country, in The Lake District and Scotland I think.'

She took some photographs of them.

'I wonder what they mean, what they're for.'

'They might be some kind of fertility symbol,' he said after a pause.

'I'll have to try and find out more. Look at the sea down there; it's the most beautiful colours. Can we go down?'

'Yes, but there's not much there, just rocks.'

'Look at this moss,' she said, stroking the soft velvety cushions. 'And all the flowers.'

There were clumps of thrift and purple thyme mingling fragrantly with violets and vetches.

At the bottom she kicked off her flip flops and stepped onto the rocks to paddle.

'Ooooh, it's so cold.'

She soon scrambled out over the rocks again and pushed her feet into the flip flops to climb back up to the flatter turfy area where Michael had sat down. Her foot slithered as she stepped onto a mossy green rock.

'Ow, ow.'

She sat down and pulled the flip flop off.

'Are you okay, what have you done?'

'I don't know, but it really hurts.'

'Can you get up here onto this flat place?'

He stood up and held his hand out to her. She took his hand and hobbled over the rock, her eyes filling with tears. He squatted down next to her and took her foot in his hand, gently feeling around her ankle.

'I don't think you've broken anything, just sprained it. Move across here a little, and you can put your foot in this pool, the cold water will help stop it swelling too much.'

She immediately shuffled over and plunged her foot into the water, gasping with the shock of the cold. She looked up at him,

'It's the silly flip flops. I slid on the sole.'

Her eyes met his and held his gaze. She was about to speak again when he leaned over and kissed her. He took her face in his hands and kissed her again. And then he drew her into his arms, brushing strands of damp hair from her face, and kissing her mouth as he stroked her face again and again.

She felt herself falling into him. She wrapped her arms around him, twisting her fingers through his soft curls. He slowly lowered her down to lie beside him, and all the while his mouth was on hers, warm and gentle. She felt his hand move softly down her neck and she was trembling, her body longing for his caress. She yearned more closely against him. He unfastened her buttons, and she tightened her fingers in his hair as his hand curled around her, stroking and gently touching. She shifted slightly, and he understood her desire and moved his hand to stroke her other breast. And then he was kissing her neck, her breasts, his breath warm, as his tongue caressed her. Her left hand fumbled to undo his shirt, and she pulled him against her to feel his skin next to hers. He kissed her mouth again as his hand moved down, stroking her belly, then her hips, and then sliding under the top of her jeans.
'Is that okay?' he murmured.

She moved herself closer to him, kissing him. He unfastened her jeans, and tugged at them and she pushed against them with her foot to shrug them away. She was shuddering with desire as his hand curved warm around her, gently easing her legs apart.
'Are you cold?'
She shook her head. He kissed her again, and she felt herself aching for him as his mouth moved over her. His fingers gently stroked her into fierce desire. He kicked out of his jeans and she felt him glide into her. At first slow and gentle, and then deeper. She felt a sharp pain and caught her breath, flinching.
'Did I hurt you?'
She shook her head again and pulled him closer. And then she was lost and there was nothing but the feel of him within her and the sensations in her own body as though the world around them ceased to exist. At last she felt him shudder, and he groaned as his body relaxed against her. She wanted more, and squirmed against him. And he kissed her again, stroked her breasts and moved his hand down over her until, curving around her again, his fingers brought her to a climax. She cried out and held him tightly to her as they lay wrapped together. She felt tears hot on her cheeks.
'You're crying,' he said softly. 'I'm sorry.'
'I'm happy, I'm crying because I'm happy.'

She sobbed against him, clinging to him as though she were drowning in her own tears.
And he kissed her tears away and held her close, stroking her as her crying gradually subsided, and they lay drowsily together. The sun slipped downwards, leaving a blanket of shadow over them.

***

She roused slowly in his arms at last, hearing again the sea wallowing and washing over the rocks below them. A soft sound of an insect exploring close to her, and grass soft and tickling on her skin. And the scent of flowers, warm thyme and musky gorse filled the air around them. His breath was soft on her neck. She lay revelling in the weight of his body against her, the warm skin of his arm flung over her. A warm stickiness between her legs. She smiled to herself. Opened her eyes and saw the great blue canopy of the sky spread over them, and she turned her face to gaze at him in adoration. He woke then, and they lay together lost in wonderment. At last they kissed again, and he stroked her hair.

'It was your first time,' he said after a while.

'Yes.'

He held her more closely, stroking her face gently.

'I thought, well, the bloke from back home, and then the commune....I didn't know.'

'No,' she said. 'There was no-one else.'

And again he kissed her.

'You should have told me. I should have been more careful.'

'It will be alright,' she said.

They lay quietly for a while, each lost in their own thoughts.

'I don't want this moment to end. I want to lie with him forever. I want him to kiss me and kiss me.' She stroked his face and he did kiss her.

'We should get going.'

They were in deeper shadow now below the cliff. They pulled their clothes on, and Lamorna winced as she moved her foot.

'My foot is so cold, I can hardly feel it.'

He held it and warmed it in his hands.

'It's still a little swollen. Can you walk do you think?'

He supported her as she struggled to stand.

'I'll have to go barefoot. I can't manage with the flip flop.'

They went slowly up the valley, Lamorna leaning heavily on him as she hobbled over the rough ground. They stopped for a while for her to rest, sitting on a hummocky bank amongst wild violets and hearts-ease. He held her close, his arm around her.

'I feel like the little mermaid in the story,' she said. 'Every step is painful.'

At the top of the hill he lifted her up and carried her across to his van. She nuzzled into his neck, kissing his warm skin, so that when he placed her gently on the ground again she could feel that he was aroused, and he held her close, kissing her and stroking her. The moment was lost when another car drew up, and they moved apart.

'We'd better go,' he said, his voice husky with emotion.

They drove along the coast in a deeper silence than before, and she was happy just to sit and gaze openly at him. He stopped by the roadside, and crossed to a small chemist shop, coming back with a paper bag. Moving around to her side he opened the door and crouching down lifted her foot onto his knee. He took a crepe bandage from the bag, and skilfully wound it around her ankle, tying it neatly.

'That should help.'

'How do you know how to do that?'

'It was part of my lifeguard training. Can you put this in your bag now?' He seemed shy as he handed her the paper bag. She peered inside and saw that he had bought two packets of sheaths, and turned to smile at him. They drove on down the coast.

'Where are we going? We've passed St. Ives.'

'A surprise.'

Some minutes later he pulled up below stone steps leading up to a small church. He went around to her door, and lifted her out.

'We're just going to look at something in the church,' was all he said as he carried her up the steps, placing her carefully down by the door. Inside the church was cool and shady. He helped her over to a wooden seat, and there she saw that someone had carved a mermaid into the wood. A rounded figure, holding mirror and comb.

'It's lovely. Who is she?'

'She's the Zennor Mermaid. She was supposed to have fallen in love with a local man when she heard him singing in the church, and he followed her into the sea. Some folks say they can hear him singing still.' She turned to hold him and kiss him.

'Not in the church.' He lifted her again and carried her across to the van. And then he took her into his arms and kissed her passionately.

'Do you want to go to the picnic, or shall we go to the cottage?'

She was flushed with desire for him.

'I suppose I should go to the picnic, it's Rosa's last evening.'

'Okay, we'll go, we should eat anyway.'

Chapter 25

They reluctantly drew apart. He turned the van around and they drove back to St Ives. The sun was a red streak across the sky as they headed down the beach, Lamorna limping along, supported by Michael.

'What kept you two? What happened to your foot?' Rosa asked.
Lamorna explained, smiling, and received a hug from her friend, and a whispered,
'I've never seen anyone in pain look so pleased.'
She sat down as close to Michael as she could get in the glow of the driftwood fire. Someone passed them both cans of beer, and there was crusty bread and salad, tomatoes and cheeses.

'We bought some fresh mackerel in the harbour,' Ced told them, 'it's almost done.'
'I thought you were all vegetarian?'
'I'm not, Rosa's not, and neither are you two, so that's half and half. Thought I should try the local fish before I leave.'

The sun had almost set when at last they ate the fish and baked potatoes. Ced piled more wood on the fire, and Martyn strummed his guitar. Lamorna could think of nothing but Michael beside her. 'I adore him, I adore him. I want to make love to him right now.' And in the flickering light she slid her hand under his shirt and touched his warm skin. He turned to her and kissed her, and then she felt his hand under her shirt, moving around her back and under her arm to caress her breast. And she was trembling again.

The others decided to go for a swim, stripped off and ran down to the water's edge.
'Are you coming?' Heather called.
'Better not, my bandage will get wet.'
And when they'd all gone they lay back together on the sand, kissing and caressing each other.
'Shall we go now?' she whispered. But the others came back then. They dressed, covered the dying embers with sand and gathered together belongings.
'Do you need a lift Lamorna?' Ced asked.
'I can bring her,' Michael said.
'Okay, come back to the house and we'll have coffee.'
He helped her back to the van. She insisted on trying to walk.
'I wanted you to come back to the cottage with me.'
'I want that too, but all my stuff is at the house. I have to go to work tomorrow. And I feel I should stay and say goodbye to Rosa and Ced.'
'I'm not sure you should go to work.'
'I can't let Phil down.'

The others had got back first and the kettle was already boiling. Michael sat with Lamorna on the floor cushions. She held his hand, and she longed for him, stroking his fingers and shifting her body so that she could feel him against her.

'Why don't you stay tonight Michael?' Laura suggested. 'We have a spare room.'

'Thank you, I have to give Lamorna a lift to work in the morning. She can't walk far.'

The conversations washed over Lamorna. All she could think about was Michael. All her senses were focussed on him, the warmth from his body by her side, the sound of his voice as he talked and answered questions, the scent of sea and sand from his skin and the touch of his hand in hers. Twice people asked her something and she had to say,

'Sorry, what was that?'

She felt the evening would never end. She was aware that there was a swapping of addresses with Rosa, and some talk about their coming trip, but it was a relief when there was a general move upstairs. Soon only she and Michael remained in the living room.

'Michael, please will you sleep with me tonight?'

They went upstairs, Michael helping her, almost carrying her. He borrowed her toothbrush, and they crept into her room together. He slowly undid the buttons of her shirt, kissing the new bare skin after each button was opened. He unzipped her jeans, and slid them down, lifting each of her feet in turn, and he stroked and kissed her, gently easing off her knickers, before lifting her and laying her on the bed. Then he took off his own clothes quickly, letting them fall onto hers in a heap on the floor, and lay down beside her. They held each other close, kissing, and she pressed herself against him.

He fumbled to open the packet and pull on a sheath. She was overwhelmed with desire for him, and he made love to her with such urgency that they were soon crying out together, and then tumbling over in the tangled sheets, clinging as they drowned in the last gasps of passion before sleep engulfed them. They roused sometime in the night, and made love more slowly and tenderly. Lamorna felt her heart was filled with joy when Michael gathered her into his arms afterwards murmuring 'my love, my love.' In the morning she was awake first, stirring him with kisses before lying on his body.

'Wait, Lamorna, wait,' he slurred sleepily, his hand groping for the packet by the bed.

'I must get going,' she whispered at last, and they rose together and shared a bath. No-one else was about and so they ate breakfast in the garden. They were about to leave when Rosa emerged, still drowsy with sleep.

'I'll miss you Rosa. Stay in touch. I want to find out what happens on your travels.'

'I will. I'll come and see you when we get back. Promise.'

Lamorna brushed away tears as she hugged her friend.

'Look after her Michael.'

He gave Rosa a farewell hug, and then lifted Lamorna to carry her over to the van. It was ten minutes after nine when she stepped up to the studio door.

'I'll pick you up tonight,' he said, kissing her, and was gone.

'What have you been up to?' Phil asked as she hobbled through the door. Over coffee she told him about the trip, and her accident.

'I know the place, it is lovely. But should you be here?'

'Yes, I can still work. I can perch on the stool in the darkroom.'

'If you're sure. Did you make a start on the brochure?'

'Yes, the weather was perfect. I took loads of shots, and I think Sam was pleased with my ideas. I'd like to process them today so that Michael can see them and choose. He's picking me up when I finish work.'

'I was wondering how you'd get home. I was hoping you could lock up again tonight. I've got a job over in St Just and won't be back in time.'

Lamorna could tell from the way he looked at her that he knew there was something between her and Michael. She caught him scrutinising her once or twice as she went about her work. And all morning Michael was in her thoughts. It was as though the touch of his body was still on hers. She imagined him coming into the studio and taking her into his arms again, and she felt herself ache with longing for him. Lost in thought she mechanically processed some of the studio work and then went on to the hotel brochure shots. She was just starting on developing her photos of Tintagel and the valley when Phil called up to her that it was time for lunch. Getting no reply, he came up stairs, and looked at her work.

'These are great. I think Michael will be pleased. Will you have chance to do some brochure mock ups for him later?'

'Yes, after I've finished your work.'

'I've bought us some sandwiches, didn't think you'd make it out for lunch. Can you get downstairs?'

'Yes, I'll take it slowly. I feel it's better to use my foot, it'll get the message it has to heal quickly.'

Over sandwiches and coffee they talked about the work lined up for the week, and then Phil said suddenly,

'I have this feeling that some other momentous event occurred at the weekend.' She blushed.

'Michael and I got together.'

'About time too. Well, I'd better be off. Sure you can lock up?'

'Of course, don't worry.'

'Okay, but make sure you rest your foot and have a coffee break.'

She spent the afternoon finishing Phil's processing, and then working on some examples of brochures for the hotel. It was getting near to closing time when she went back to the dark room to print a few more of the weekend shots she'd taken. She was just pegging up her images of the beach barbecue when she heard a sound. Someone had come quietly into the room, and was crossing the floor towards her. She froze with fear.

Chapter 26

'I locked the shop door, I know I did,' she thought wildly.

And then she felt a warm hand slide under her top and around to enfold her breast, and Michael was kissing her neck. She felt his other arm fold around her and cradle her.

'I couldn't stop thinking about you all day. I wanted to be here with you, making love to you.' And then he was kissing her. After a while she managed to speak.

'You scared me, how did you get in?'

'Phil called by on his way to a job, dropped me a studio key off. He thought it would be too much for you to hobble downstairs and let me in. He says you've got some good photos for the hotel.'

His hands were caressing her again, and she felt the flush of desire creep warmly over her.

'I have to finish these, and then I'm ready to go. Five minutes.'

'I wasn't thinking of leaving just yet,' he said.

It was an hour later when they locked up and set off. Lamorna had gathered the photographs and brochure ideas, and they drove in silence, not needing words.

She barely listened to the conversations around the dinner table. After dinner they all studied her photographs.

'You've got some great ideas Lamorna,' Sam said after a while. 'I think you and Michael will make a good job of this together.'

'I promised Mary I'd meet her in the pub tonight,' Lamorna suddenly recalled.

'Shall I come with you?'

They left together, he supporting her as she limped along. Mary and Chris were already in The Ship, sitting together by the window. They joined them, and Mary's eyebrows arched upwards when she saw them.

'What's been happening?' she whispered.

The two men were already deep in conversation. Lamorna heard the words *Test, Headingly and Illingworth.*

'What are they talking about?'

'Test match, they're all fed up, England drew, even though Illingworth took 6 for 87.'

It was a strange language to Lamorna. Cricket had never imposed on her life.

'I did the hotel pictures with Michael yesterday, and then we went to see the rock marks near Boscastle, and he showed me the mermaid in Zennor Church.'

'And that's not all, I'd say,' Mary said, grinning.

Before any more questions could be asked the door opened and in walked Rosa and Ced.

'Rosa, what are you doing here?'

'Had a problem with the magic bus, had to take her in for repair. So we're not leaving until tomorrow now.'

'Come and sit with us.'

'Drink, anyone?' Ced asked, and went over to the bar to buy a round.

'Are you the bloke with the camper van?' Chris asked. 'I've been thinking we should get one, do some travelling after we're married. We should see a bit of the world before we're too old.'

'Chris, you've never said a thing to me!'

'If you hang on until next year I'll be over here before I head back to the States. You'd be welcome to the bus if she's still on the road.'

'Sounds good to me. Thanks.'

'Where's this idea come from? It's the first I've heard,' Mary said.

'I just thought it'd be a good way to get around, see some other places before we start a family.'

Mary looked at him. Then delved into her bag and pulled out a letter.

'I nearly forgot,' this came for you today.'

'It's from Jude.'

She read through it quickly.

'She's found a house for us next year, and we're going to share with her friend Joy. Oh, she says Joy is doing a project on bridal wear, she's a fashion student, and, guess what? Jude has suggested she could design your wedding outfits, listen,' *Mary would only have to pay for the material, and that would be at cost price through the college.'*

'That sounds wonderful, but how would it work, it's so far away?'

'Well, she says you'd have to come up for a consultation and measurements. And then Joy will bring the dresses down for a final fitting. You could give her the bridesmaid's details, and you'd all get to try them on.'

The three men disappeared to the bar at that point.

'I wonder if Ian would drive me up. He could see Jude then. Does she mention him? He got a postcard from her today.'

Lamorna scanned the letter.

'Yes, she says if Ian could come we could all go for an evening out. *"But don't bring Chris. The dress has to be a secret."'*

'He wouldn't want to anyway; you can see how interested he is in weddings now.'

'It sounds really special,' Rosa said, 'It will be a one-off designer dress.'

Lamorna was still reading.

'She says she'd like to come and take photos at your wedding too, get some pictures of the fitting, etc.'

'I can't let her. Chris asked Phil to do the photographs.'

'She's not charging you; these will be for her course portfolio. They'll be ordinary shots just recording the preparations, showing the dresses and the process.'

'Well, I have to say yes then, it sounds amazing. I can't believe all this.'

The pub was filling up now, some of the men casting a disapproving glance over at Mary when they saw the company she was in.

'I can't wait to tell my Mum, she'll be thrilled. She wanted me to have a lovely wedding, but the cost is too much for them. We've put some money by, and we're not having a honeymoon. Moving into the cottage will be enough. And now Chris's talking about travelling. It's not like him. I can't believe it.'

The men joined them again, bringing drinks over. Lamorna went to the toilet. The conversation had turned to travel when she got back to their table, and slid onto Michael's knee. Ced was talking about places he'd visited on his trip around Europe.

'I'll be glad to get home eventually though, and I'm hoping Rosa might come over with me.'

'Try to stop me!'

'Where are you from?' Chris asked.

'Minnesota, little place called Northfields. It's near the Great Lakes; I guess that's the closest we get to a sea. That's why I love it here, so much ocean.'

The conversation meandered on in the theme of travel. Ced looked at his watch after a while.

'Well, I guess we'd better hit the road, we want an early start in the morning, come on Rosa.'

Mary and Chris followed them out.

Laura and Jean appeared and took their seats.

'We've just come back from Newquay, selling stuff again. We did really well.'

Michael went up to buy them drinks, and then turned to Lamorna.

'I'll be back in a few minutes, got something to do. Don't go away.'

They talked about their plans for chickens at the commune.

'We've nearly got enough money now,' Jean said.

Then the conversation turned to Rosa and Ced.

'We'll miss Rosa. Hope she'll come back her after her travels.'

'Will you look for anyone else to come and stay?' Lamorna asked.

'We might,' Laura said. 'Suki knows someone who needs a place for a while.'

Michael came back, a broad smile on his face.

'Come on, let's go home.'

'I'm staying with Michael in the cottage tonight. See you tomorrow.'

He took her hand and led her through the village. As they turned the corner she cried out,

'Oh, it's lovely. What a wonderful surprise.'

The path to the cottage, and steps up to the door were lit by candles in jars, shining out in the twilight, like the lights showing a safe channel for boats returning to harbour. He lifted her over the threshold, and placed her on the settee. The room was lit by candles too, and a fire was beginning to blaze in the grate.

'It's so special; it feels as though it's my birthday.'

'When is your birthday?'

'Oh, ages away. February. Mary and Chris will love it here.'

'I wish it was you and me going to live here.'

'I would love that too, but not now. I have to go back and finish my course. I want to be a photographer.'

'I know. I know it's important to you. But I'll miss you so much.'

'Michael. You are more important to me than anything. But I have to do this. I have to prove to myself I can do it. We can see each other sometimes.

"I'm not earning enough here to keep you anyway. Maybe I should come with you and get a job.'

'You'd hate it! But do you understand? I have to be independent too. I don't want to have to rely on a man to keep me.'

They sat in silence for a while, watching as the logs caught and flared in the fire.

'It's hard, because I want you too. I want you so much.' She wrapped her arms around him. 'I want to be with you and never let you go. And I'm so afraid that you'll meet someone new and forget me.'

'I won't. I won't do that. You're more likely to meet someone at college.'

'I want to work hard, I won't have time.'

Later they shared a bath, and Michael examined her ankle.

'I think it's getting better, the swellings gone down a little. I'll put you a new bandage on in the morning.'

He lifted her out of the bath, wrapping her in a towel.

'Closest I get to being a fisherman.'

'What am I then, a mackerel?'

'More of a pilchard I think.'

Chapter 27

It was late when Lamorna roused on Wednesday morning. She had stayed another night in the cottage. They were still curled up together. She lay for a while looking at Michael sleeping, tempted to wake him with kisses and make love. But he was so peaceful. She made do with a light kiss on his cheek, and snuggled down beside him. When she stirred again Michael was coming in with a breakfast tray.

After they'd eaten he put the tray on the ground, and went to hold her, but she slipped out of his grasp. She smiled.
'No, we've got work to do, come on.'
So they got up, dressed and sat down together to discuss the photographs they would need for the cottage brochure. Michael had remembered her suggestions, and produced a bundle of windmills and child's bucket and spade.

She placed the windmills in a jar on the kitchen window sill first, and took photographs in there, before carrying them out to the front steps, and arranging the bucket and spade, and one windmill together. Michael had bought tubs of red geraniums and they contrasted beautifully with the blue of the door. It was a perfect day for photography. Sun streamed in through the windows and she quickly moved through the cottage, taking images in every room, and close up shots of the pebbles on a sill, some little wooden boats on another, a vase of flowers by the bed. She had to make the bed first, but pulled back the sheets a little for an inviting look, and got Michael to make a pot of tea on a tray, before pouring a cup and photographing it by the bed.
'No-one will guess that we rumpled up those sheets last night.'
'Maybe we need to try a bit harder then.' he said, grinning.
And in reply she put her camera down and pulled him down with her onto the bed.

Later they called into the hotel and were given lunch. Michael could have the rest of the day off with her.
'Where would you like to go?'
'Can we go to St Michael's Mount? I was there with Phil doing a photo shoot, but I don't think I've ever been across to the island.'
'Another place where we can be cut off by the tide it is then!'

Michael drove her back to the commune that evening after they'd eaten out in Marazion.
'I've got washing to do, and some other jobs,' she told him, 'but I'll come to the cottage tomorrow night.'
'I'll pick you up in the morning then. I'll miss you.'
She limped through the door, and immediately sensed that something was wrong. There was no music playing, and the whole place was strangely quiet.

'Hi. Where is everyone?'

'In here,' came a voice from the living room. Laura and Jean were sitting on the sofa, Heather slumped in an armchair.

'What's wrong? What's happened?'

'This.' Jean waved a piece of paper. 'We've got to leave the house at the end of the month.'

'No. Why? What's happened?'

'The landlord is selling up, and you'll never guess who the new owners will be.' Lamorna put her bag down and sank onto the cushions.

'It's a local consortium,' Laura told her. 'Some hotel owners from Penzance and Sam Tremayne. The landlord says they're going to turn it into holiday flats.'

'How could they? Why hasn't Michael told me?'

'It's a blow. We thought we'd be here for years. I was over in Newquay with Heather earlier, arranging to buy the chickens. Martyn's already started building the coop,' Jean said.

'The letter came in the afternoon post. We've been talking ever since. We all feel we no longer have the heart to stay now. We don't want to pay the next month's rent. Jean and I are thinking of going over to Spain straight away, to the commune we know about.'

'My parents have been trying to persuade Martyn and me to help with their business,' Heather said. 'They've bought a small gallery, and as we both studied art and art history they reckon we'll make a go of it. I haven't told Martyn yet, he went to work before the letter came, but I think he'll be willing.'

'I suppose that's all good news, but I'll be sad to see the commune close,' Lamorna said. 'I don't know what I'll do.'

'What about Michael and the cottage, could you move in there?'

'I don't know any more. I don't know what to think. Michael must know about the plans. I saw Sam today too, and he never said a thing.'

She sat with her head in her hands, uncertain what to do or say.

'I'll look for somewhere in Penzance I suppose. Phil might have some ideas.'

'Why don't you ask Michael before you jump to conclusions? He may not know.'

'I suppose so. But if he did know I don't see how I can see him again.' She brushed away tears.

'We thought we'd all leave on Sunday, and we're thinking of a party on Saturday night. We'll ask Michael, and you can see if Mary and Chris will come.'

'It would be nice. I could come and see you in Spain if you're there next summer.'

'You know you'd be welcome. I'll give you the address, and you must share your home address with us. We'd like to keep in touch.'

'Come on,' Jean said, 'We have to eat. I'll make us omelettes.'

'I nearly forgot,' Lamorna said,' Michael and I brought a lemon meringue pie from the hotel. His Mum baked it for us, and he said to share it, if you can bear to eat something from there.'

'Of course we can, we just won't think about where it came from.'

Later they made coffee, Heather and Martyn taking theirs up to bed with them to talk about the business plan for the Gallery.

'We had a letter from Suki, and you'll never guess. They went to a party at another squat and it turned out Paul had been living there. He got thrown out because he never did anything to help, and the women got fed up with his attitude.'

'And,' Jean added, 'after he'd gone they found a few things missing, a transistor radio, a watch and some Beatles albums.'

'What will become of him?' Lamorna said. 'I wonder where he is now.'

'We're hoping he doesn't turn up in Spain. I told him about the commune there once,' Jean said.

'Will you be able to help us clear the house on Sunday Lamorna?'

'Of course.'

Later in bed she curled up under the blankets, feeling very alone, thinking about Michael, about the letter. 'I can't believe he knew about it. He would have said something. But how can he not know, it's his Dad?' A confusion of thoughts cluttered her head. She struggled to relax. She thought about the way he made love to her, and she imagined him coming into her room now, climbing into bed with her. She thought about the way he would hold her and kiss her, the softness of his hair, his blue eyes, and the way he held her in his arms after they'd made love. 'I could go to the cottage now. Climb into his bed. Ask him.' She was drifting into sleep. Suddenly there was a banging and shouting. Someone was hammering on the door. She heard voices, Laura and Jean's door creaking open.

'Police, Open up. Open the door.'

Chapter 28

Lamorna jumped out of bed, her heart beating wildly. She pulled on her pyjamas and hurried out, straight into Martyn and Heather.

'What is it, what's going on?'

'We don't know, think Laura's down there,' Martyn replied.

They hurried downstairs. Three men, two in uniform were in the hallway, and she watched as they split up and moved into different rooms. One of them had a dog. It strained at its leash, nose to the ground, pulling the police officer behind it into the kitchen. Laura and Jean were there, a stunned and angry look on their faces.

'What's happening?' Martyn asked.

'It's a raid, they're looking for drugs,' Jean said. 'Someone's tipped them off.'

'We haven't got any drugs,' Lamorna protested.

'No, we haven't, but they're not going to believe that,' Laura said.

They stood helplessly by as the men searched every room downstairs, turning out all the drawers, tipping over furniture, pulling books off the shelves. The dog ran sniffing around the rooms, jumping onto the chairs and settee, dragging away cushions, rooting under rugs and throws

'We'll do the upstairs now,' one of them said.

Lamorna rushed up to her room, thinking to protect her camera. They went into Laura and Jean's room first. One of them came into her room with the dog. It began digging into her bed, pushing blankets and pillows around, then jumped down and, tail wagging sniffed around the floor. The policeman emptied out her drawers, tipping everything out, picking up her knickers and smirking at her.

'You'd better give me that bag you're holding.'

'It's my camera, I need it for my course, please don't damage it.'

He opened the bag, and she held her breath as he tipped the camera out onto the bed, and held the bag open for the dog to examine.

'Hmm, nothing,' he said, bending over to empty the contents of her bin onto the carpet. She was mortified when used sheaths slid from under tissues. Her face was scarlet. He leered at her.

'You're not one of those then, like that other pair.'

He went on staring at her, looking her up and down. She was aware that her nipples were showing through the thin pyjama fabric, and she folded her arms across her chest. And then he was gone.

She began to clear up, scraping the rubbish back into the bin, piling things in haphazard heaps into the drawers. She heard them in Paul's room, and someone shouted for assistance. She quickly dressed and went downstairs. The others were in the kitchen, no-one was talking. Heather was making cocoa, stirring milk in a pan.

'They're all in Paul's room.'

They heard a clattering on the stairs, and the sound of the front door opening. The plain clothes officer strode into the kitchen.

'Whose is the room at the back?'

'It was a friend's. He's left now,' Laura told him calmly.

'The dog was most interested in that room. We think there were traces of drugs, but we didn't find anything. You've got away with it this time.'
He turned on his heel and walked out, slamming the door behind him. Martyn went to follow him, his face red with anger. Jean held him back.

'Don't Martyn. Don't let it get to you. That's what they want. A response. They want to spook us, make us afraid. But we've got nothing to hide. We've not done anything wrong.'

'We're lucky they didn't come a couple of weeks ago,' Jean said. 'They would have found stuff then. The pot Rog and Nick brought down.'

'Cocoa's ready.' Heather plonked a tray of mugs on the table, and they all sat round. No-one felt like talking any more.

'The kittens, where are the kittens?' Laura jumped up, and everyone followed. There was a mad search around the rooms until Martyn found them cowering under the kitchen dresser.

'You poor little things,' he soothed. 'Nasty dog.'

The kittens mewed pathetically and he put them gently in their basket by the range, and poured milk into a saucer for them.

A clock chimed two.

'We'd better get to bed,' Laura said. They piled their mugs into the sink and went upstairs together. Lamorna was alone in her room and felt desolate.

'Who sent the police?' she thought. 'I can't believe it was anyone from round here. I couldn't bear that. But it must be. There's no-one else. They're doing their best to get rid of us. Oh Michael, I can't believe you knew, but how could you not?' It seemed a long time before she fell into an uneasy sleep.

Chapter 29

Thursday morning's weather echoed the mood in the house. Lamorna woke to a grey mizzle. She bathed, and then ate a desultory breakfast of toast and jam, shivering at the kitchen table. Already the house seemed to be losing its warmth. The kittens were huddled together in their basket. Laura and Jean joined her. No-one spoke much. And then Lamorna heard Michael's van.

'I can't face him, I can't. Please tell him I'll go on the bus,' she said, and hurried upstairs. A few minutes later Jean came into her room.

'Michael won't go without you. He seems shocked. I believe that he didn't know about the plan to buy the house. He was really angry when we told him about the police. Please, come down and speak to him.'

Lamorna came down, but she couldn't look at Michael.

'I can't go with you. Not now, not now I know your father wants to evict my friends. Not now I think he might have been responsible for sending the police round here.'

'Lamorna, I didn't know about this, I promise. I'm just as angry as you are. I can't believe Dad would be involved with the police. He knows you're here. Please come with me. You can't walk with that foot. Don't be silly.'

'I'm not silly. These are my friends. They took me in when your Dad forced me to leave the hotel with his attitudes. I won't come with you.'

She walked past him and out of the door. Despite her limp she walked quickly, ignoring the pain, choosing the narrow streets and the beach where he couldn't follow in the van.

'Whatever's the matter?' Phil asked, as soon as she arrived at the studio. And she burst into tears.

'I can't finish the brochure now. I can't go near the hotel.'

'Sit down,' he said. 'I'm going to make you a coffee, and you can tell me about it.'

He handed her a box of tissues, locked the door and turned the notice round to CLOSED again. He sat her down in the studio, let her drink her coffee.

'Now, tell me what's going on.'

So she told him what had happened.

'That's bad,' he said after a while. 'But I can't believe Michael knew. He would have said something. He's just about the most honest and straight bloke I know. You're doing the brochures for him, not Sam. We have to resolve this. I haven't time to pick up the job, and I need you to finish it. I've already spent a lot on resources and time.'

'I know. I'm sorry. I don't know what to do.'

'Did you ask Michael if he knew?'

'Yes, he said he didn't.'

'Do you believe him?'

'I'm not sure. It seems crazy that he wouldn't know. But he seemed sincere. I can't believe he would lie to me.'

'Well, there you are then. Is he picking you up tonight?'

'I don't suppose so. I was horrid to him. I wouldn't let him bring me this morning.'

'I think he'll come. He won't give up on you if I know him. I'll talk to him. Now, are you ready to get some work done? There's tons of processing to do.'

'Yes, I'm sorry.'

'Don't worry; just work steadily through it, it'll get done.'

She was soon immersed in her work, and Phil had to come up to persuade her to stop for lunch.

'I'm coming with you.'

He helped her along to the coffee bar, and over bowls of spaghetti they talked.

'I phoned Michael. He's had a blazing row with his Dad. He asked me to see if he can give you a lift tonight.'

'I didn't expect him to fall out with his family. I feel I've been nothing but trouble for them since I got here.'

'Now you're being silly, none of this is your fault. Shall I tell him to come for you?'

'I should ring him, but I'm scared Sam or Aileen might answer, and I won't know what to say.'

'Problem solved, Michael is ringing me again at two o'clock, and you can answer the phone.'

Exactly at two the phone rang. Phil picked it up. After a brief word he handed the phone to Lamorna and left the room.

'Yes,' was all she said, and replaced the receiver before bursting into tears.

'You know what,' Phil said, coming back in with a box of tissues, I think I should put a new sign up outside, *"Photography, and Counselling, services on the studio couch,"* what do you think?'

She couldn't help but smile then, and after blowing her nose she retreated back to the dark room to finish her work. She didn't feel like doing the brochures though, or processing the photographs she'd taken of the cottage. It felt like a long day, and she was glad when she could lift the last prints out of the trough and hang them to dry. She was remembering the night when Michael had arrived and crept up on her.

'I wish I could turn back the clock and make everything alright again, make none of this bad stuff happen.'

Phil appeared and broke into her thoughts.

'Michael is here. Shall I send him up?'

'No, I'll come down.'

She washed her hands of chemicals, and followed him down the stairs.

'I'll leave you to lock up Lamorna. See you tomorrow.'

Then he was gone, the doorbell jangling in his wake. She stood looking down at her feet. Michael was standing awkwardly by the counter.

'Lamorna, please believe me, I didn't know what was going on. Even Mum didn't know. She's had a real rage at Dad.'

After a while she answered.

'I believe you. I don't think you would lie to me. But it's still just as bad. They're my friends. I can't be involved with you now. It's like sleeping with the enemy.'

'Don't say that, please don't say that. We'll sort it somehow.'

'How can we, what's done is done?'

'Dad says he'll drop out of the group. He's got to, or he thinks Mum'll kill him.'

'But it's still too late. The house is sold. They've all got to go.'

'I know. I can't change that. I can't bear it Lamorna. I don't want this to drive us apart.'

'We're having a farewell party on Saturday. The others want you to come.'

'Do you want me to come?'

'Yes. I want to be with you.'

'Will you forgive me for having a Dad with such poor judgement?'

'I should have realised that when he gave me a job.'

She half smiled, and he must have noticed the chink in her defences, because he reached out and took her hands.

'Will you let me drive you home now?'

'Where's home?'

'Wherever you want it to be.'

'Will you take me to the commune? I need to see everyone. To tell them you didn't know.'

'I already told them this morning, and they believed me.'

'I'm sorry I didn't believe you.'

She looked down at her feet.

'It's harder for you.'

'But I should have trusted you. I was just so upset and confused.'

'It doesn't matter. Come on, I'll take you there anyway. Then you can decide what to do. I'd rather delay going back to the hotel. Can't face the atmosphere.'

They didn't talk on the journey.

'Come in with me please,' she said when they reached the house.

It was strangely quiet. Michael drank tea with them.

'I'm sorry you've all got to go.'

'Michael, it's not your fault. It's happened. We can live with it. Heather's gone home to her parents tonight, and Martyn is meeting her there, so Laura and I thought we'd eat in the pub, we don't have the heart to cook tonight. Why don't you join us?'

'Shall we Michael?'

'Don't see why not. It'll give the locals something to talk about.'

Michael drove Lamorna down to give her foot a rest, and they met up half an hour later. There was no sign of Mary or Chris. Ian was propping up the bar, and came over for a quick chat, sharing news from Jude.

'Looks like I'm roped in to drive our Mary up to sort the dresses out.'

'Are you coming up Michael?'

'Not been invited.'

'You can come,' Lamorna said. 'You can come any time.'

'Come up with us, should be fun,' Ian said. 'Well, I'd best be off then, I'm late for dinner.'

They were aware of a few glances in their direction during the evening, but managed to ignore them.

'After all,' Laura said, 'they're happy to take our money in here.'

'Well,' Jean said later, 'we'll see you both on Saturday night then. Don't forget to ask your friends Chris and Mary.'

'But......' Lamorna began.

'You'll be staying with Michael,' Jean said, and they both got up and left.

'Shall you?' he asked.

'Yes. I want to.'

'Come on then.'

Chapter 30

'Will you work on the cottage photos today Lamorna? I need to get moving on the project.'

'Yes, I'll get them finished, and do some more on the hotel brochure too.'

'Thanks, I'll pick you up later. I need to escape, I'll be stuck at the hotel all day, have to clean the chickens. They're missing your tender care by the way!'

'As if!'

She watched him drive away. Paused for a moment to look around. The sun was just breaking through the clouds, and a chorus of gulls were shouting from the rooftops. She pushed open the door and began her busy day in the dark room.

It was almost closing time when she had finished the last proofs for the brochure. The cottage photographs were ready and placed in an album for Michael. He arrived early, and browsed around the studio.

'I've not seen these before. It's the lifeguard group.'

'I printed them. Who's the girl you're with?'

'That's Ellen. Were you jealous?'

'Only a bit.'

'Will you do a copy for Mum, she'd like it? I'm to invite you back for dinner. Dad insists. Please come Lamorna. It'll be hell if you don't. He's done his best to placate me. I can't bear another day of it. Mum won't leave him alone until he apologises to you. She told him he's ruined my life.'

'I don't know.'

'Please, it'll be okay. Anyway, Mary's expecting you. I told her you have an invitation for her.'

'You're wicked Michael, you know I can't refuse now. But you have to grovel at my feet first.'

He knelt down on the floor and kissed her feet.

'Your foot's looking better,' he said, 'how does it feel now?'

'Don't change the subject! It is better. Still hurts a bit though. Come on, you win, let's go.'

Aileen seemed genuinely pleased to see her, giving her a warm hug that made tears spring into her eyes.

'What's this invitation then? Don't tell me you're getting wed next,' Mary asked.

'No,' I'm inviting you and Chris to a party at the house I'm living in on Saturday night. It's a leaving party. We've all got to go. Ian can come too.'

'Oh. I'm not sure. We don't know all those people.'

'It was their idea, they asked me to invite you. Please come.'

'Well, I'll ask Chris. Why are they leaving?'

'The house is being sold.'

'Oh. Where will you go?'

'She'll stay with me in the cottage,' Michael said, making her blush.

'A good thing too,' Aileen interrupted. 'Someone to keep you out of trouble. Come in and sit down you two, dinner will soon be ready.'

'Where's Dad?'

'Hiding in the bar, will you fetch him?'

Michael left the room.

'I'm sorry about all this upset Lamorna, about your friends having to leave. Believe me I knew nothing about it.'

'It's alright. I know you're not to blame. Maybe it will be all for the best.'

'It will be for the best for Michael. I'm glad you two have got together. You're good for him Lamorna; I've never seen him so happy. Now, let's be getting this dinner on the table.'

Michael reappeared then, Sam close behind him.

'I'm sorry about your friends, Lamorna,' he said straight away. 'I think I've made an error of judgement. I tried to back out of the deal, but it's too late. As soon as I can I'll sell my share.'

'What's done is done,' she said, after a pause. 'You misjudged my friends. They haven't done anything wrong or committed any crimes against the village. They were just trying to lead a peaceful life together away from the rat race.'

'That's what Michael tells me.'

'They're all leaving on Sunday, so you've all got your wish,' she said quietly.

'They don't have to go so soon.'

'They don't have the heart to stay longer.'

'I'm sorry for that. What shall you do? You could have the cottage here again.'

'She'll be staying with me,' Michael said.

'Aye, well, that's alright then. But none of us had anything to do with the police raid. We're all shocked.'

'I didn't really believe it would be you,' Lamorna said.

'Sit down all of you, the dinner's spoiling.'

Aileen spared him from having to make further comment.

After they'd eaten Lamorna produced the proofs for the hotel brochure, and they were delighted with what she'd done.

'Well, Michael,' Sam said,' will you be giving this young lady the job then?'

'I think so,' he smiled. 'Wait till you see the cottage photographs.'

She opened the album for them.

'They're really lovely,' Aileen said. 'I can see your touch Lamorna.'

'It looks handsome. I could move in myself,' Sam said.

'Yes, especially when someone brings you tea in bed. Can't remember the last time that happened here.'

'It was only a pretend cup of tea,' Lamorna said, embarrassed.

'I think we'll get lots of bookings. Pity, because I'll have to move out then!'

'Well, I daresay you'll move out soon enough for Mary and Chris, they won't want you there with them I'm sure. When I sell my share in that other place we'll maybe buy another cottage for you to renovate. They keep coming up for sale.'

'There's a leaving party up there on Saturday,' Michael said. 'I've been invited.'

'Well, maybe I can find you a crate of beer to take.'

'Thanks Dad. Time we went Lamorna. You've got a busy day tomorrow.'

'Thank you for dinner, I'll get the work on the cottage brochure done tomorrow.'

'You're welcome any time, you know that. Do you need anything?'

'Maybe some milk for breakfast?'

Aileen opened the fridge and handed her a bottle.

'When will we see you again?'

'I don't know. I could call in one day after work.'

'Why don't you both come for dinner again on Sunday night? You'll be packing and moving won't you Lamorna? You won't feel like cooking.'

'That would be nice. I have to help clear the house up too.'

'And Michael will be busy helping us up here. You will come then?'

She looked at Michael enquiringly.

'Yes, we'd love to.'

'Good. Take care now both of you,' and she kissed them.

Chapter 31

Michael picked Lamorna up again at the end of the next day. She'd managed to finish a mock up for the cottage brochure, and he was really pleased with it. Phil was equally impressed.

'She's got a real artist's eye,' he said. 'I would never have thought of these little touches, the kid's stuff, and the tea by the bed. It makes the place look really homely. I'm ashamed of my effort for the holiday camp now. Just hope they don't see this. Wish I could keep you on for future contracts.'

'Well maybe I could help in the holidays?'

'Come on, we need to get going, I promised Dad we'd drop him this off to look at, and he's got some beer lined up for the party tonight.'

'Party?'

'Yes, we're all leaving the commune house, it's a farewell party, our last night. Why don't you come?'

'I've got a date, not sure she'd go for that kind of thing.'

'Oh well, see you Monday then.'

Sam had got ready a crate of different beers and cider as he'd promised. He seemed determined to make amends for his previous actions. And he was pleased with the brochure she had produced, only suggesting a couple of small changes to the text.

'If you're happy with it Michael, then I think we should go ahead and get it done. It's a good idea leaving the prices off, that way it can do for a couple of years.'

'I think it's brilliant,' Michael said. 'Thanks for the beer. See you tomorrow.'

'I'll need you at eight thirty; do you think you'll make it?'

'Do my best.'

Lamorna sought out Mary, who was just hanging up her apron and ready to go.

'Are you coming tonight?'

'Yes, I talked Chris into it. He reckons that Ced was okay, and Rosa, so he's come round to it.'

'See you later then. Why don't you meet us at the cottage and we can walk up together?'

They went back to the cottage, Michael taking the van as Lamorna was still troubled by her ankle.

'It's getting better, but I've been standing up too much all day,' she said. 'I'm going to make some tea, what about you?'

'I'll just have a beer, and then shall we have a bath? And you shall sit down while I make the tea.'

He lifted her off her feet and swung her round impulsively.

'Put me down; put me down,' she laughed, 'I'll be dizzy.'

***

The evening was warm after the hottest day of the year. Mary and Chris came, and they went together up the hill, Chris and Michael carrying the crate between them. Michael with his guitar slung over his shoulder.

'Do I look okay?' Mary asked.

She was wearing a floral skirt and white blouse, a shawl around her waist, and she'd put on some hooped ear rings.

'You look great, like a sultry gypsy,' Lamorna told her.

'Is that a good thing?'

'Don't worry Mary, I just meant you looked summery and beautiful.'

They reached the house and turned off the lane into the garden. Although it was a hot evening a fire had been lit, and rugs spread out on the grass. Laura and Heather were tending the fire, and called them over.

'We've got beer, we'll take it into the kitchen,' Michael said.

'Great, the others are in there getting food ready. We lit a fire to make it a celebration, and we've burned some rubbish! Come and sit down. Hello Mary, I'm glad you could come.'

'Thank you for asking us, it's lovely here.'

The four girls sat down together.

'It'll be hard to leave if the weather's like this tomorrow,' Heather said. 'I'd rather be relaxing in the garden, not packing and clearing away.'

'What will you do?' Mary asked.

Lamorna left them talking and went in search of Michael. He and Chris were helping Martyn get plates and glasses together, talking about cricket. Martyn spotted the guitar.

'Do you play?'

'He's good,' Chris answered for him. 'Plays in a local folk group sometimes.'

'That's great. I hope you'll play tonight.'

The food was ready, so they all took something outside, and spread the feast on the waiting bedspread that served for a tablecloth. Jean opened beers and handed them round.

After the meal was finished Martyn and Michael picked up their guitars and found some common music to play. Martyn's enthusiasm was traditional folk songs, and most everyone could join in.

'Play some of your songs now Michael,' Mary said.

So he played and sang some of the newer songs he'd been learning. Songs by Paul Simon and Bob Dylan. They were joined by Martyn's friends from work, who had also brought some offerings of beer and a big apple pie left over from the pub meals. Mary and Chris were reluctant to leave when they realised it was past midnight. They were enjoying themselves so much, and so unexpectedly.

'We'll have to go,' Mary said, yawning.

'Why don't you both stay, we've a spare room?' Laura asked.

'Whatever would my Mum say? No we should go. Thank you.'

It seemed that everyone was ready to end the night. Martyn's friends had to walk back into town.

'We've got a busy day too,' Jean said, 'All the packing and moving. Are you staying Lamorna?'

'Can we Michael? I won't have to walk up in the morning then when you've gone up to the hotel. Can we sleep in the hammock? It's such a beautiful night.'

Someone cleared a few bottles away, but most were too tired to do much. It was almost one thirty when Lamorna and Michael climbed into the hammock, and lay together looking up at the stars.

'The sky's wonderful,' she said. 'It's like a jewelled eiderdown covering us for the night.'

And they fell asleep, lulled by the swinging motion and the stars lurching in the heavens.

Chapter 32

Lamorna lay looking at the dawn sky. Low clouds spread across the horizon, striped with pink like strawberry ripple ice cream. Light flashed on the house windows. The birds were waking, and three white doves settled on the roof and began preening their feathers. She watched as one feather flew down into the grass. The garden seemed forlorn after last night's gathering. The ashes from the bonfire lay dull and grey on the grass, and around them were spread the rumpled rugs and blankets.

She turned now to look at Michael. He was sleeping still, his mouth slightly open, dark curls damp on his forehead. One arm was slung over the side of the hammock, the other across her. She looked at the hairs on the dark skin of his arm, the way his eyebrows curved. She studied his nose and ear, deciding they were perfect. She longed to lean over and kiss him, but didn't want to wake him, so lay beside him quietly, feeling his breath in the air between them, breathing in the scent of his warm skin. She drifted into sleep. The sun was higher in the sky when she woke again. And then Michael did wake. He turned so that he was facing her, making the hammock swing wildly so that they were tumbled together as he kissed her. The church bells clamoured their call to communion, sending the doves on the ridge up like a cloud into the clear sky. And they lay still and quiet again, drowsing together as the hammock swayed. After a while Michael spoke.
'I could lie here with you all day, but I need the loo.'

He rolled onto the ground and gave the hammock a gentle push to set her rocking. Half an hour later he was back with a tray of tea and toast. Lamorna clambered reluctantly out of the hammock, and they sat together on the rugs.
'The others are getting up now,' he said, 'and I need to go. I'll come back for you later today.'
He kissed her and then stooped to gather the empty bottles into the crate. Slinging his guitar over his shoulder he was gone.

Half an hour later the great clear up began. Lamorna packed her belongings and cleaned her room. She was finished first, and so volunteered to start on Paul's room. She took a rubbish bag and filled it with all the dirty clothing and debris he'd left strewn around. She found a reel of film under the cupboard, and realised it was the one that had been in her camera the last time she'd used it. She looked at the butterflies trapped forever in their boxes. No-one wanted them, so she decided to throw them out. But something stopped her, and she retrieved them from the bin bag.
'They will have died in vain if I throw them away. Maybe we can use them at college.'

They all worked together to clear up and clean the communal areas. Martyn had managed to borrow a friend's van, and they loaded up with furniture and items for storage in a barn at Heather's parent's place. It took three trips. At last they were finished. The door was locked. Martyn was back with the van for the last few things. There were farewell hugs and a few tears and then he and Heather set off for the north coast, taking the protesting kittens with them in a cardboard box. Laura and Jean went down to catch the bus into Penzance.

The house was an empty shell now, curtain-less windows like glassy eyes stared bleakly over the garden. Anyone chancing to pass by would never have realised that it had been occupied only that morning. Lamorna wandered around. She dawdled in the fruit garden, picked and ate a few strawberries. Then noticed the hammock still strung under the tree.

'Oh no, we've forgotten it. Maybe we can take it to the cottage.'

She piled her bags underneath and climbed in to wait for Michael. She suddenly felt very alone, and the rocking was soothing. She lay swinging gently, watching a patch of blue sea appear and disappear as she moved.

'This has been such a special time, so many new friends. I hope we'll all meet up again. The house looks forlorn,' she thought, looking over at its stone face, the pillars standing guard each side of the door, which was closed for the first time she could remember in the daytime.

She must have drifted into sleep. A sudden sound jolted her awake. The sun was beginning to sink to the horizon, and the air felt cooler. She struggled to slide out of the hammock, and saw someone trying the door of the house. It was Paul. She called over.

'What are you doing?'

He started.

'I was wondering where everyone was.'

'Why are you here?'

'I came back for some of my things. I didn't get to Paris. Things didn't work out. Where is everyone? Have the police moved you on?'

'What do you mean police? Did you send them Paul? It was you wasn't it? You told the police to raid the house. How could you? How could you do that to your friends?'

'Some friends. They chucked me out. They're no friends of mine. Why should I care?'

'It wasn't the police. They didn't find anything so you wasted your time. They've all left now, the house has been sold. Why did you take my camera Paul? You knew I needed it for my project. You knew I had no money to buy another one.'

He walked over to her.

'I was desperate. They kicked me out and I had nothing. I'll pay you back. Tell me your home address and I'll send you money. What are you doing here, all on your own?'

He came up close to her, grabbed her arm and pulled her towards him.

'I'm waiting for Michael. He'll be here any minute.'

'Oh, it's you and Michael now, is it? I think you and I have some unfinished business.'

She was struggling to free herself from his grip, kicking his legs, stamping on his foot. She shouted out, hoping someone, anyone would hear. Not caring how embarrassing it would be. And then someone did come. Michael was there, dragging Paul away by his collar.

'Get out of here before I really do some damage.'
He gave Paul a push, and he slunk away, heading off down the lane, surprisingly quiet.

'Are you alright?'
'Yes, but only because you came at the right moment. I couldn't fight him off. He was too strong for me. I couldn't stop him.'
He took her into his arms.

'You're always having to rescue me.'
'Come on, let's get home.'

They walked over to the van, Michael carrying her bags. There was no sign of Paul.

'What if he tries to break in when we've gone? Michael, he asked if the police had got us moved out. He was the one who told them.'
'That doesn't surprise me. He has no morals. I'll ask Brian to keep an eye on the house.'
'Who's Brian?'
'Local bobby. And you know, I think we should tell the Police about Paul, we should report him. He's gone too far.'
'I don't know. Everyone will get dragged into it if I do. And I can't imagine the police will want to help, not if they're all like the ones who searched the house. They were horrid.'
'We'll talk about it when we get home.'
'Get home,' she thought. 'Our home. I've never felt I had a real home for a long time.'
'What are you smiling about?'
'You said 'home', I like that.'
And soon they were at the cottage. A vase of flowers filled the room with their scent.

'Michael, they're lovely.'
'Mum picked them for you. She said you'd need cheering up.'
'I'd better unpack, we've not long before we're expected for dinner, and I feel really dirty.'

He carried her stuff upstairs for her, and sat watching as she stowed her clothes in drawers and placed her few belongings around. She looked at the butterflies in their boxes and then arranged them on the shelf.

'They were Paul's butterflies. He left them, and I couldn't let them be tossed away.'
'I mean it Lamorna, we should report him.'
'Michael, I don't know. Let's talk about it tomorrow.'
'That may be too late. He may leave the country.'
He watched as she continued to put her things away.

'I love being here with you. It feels so right, us together here.'
She came and sat next to him, taking his hand in hers.

'Dad says we can stay here.'

'We can't Michael, you promised it to Mary and Chris, and we can't let them down. They'd be so disappointed.'

'I know. But I wish we could. I want you to stay here with me.'

'Oh Michael, you know I want that too, but I have to go back to college, finish my course.'

'Phil says you can keep your job.'

'He's great, and I love the work, but I have to go.'

'But why do you? I want to live with you. I want us to be together.'

'I have to prove something to myself. At school no-one thought I would make anything of my life. I have an opportunity now. I don't want to waste it. I want to make you proud of me. In a way I'm doing this for my Dad too. He wanted me to go to university. He put money aside for me, and he was always telling me that education is important. No-one else in the family, even my Mum thought it was important for me to go to college. They kept saying it was a waste, educating a girl. They'd say things like, 'what's the point, she'll only get married,' but my Dad was determined. I didn't know until after he'd died that he'd started to save some money for me. That's how I got my camera. My Mum was livid. She thought it should all go to her. So you see I have to do this for him.'

'I'm sorry,' he said, as her eyes filled with tears. 'I was being selfish. I wish I could have known your Dad. Of course you must go. You're going to be a brilliant photographer.'

'You would have liked my Dad, I think. In a way you remind me of him, you're so modest, but you have a passion for the things you care about, and you're so practical, so skilled.'

'But I'm not educated, like you. I never had your ambition. I just got sucked into the family business. I feel I have to help them, even though it's not really what I want to do. Come on, we need to get moving. Look at the time.'

Lamorna quickly bathed and then changed into the dress she'd bought in Penzance on the day Jude had left, before all the changes in her life. Before Michael. She had forgotten all about it.

'You look beautiful; it's a pity we're going out.'

'Well, we're coming back again, aren't we?'

And so they walked out into the warm evening, making their way around the harbour. She stopped to look down at the boats. The tide was out, and the mooring ropes stretched out across the sand.

'Look Michael, the ropes are like a music score, with the little clumps of seaweed and stones making the notes. Could you play the tune? Could you play it on your guitar?'

'I don't know,' he laughed. 'You'd have to work out what the stones and seaweed stood for, which are crochets and which are quavers. Where do you get your ideas from?'

'The seaweed has to be the quavers, in the absence of jelly fish.'

'You're mazy!'

Mary and Chris were just heading into the pub.

'Fancy a drink?' Chris called.

'No, sorry, we're expected for dinner with the folks.'

'Why don't you two come for dinner with us?' Lamorna asked. 'You could come tomorrow.'

'I'll cook,' Michael said.

'I was going to say yes before you said that,' Chris quipped.

'Oh please come, it would be lovely.'

'We'd love to, wouldn't we Chris? We can see the cottage again.'

'Yeah, we'll come, thanks.'

Dinner was almost ready by the time they arrived at the hotel. Aileen had cooked Lobster Thermidor, remembering that Lamorna had never tried it. She was a little apprehensive, but discovered that it was delicious. Afterwards there was Pavlova with raspberries.

'How did your moving go?' Sam asked. 'I'm still feeling bad about it all.'

'Everyone was sad to be parting, but they've all got other plans, so maybe it will all turn out for the best. And I get to stay with Michael.'
Michael squeezed her hand under the table.

'I don't suppose they did any real harm,' Sam went on, we all just got carried away and lost all common sense.'

'Maybe they would have found it hard to all stay together and make it work,' Lamorna said. She was thinking about Paul.

'Ellen is on her way home now. We had a call from her yesterday. She left the hippy cave in Crete, and she's back in Athens.'

'We'll expect her around the end of September,' Sam added. 'And she's bringing one of her hippy friends with her.'

'Oh, I'll be sorry to miss her. I'll be back in college then.'

'Oh, I thought you might be stopping down here now, what with your new job and all. I told Michael you could both have the cottage.'

'Lamorna needs to finish her course,' Michael said.

'It's a difficult thing, because I love it here. The cottage feels like home, and you've all been so kind. Phil's great to work for. And it's hard to think of leaving Michael now. But I have to get my qualification.'

'Well, you are a sensible young woman,' Sam said.

'You know you're always welcome here. Come down in the holidays. I know it's not the same as staying in the cottage, but Mary and Chris will be there soon. There's always space in the hotel in winter, or there's our cottage here,' Aileen said.

'Thank you, I'd love to.'

'What about your parents?' Sam asked.

'They won't mind. The house is so crowded now. They're glad I'm thinking of moving out to share with Jude and our friend Joy when I get back. Did Michael tell you that Joy is going to design Mary's wedding dress?'

'No, but Mary said something about it. I think she's a little worried that it might be a bit weird,' Aileen said.

'Oh, they're coming for dinner with us tomorrow, so I'll have to reassure her.'

Sam and Michael cleared the rest of the dishes away and went off to do a couple of jobs.

'We should talk about weddings more often,' Aileen laughed. 'Might get a few more things done around here! I'm not hinting sure, but I'm really glad you've got together with Michael.'

'I don't know why it took so long, but he did seem so against me at first.'

'Well you know what that was all about. And I hear you became friends with the girl he was mixed up with.'

'Rosa, yes. She's a lovely person. She told me she was fond of Michael, but she was involved with another man, and she'd got pregnant. She said Michael was so kind to her, but she didn't love him, and she didn't want him to feel obliged to her, to the baby. And she's found a new man now, an American who stayed with us.'

'Well I'm glad that Michael didn't get too involved. I wouldn't be happy about him bringing up someone else's baby. What happened to the baby's father?'

'He wasn't the nicest of people. He didn't want commitment. He wasn't interested in Dylan, that's the baby. I don't know if Michael told you, but he left the commune in disgrace, and he stole my camera.'

'He didn't tell me. He never talked about the people there. What happened, did you tell the police?'

'Phil was really kind. He gave me his old camera, and it's a million times better than mine.'

Sam and Michael came back in.

'Lamorna was telling me about her camera being stolen,' Aileen said, and Lamorna had to tell Sam the story.

'You should report him,' Sam said. 'He shouldn't be allowed to get away with it.'

'I think I will, but let's not talk about him now.'

It was ten o'clock when they left the hotel and set off to walk back down through the village.

'Let's go down through the garden and along the shore,' she said.

The scent of the roses was still strong in the warm night air. Michael drew her into his arms and kissed her.

'I've been wanting to do that all evening,' he murmured.

The harbour was busy with people emerging from the pub. They stopped to chat to some of Michael's friends, and then lingered awhile, watching the lights reflected in the water. Lamorna realised it was the exact spot where she'd been standing when Gary had assaulted her.

'It seems a lifetime since that night you rescued me from Gary.'

'I'm sorry I had to hit him. I seem to be doing a lot of that recently. It's not like me. I'm not usually the violent type. I wasn't admitting it to myself, but I think I'd already fallen in love with you. I felt it from the moment I first saw you.'

'That's how I felt too. But I really thought you hated me.'

'And I thought you hated me, and all blokes. I kept hearing you say things like men were a waste of space. But I couldn't get you out of my mind. I was so happy when you said you'd go with me to Tintagel.'

'All that time we wasted when we could have been together.'

'Let's not waste any more.'

Back in the cottage he went to make coffee. Lamorna lit the candles, and then on an impulse ran upstairs to get her camera, managing to catch Michael as he came through with the mugs on a tray.

'Oh no, if that gets about it'll ruin my reputation.'

'You're the one who volunteered to make dinner tomorrow. What will you cook? Fish?'

'No, Chris won't eat fish. He hates it.'

'But he's a fisherman!'

'That's probably why he hates it. I'll make spaghetti.'

'Spaghetti? Do you know how to?'

'Yeah, we've had it at the hotel. I can scrounge some ingredients from Mum. We had an Italian working here last summer, gave us some ideas for different meals. He's set up a restaurant in Penzance now.'

'I'll make a cheesecake then, I'll go shopping at lunch time. It'll be lovely. I've never entertained friends like this before.'

'Michael,' she said after a pause. 'I've just remembered we left the hammock at the house. We should bring it down here. And there's some fruit to pick, raspberries and strawberries, we could eat them with the cheesecake.'

'I'll go up there in the morning and get them.'

'We could ask Mary and Chris to stay the night.'

'We could ask, but I don't think they will. Mary wouldn't know what to say to her Mum.'

'Why don't your parents mind us sleeping together?'

'I don't know. Maybe it's because I'm a bloke. There's less risk. They'd be worried if it was Ellen. Mum did ask if I was being careful.'

'What did you say to her?'

'I told her I was taking precautions.'

'I wouldn't want her to think I was on the pill. It makes you look like a loose woman.'

'I don't think Mum would say that about you. What about your parents?'

'I wouldn't tell them. They'd freak out. My brothers can get away with far more than I ever could. They go to the Saturday films on their own, and they're allowed to go to the fair. I was never allowed anywhere near it. She thought I'd run off with a gypsy or something. She'd probably think you were a gypsy with that dark hair and brown skin. But now she's got the boys she's not so bothered about me.'

'She would be if you got pregnant.'

'I suppose so. Shall we go to bed?'

Chapter 33

Michael was up first, bringing her breakfast in bed before setting off to the house to pick up the hammock. Lamorna had to run for the bus, and only just caught it. She'd got used to having a lift every day.

The studio was busy all day. There were two lots of wedding photographs to be developed. She was surprised when Phil called up at lunchtime,
'You've got a visitor.'
It was Michael, of course, and she could see straight away that something was wrong.
'What's happened?'
'I was just telling Phil. Someone has broken in at the commune house and daubed paint on the walls. I don't know whether to tell the police.'
'You should.'
'Some of the words are about us, and they're not nice. I told Dad, and he doesn't want to involve the police, reckons it was a one-off.'
'Did you tell him the bits about us?'
'Not in detail. I've been up and painted it out. You can't read it now.'
'It must have been Paul. I knew this would happen.'
'Yes. I think it's a parting gesture. I can't see him hanging about round here now.'
'If that's the same guy who took your camera Lamorna, I think you should go to the police.'
'Phil's right. We should report him for the camera and what he's tried to do.'
'I don't want to talk about him. Come on, we've got shopping to do, is it okay if I take a bit more time for lunch Phil?'

They shopped in the market before ending up at the usual coffee bar for lunch, perching on her favourite window seats.
'How come you've got time off?' she asked.
'I've got some errands to do for Dad, and I'm getting wood to board up the windows at the house.'
'It'll look horrible and unloved, and it was such a lovely place.'
'Yes, all this would never have happened if everyone had stayed. It'll make a great place for family holidays though when it's all done up.'
'What do local people think about all these houses turning into holiday cottages?'
'Mixed views really. Some folk want the village to stay the same for ever, but a good many people don't want to live round the harbour now. I think most of them see that it's better to have emmets than leave the houses empty. And a lot of people make money from the tourists, the galleries, the pub, and the shops. It makes the harbour seem dead in the winter, although the Christmas lights are bringing some people down now.'
'A local family could live in that house, it's big enough.'

'Yeah well, they all want a modern house, up at the top of the village where it's quieter.'

'I would want to be down near the sea.'

'That's because you're an emmet really. It's different in winter. We have to close the harbour entrance up. The waves crash over the harbour walls. It's cold, wet and dismal. No new girls to chat up.'

'Michael!'

'Only joking.'

Suddenly she grabbed his arm.

'Look, it's Paul, don't let him see me.'

She slid off her stool and hid behind him. Paul was hurrying along the street, a duffel bag slung over his shoulder.

'I'm going after him.'

She held onto his arm.

'Please don't Michael, just let him go.'

'Alright, but I would like to have asked him why he wrote those things. Made him apologise.'

'It doesn't matter. Come on, I have to go back to work.'

'Okay, I'll see you later. I've got a surprise for you.'

'Oh, what is it?'

'A surprise.'

The afternoon was busy again, and she was amazed when Phil called up,

'Michael's here to take you home.'

She came down with the albums she'd been putting together.

'Where does all the time go? Nearly all done, not much left for tomorrow.'

'Well, you can come with me to the printer to sort out the hotel brochures, and I've got a family coming in for a portrait session.'

'Oh good. I'll see you in the morning then.'

They walked together to the van.

'I followed him. He went to the station and got a train to London.'

'Michael, you promised you'd leave him alone.'

'I didn't go near him. I wanted to see what he was up to.'

'How do you know he went to London?'

'I asked the bloke in the ticket office, and he told me he bought a one way ticket. It looks like he's gone for good this time.'

Back at the cottage she was unloading the shopping.

'I'm looking forward to this evening. I can't wait to see what Chris thinks of spaghetti.'

'Come and see the surprise.'

She went through into the living room, and there was music. A record player was installed on the chest.

'I found it at the house, pushed to the back of a cupboard.'

'I never saw it there, they used a newer one. But where did you get the LPs?'

'Brought them down from the hotel. Some of Ellen's too.'

'It'll be great to have music this evening.'

They propped the kitchen door open so that they could hear music while they worked. Lamorna chose the Paul Simon Songbook. Soon there was a pan of spaghetti sauce bubbling on the cooker, and cheesecake in the fridge. Michael had picked lots of fruit, and he went outside now to sling the hammock up. There was banging and some cursing as he fixed hooks into the walls.

Mary and Chris arrived dead on time, and insisted on a guided tour of 'their' cottage.

'It's so nice, I can't wait to move in,' Mary said.

'You could stay here tonight, there's a spare bed and a hammock,' Michael suggested.

'Why not?' Chris said.

'And you'll be the one to tell my Mum?'

The spaghetti proved a great hit, and there was lots of laughter as they all struggled to keep it on the fork. Chris was reprimanded by Mary for sucking it into his mouth. After they'd washed up Chris and Michael went to make coffee.

'It'll be great here, just Chris and me. You're so lucky Lamorna. But what does your Mum think?'

'She doesn't know. And I won't tell her. After all, I'm nineteen now, I can marry without their permission.'

'Will you marry Michael?'

'I have to finish my course first. I want to be independent, be able to earn my own salary. And then he might not wait for me, all these girls that come down here every summer.'

'I think it's different with you. You're more important to him. Why don't you marry him anyway, you could still finish the course?'

'He hasn't asked me!'

'He would if he thought you'd say yes. He told Chris you were the one for him. He asked Chris how he proposed to me. But don't tell him I told you.'

'Of course I won't. I do love him Mary, but I don't know what I'd say if he asked me. It doesn't seem the right time somehow.'

'You are odd.'

Michael and Chris reappeared. Lamorna lit the candles around the room, and they handed round the chocolates the visitors had brought with them.

'Will you stay here when Lamorna's gone off to college?' Mary asked.

'I don't think so, I'll finish off the last few jobs, make sure it's all ready for you two, and I'll go back up to the hotel. I'd be too lonely on my own here now.'

'Plenty of girls willing to share with you round here,' Chris said, and was whacked over the head with a cushion by Mary.

'Not all blokes are like that!'

'Only joking. I heard there was a break in at the hippy house on Sunday night,' Chris said.

'How did you know that?'

'Brian told me.'

'It wasn't bad, just a bit of paint splashed around.'

'How terrible, if the hippies had stayed it wouldn't have happened,' Mary said.

'Well, what's done's done.'

'What will everyone talk about now? There's never been so much gossip.'

'There's your wedding,' Lamorna said.

'They'd only be talking if I was pregnant.'

'Come on, I'd better get you home before they send out a search party,' Chris said. 'Thanks for the dinner, it was great.'

'I nearly forgot, Mum says will you both come for lunch on Sunday, she says she won't take no for an answer?'

'Well then we must. Can you make it Michael?'

'Yeah. Guess I could.'

'Well, we'd love to then, tell her thank you.'

Lamorna washed up the mugs, humming to herself in the kitchen. Michael suddenly wrapped his arms around her.

'Lamorna, will you marry me please?'

She twisted round and took his face in her hands.

'Michael. I love you, but it seems like the wrong time. We should wait until I finish college.'

'I want you to wear my ring so that all the other blokes won't be chasing after you.'

'They won't, they never do, and I don't want them. I want to work hard and get a degree. Don't you trust me?'

'I don't know. You might forget me.'

'I won't forget you, but I don't know what will happen. I'm only nineteen. I don't have any experience like you. And you might find someone new. Getting engaged won't stop that. We shouldn't need that if we really love each other.'

'Don't say those things, I can't bear it.'

'I'm trying to be realistic. We don't know how it will be when we're apart. You could forget all about me.'

'Mary is sure of Chris.'

'Yes, but she doesn't have a course to finish like me. Right now you are the most important person in the world to me. I love you so much. And you make me so happy. But please understand. Getting married isn't the right thing to do just now.'

'I'll pine away without you.'

'Of course you won't, you're too sensible.'

'That's my problem then. I'm too sensible for you.'

'Oh Michael, that's not it. Can't you see that I'm taking the biggest risk? There'll be so many women falling at your feet in this romantic place.'

She knew she couldn't convince him, but didn't know what else to say. Instead she kissed him.

***

Marriage was the topic of conversation at work the next morning too. She and Phil were putting together another wedding album.

'I often wonder how long these marriages will last,' he said. 'You see them all in their wedding finery, all smiles, and the next thing you know they're splitting up.'

'Have you ever thought about getting married?'

'I'm only twenty six. Give me a break.'

'Sorry, I just wondered.

'Look at this couple, I'd give them two years at the most, they just don't look right together. Looks like she might be pregnant.'

'Phil, that's terrible!'

'Doing this job makes you cynical. Puts me off marriage I suppose.'

'Maybe you've just not met the right person?'

'I haven't met anyone I'd want to spend the rest of my life with. What about you?'

She thought for a while before speaking.

'I really love Michael. But I can't settle down yet, I want to finish my course. I'm too young. Everyone seems to be asking me now.'

'You started the subject!'

'It's on my mind. I'm trying to work out how I feel. I can't bear the idea of being away from him, but I want to do the course. How can you really know, really, really know that someone is the right person for you?'

'I don't know that. Maybe you have to take a chance if it feels right. Maybe most people think they won't get another chance. There's all sorts of reasons, escape from home, money, getting pregnant.'

'Rosa at the hippy commune was pregnant, but she didn't push Paul to marry her.'

'Good job too, isn't he the one who took your camera?'

'Yes, she was so sad about the way he turned out, but she did care for him at first.'

'Have you told the police yet?'

'No, we saw him yesterday. He got a train to London. They'd never catch him now.'

'You've got photos of him, you should report him.'

'Maybe you're right, I'll think about it.'

They were finishing the last album together when Michael appeared.

'We were just talking about that Paul bloke. I told Lamorna you should go to the police.'

'I think Phil's right. We should report him before he does any more harm.'

'Okay,' she said reluctantly. 'Let's go now and get it over with.'

Lamorna went upstairs again to rummage through her portfolio for a clear photo of Paul, and carefully cut out his image, and they walked around to the Police Station.

'We should tell them about the attack first. It's the worst thing.'

There was a sergeant behind the desk. He took her name and details, and then she told him that she wanted to report an assault. He listened as she described the incident at the commune house.

'An assault, in a hippy commune? I thought those places were all about free love.'

'You're treating her like she's the criminal. I was there, I saw what happened,' Michael interrupted angrily.

'You'd better come through to the interview room.'

He led them through, and summoned a constable to take her statement. Like the sergeant he didn't seem to take the assault seriously. But when she mentioned the theft of her camera he became animated.

'That's something we can get our teeth into. When did this happen?'

'It was the beginning of the month.'

'Why didn't you report it earlier?'

'Come on Lamorna,' Michael said then, 'he's not taking you seriously. 'We didn't report it because we thought this would be your attitude. The bloke took the camera and said he was going abroad. He came back and assaulted her, and now he's gone to London and we're wasting our time.'

He stood up.

'Wait Michael. I've got a photo of him. You can use that to find him.'

She pulled the picture out of her bag.

'He looks like a description we have of someone we're looking for. He's been seen stealing charity collection boxes. I think we need to get your statement.'

Michael sat down again.

'I don't know his second name, but he did say he was arrested in the Grosvenor Square demonstration in March. Maybe there'll be a record of it.'

'There will be. I'll phone and check. Wait here.'

'I can't believe how bad this is,' Michael said, they don't want to take the attack on you seriously, and it's the worst thing he did.'

The constable came back after some while.

'No record of a bloke called Paul with that description getting arrested, so that doesn't help.'

'That's odd.'

Michael's witness statement was taken seriously, and Lamorna felt slightly better when they finally left. They went for a coffee before heading home.

'I'm really scared, but I hope they catch him. I wonder how much he got from the charity tins.'

'Enough to buy a ticket to London.'

'What will happen if they catch him?'

'It will come to court, and we'll have to be witnesses.'

'Oh no, I'd hate that.'

'Don't worry, they'll probably never find him.'

'I want them to. It's not the worst thing.'

She told him then about his attempt to seduce Marie.

'My god, that's bad. Rosa should have reported it.'

'She couldn't, she was worried about her Mum's reaction, and the impact on the commune.'

'She was wrong. He might try something like it again, but come on let's go and get some fish and chips and eat them on the beach.'

Chapter 34

Michael was needed at the hotel in the morning.

'I'll ask Mum to pack us a picnic, and I'm taking you out for the afternoon.'

'Where are we going?'

'It's a surprise.'

He left her relaxing in bed with a cup of tea and a book. She had a peaceful morning, getting some washing and cleaning done, and then sitting down on the garden bench to write some letters. She wrote a short note to her Mum, telling her about her new job. And then she started on a much longer letter to Jude. There was so much to tell her.

'I don't know where to start, so much has happened. The commune has broken up. Someone bought the house and we all had to leave. We had a party, and even Mary and Chris came. Rosa went off with a new man, Ced, an American friend of Laura's. The one who sent her those LPs. I nearly forgot about Paul........' At last she got around to mentioning Michael.

'You were right Jude; I did fall in love with Michael. And it's the most wonderful thing that's happened to me. I'm staying with him in a little cottage that Sam owns. Mary and Chris came for dinner. And Jude, Michael asked me to marry him. I said I couldn't, I have to do my course. But I don't know if that's the right thing to do. I wish you were here to talk to.'

She had just finished addressing the letter and sticking the stamp on when Michael arrived.

'Come on, you're missing the sunshine, the picnic's ready and I've got some old towels from the hotel.'

'Towels?'

'Yes, we're going to the beach.'

'Can I post these on the way?'

'Yeah, we're going down to the harbour.'

They walked down, and she was surprised when he led her to the quay.

'Here we are. I'll go down first with the bags.'

He climbed down the flight of stone steps, and she followed. A wooden boat was bobbing against the wall.

'Oh, a boat!'

'Yes, it's Chris's boat. I've borrowed her for the afternoon, come on, we need to go before the tide's right out.'

'Oh, look Michael, the boat's called Mary.'

'It was his Dad's boat, probably named after his Mum,' he told her matter of factly.

She clambered into the boat, and it rocked violently.

'Sit down quickly and you'll be okay,' he said, and he jumped out to untie the painter, push them off and jump back on board.

He sat in the stern, and turned on the outboard motor, and soon they were chugging out of the harbour, turning right to head along the coast. She noticed how at home he was in the boat, and happy. He was smiling broadly as they motored along. He pointed out landmarks to her.

'There's the cave. There's the coastguard look out.'

He told her the names of all the headlands as they passed, Penzer Point, and Carn Du, and then she recognised the little cove they were passing.

'It's Lamorna,' she cried excitedly. 'Can we go there?'

'Another day.'

They went on, past Tater- Du and Boscawen Point.

'That's Penberth Cove now,' he said, pointing to a beautiful narrow inlet. She looked over and saw a stone slipway with little boats pulled up. They passed another rocky headland, and then Michael turned the boat to shore.

'I know where we are, it's my lagoon beach, it's Porthcurno,' she said, smiling.

'The tide is still quite well up the beach here, we've still got time before the way round is clear and the emmets invade.'

She was looking up at the cliff, wondering how they had managed that climb, when she felt a lurching, and the boat slipped onto the sand. Michael lifted the outboard motor clear and then jumped out into the water, and secured the bow painter with a small anchor. Lamorna clambered out. The water was clear, and she paddled through the small waves rippling onto the warm sand.

'I'm so hungry,' she said, reaching into the boat for their bags.

'Work first, then picnic,' he said. 'Swimming lesson number one will commence in one minute.'

'Swimming! You didn't say. I can't, I didn't bring any swimming stuff.'

'You don't need it, there's no-one to see.'

He took his own clothes off first, dropping them in a heap on the sand. She threw her flip flops at him, but resignedly pulled off her clothes, folding them onto his, delaying the moment when she'd have to take the plunge.

'Don't look so worried, I'll look after you. I'm a qualified life-guard, remember. It's going to be hard to concentrate though,' he added, looking at her standing there bereft of clothes.

But he took her hand, and led her into the water until they were waist deep. The coldness made her catch her breath. She held his hand tightly. She could feel the soft sand slithering away beneath her toes. A clump of slimy seaweed wrapped itself around her ankle.

'I'm going to hold you and let you float gently,' he said. 'Just close your eyes and relax, let the water support you. I won't let go of you, I'll hold you all the time.'

She closed her eyes, and felt him take her shoulders and ease her gently back, his hand moving under her back to reassure her. He moved her gently backwards, towing her, and her hair spread out across the water.

'Let your legs float up, let them relax.'

She followed his instructions, and she felt herself floating now, the sun warm on her body, his hands reassuringly holding her. He leaned over and kissed her.

'Imagine you are that mermaid now, floating off the shore. I'm going to keep moving backwards, and you'll float along. Try kicking your feet gently like flippers.'

She loved the sensation of floating. Even with her eyes closed she was aware of the sun glinting on the sea around her. She listened to the waves rippling against her face. And then she was aware that he was floating with her too. He supported her with just one hand now, and she felt confident to lie back in the water, and be led by him.

'You are really floating by yourself now, you don't need my hand, but don't worry, I'll keep it there.'

They had travelled some way from the beach, and he began to swim back in now, a gentle back stroke, still supporting her. They floated together onto the warm sand. She rolled over to him, and wrapped her arms around him.

'That was lovely.'

'You see, you'll soon be swimming,' he told her. 'The salt water helps to hold you up.'

'It's because I feel safe with you.'

'I don't think you should,' he said then, and he was suddenly on his feet, and carrying her up the beach to their clothing. He placed her carefully down, and then spread out a huge bath towel.

'Lie down here for lesson number two.'

'What am I learning about now?' she said.

'Resuscitation and recovery position,' he said, kissing her.

He lay down beside her and made love to her. Only hunger drew them apart at last, and they hastily dressed as a few distant figures appeared around the headland.

'We need to get here earlier next time. And maybe bring swimming stuff,' he said. 'Mustn't get distracted again. I daresay we kept the coastguard entertained.'

'Coastguard?'

'Yes, the bloke up there on the cliff.'

'I can't see anyone.'

'You can see his binoculars glinting when the sun catches them.'

'Binoculars! Michael!'

'Only joking, he's further round, he couldn't see us.'

They sat down to unpack the picnic. Aileen had made them coronation chicken sandwiches, and there were two small pasties and a variety of fruit. Michael unearthed a couple of splits with jam and cream from the bottom of the basket.

'I made these, and Mum said they weren't fit for the guests.'

'They're a funny shape, but they taste good,' she said.

The beach was filling up now. A crowd of children were splashing in the lagoon. She looked up at the cliffs again, trying to remember where they'd climbed.

'I knew I was in love with you that day we were here, we were lying in the bracken at the top of the cliff, and I wanted to touch you. I could feel you lying there with all of my body and I wanted you so much.'

'Me too, I had to lie on my hands to stop myself.'

'I thought you still hated me.'

'I never hated you. I was trying not to love you. Shall we go home?'

'Yes, lets.'

'Do you mind paddling?'

'No.'

They went down to the boat and loaded up their belongings before pushing her out into deeper water. Lamorna found herself almost waist deep before Michael helped her to clamber into the boat. Still holding the painter he too climbed in and lowered the motor. It started first time, and they headed back along the coast. Lamorna recited the names of places she'd learned on the way, and he was amazed at how well she did.

'There's the little lighthouse again, what was it called?'

'Tater-du. It was only built a few years ago after a Spanish coaster went on the rocks at Boscawen.'

'How terrible, were any lives lost?'

'Yes, about ten, I think.'

At home they shared a bath and then went to bed for a couple of hours. Lamorna cooked them chilli and rice for dinner, and then they walked down to the pub. Ian was there.

'What's this about you and the police in Penzance?'

'No point asking how you know,' Michael said, sighing. 'I suppose Mum and Dad'll have found out.'

'I dunno. It was my cousin told me, I ran into him in Newlyn. He's a copper. Don't think anyone else has heard. I won't tell.'

'Thanks Ian. We went to report the bloke who stole Lamorna's camera.'

'Neil said something about assault.'

'Yeah, there was that too, but we'd rather not talk about it. No real harm was done'

'Why didn't you tell them before now?'

'I don't know, didn't want to get the group a bad name I suppose.'

Mary and Chris arrived then, and the conversation turned to fishing and weddings.

'This came for you today,' Mary said, producing a letter from her bag, 'I hoped we'd see you'

'It's from Jude again.'

She opened it and read it quickly.

'She's sent me a reading list for next term, as if I'll get any done down here. She says she's writing to you Ian. The house we're going to share sounds good. She's been out and bought a twin tub washing machine and a TV. She's had a phone put in. Her Dad insisted. I'll be able to ring you all. That's it.'

She folded it back into the envelope and stuffed it into her pocket. They didn't stay long. The pub was filling up with visitors and it began to feel hot.

'Don't forget, Sunday lunch, one o'clock,' Mary called after them.

'I've never had so many invitations. It's your popularity,' he said.

'They're probably just curious about what's going on. No, I wish I hadn't said that. I like Mary's Mum and Dad, they're genuinely welcoming. I've taken a lovely photo of Mary. I'll get it printed for them. I need to do some prints for the cottage walls too.'

Later, when they were snuggled together in bed, Michael asked,

'What was it that upset you in Jude's letter?'

'Oh, she said something about Gary. He was talking about me in the pub. Seems to be thinking we'll get back together again.'

'I'll come up and sort him out.'

'Michael, don't worry. I'll deal with him this time.'

There was silence for a while, and then Lamorna spoke again.

'Michael, what did Paul tell you about me that made you hit him the day you came to Porthcurno?'

'He told me he'd seduced you. Not in those words. I didn't want to believe him. And then when we were together that first time I knew he'd lied to me.'

'Why did he tell you?'

'Because I came looking for you to give you the letter. He sneered at me, said I needn't bother trying it on with you. Said you were already his. Something like that.'

She lay thinking for a while.

'He tried to Michael. It was when we were all on the beach at Sennen. The others all went for a swim. He came out first and tried to force me. He talked to me as if it was his right, as if I'd encouraged him. I didn't Michael. I didn't encourage him.'

'What did he do?'

'I can't tell you. I'm too ashamed. What's wrong with me? Why did he think he could do that?'

'You shouldn't be ashamed. It's not your fault. Maybe he saw you as a challenge because you're not easy like some women.'

She buried her face against him.

'He only stopped because I'd got my period. I had a tampon. He seemed disgusted.'

'How horrible for you.'

'And then he made me, he made me......'She couldn't say the words. 'He made me do this.'

She placed her hand over him and showed him.

'I want to do that with you, but I couldn't bear him.'

And she was crying now. He held her more closely and kissed her.

'I was so ashamed. I didn't tell anyone for ages, not until the day he left. I told Rosa then. She couldn't understand why he'd do that. I think to be honest she thought I should be sleeping with him. But I couldn't. I didn't like him. The trouble is there was no-one else. Rosa was involved with Ced. He was jealous. He tried it with Jude. She might have been interested if she hadn't got involved with Ian. There must be something wrong with me. Jude seems happy to sleep with random men. Rosa does. Everyone tells me I should get into free love. But I can't.'

'Free love sounds good, but it can only work in the right situation. None of the men I know would respect a girl who sleeps with loads of men. She'd be called a slag, even if they'd taken advantage of her. No-one would marry a girl like that.'

'Men want it all their own way. They want to go with lots of women, but they only want to marry virgins. It's so unfair.'

Michael was quiet for a moment.

'You make me feel terrible. I wish I could undo everything. I wish you could be the first person for me. Loving you makes me see how cheap all the other times were. Will you forgive me?'

'Of course I do. It's the way things are. It will probably always be like that for men. It's so easy for them. Maybe the hippies have got it right. Maybe we set too much store on it, on virginity. They aren't interested in marriage. They think it's a form of prostitution.'

'Well, I suppose that's okay as long as they all agree. Do you agree with them?'

'I don't think so. I understand what the feminists say. There are men who dominate women, women who have no rights. Even my own Mum never knew what my Dad earned. That's why I want to be independent before I think about marrying or having children. I want to be sure that we can be equal. I don't want to feel dependent on someone else. Do you understand?'

'I think I do. I wouldn't want a marriage like that. My Mum and Dad aren't like that. They share everything.'

'But even your Dad didn't tell her that he was buying a share in the commune house.'

'You're right. He didn't. Maybe it's not so equal.'

'Michael, I'm glad you were the first for me. You make it so lovely. I would never want anyone else.' She brushed her lips across his neck, breathing in his scent. 'We should go to sleep. Thank you for listening to me.'

'I always want to listen to you. I want to understand.'

'You sound too good to be true.'

'Don't say that. I'm trying, but I find it difficult. Sometimes I want to just say that you will marry me tomorrow, and that's that.'

Chapter 35

Kate was pleased to see them when they arrived for dinner on Sunday.

'Come in, come in, I want to hear all your news, you love-birds. Who'd have thought that you two would get together?'

Mary and Chris were both in the little parlour.

'Thanks for the boat on Wednesday Chris. Any chance of borrowing it this Wednesday?'

'No, sorry, need it myself.'

Mary and Lamorna went into the kitchen to help her Mum.

'I'll help,' Michael offered.

'She won't want a man in the kitchen!'

Mary's Dad came in then.

'Hello Michael. I see you've your maid with you. That was a long job Chris. The trailer were caggled. Shan't lend it to that great dobeck again. Best get cleaned up before Kate catches sight.'

He left the room.

'What was that all about?' Michael asked.

'Oh, Frank lent Edwin his trailer last week, and he used it to move a load of muck. Came back in a right state.'

'What have you done with Ian today?'

'He had a letter from Jude, and he went up to see her last night. Don't know what it's about.'

'It's only love,' Mary said. 'It's catching round here.'

After all the washing up was done and they'd gone back into the living room for cups of tea, Lamorna presented Kate with the framed photo she'd made of Mary.

'That's lovely, thank you my lover, I didn't have a good one of her, and she'll soon have flown the nest.'

She placed the photo on the mantel piece, alongside pictures of two other girls, and one that looked like a younger version of Mary.

'Tell me about these other pictures Mary,' Lamorna said.

'That's me when I was about thirteen, I was May Queen. Those two are my sisters. This is Catherine. She lives over in Cambourne; she's married with two kids. This is my other sister Tamzin. She lives with some friends up the road. She works at the bird sanctuary. Started there last year when they were busy after the big disaster.'

'What disaster?'

'The Torrey Canyon. She went aground off Land's End. They got lots of birds in all covered with oil.'

'I remember reading about it,' Lamorna said. 'Didn't it spoil all the beaches too?'

'Aye, it did that, they were clagged with it, and it ruined the fishing,' Frank said.

'The smell was awful; you could breathe it in miles away. Don't blame the emmets for staying away.'

'Didn't stop the hippies coming down for the summer of love,' Chris said.

'There you are,' Mary said. 'They all moan about them, but they were spending money down here when other folks weren't.'

'We didn't expect them to stay down here forever,' Frank said, and was ignored.

'The worst was all the chemicals,' Chris said. 'Don't reckon they knew what to do.'

'They even got the RAF to bomb the ship. Thought they could burn the oil off.'

'There's still some oil coming up on the beaches. But we've been quite busy again in the hotel. Our regulars want to support the place.'

'They do say we won't be clear of it afore a good many years,' Frank said.

There was no time later to carry out Michael's plan and go for a swimming lesson, and they set off back up to the hotel to help out for the evening.

***

Lamorna planned to lie in on the Wednesday morning. Michael was up early and brought her tea in bed.

'I have to get going, or I won't get the afternoon off,' he told her.

She lay back on the pillow, watching the dust motes dancing in a shaft of sunlight. She pulled his pillow into her arms and hugged it, breathing in the faint smell of his hair.

'I don't know how I'm going to make myself leave him, and there's hardly any time left now.'

She got up and went out into the courtyard to eat her breakfast, before cleaning up the cottage. At half past eleven she was outside again, writing postcards to send to Jude and her family. She chose a harbour view for Jude, and marked a cross on the beach, writing on the back: *'x marks the spot.'* And then she walked round to the post office to drop them in the box. Michael was by the memorial with Ian, but by the time she'd reached them Ian had gone.

'Did Ian say why he'd been up to see Jude?'

'No, he didn't mention it, and I didn't ask. Come on, I've borrowed Ian's boat.'

They went back to the cottage, and ate beans on toast, which was just about all they had.

'I need a serious shopping trip,' she said, peeling a banana and handing half to him.

'You eat that. Mum already forced me to eat a sandwich.'

'She must think I'm starving you to death.'

'No, she's just being a mother, come on, get your swimming stuff.'

'Oh no, not another lesson.'

'You're not leaving until you've learned to swim.'

'How did you learn?'

'Mum was a schoolgirl champion, she taught me and Ellen.'

They got their things together and headed down to the harbour. Lamorna was wearing her old jeans and a tee-shirt, with flip flops.

'Those flip flops again.'

'I need to keep my sandals for work. I don't want to ruin them with sea water.'

The boat was moored on a buoy, so they hauled her up and clambered on board.

'The boat's called Lamorna,' she said, amazed, noticing the word painted on the stern.

'No, she's Merry Maid. She's from Lamorna. She used to belong to a fisherman over there.'

'Oh, well I like Merry Maid. How do you know where she's from?'

'She used to belong to me. I didn't have time for boats so I gave her to Ian.'

Soon they were passing Lamorna Cove.

'We walked over to Lamorna every time we came down here, and we had to have a picnic in the same little field every time. My Mum never told me, but I think it must be where I was conceived. I remember thinking that they would get all soppy when we were there. I wonder if I could find the place now. I used to sit and make daisy chains.'

'Your Mum and Dad must have been a bit daring.'

'Not really. I just think there weren't many people about back then. I never remember seeing anyone else when we did the walk.'

'Are you like your Mum?'

'Not really. I'm more like my Dad I think. Except that he could swim.'

'Well I reckon you'll soon learn.'

'But I won't ever want to swim where people can see me, see my leg.'

'After a bit they'd stop noticing. And anyway, the rest of you is more interesting to look at!'

They were passing the last headland now, and began to turn towards the shore. The sea was turquoise, sparkling in the sun. She leaned over the prow, trailing her hands, trying to catch one of the small fish swimming below. She saw strands of seaweed swaying in the current like long hair blowing in a breeze, and reached over to try and touch them.
A speed boat rounded the headland, sending huge waves under them in its wake.

'Hold on,' Michael called.
The boat lurched in the swell.

She reached out to grab something. But it was too late. She was tumbling out, falling head first into the waves. She tried to cry out. Her mouth filled with water. She felt herself being sucked down. The seaweed was tugging at her ankles. Pulling her down into its slithering depths. The sound of Michael's voice was a muffled roar in her ears. She struggled and spluttered back to the surface. A gurgling in her head. Sudden shriek of gulls. And then down, down again. She felt Michael's hand around her wrist. He was beside her in the water now, pulling her up, holding her against him. She heard his voice, calm, reassuring, but she was struggling against him, fighting against the sea, fighting to stay afloat.

'I've got you. I'm holding you now. I'm taking you to the shore. Remember last time when I held you? Let yourself float.'

She stopped struggling and let herself fall limp against him. She was gasping still, fighting for breath. After a moment she felt him moving her through the waves, and let her legs and feet float up. They reached the beach, and he lifted her up and carried her to the dry sand. She coughed and spluttered.

'I'm going back for the boat. Stay here and don't move.'

She wanted to say 'don't leave me,' but couldn't get the words out, and then he was gone, running down the beach and into the waves. The boat was drifting, bobbing towards the rocks. She saw her flip flops riding the waves like two miniature surf boards. She watched him swimming over to the boat. Watched as he held onto the gunwale and begin to pull himself up. And then there was a roar, and the same speedboat came hurtling round the headland again, sending waves rushing towards the rocks. The boat lurched and tipped. Michael disappeared under a wave. She ran down the beach calling to him. The boat seemed to be sucked back out again. And then another wave came in. The boat crashed back onto the rocks. She couldn't see him now. She scrambled over the boulders.

And then he was there, floating face down against the rocks. The water was too deep for her, but she managed to grab his shirt and pull him along until she could get into the sea beside him. She slithered down the rock, grazing her arms and elbows, and was chest deep in the water now. She lost her footing. Slipped under the water. Then recovered herself, gulping air into her lungs. Holding him up, and struggling to turn him over. Wading. Knee deep now. Hauling his weight against her. Dragging him through the waves by his shirt. She reached the sloping sand and fell down beside him, sobbing and crying his name.

'Help me, help me,' she heard herself cry out as she cradled his head, and saw the blood pouring from a gash above his ear. She was kissing him, kissing the blood away. Someone prised her away from him and wrapped her in a towel. She watched numbly as he turned Michael over and began resuscitation. But she couldn't just sit shivering. She shuffled over to him and lay down beside him, holding onto his arm. His hand felt cold and lifeless.

'Will he be alright, will he be alright,' she was crying.
Then at last she heard a familiar calm voice. It was Ian. He was lifting her to her feet.

'Come now, come now, he'll be fine.'

'We lost your boat. We lost your boat. It was a speedboat......'

'I know, I know, don't worry,' his voice soothed her. He lifted her and carried her onto a boat, and she realised it was the lifeboat.

'I'm sorry, I'm sorry,' she kept on saying through clattering teeth.
Someone wrapped her in a blanket, and the lifeboat was underway. She saw Michael now, lying nearby, someone was attending to him. She stumbled over to him, her feet tangling in the blanket, and sat down beside him, tears streaming down her face. She found his hand and held it, kissed it, her hot tears streaming over his fingers. And then she felt herself slipping away.

***

She couldn't think where she was. A darkened room. She felt the weight of blankets over her, and pushed to free her feet and legs. She struggled to sit up, and sent something crashing to the floor. A curtain was drawn aside, and a nurse appeared, an anxious look on her face.

'Now now, you're not to get up, we're keeping you under observation for the night.'
Lamorna pushed her feet out of the bed, found the floor and tried to stand, but a dizzying sensation sent her slumping back down.

'Come on now, you're to stay in bed for the moment. Can I get you a drink?'

'I have to get up. I have to find Michael. Where is he? Where is he?'

'We're looking after him, he'll be fine. You can maybe see him in the morning.'

'I want to see him now. I have to be with him.'

'His mother and father are here, they're with him, but he needs to rest now. You can see him tomorrow. You need to rest and recover too. You've had a nasty shock.'

The nurse tucked her firmly into the bed again. And then Aileen appeared beside her.

'Michael, Michael, where is he?' she was crying.

'He's fine Lamorna, he's sleeping now. We're going home, and we'll be back in the morning to see you both again. You must listen to the nurses. You need to get some sleep too. Michael will need you to be awake and strong for him.'

'It's all my fault, it's all my fault.'

'It's not your fault, it was all an accident. And I hear you did a pretty good job of rescuing Michael. I want you to promise to get some sleep now. You don't want him waking up and seeing you look a wreck now, do you?'

And then she was sobbing again, and Aileen lifted her into her arms and held her, soothed her.

'He will be fine. He's a strong young man. He has a nasty knock and the doctors think he needs to rest and recover. They are doing everything they can for him. I'll bring you some clothes in the morning and you can come home with us.'

'I can't come. I have to stay with Michael.'

'I know, I know. We'll talk to the doctor in the morning. Now promise me you'll get some sleep.'

Lamorna nodded, and sank back onto the pillow.

'I'll come in and see you first thing.'

The nurse reappeared with a warm mug of cocoa and some tablets.

'These are to help you to sleep, and we'll see about your young man in the morning.'

Chapter 36

Trolley wheels squeaked across the ward. Someone was speaking in a hushed voice. Lamorna clambered a little unsteadily out of bed, and padded across the floor to pull the curtains open. A nurse was beside her immediately.

'We can't have this. You must get straight back into your bed.'

'I've got to find Michael.'

'You have to let the doctor examine you first.'

She was allowed to visit the toilet, and was shocked when she saw the wan face staring back at her from the mirror. Someone brought her breakfast, a bowl of cereal and some toast, but she couldn't eat. A nurse appeared and took her temperature, checked her blood pressure.

'When will the doctor come?'

'He's on his rounds now. Maybe half an hour.'

It seemed the longest half hour in the world, but at last the Consultant arrived. The nurse drew her curtains round again.

'Now then young lady. Let's take a look at you. Nurse tells me you had a good sleep.'

He examined her, listened to her chest, and studied her chart.

'How are you feeling?'

'I'm fine. I just want to see Michael. When can I see him?'

'Well, nothing much wrong there. I think you'll be well enough to go home today.'

'I don't want to go home. I need to stay with Michael.'

The Consultant pulled up a chair, and sat down beside the bed.

'Michael is fine. He's had a nasty knock on the head. We've stitched him up, and we're looking after him. His parents are here with him at the moment. His mother tells me that you're a determined young lady, and if you can convince me that you can stay calm then I will allow you to see him. Even though he is unconscious he can hear and probably understand what he is hearing.'

'I will be calm. I won't upset him. Please can I see him?'

'Come with me now, and we'll talk to Mr and Mrs Tremayne. I know Mr Tremayne was anxious to take you home with him.'

They went together down the corridor and turned into a side room. Aileen and Sam were sitting beside a bed. Lamorna saw that Michael was lying on his back, wired to various pieces of equipment. He looked pale, and his head was bandaged. The Consultant indicated that he wished to talk to Aileen and Sam, and gestured to Lamorna that she might sit down with his patient. The three of them left the room and were talking quietly in the corridor. Lamorna sat down and lifted Michael's hand. She stroked and kissed it.

'Hello Michael, it's me. I'm allowed to come and talk to you now. I had to sleep on another ward all night. I missed you so much. I'm going to kiss you now, whilst the doctor is out of the room.'

She leaned over and gently kissed his cheek. For a moment she was sure she felt him make some small movement.

The Consultant re-appeared.

'We have just been discussing Michael's treatment, and his parents have agreed with me that you might be the best one to help him. I think if you were to stay and talk to Michael, perhaps read to him it may help him. How do you feel about that?'

'I want to do that, I want to be with him,' she said quietly.

'Sam and I will be here sometimes, and we'll take you home at night,' Aileen said.

'Can't I stay here all night too?'

'No. He needs to have a normal daily pattern. We like patients to have a quiet night, and the staff too. And you will need to sleep if you are to be any good for him.'

'We'll bring some clothes for you and pick you up later today,' Aileen added.

After a farewell hug she was alone again with Michael. She sat down once more and took his hand in hers again.

'I can see some lovely birch trees through your window,' she said. 'The leaves are golden in the sunlight, and there are two small blue tits exploring. Do you remember the birch trees up on the heath near Men- an-Tol? They were still on that calm day, and their trunks were so white against the sky. The wind is blowing in these trees here, and the leaves are fluttering and dancing. There's a blackbird now...'

Nurses came and went, examining Michael, taking his temperature, scrutinising the machines. And still she stayed by his side. Someone brought her a drink, but it was left untouched. And then Aileen was there beside her.

'Hello Lamorna, I hear you've not left the room all morning. I've come to see Michael for a while. I've got some clothes for you, and I'm told I must send you down to the café to eat some lunch.'

'But I don't want to go, what if Michael wakes up and I'm not here?'

'I'll tell him where you are, don't worry. You need to eat Lamorna. You'll be no use to him if you waste away with hunger, will you? And I need some time with Michael too.'

'I'm sorry, I wasn't thinking. Thank you.'

She reluctantly let go of his hand, and bent over to kiss his cheek.

'I'm going to get a sandwich now. Your Mum is here. I expect you know. I'll soon be back.'

She left the room quietly as Aileen sat down and picked up Michael's hand in hers and began to tell him about her morning at the hotel.

Half an hour later Lamorna was back.

'Here I am again, the sandwiches here are not much good Michael, so you're not missing anything. Aileen, how are you managing at the hotel? I need to ring Phil, I'm letting him down.'

'You're not to worry. Mary's Mum has come in to help us. Ian phoned Jude and she's arriving this afternoon. Chris and Ian are both mucking in when they can, helping in the garden. Everyone has been marvellous. What about your parents, shouldn't we phone them too?'

'I don't know. They won't know anything about what's happened. It would probably worry them more if I rang. They won't be expecting it.'

They sat together for an hour or so, talking together about Cornwall, about Aileen's childhood. Someone came round with a tea trolley. At last Aileen rose to leave.

'Well Michael, I need to get back to the hotel for the dinner shift. I'll leave you here with Lamorna and see you again tomorrow. Your Dad will call in later to see you and take Lamorna home. Get a good night's sleep.'

She gave Lamorna a swift hug. Leaned over to kiss Michael's cheek and whisper to him.

Later the Consultant came round again.

'You seem to be doing a good job young lady. You haven't raised his temperature yet. I think it will be fine for you to sit with him again tomorrow.'

'Please can't I stay tonight?'

'No, as I said earlier he needs a night time phase. We don't want to tire him with endless talk.'

Sam came in at 7 o'clock. She went out to the toilet and for a cup of tea in the cafeteria, coming back to overhear Sam talking about cricket.

'Come on then,' he said. 'We're expected for dinner Michael, your Mother will be after us.'

Lamorna leaned over and kissed Michael.

'I'll see you tomorrow, I love you.'

Chapter 37

Mary's mum was still at the hotel when they arrived.

'I'm so sorry about Ian's boat,' Lamorna said.

'You're not to worry about that my lover. The main thing is that you and Michael are alright.'

Lamorna suddenly found herself bursting into tears.

'There there now, he'll be fine,' Kate said, folding her into her arms. 'He's a strong young man. You'll see. Come on now, your dinner's on the table, and I'm off back to my brood.'

Despite the presence of Jude, who had arrived half an hour before, the atmosphere was subdued that evening. They were all lost in thought and concern for Michael.

'I must phone Phil, the Doctor says I can sit with Michael again in the morning.'

'It's all taken care of, I'm going to work for him until Michael's back home, so don't worry,' Jude told her.

'I thought you'd be helping out here.'

'I can help out in the evenings and on days off.'

'It's not too bad here,' Sam said. 'We're still not back to normal since the Torrey Canyon. Folks are still staying way. And Kate is a real help. Mary is doing more hours, she's glad of the money to put towards the wedding, so you've no need to worry.'

'I thought you two would like to share the cottage here again,' Aileen said. 'It will be easier than picking you up from the village.'

'I'll need to go down and get some things, some clean clothes,' Lamorna said. 'Will you come with me Jude?'

The two girls walked around to the cottage, avoiding the road where possible.

'I don't want to meet anyone, I can't face questions yet.'

'It's lovely,' Jude exclaimed when they arrived at the cottage. 'I can't believe everything that's happened since I left. Are those your photos on the walls?'

'Yes, we thought they'd be perfect for Mary and Chris, they're going to live here for a while after the wedding, until they get their own place. I'll just go up and find my stuff.'

She walked into the bedroom. The bed was still rumpled, the way they'd left it that last morning. She flung herself onto it and cradled Michael's pillow against her.

'Oh Michael, Michael, please be alright, please come back to me.'

That's how Jude found her a few minutes later. She was crumpled in a ball, sobbing into the pillow.

'Come on, it'll be alright. He's going to be okay, you'll see.'

'What if he isn't? What if he never wakes up?'

And they were both crying then.

It was Lamorna who roused first, grabbing the tissues from beside the bed, wiping her eyes and nose.

'I'm sorry Jude.'

But Jude had cried herself to sleep. Lamorna crept downstairs and made a pot of tea. There was still fresh milk in the fridge.

'Better take these odds and ends back up to the hotel. Don't know when we'll be back.' Her eyes filled with tears again. She fought them off.

'Pull yourself together. You're no use to Michael if you're blubbering all the time.'

She carried the mugs of tea back upstairs and woke Jude.

'Sorry, I must have dropped off. Are you alright?'

'Yes, I needed that cry though. I couldn't in the hospital or back at the hotel.'

They sat together on the edge of the bed, sipping their tea.

'I'm so scared Jude.'

'I know, I know. But you've got to believe he'll be okay.'

'I do. When I was sitting with him I was sure he was listening and trying to tell me he would be alright.'

'I got your letter. I want to hear every detail about what's happened.'

'We'll talk on the way back. We should get going. Aileen will start worrying.'

They washed up, gathered the left-over food items and set off back to the hotel. Lamorna had found the book of poetry she had borrowed from Laura and Jean, and popped it into her bag, thinking she might read to Michael. They dropped their things off at the hotel cottage and then went over to the kitchen again.

'I wondered where you'd got to. I'm making Horlicks. Would you like some?'

So they sat quietly around the table, no-one having the heart to make casual conversation, until suddenly it was almost eleven o'clock.

'I'll take you into the hospital at nine in the morning,' Sam told her.

The two girls went over to the little cottage, and too tired to talk climbed straight into bed.

***

After breakfast the next day Lamorna asked to go up to Michael's room.

'I want to choose some books to read to him,' she said.

'Treasure Island was always a favourite,' Aileen said.

She moved softly around his room, looking at the posters on the wall. A faded picture of Francoise Hardy. Sports posters, a cricket team. On the window sill was a fleet of little model boats that he'd made. She lay down on the bed and thought about him. Thought about him lying in this bed as a young boy, watching the little model aircraft fly through the dust motes near the ceiling. She noticed a photo pinned near to the bed head. It was a copy of the photograph Phil had taken of her for the holiday brochure. Someone was calling her. She jumped up, took 'Treasure Island' from the shelf, a book about ships, and on a sudden impulse a Rupert Bear annual. Stuffing them in her bag she ran down the stairs.

It was just after nine when they arrived at the hospital. Aileen and Sam went to talk to the Consultant, and Lamorna sat with Michael and talked to him, telling him that Jude had arrived, and was working at the studio.

'There's good news,' Sam said, when they eventually came into the room. 'The x rays have not shown any serious damage. It's just a matter of time.'
He stayed for a while, and then went off back to work. Aileen and Lamorna sat together talking for a while, and then Aileen got up to go.

'I'd love to stay, but I think he's in good hands with you. I'll be back later.'
She bent down to kiss Michael and whisper a few words to him, and then she too was gone. Lamorna took Michael's hand and stroked it, before pulling the poetry book from her bag and beginning to read.

At lunch time Aileen came bearing sandwiches for her, and she went into the hospital garden to eat. It was a bright day. She sat in the shade of the birch trees, trying to decide which window was Michael's room, thinking of him, wondering what was happening and then deciding she had to get back.
Aileen stayed for a little longer.

'I'll be back later with Sam. Make sure you have a break during the afternoon. There's some Saffron cake for you in the box.'

***

Saturday was much the same. Lamorna carried on with 'Treasure Island, attempting to read with appropriate voices. There was still no change in Michael, but the Consultant, a different one this time, seemed satisfied that there was no cause for concern. Lamorna was driven to almost hyperactive activity. She insisted on helping with the work at the hotel in the evening, and had been up early that morning weeding in the garden. Aileen came over to the little cottage later that evening.

'The Doctor has given me something to help you sleep Lamorna.'

'I don't want to take it,' she said. 'I might not wake up in time in the morning.'

'You should,' Jude urged, 'you need some sleep. And it would give me some peace too, instead of hearing you thumping around at six in the morning.'

'I can't, I'm sorry. I'll try not to disturb you.'

'What would Michael think if he wakes and sees you looking like this, come and see,' Aileen said then, leading her across to the mirror.

'I look horrible,' she said, her eyes filling with tears.

'It wouldn't be good for Michael to think you're making yourself ill now, would it?'

'No, I'm sorry, you're right.'

Chapter 38

Lamorna slept soundly that night for the first time since the accident. It was past ten o'clock when she woke. Jude's bed was empty. She jumped out of bed, hastily washed and dressed and hurried over to the kitchen.

'I'm late, I'm sorry,' she cried, hurling herself through the door and almost sending Mary flying with a tray of cups.

'What are you doing here Mary, it's Sunday?'

'I'm here to help. I'll talk to you when you've calmed down. Sit down here and I'll get you some tea.'
She put the tray down and went to fill the kettle.

'I can't wait for tea. I have to get to the hospital.'

'You're not going anywhere until you've had some breakfast,' Mary said in a firm tone that was so unexpected that Lamorna sat meekly down again. Kate appeared from the dining room.

'I can see you're fretting, but there's no need. Aileen and Sam are with Michael at the moment. Don't you think they need some time with him?'

'Of course, I'm sorry.'

'No need to apologise my lover. I'm under strict instructions to make sure you eat a good breakfast and then you're to have a nice bath. Aileen says to tell you that she won't have Michael waking up to see some awful fright.'
Lamorna couldn't help but laugh then.

'Do I really look so terrible?'

'Nothing that a good bath and clean hair won't put right. Why don't you go up now, and we'll have a breakfast ready when you come down. That young maid Jude is out getting eggs, I daresay that's what you could do with.'

'Jude, getting eggs?'

'Yes, she's been out working in the garden all morning with Ian.'

So it was an astonished Lamorna who went up to the bathroom. There was a note from Jude.

'Some special pampering stuff to restore you.'
There was a collection of small glass bottles, special shampoo, bath oil and body lotion.

Whilst the bath was running she crossed the landing and went into Michael's room. She stood for a moment, thinking about him, thinking about the future, wondering if she should abandon her course and stay with him, thinking she wouldn't be able to be without him for a moment now. And then she was lying in the warm bath, feeling the bubbles popping around her ears, remembering the first bath she'd had in this room. Today she couldn't sing. She was too filled with sadness and worry. But the bath soothed her, and she felt so much calmer when she reappeared in the kitchen half an hour later.

'Well, you're looking much better,' Kate said, 'sit you down, breakfast is almost ready.'

For the first time since the accident Lamorna had an appetite, and ate everything put in front of her.

'Where's Jude?'

'She's cleaning out the chicken run with Ian. Do them both good that will.'

The door opened, and Sam appeared. He smiled at her.

'You're looking much better, ready to go in ten minutes?'

'How's Michael?' A chorus of voices bombarded him.

'He's fine, much the same.'

Aileen scrutinised Lamorna when they arrived at the hospital.

'Yes, I think you're looking presentable,' she smiled. 'I've been telling Michael that you've been having a lie in. I've enjoyed my time with him. Bye now Michael, I'm off back to work. I'll see you later on.'

She bent to kiss his cheek, and turned again to Lamorna, giving her a quick hug before leaving. Lamorna sat down in the still-warm chair, taking his hand in hers, stroking his arm.

'Can you believe it Michael, Jude is cleaning out the chickens with Ian? I never thought I'd see that. She's working so hard. I'm going to read to you now, first some more Treasure Island. I never read this before. Thought it was a boy's book I suppose, but it's really exciting.'

After an hour or so a nurse came to change his dressing and send her to get a cup of tea. After another section of Treasure Island she embarked on a Rupert Bear adventure, just for a change.

It was then that she felt something. Michael's hand was moving in hers. She held her breath, and squeezed his hand, looking up at him. He opened his eyes slowly and looked at her.

'Michael, Oh Michael,' she cried, standing and bending over to kiss him. He was trying to speak but couldn't get the words out.

'Hush, hush,' she whispered, 'don't try too hard, let me get someone.'

She walked over to the door, and called. She was back by the bed once more when the nurse appeared. Michael had closed his eyes again. She stroked his hand, and felt his fingers move.

'He opened his eyes. He moved and tried to talk.'

The nurse went over to Michael, touched his hand, and received a squeeze in response.

'That's good Michael. Don't try to do too much. I'm going to fetch your doctor.'

As soon as the nurse had left the room Lamorna carefully climbed onto the bed and lay down beside him, holding his hand and kissing his neck. He opened his eyes and gazed at her.

The Consultant appeared.

'Now young lady, we only allow one patient to a bed here, let me see this young man.'

She reluctantly slid off the bed, still holding his hand whilst Michael was checked over.

'Hello Michael. Will you squeeze Lamorna's hand if you can hear me?'

He watched as Michael slowly obeyed.

'That's good, but you mustn't rush and do too much. Your head has had a nasty knock, and you need time to heal and get over it. Can you squeeze Lamorna's hand again if you can answer yes to my questions? Do you remember what happened to you?'

There was no response.

'Hmmm, that's normal in this kind of thing. You may never remember the detail of what happened. But you are a strong young man. You seem to be recovering well. I need to do some more thorough checks, so I'm going to send your young lady off for a cup of tea and to phone your parents. Is that okay with you?'

He squeezed Lamorna's hand and turned slightly to look at her.

'Can I tell them to come and see him?'

'Yes, of course. But we still don't want too much excitement.'

'I'll be back soon Michael.'

Half an hour later Aileen and Sam arrived. Lamorna saw that Aileen was fighting back tears when Michael squeezed her hand. After a while they left with the Consultant, and Lamorna was alone again with Michael. His eyes were closed now, but she bent over to kiss him and for the first time felt a response.

'Oh Michael, I love you so much.'

And she felt him squeeze her hand again.

'Shall I read to you?'

He opened his eyes and looked at her. Then squeezed her hand. When the doctor reappeared with Aileen and Sam she was still reading Treasure Island. Michael's eyes were closed again.

'Michael is sleeping now,' the Doctor said. 'I think you may all feel able to leave him with us for the night. We'll do some more tests tomorrow. You will be able to see him again in the morning.'

A reluctant Lamorna allowed herself to be led away. Back at the hotel everyone was thrilled by the news. Kate had cooked them a dinner.

'Give our love to him for us tomorrow,' she said, 'I must be off home now.' Afterwards they all sat around with coffee, enjoying the feeling of relief at the good news.

'We don't know yet when he can come home, but they are amazed at his progress. The Consultant thinks there will be no long term problems,' Sam told them.

'He may take time to get his strength back and may have some difficulty putting words together at first, but it all seems very positive,' Aileen added.

Chapter 39

Michael continued to make progress. By Thursday he was up and walking and his speech was almost back to normal. Sometimes he struggled to find words, or muddled them up still. His gash was healing well. Lamorna was constantly by his side. She finished reading Treasure Island.

'Would you like some more Rupert Bear?'

'Rupert Bear! Is that what you've been reading to me?'

'That's what I was reading when you woke up.'

'No wonder I came round, probably wanted to stop you!'

On Saturday they were allowed to take Michael home, under strict instructions that he was not to do anything. It had been decided that Lamorna would be happiest staying in the hotel, helping out a little as needed. The doctor seemed to think it a good plan. He was convinced that Lamorna's devotion had contributed to Michael's recovery. Jude was keen to carry on at the studio for another week, and Phil's new assistant was due to start the following week.

Michael sat in the private garden for some of the afternoon, enjoying the fresh air and sunshine. Mary and Lamorna were busy serving teas, and Michael was the first to be served. Lamorna presented him with splits she had baked that morning, and a few kisses.

'I hope you don't kiss all the customers.'

'Of course I do, that's why we're so busy.'

And in a way she was right. Aileen said they were extra busy because news had got around that the young man who'd had an accident was back home.

'They've all read about you in the paper and they want to come and look, catch a glimpse of you both,' she said.

Michael was immersed in the papers too, reading various accounts of the accident. He could remember nothing of that day. Lamorna had told him that he had rescued her, and had then gone back to salvage the boat, but she had not mentioned her own part in his rescue

After dinner that evening Aileen sent him up to bed.

'Doctor's instructions, you're not to overdo it,' she said sternly in response to his protests.

Lamorna couldn't wait for the evening to end. She helped clear up, and then after a while was allowed to take him a mug of cocoa. He had been sleeping, but was awake now, reading the evening paper. There was yet another article and a blurred picture of Lamorna serving teas, alongside a mention of her brave part in his rescue. Aileen stuck her head round the door later and found Lamorna lying beside him on the bed, her arms around him.

'Well, you're certainly looking better, but remember the doctor's orders, not too much excitement.'

Lamorna felt a flush of red creep up her neck and over her face.

'Nurse West seems to be looking after you well. Goodnight both of you.'

She kissed them both on their cheeks, and went to leave the room. She opened the door, then turned, smiling,

'You'll find the medication that was in your pocket popped into your bedside drawer Michael.'

With that she was gone.

'What does she mean, medication?'

'Don't know,' Michael said. 'Have a look.'

Lamorna opened the drawer, and saw that on top of an assortment of odds and ends were two silvery packets of sheaths. She held them up, smiling, but blushing profusely.

'I think Matron has just reminded me of the treatment you need.'

And she quickly removed her clothes and laying down beside him again gently unbuttoned his pyjamas. Kissing him softly she moved over him.

'What are you doing, it's tickly?'

'I'm writing I love you with my nipples,' she said. 'Lie still, you're not allowed to move during the treatment.'

Afterwards they lay peacefully together.

'Are you okay?' she asked.

'Yes. It was lovely. And thank you Lamorna. Thank you for saving my life.'

'I don't think one treatment can do that. I think we need a daily dose.'

'You know what I mean. I'm sorry I don't remember what happened. Ian has been telling me all about it. You were so brave.'

Aileen brought them mugs of tea at ten o'clock the next morning, and found them wrapped together under a tangle of blankets, looking for all the world like a couple of shipwrecked waifs. But they were both flushed and very much alive.

'Wakey wakey. Doctor Davy is calling at mid-day, so I think Nurse West needs to get you up. There'll be a good breakfast waiting for you in an hour. Before you say anything Lamorna, we've plenty of help today, so you can relax for a while too.'

They sat up and drank their tea, Lamorna got up to pull the curtains back and let in the sunlight.

'Are you okay Michael?' she asked.

'It wasn't too much for you last night?'

'No, you did all the work. I enjoyed the treatment. It's done me good. But I think we're almost out of medication!'

She pulled open the drawer and peered inside.

'No, you're wrong, there's a brand new packet.'

She held it up to show him.

'I didn't buy those.'

'It must be your Mum. I can't believe how amazing she is. She's encouraging us under her own roof. I can't imagine my mother ever thinking of it.'

They shared a bath together, and then went down for a late breakfast. Soon afterwards the family doctor arrived and spent some time with Michael. Lamorna helped with the lunches and afternoon teas, and Aileen sent Michael up to rest at the end of the afternoon. Lamorna tiptoed in to look at him at five o'clock, and found him sleeping. She went down to the kitchen for a cup of tea with Aileen. Mary had gone home, and Sam was busy in the bar.

'Doctor Davy is pleased with Michael,' Aileen said. 'We just have to make sure he doesn't do too much too soon. He told me that the police have been questioning the motor boat owner who caused your capsize. He may be charged.'

Lamorna plucked up her courage.

'Thank you for the package in the drawer.'

'Well I think you have the best medicine for Michael, but I wanted to be sure that there were no side effects,' she said, smiling.

Sam appeared, wondering where his tea was, so there was no more discussion. Lamorna washed the teapots up, and just as she'd finished Michael came down. She made them some tea, and they went out together into the garden to drink it. ***

The days passed quickly, and Michael grew stronger. Doctor Davy visited again on Friday morning. Michael was concerned that he still could not remember the accident, but was told that he shouldn't worry, and that he might never remember.

'I sometimes feel that our brains are protecting us from traumatic experiences, perhaps it's all for the best that you don't remember.'

Lamorna was thinking about her future. She managed to talk to Jude about her worries as they drank tea in the garden at the end of a busy Wednesday lunchtime.

'What shall I do? I want to be with Michael, I can't bear the thought of leaving him. But I'm torn. I want to finish the course too. We should be getting back at the end of next week. Maybe I should defer the second year.'

'Why don't you see how Michael is in a couple of days, and then decide?'

'Yes. Maybe I will. You never did tell me why Ian went rushing up to see you that weekend.'

'Oh that. I had a bit of a scare. I thought I was pregnant. I told him, and he insisted on coming up. In the end it was okay, just a late period.'

'I thought you were on the Pill.'

'I am, but I forgot to bring them with me to Cornwall. I thought there'd be enough in my system to stop me getting pregnant. Before you say anything I brought them this time.'

'What happened when you saw Ian?'

'He said he'd marry me, can you believe it? But I know he doesn't really want to. He's been courting a local girl for years.'

'Oh Jude, that's you all over. When will you ever meet the right man?'

'Well actually, I've got something going with Phil. It feels different this time.'

'Jude! What about Ian?'

'I told him. He's fine with it. I told you, he's got this other girl.'

Lamorna was silent for a moment, taking it all in.

'You amaze me Jude. But it's great. Imagine. We've both lost our hearts down here. Maybe we'll both end up living here.'

'Well I'm definitely going back to college, I want the qualification. If things work out I'll come down and work with Phil. I've got lots of ideas about the business, especially the studio work.'

'Are you sure about Ian, what will he think if you're down here with Phil?'

'I told you, he's okay. I think his mum will be relieved we're not serious too. She thinks I'm a flighty wench.'

'I wonder what Aileen and Sam really think about me. I'm sure Sam would prefer Michael to find a local girl.'

'Well that's just where you're wrong. He was telling me that you're the best thing for Michael. He wasn't keen on some of his previous girlfriends. He's very impressed with the work you did on the brochures too. He thinks you're a good influence. Aileen thinks Michael might get more ambitious now he's met you.'

'I thought they were keen for him to work with them here and develop the hotel.'

'Why not talk to Aileen? She knows his heart's not in it. I heard her talking to Sam. She says they shouldn't pressure him if it's not what he really wants.'

'What he always wanted was to be fishing on the boats. But I'd be so afraid. It's so dangerous.'

'Ian seems happy with that way of life. So does Chris. It's part of the culture isn't it.'

'I suppose so. I'm just being selfish.'

'Maybe you should talk to Michael.'

'I will when he's fully recovered. He understands why I want to finish my course. I'm the one who's having doubts. When you nearly lose someone you realise how important they are.'

'Yes, but the course is only two more years, the time will just whiz by. Anyway, I'd better get a move on. Phil's picking me up, we're going out.'

***

Lamorna carried their mugs back to the hotel kitchen, and found Michael there. He was heading out to do some light work in the garden.

'Why don't you help Michael?' Aileen suggested. 'We're not too busy in here now. We need some vegetables and fruit, and I'd be happier if you were out there keeping an eye on him.'

So they went hand in hand up the garden together.

'What shall we start on first?' she asked.

'Potatoes and roots that keep well, then beans, peas. We'll get the fruit and salads last.'

They worked together side by side, Lamorna keeping a watchful eye on him. She talked to him about Jude and her plans.

'I didn't know,' he said, 'Phil's a dark horse. I thought he had his eye on you.'

'I don't think so; he seemed to believe all along that you and I were together.'

'He's always been shy with women. I don't know what's come over him.'

'It's Jude, that's what's come over him. She always has that effect on men. She's so bubbly and confident. But she's so independent; I can't believe she's thinking of settling down.'

'I thought she had something going with Ian still.'

'Oh, he knows all about it. Jude says she was just a bit of a fling. He's got some local girl.'

'I'm beginning to think I don't really know my friends at all. You girls come down here for a few weeks and turn the world upside down. I believe you had something to do with Chris naming a day too.'

'Is that enough potatoes?' she asked.

'You're changing the subject. We'll do carrots now.'

'Are you okay?'

'Yeah, fine.'

They worked on along the row, pulling the carrots and dropping them into a basket.

'I've been thinking a lot over the last few days,' he said. 'I want to try and get into agricultural college, then maybe get a smallholding somewhere. The hotel business isn't really my thing. I don't want to be cooped up indoors the whole time. I couldn't do what Dad does, it would drive me crazy.'

'That sounds fantastic. I can imagine you doing that. Would you keep animals?'

'I'm not sure. There'd have to be chickens for you to look after though.'

'Michael. You're cruel! Have you told your Mum and Dad?'

'Not yet, but I think they'll support me. Could you imagine living on a farm?'

'I don't know. I would live anywhere with you I suppose. It's so different from anything I imagined. Where would it be?'

'That's some way in the future. I don't really know. Let's pick the beans now.'

They walked behind the bean rows and Michael took advantage of the cover to grab hold of her and kiss her.

'I could imagine growing beans,' she said.

'I'd be my own boss, outdoors all the time. It would be a great place to bring up children.'

'I do love this.' she said. 'Out here with you, picking the stuff we've grown. I planted those salads. I'm really proud of them.'

'I can apply to a college near to you maybe, and we can meet at weekends. We'd better take this stuff down to the kitchen. They'll be starting to cook the dinners.'

The sun was lower now, casting shadows across their path. They reached the kitchen door and stepped into a world of bustle.

'That was a hard evening,' Lamorna said later. 'Some of those people were so rude tonight, complaining about everything. It's so difficult to be nice to them when you know they're in the wrong most of the time.'

'You get some days like that,' Mary said. 'It's like it's catching. One person says something and they all start. There was nothing wrong with that fish. They'd just never tried it before. It's such a waste when you have to go along with them and throw it out like that.'

Mary ate some dinner with them and then set off for home. Aileen and Lamorna cleared away, and they sat together later over a cup of coffee. Sam was in the bar again with Alec. Michael had been sent to bed.

'Michael has been telling me about your conversation. I'm so glad he's made a decision about his future.'

'What do you think about his idea?'

'I think it will suit him. He's not really cut out for this business. He's been an angel, helping us out when we needed him, but this is his time now. Sam will be disappointed. But I think he'll understand. He knows Michael hates to be stuck indoors. He's never really shown any interest in the business side of the work.'

'Michael asked me how I'd feel, working with him on a farm, and I didn't know what to say. I want to be with him, but I never imagined myself as a country girl.'

'You need to follow your dream too, see if it's really what you want. Then you'll know whether to follow your heart or your head. Sometimes we have to make sacrifices in our lives. For me it was giving up the plan of going to London and nursing. I met Sam. This was his dream, and when it came down to it he mattered more than my ambition.'

'Do you ever have any regrets?'

'Sometimes I wonder what might have been if I'd travelled that road, but I'm happy here.'

'I feel that I've grown up since I came here. I've learned so much.'

'I think you have, and we'll miss you. I hope that things will work out between you both. I'd enjoy having you for a daughter.'

'You feel more like a family to me now than my real one,' Lamorna said, her eyes glistening with tears. 'I can talk to you more than my own Mother.'

'Don't be hard on her; she's not had it easy, losing your Dad, bringing you up alone.'

'No, I'm sorry.'

'You know, I wonder if Michael has something of my family in his blood, they were all in farming, and a bit of fishing too. Well, we'd better get some sleep. I'll see you in the morning. Don't worry. When the time comes you'll know what you really want.'

Lamorna popped over to the cottage to get a few things. There was no sign of Jude.

'She must have stayed with Phil. How come she can be so sure of what she wants?'

Chapter 40

Lamorna watched whilst Doctor Davy examined Michael the next morning.

'Well, everything seems fine. You'll be due back in the hospital in a few days for a thorough check up, but I'd say you've recovered well. The gash has healed nicely. You'd hardly know it was there now. I don't want you rushing back to work though, so don't even think of it. Why don't you try to have a holiday for a couple of days? They can manage without you here. Take your young lady with you. Now how about you see if you can get me a cup of that wonderful coffee your mother makes. I'll be down in a few minutes.'

Michael went off, and he turned to Lamorna.

'How do you feel Michael is doing?'

'He seems great, he gets tired, and he has to take things slowly. He still doesn't remember what happened.'

'No need for concern about his memory, it's normal in this sort of case. What about you?'

'I'm fine.'

'I can see that you're close to tears.'

'I'm okay, but I feel so tired suddenly. I don't feel that I'm any use any more.'

'I think you've worn yourself out with worrying and caring for Michael, and I hear from Aileen that you've done a wonderful job. I could give you some medication, but somehow I think you're strong enough to make your own recovery.'

'I don't want any pills.'

'I'm going to prescribe a few days away with Michael. You're trying to do too much, and Michael is champing at the bit to get back to work. I need to keep him quiet until after his next hospital appointment. I think he'll get the all clear then. But we need your help still to keep Michael in order. Can you stay and go away with him?'

'I don't know. I don't know where we'd go. I'm meant to be working.'

'I'll have a word with Aileen before I leave.'

It had all been sorted when Lamorna arrived in the kitchen. Aileen had phoned Sam's sister Ellen on the Isles of Scilly, and they were to go over for a few days together.

'You'll be in good hands. Ellen nursed with me up at Truro. Couldn't think of a better idea myself,' Dr Davy said.

At half past four they were taking off. Neither had been on a helicopter flight before and they were really excited. They watched as familiar landmarks appeared below them, the hotel and harbour, Lamorna Cove, the sweep of sand at Porthcurno. The cliff looked much less daunting from up in the air. And then they left the coast behind and headed out to sea. The islands came into view, little rocky outcrops with wooded slopes surrounded by a fringe of white sand in a beautiful emerald green ocean.

Aunt Ellen was there to meet them.

'Michael. Let me look at you. I haven't seen you in ages.' She hugged him, and then stood back to look him up and down.

'Well, you look right as rain, I must say, but be warned, no overdoing it while you're in my care, or I'll never hear the last from your mother.'

'And you must be Lamorna,' she said, smiling, and then stepping forward to hug her too.

'You've found yourself a beautiful young lady Michael. Come on then, let's get your bags and get going. I've brought Ruby along to get us home.'
Ruby turned out to be an old Austin car. Ellen drove them around the island to a small village and harbour that was Old Town, parking beside a small bungalow.

They awoke next day to grey skies and rain. Michael got out his guitar and sat playing whilst Lamorna browsed Ellen's bookshelf.

'I'm meeting up with an old friend on St Agnes, and she's invited me for dinner tonight,' Ellen told them. 'I hope you don't mind, I've booked you into my favourite restaurant. It's in a great location, overlooking the harbour in Hugh Town. They owe me a few favours. I'm always sending them guests, so the meal is free.'

'Thank you Ellen, it sounds wonderful.'
She set off then to catch the 2 o'clock boat, leaving them to wash the dishes. The sky was clearing now, and a good afternoon was promised. They sat together on a garden bench with mugs of coffee.

'Your Aunt is lovely. Is your sister named for her?'

'I don't know, I never thought about it. I suppose she must be.'

'She looks very like your Dad, doesn't she? Same brown hair and eyes. I loved it when you sang and played Michael. It reminded me of when I was a girl, and I used to sneak out to the fair with my friends. They had all that music on the rides, Del Shannon, the Everly Brothers.'

'They're easy to play. I was in a pop group at school, that's low I learned them. I was lead singer. Don't think we would ever have got anywhere though.'

'But you have a lovely voice Michael.'

'It's a Cornish thing. A lot of fishermen down here sing. It's a tradition on the boats, singing when you haul in the nets. There's a big choir back in the village too. You'll hear them when you come down at Christmas. We all used to take our guitars to the beach. It was a great way of attracting girls. The others are all married now, so no chance of getting a group together again. And I was just waiting for you to come along.'

'Michael Tremayne, you're such a charmer!'

They set off for their walk, hand in hand around the cliffs to Porthcressa Beach, where they sat for a while watching children playing. Lamorna collected small sea shells, dropping them into Michael's pocket. And then they walked on around the headland where Star Castle rose up gaunt and grey, and down into the harbour at Hugh Town. They strolled down the quay. The boats were returning from the other islands now, and holidaymakers burdened with beach equipment and bags, towing children with faces smeared in ice cream struggled up the steps.

Michael suggested a quick drink in the pub before dinner, and they stepped into the nearest, right by the quay. The Mermaid was a real local, the walls adorned with flags and memorabilia from boats. A few people came up to talk to Michael, nodding an acknowledgement to Lamorna. She was introduced to all sorts of men, a few boatmen, and the crew from a racing gig, an occasional girlfriend of one or the other.

'How do you know so many people here?'

'Ellen and I used to come over and stay with Aunt Ellen and my Uncle every summer for a week or two.'

On Thursday they walked all around the island, stopping in Porthellick for a picnic. Lamorna was fascinated and appalled by the memorial there and the story of the loss of The Association in 1707.

'How could so many ships get wrecked? It's terrible.'

'It was before they knew about longitude; it was more difficult to know your exact position. Shall we go swimming?'

'I don't know. I don't know if I could after......'

'Lamorna, it will be okay, I'll look after you. I won't let you come to any harm. You made a promise to me.'

'Alright. I'll try.'

So they waded out together, hand in hand into the calm sheltered bay, and then once again he held her whilst she floated against him. After a while Michael walked further out until he could swim with her, and he slowly floated, supporting her. He took a further step so that she was supported by just one hand below her back, but she panicked, and he had to encircle her with his arms again.

'I'm sorry, I suddenly got scared.'

'You don't need to apologise. I'll just hold you and swim with you back to the shore now.'

They sat on the warm sand, letting the sun dry their bodies. Lamorna was making a little pile of stones, balancing them one on top of the other. She found a grey pebble with a complete band of white around it. She rooted in her bag for a pen, wrote 'I love you' around the white stripe, and gave it to Michael.

'Thank you. I'll always keep this.'

There was time for a quick drink in 'The Mermaid' before heading home.

'Look Michael, there's a poster. There's a folk night at the club here tonight. Why don't we come? You could bring your guitar.'

'Yeah, we could. Sounds fun.'

'Let's ask Ellen to come with us. Do you think she would?'

'She might. She used to sing when she was younger.'

Ellen was pleased to be invited, and she drove them all over in Ruby. A local band was playing, and then a couple of islanders got up to sing. Someone persuaded Ellen to sing, and Michael accompanied her for a beautiful rendition of 'The Water is Wide.' As they finished to rapturous applause Michael looked across at Lamorna. Tears were streaming down her cheeks.

'Lamorna, I'm sorry, I didn't mean to make you sad. Maybe it was a bad choice of song.'

'It's okay. It was beautiful. It made me want to be in a boat with you again. And then I thought about going away and leaving you. And then it was about love growing old and fading away. It made me feel sad.'

Ellen came over, and they sat together whilst Michael was dragged back to perform again, this time joining in with a group of locals, before accompanying himself on guitar for a couple more songs. Lamorna sat with her legs drawn up, totally entranced by him. Her eyes were bright with tears still. And she was completely overwhelmed when he dedicated his last song 'to Lamorna who saved my life.'

It was a lovely version of 'The First Time Ever I Saw Your Face.' She sat listening; and the whole way through his eyes were on her. There were cries for more, but he left the stage and came over to her. He sat beside her again, and took her hand in his.

At the end of the evening Michael was suddenly surrounded by a crowd of young people, all clamouring to talk to him and hear about his accident. Michael introduced Lamorna to them. She was completely overcome and struggled to speak, holding tightly onto him, wishing the earth would swallow her up.

Back home Ellen made them hot drinks, and they talked together for a while before bed.

'It was the most wonderful evening I've ever been to,' Lamorna said. 'You and Michael were amazing. I didn't want it to end.'

Later he made love to her so tenderly. She felt spellbound by him. And afterwards he held her close to him, stroking her face, her hair again.

'I wish I'd been the one to write those words for you,' he said. 'That's just how I felt when I first saw you, when I kissed you. It's how it will always be.'

Chapter 41

Suddenly it was Lamorna's last weekend. She and Jude had to travel back up for college on Monday morning.

'I'd like to spend the last weekend at the cottage,' Michael said.

'Well okay,' Aileen agreed, 'but you must come up for dinner every night.'

Saturday started strangely. They ate breakfast and couldn't think what they might do for the day. It seemed so important to make each moment special that they were daunted. In the end Lamorna suggested St Ives.

'I'd like to buy presents for everyone back home, and maybe explore the galleries,' she said. 'We can take a picnic.'

'And go swimming,' Michael added.

So he went off to borrow a car whilst she made the picnic.

'We've had a letter from my sister Ellen; she'll be home in a couple of weeks. I'm sorry you'll miss her,' he told her when he got back.

'Won't she be here when I come down for the wedding?'

'Maybe, who knows with Ellen?'

St Ives was crowded. They roamed the higgledy-piggledy little streets. Lamorna found a Troika vase for her Mum. She decided that her Step-dad Tom would like a book about shipwrecks, but she couldn't think what to get for her brothers. Michael suggested kites, and she thought that was an inspired idea. He was interested in looking around at the boats, and she took some photographs of him engrossed in talking to a group of fishermen on the quay. She persuaded him to visit a gallery, and they fell in love with some quirky little paintings. They were by a local fisherman who it seemed had been self-taught, painting fishing boats and harbour scenes on whatever came to hand. Lamorna had just enough money still to buy one for Michael, and she chose a small harbour scene with boats heading out to sea. It took all of the earnings she had saved.

'It will be the first painting for the walls of the home we have together one day, along with your photographs,' he said.

In a nearby shop he bought her a quirky little mermaid, carved in wood and painted.

They decided to drive to Penberth Cove for their picnic.

'I remember seeing that when we went to Porthcurno.'

'It'll be more peaceful,' Michael said. 'I want you to myself now, away from these mad crowds.'

They watched the fishermen hauling up their boats whilst they ate. Lamorna had to get some photographs. A little stream slipped between graceful reeds down to the sea, and colourful floats were bunched like strange sea plants on the granite cottage walls. It was one of the most photogenic places she'd been. Michael swam off the rocks, and she waited, heart in mouth for his return. And then they went for a short walk along the cliff top, leaving their bags in the care of the fishermen. They found themselves on the cliffs above her lagoon cove.

'So much has happened since I met you, since I got here, it feels like a lifetime's experiences, I can't believe anything so interesting could happen to me ever again.'

'What about marrying me? Wouldn't that be a bit interesting?'

'Of course, but that's something I'll choose, it won't just happen.'

They set off for home then.

'I know a great place for cream teas,' she said.

And they surprised Mary by turning up at the hotel and sitting in the garden to be served. Mary was suddenly shy, blushing when she brought their teas.

There was a sudden surge of guests, and Lamorna and Michael found themselves helping out. Michael went to collect produce for dinner, and Lamorna was back in the kitchen.

'You two are supposed to be resting,' Aileen said, concerned. 'I feel we should be paying you a wage again Lamorna.'

'Don't be silly, we're family. We've been relaxing all day, we're happy to help.' Lamorna said.

Lamorna and Michael spent Sunday around the village. They stayed in bed late, making love, and talking about their future. Lamorna made them breakfast in bed. They called in at Mary's for a late morning coffee and for Lamorna to say goodbye. She would not see much of Mary in the morning. Then they spent the rest of the afternoon packing to return to the hotel for their last night.

Aileen had made a special meal. The hotel guests had all eaten at lunch time, so it was a family gathering. Phil had been invited, and there was talk of brochures, the plans for the studio and Mary and Chris's forthcoming marriage. Michael held her hand under the table. Lamorna was worrying that there was no plan for a future with Michael. She had not wanted to be tied down, but now she was feeling forlorn. She was glad when the conversation turned to the news about Ellen.

'She phoned today,' Aileen told them. 'She says she's got lots of news and we'll never believe it. I can't imagine what she means.'

'Knowing her, it'll be some mad scheme,' Michael said.

Phil went off home at ten o'clock, and Jude disappeared back to the little cottage. The plan was for Michael to drive them both to the station in the morning.

***

'It's a horrible grey day,' Lamorna said, opening the curtains. 'The weather is in the same mood as me, it's all misty and mizzly.'

Michael groaned and burrowed under the bedclothes again. She jumped on him to get him moving, and they both got through the bathroom and went down for breakfast. Neither of them felt much like talking, and they sat in silence whilst an irrepressible Jude chattered on.

Everyone fought back tears as they piled into Sam's car. Lamorna sat in front with Michael. She was silent, dreading reaching the station. But they did arrive, and found the platform desolate. Only a few people seemed to be travelling. The train pulled in, and it was time to get on board. Michael gave Jude a goodbye hug. And then Lamorna flung herself into his arms. She held him and kissed him until the guard began to slam the doors shut, and then she had to run and throw her bags into the corridor, jumping up after them.

She pulled the window down straight away and hung out, waving, her face streaked with tears. The train gathered speed, curving away from the station, and Michael was suddenly lost to view. She stood by the window. St Michael's Mount was once more a grey mysterious shadow looming through the mist. She looked back towards the town, and then across the shore again, staring intently as Marazion came hazily into view and then disappeared again as the train swept inland away from the sea. It was as though she was trying to retain each image in her head. And only when she could no longer see Mounts Bay, and the train was cutting between fields and banks, did she go to her seat opposite Jude. She couldn't speak. She gazed out of the window, watching the stations come and go, lost in her desolation.

The train rattled onto the bridge over the Tamar. The tide was in today and the boats were shrouded in mist.

'We're leaving Cornwall,' she sobbed miserably.

'What are you moaning about? You'll see him again in a couple of weeks.'

'Yeah. You're right Jude. But I'll miss him so much. I'll miss Cornwall.'

They reached the Devon coast. She saw children paddling at the sea's edge. The sun suddenly emerged, transforming the blue sea and the red cliffs, the brightly painted beach huts into a newly painted canvas. She dried her tear streaked face and watched the glimpse of seaside disappear as they entered a tunnel.

'If the train had stopped there I could have got a brilliant photograph,' she thought. 'I want to work really hard this year. I have to finish college. Then Michael and I will be together.'

She turned to Jude.

'I wonder what we'll be doing on the course this year.'

PART TWO

1972

Lamorna wandered alone through the glasshouse. Breathing in the warm exotic scents. Soft leaves brushed against her face. She perched on the edge of the water lily pool to sip her wine and dip her hand into the water. Droplets trickled through her fingers. She could hear the distant drone of the speeches and for a moment felt a pang of guilt. She should be in there, taking photos. And yet she'd chosen to drop off her camera at home before coming out for the evening. Wanting just to be there in the moment. Enjoy it.

'We've achieved so much,' she thought. 'I can't believe that we've opened the Women's Centre at last. It's going to mean so much to so many women. It's like the most important thing I've ever done. Bigger than my work and all of that.'

A carp leapt and splashed in the pool. She felt the sudden rush of water over her hand. And suddenly she was back in the boat in Cornwall. Back in that moment when she'd been trailing her fingers through the waves. When the speed boat had swept around the headland and tipped the boat, sending her over into the sea. And Michael had leapt in and swam with her to the beach.

She thought about that summer in Cornwall when she had fallen in love with him. How she had believed they would be together forever. Until everything went wrong. Until he had betrayed her.

'All I have now is this. And my work.'
Someone called her. Sighing she picked up her glass and went back in for the final photo call.

Chapter 1

September 1968

'Oh Michael I got really high marks for my commune project and my tutor thinks I could sell the photographs. He's got a contact on a national magazine. He thinks they'd be interested.'

'That's fantastic! Will you need permission from the people in the pictures?'

'I suppose I should try, but they didn't seem to mind when we talked about it before. Phil thought I could sell them, and when I mentioned it everyone said it was a good idea. They thought it might show hippies in a good light.'

'Hard to see how you could contact them anyway. Well, we know where Heather and Martyn are. The others are probably still in Spain. And there's Paul. Who knows where he is. We never heard anything from the Police about him did we?'

'I don't suppose they'll catch him. Will you help me put some pictures up Michael?'

She rooted around for a hammer and some picture hooks, and they went into her bedroom to hang her photographs of Cornwall, pictures Phil had taken of herself and Michael on the beach in Mousehole harbour, and the one of her with Rosa and Marie, all of them smiling, wearing studio costumes and absurd hats.

'This is a great place you've got,' Michael said.

'Thanks to Jude's parents. They bought the house for her and it's the most luxurious place I've ever lived. Not the loveliest though. It can't compare with our little Cornish cottage.'

'It beats the poky little room I'm in at college. I'll try and find somewhere better next term. Can't complain though, I'm lucky to have got on the course at such short notice.'

'What's it like?'

'I think it's going to be interesting. There's lots of theory, but we get lots of hands on practical experience too.'

'Have you made any new friends?'

'Give me chance. I only got there on Wednesday. I met a couple of blokes in my Hall. We went out for a drink last night. Hardly any women on the course though.'

'That's a good thing!'

*

Jude and Joy were still in bed when they'd finished breakfast next morning and set off to walk into the town centre. They had lunch at 'The Seven Stars' where all the students congregated, and she introduced him to some people.

'He's gorgeous,' whispered Elaine, 'let me know when you're fed up with him.'

'I never will be.'

She noticed her ex-boyfriend Gary. He was sitting at the far side of the pub with a group of other men. He appeared to be avoiding eye contact with her. Michael impulsively drew Lamorna into his arms and kissed her.

'That was especially for Gary's benefit,' he whispered, and then kissed her again. 'I ought to go over and thank him for making you run away to Cornwall.'

'Don't bother. He's a waste if space. I want to take you rowing on the river now,' she said.

'Sounds great, is it far?'

'No, we'll take this stuff back to the house, and it's only a short walk from there.'

The others were only just having their breakfast when they got back.

'We had a great night,' Jude said. 'Never stopped dancing. Come with us next time you're here Michael. What are you two doing tonight?'

'Haven't thought,' Lamorna replied.

'There's a Folk Club at the Greyhound. We thought we'd go. Come with us.'

'Shall we go Michael?'

'Yes, why don't we?'

They unpacked the shopping and then set off for Darley Park. The river was flowing smooth and brown below the grassy slopes, and along the bank, tied to a wooden jetty was a fleet of rowing boats. It was the end of the season, but Lamorna knew the boatman, and he let them take one out. She insisted on rowing Michael on 'her' river.

'You're good at it, aren't you,' he said, sounding surprised.

'My Dad used to bring me here, and he taught me how to row when I was seven. At first I could only manage one oar, and we just went round in circles. And we all came out on the boats a lot before I came down to Cornwall.'

They moved peacefully down the river. It was in full spate and their progress was swift. Michael took the oars for the harder row back upstream. Lamorna leaned over and trailed her hands in the water. The only sound was the creak of oars in the rowlocks and the trickle and splash of water falling back into the river as the blades were lifted.

'Let's row together for the last stretch,' she said.

The boatman caught their rope and pulled them alongside the jetty, and they clambered ashore. The sky began to darken as they walked back to the house.

Jude had cooked for them all that evening, a huge pot of chilli with rice. They talked for a while about the commune and Lamorna's photographs.

'I only saw a small part of it all,' Lamorna said. 'I was there for such a short time, and I was out at work a lot too, or with Michael. I can't imagine many groups of people just welcoming any waif and stray like they did.'

'A bit risky, when you don't know anything about them,' Joy remarked.

'Yeah,' said Jude, laughing, 'they had no idea just how crazy Lamorna is.' Lamorna threw a beer mat at her.

'I need your friend Mary to come up and see me,' Joy said. 'There's not much time to get the dresses made if they're still intending to get married at the end of October. Barely a month. Could she come next weekend?'

'I'll phone her this evening before we go out. I hope Ian will be able to bring her.'

'It'll be great to see him again,' Jude said.

'I thought your bloke was called Phil,' Joy said.

'He is, but I'm very fond of Ian. We could all go to the club on Friday night.'

'Guess who was in the Stars at lunchtime?' Lamorna said. 'Gary. And he ignored us.'

'I heard he might get thrown off the course,' Jude said. 'He didn't do enough work last year, and he didn't finish his summer project.'

'That'll make life easier. I won't miss him. I'd better go and phone Mary.' Lamorna got up and went into the hallway. Michael went off to do the dishes.

Several minutes later she was back in the kitchen.

'She thinks they can come up on Saturday, but she'll talk to Ian and confirm it. And guess what Michael; your sister's got home. You'd better phone your Mum.'

'Is it okay to use your phone, I don't have one back in my place?'

'Of course,' Jude said. 'My parents pay the bills.' Lamorna took over his washing up tasks, and she was putting the kettle on when he reappeared.

'You won't believe this. Ellen's brought a hippy boyfriend home with her. She met him in Greece. He's Dutch. She's talking about staying to help with the hotel. She's changed her mind about going to London and getting into journalism. Dad's really pleased.'

'That's amazing, isn't it incredible how everything works out for the best in the end?' Lamorna said, hugging him.

*

The folk club was in a small grey stone built pub in Friargate. A local band was playing, and then the stage was thrown open to the floor. One or two people got up and sang, and then Jude pushed Michael forward.

'You're better than all of them, go on Michael.' He protested, but it was impossible to resist Jude. He went up to the stage, borrowed a guitar, and sat down to tune it.

'I'll just do a couple of songs I've recently been learning. This is one by Van Morrison.

He launched into 'Brown eyed girl,' and Lamorna felt he was singing just for her. It sent a shiver down her spine. She drew her feet up to the edge of the bench and leaned her chin on her knees, gazing at him in admiration. His dark curls framed his face, still tanned from the summer, and the stage lights lit up his beautiful blue eyes. He was looking at her alone as he sang.

He was persuaded to do two more songs by the enthusiastic crowd, and then stepped modestly down from the stage to the greatest ovation of the evening. The band went up for their final set. There were some familiar songs and pretty much everyone joined in. Lamorna had drunk more than usual, and was feeling light-headed and uninhibited. Much to Michael's surprise she insisted on sitting on his knee and kissing him.

'Maybe we should go home,' he said.

The others tagged along too. And they crunched their way along under the trees, gathering the dry fallen leaves and throwing them at each other.

There was no rush to get up in the morning. They lazed in bed, reading yesterday's paper.

'What shall we do next summer?' Lamorna asked. 'We could go on an adventure, unless we're needed to work in the hotel.'

'I don't think we will be; not now Ellen and Klaus are around. We could go travelling. And I've got to teach you to swim remember. Unless you book some lessons here.'

'I want you to teach me. I hate swimming pools. All that horrible chlorine smell.'

'Okay, let's go somewhere on the Mediterranean. The salty water is good for buoyancy, and it's warm.'

'Michael, can you come next weekend? When Mary and Ian are here.'

'I suppose I could, but won't it be all about planning weddings and dresses?'

'No, I just need to be measured. I want you to come.'

'Then I will, I want to come often, I'm going to miss you.'

'Me too, I can't imagine even just one whole week without you.'

Chapter 2

Michael picked up the three girls to drive them down to Cornwall for the wedding. Rooms had been reserved for them at the hotel, and Phil, who was to be the official photographer, was to share with Jude.

They arrived in time for a late dinner. Aileen was thrilled to see them all, especially Michael who had not managed to get home since leaving for college. Lamorna was meeting Ellen for the first time.

'I've heard so much about you, I couldn't wait to meet you,' she said, greeting Lamorna warmly. 'You and Michael seem to have had an even bigger adventure here than I had on my travels.'

'I don't think it felt like much of an adventure at the time,' Michael said.

Ellen and Klaus had taken over all the arrangements for the wedding, picking up on the sea theme Joy had designed for the dresses by decorating the hotel with driftwood and shells adorned with strings of pearls begged and borrowed from everyone's aunts, displays of lilies and drapes in different shades of blue and green. It looked stunning and so unusual.

By the end of the meal everyone was relaxed, and Lamorna had warmed to Ellen. They had a good discussion about Lamorna's course and discovered a common passion for beach combing.

'I got masses of shells in Greece, I'll show you them. Some of them are around the hotel in the decorations.'

'I love being in your room Michael,' Lamorna said when they were lying together in bed later. 'All the little boats and planes you made. Where's the little picture of me?'

'I took it to college with me.'

He pulled her into his arms, kissing her.

'I wish it was us getting married tomorrow,' he said after a while.

'I don't, I'd be terrified. And we wouldn't be sleeping together now.'

'Who said you can't sleep together the night before? I'd break that rule.'
***

The hotel was a scene of bustling activity the next day. The bridesmaids were gathered there to be dressed, with Joy and Lamorna adjusting the mermaid dresses and tiaras for the three little 'merry maids.' Jude was capturing each moment on camera; the smallest bridesmaid wiping her tears away when Lamorna had found her lost teddy, Tamzin sneaking outside for a crafty cigarette and one of the bridesmaid's Dads snoozing in a lounge chair. Michael, looking devastatingly handsome in a dark grey suit, came to find Lamorna.

'You look wonderful,' he told her, kissing her. 'Are you sure you won't marry me today?'

'Not possible,' she said, laughing.

'Hope he's calmer than he was last night,' he said as he left for Chris's house. Mary of course was at home, and Joy set off after a while to help her, with Jude and camera in tow.

At last they were all ready. The sun was shining on one of the warmest October days that anyone could remember. They all walked together up to Mary's house. Mary's mum had done a brilliant job and the bride was calm and smiling, with no last minute nerves. Soon they were at the Church, and processing down the aisle, Lamorna holding hands with the two youngest little bridesmaids. She looked for Michael, and he turned to smile at her and mouth 'I love you.' Chris had overcome his nerves, and spoke out so clearly that Lamorna was awed. Michael produced the wedding ring at just the right moment, and the newly-weds kissed for the first time in front of all their families. Phil was ready outside the church for the photographs, and Jude was there too, capturing the informal moments.

The reception went without a hitch too. Aileen and Mary had planned the menu, and of course 'harvest of the sea' was the theme. They'd had to provide a meat alternative for Chris as he didn't eat fish. For dessert there were Pavlovas shaped as scallop shells with fresh raspberries and clotted cream. Lamorna sat next to Michael, and she was overwhelmed with emotion, and a rush of love for him. She wrapped her leg around his, and in between courses sought out his hand, or pretended to drop a napkin so that he would bend to find it for her and she could kiss him.

Mary's dad embarrassed her in traditional style by extolling her many virtues.
'I'm so proud of our Mary today. I shall be sorry to lose her, but she's found herself a good local lad, and I know she'll be in safe hands for the voyage.'
And then he amazed everyone by adding;
'A good many folk condemned the hippies and young people coming down here, but they've been good to our Mary. I'll leave it now, because Chris will have summat to say about that too.'

Chris did have something to say on that subject. He began by thanking Frank and Kate for allowing him to marry their 'beautiful daughter' and talked about his good fortune in having the loveliest girl in Cornwall for his wife.
'I want to thank my Best Man, Michael, who helped me to have the nerve to stand up here today and do this. I couldn't have done it without him. And I want to thank Lamorna here who gave me some wise words which prompted me to name the day.'
He turned and smiled at her, making her blush.
'All of the bridesmaids have done a wonderful job. Tamzin has looked after Mary so well, and these three little maids have done us proud. I hope we shall have a little family as handsome. Thank you to Joy. I've never met her before, but she's made a proper job of all the dresses. I want to thank someone who's not here today. He's one of these hippies that we met in the summer. He's giving us his camper van when he gets back over here, and I shall take Mary away in it for our proper honeymoon next summer. Some folk didn't like them, but we found them to be helpful and generous. This is the best wedding I've ever been to. Thank you to all of you for sharing it with us. That's me done.'

A round of applause and cheering greeted his words as he sat down with obvious relief. Michael kept his promise about being brief, but couldn't resist one or two stories relating to the groom's misspent youth which caused a great deal of laughter. But he spared Chris any real embarrassment. He led the toasts, and then invited the couple to cut the cake. This was a three tiered and splendid concoction which Ellen had commissioned. It was decorated with icing shells and topped by fine silver wires bearing small birds made of white card that bobbed and floated like gulls over a fishing vessel.

More photographs were taken, and then the doors to the garden were opened and people drifted out to enjoy the sunshine. Michael was busy helping with the guests, making sure people had drinks, and tending to the needs of elderly relatives, so Lamorna took the three little bridesmaids into the garden with some of the driftwood and shell decorations, and they sat together on the lawn playing with them, arranging them on paper plates and pretending that they were mermaids enjoying a feast. Michael appeared after a while and gave them a box of little toy cars and boats.

'Sorry girls, Lamorna is needed for a few moments, she'll soon be back.'
He took her hand and led her into the hotel.
'What is it? Where are we going?'
She followed him upstairs and into his room.
'What's the matter Michael?'
He didn't reply, just took her into his arms and kissed her.
'I've been wanting to do this all day.'

He carefully took the headdress from her hair and placed it on the bookcase, and then he unzipped her dress so that she could step out of it. He hung it carefully over his chair, and then lifted her up, still wearing her under-slip, and just as tenderly set her down on the bed before quickly stripping off his own clothes and laying down beside her.

***

At last they had to move, and rose, silently pulling on their clothes. Michael placed the crown back onto her hair, slightly askew. Lamorna plucked some Rupert Bear books from his shelf, and they left his room, still flushed and a little tousled. Ellen was just on her way up the stairs.
'Wondered where you two had got to.'
'Just went for a short break,' Michael said.
'Is that what you call it?' she said, smiling.
'I've got some books to read to the mermaids,' Lamorna said, embarrassed.

She left Michael at the garden door and went out to find her little charges, gathering some sweets for them from a bowl on the way. They wanted Lamorna to put them to bed, so she went up with their Mum's, Mary's sister Catherine and Chris's cousin Nora, who was Aunt Dolly's daughter, to help with their baths and tuck them in, before reading them another story.

Once the children were settled she and Nora went together into the garden with mugs of coffee.
'I love your girls Nora,' Lamorna said. 'They have such imaginations.'

'Yes, they enjoyed the mermaid games you played with them. And my Mum's great. She loves to play dressing up games with them. I just wish my Dad had lived to see them.'

'Mary told me that he died when you were young. My Dad did too. Isn't it strange that we both lost our fathers in tragic accidents?'

'What happened to your Dad?'

'He worked on the railway. He got knocked down and killed by shunting wagons.'

'Do you miss him?'

'Yes. We were really close. And my mum would never talk about him. I got this idea in my head that it was all my fault. I think they'd been arguing about me. She married again, and I've got two brothers now.'

'My mum never married again. She said she'd had enough of men. I don't know whether you've heard. My dad was a bit of a womaniser. He was so good looking. He couldn't resist the women who fell for him. He always won my Mum back round afterwards. She says she always knew when he'd been seeing someone.'

'That must have been hard for her. Why did she stay with him? I'd have sent him packing.'

'Me too. I think she stuck it out for our sake. We adored him when he was around. After we'd got over losing him things got better. There was less of an atmosphere at home, no rows. And mum seemed to relax and enjoy us more. I still miss my dad though. I'd like to ask him why he did what he did. Why he got involved with other women. Sometimes I wonder what might have happened if he'd lived.'

'I know what you mean. When my mum got married things were calmer. I hated it at first, but it took the pressure off me. And she seemed to be happier than when Dad was alive. I resented that, I felt she was betraying him. But it made it better for me. The new babies got her off my back, and I had more freedom.'

'My mum said she wouldn't be surprised if there aren't some other kids around that are my Dads. We used to think we could track them down. But we wouldn't really know where to start. Best not to know really. Come on, we'd better get back into the fray.'

Back indoors a space had been cleared for dancing, and Mary's cousin's folk band was tuning up for the evening entertainment. Lamorna managed to share a few moments with the bride.

'I'm so happy,' Mary said, 'This is the best day of my life.'

'It's a lovely wedding, and Chris's speech was amazing. You're so lucky to have him.'

'Well it has to be you and Michael next. Why didn't you try to catch my flowers? I was aiming them at you.'

'I thought Tamzin was the priority, she hasn't got anyone at the moment, and I know I will marry Michael one day soon.'

Mary was called away to join Chris in farewells to some family members. Lamorna looked around for Michael, but couldn't find him. She wandered into the kitchen, looking for a job, and found Aileen with her feet up.

'I'm whacked, fancy a cup of tea?'

Lamorna put the kettle on, and they sat together at the table, chatting about the day. That was where Michael found them when he reappeared wearing a tee shirt and jeans, guitar in hand.

"Are you playing tonight?' Lamorna asked.

'The band asked me to join them for a few songs.'

'Well, that will be lovely, I never get to hear you,' Aileen said. 'Will your Aunt Ellen be persuaded?'

'I hope so, I'll ask her.'

He went off then to sort out the lighting with Klaus. The guests were all in the bar now, Sam and Alec serving drinks.

'We could do more weddings,' Aileen said. 'Never really promoted that idea before.'

'It's a perfect place,' Lamorna said, especially on a day like this with the garden.'

'Can't guarantee good weather though.'

'It's lovely to see Michael's Aunt Ellen again; we had such a good time with her in the summer. I didn't realise she would be here today.'

'Her husband was Chris's Dad's brother,' Aileen told her.

Lamorna danced with Michael, and then he left her with Mary and Chris whilst he went up on stage to accompany Ellen in a couple of songs. Aileen managed to get out of the kitchen to hear them, and there were tears in her eyes as she listened to Michael sing.

'This is a request from the groom for his bride,' he said, launching into a haunting version of 'Can't help Falling in Love.'

As he sang he looked at Lamorna from time to time. Aileen had to go and find tissues for them all. Eventually the night had to end, and the bride and groom went off to their honeymoon suite at the top of the hotel. The room had just been created by Ellen, and had its own private bathroom and a magnificent four poster bed with filmy net curtain drapes. There were arrangements of lilies in the room, and a shelf of books, mainly love poetry that Ellen had read for her English degree.

'Don't suppose anyone will read them, but you never know,' she said.

Michael and Lamorna tumbled into bed together, and she lay caressing him.

'I'm sorry,' he said after a while. 'I'm no good for anything, too much to drink.'

He kissed her, and then was almost immediately asleep. She lay awake for a while, thinking about the wedding, wondering when she and Michael would marry, wondering if Mary and Chris were making love, or were too exhausted and sleeping now. She thought about Michael's singing, and hugged herself at the memory of the way he had looked at her. She rolled over to hold him in her arms, and lay stroking him as he slept.

Chapter 3

She woke to sunlight streaming through a gap in the curtains and a chorus of gulls. And just as if he knew she had woken Michael came through the door with a mug of tea for her.

'What would you like to do today,' he said, as he opened the curtains to let the day in, and leant over to kiss her.

'I would really like to spend the whole day in bed with you, but maybe people will think we're trying to upstage the happy couple.'

'Not sure I'm brave enough under this roof.'

'Well, I would like to walk to Lamorna Cove with you.'

'Okay, that sounds good. I'm just helping to clear up downstairs, and then I'll come and get you for breakfast.'

Lamorna was emerging from the bathroom when Michael reappeared.

'Breakfast is served, I'd better go, or we'll end up following your first plan,' he said, as she dropped the towel she was wearing to start dressing.
The dining room had been transformed again, with clean white cloths and lilies on each table. She found Michael sitting with Jude, Phil and Joy. There was no sign of the newlyweds. They were talking about the wedding, all agreeing that it was the most amazing they'd been to. Joy was pleased with the dresses, and said she had received many compliments and possible orders for the future.

'What are your plans for the day?' Jude asked. 'We're thinking of going over to St Ives.'

'I've got some more to do here,' Michael said. 'Then we thought we'd walk along the coast.'
He went off to help sort out the bar with Sam, and Lamorna headed for the kitchen with the breakfast dishes. She loaded them into the dishwasher and set it running. The weekend girls were at work, busy upstairs doing the bedrooms vacated by wedding guests.

'You shouldn't really be working,' Aileen told her. 'You're a guest. But I'm glad of your help.'

'I like to think of myself as family, if that's alright with you.'

'Of course, and I hope it will be official someday soon. Would you want a wedding like this one?'

'I don't know. I never imagined such a grand occasion, but it was lovely, wasn't it?'

'Your friend's designs for the dresses were so unusual. I can't wait to see the photographs.'

'You did a great job with the little bridesmaids Lamorna. They've left you some pictures.'

Lamorna looked through the drawings. There was one picture of three little mermaid figures in blue, and a picture of her with her name and 'I love you' written in a childish hand and a line of little kisses along the bottom.

'They're lovely, how sweet of them.'

Michael appeared.

'Shall we go for our walk now? We could do a circular walk, start off on the field paths and then come back along the cliffs, what do you think?'

'That sounds nice.'

They drew level with the house where the commune had been set up.

'It's hard to believe that it's only a couple of months since I was living there,' Lamorna said. 'It seems a lifetime ago.'

The house was being renovated. There was scaffolding around the walls and the garden was piled up with building materials, heaps of sand and roof slates. The vegetable plot was covered in a heap of building stone.

'I wonder if we'll meet any of them again.' Lamorna said.

'Dad managed to sell his share in the house. He's trying to decide how to invest the money. He asked me if I wanted to help choose a cottage that he could renovate and maybe one day we could live in when we're married.'

'What about Ellen and Klaus?

'They don't want a cottage. They're talking about finding a flat in Penzance.'

'A flat?'

'Yeah, Ellen's an ambitious type. Mum's upset because she told her she doesn't want children.'

'Michael, do you want children?'

'I would I think, but it depends on you.'

'I would someday, especially if they were like you. I loved playing with the little bridesmaids. What about your Dad's idea? Won't you want a farm? A cottage here wouldn't be much use.'

'I suppose. But it all seems so far into the future. I've got three years of this course yet.'

They were walking through a farmyard now. The sea a distant blue line above the fields. A group of black and white cattle stared at them over a fence. Michael carried her across a yard thick with mud and slurry. At last the path began to climb down to the village of Lamorna.

'I haven't noticed the field where I used to picnic with Mum and Dad, the one where I was supposed to have been conceived,' she said.

'Maybe some of the hedges have been taken out. That's happened in some places round here.'

'It was a field full of wildflowers.'

'They may be gone. The farmers use chemical fertilisers now and weed killers.'

'That's a shame.'

The 'Lamorna Wink' was open, so they called in for a drink. Neither of them was hungry, so they just shared a packet of crisps. And then it was a downhill walk to the harbour. Lamorna spotted Chris's Aunt Dolly's house just as two young women were walking up the path.

'There's Dolly's younger daughters.'

'I went out with one of them once. The one with hair a bit like yours.'
Lamorna looked back, and glimpsed the girl as she went in through the door. Her hair was similar, a dark auburn shade, but cut short in a neat bob.

'I was talking to Nora about their Dad. About him dying.'

'Yeah, he was drowned. They think he got his legs tangled in his lobster pot ropes and pulled overboard. But you know he wasn't well thought of. Had a bit of a reputation. He was one for the women.'

'Nora said.'

They reached the small beach and kicked off their shoes to paddle together at the water's edge before setting off to climb the steep path up from the bay.

Aileen was preparing the evening meal with Ellen when they arrived back at the hotel. The others had not yet come back from their expedition.

'Where's Dad?'

'Gone down to 'The Ship' with Klaus.'

'That's unheard of.'

'I sent him to get him out from under my feet. I thought he needed a break. We've been so busy. Alec's already in the bar, so he wasn't really needed. And Aunt Ellen's gone for a rest.'

'Where are Mary and Chris?'

'They got up at lunch time, and then went back up to their room. Haven't seen a sign of them since,' Aileen said, smiling.

'Can I do anything to help?' Lamorna asked.

'You could get me some herbs if you would. Take Michael with you out of the way.'

'Sounds like an anti-men thing going on. Let's get out of here,' Michael said, laughing.

They picked up a basket and wandered up the garden. There was parsley and mint to gather. And then they sat on a bench together for a while, holding hands and looking out over the sea.

There were seven of them round the table for dinner. Jude had rung to say they would be eating out in St. Ives, and Klaus and Ellen were out with an old school friend of hers in the village.

'That was the best wedding ever,' Lamorna said.

'It was lovely,' Aileen said. 'I can't believe everything went like clockwork.'

'And no fights,' Chris remarked. 'Every wedding I've been to somebody got into a fight.'

'Tamzin can't believe she caught the bouquet. I told her I was aiming it at you Lamorna.'

'But I don't need a good luck charm, I've got Michael.'

'Klaus seems like a good bloke.'

'He is Michael. His parents run a hotel in Amsterdam,' Sam said. 'He's got some good new ideas for the hotel. I worry that he and Ellen might try to do too much too soon though. We need to be sure we can sustain the business, especially with the two of them to support out of the profits.'

'It's only like you and Mum supporting me and Ellen though, what's the difference?'

'Well, they want a place of their own for a start.'

'Klaus is paying for that,' Aileen said. 'What we have to realise in this business is that most of our guests are older people who've always come down to Cornwall. We're hoping the new brochure that you made Lamorna will attract some younger visitors, but it's hard to see how a small village like this can compete with Newquay and the bigger resorts.'

'I suppose there's not much here for young people to do, you can't surf, there's no clubs for dancing,' Lamorna said.

'The honeymoon suite's a good idea,' Chris said. 'Honeymooner's aren't needing all that stuff.'

Mary blushed profusely.

'I think we'll get families booking the cottage,' Sam said.

'You could provide some children's games and beach stuff for the families coming down by train,' Lamorna suggested. 'When I was a child we stayed up the road in a caravan once, and you even had to bring your own sheets and towels. It was a lot to carry on the train. My poor Dad used to have to carry two big cases up and down the train so that Mum could find the perfect seat.'

'Good point Lamorna. We already provide the linen, but it's a bit too late to mention the games and toys in the brochure.'

'I'm thinking of getting the cottage into the local tourist guide, so we can put it into that. Don't see why we can't provide all of that at the hotel too.'

'I'll donate my Rupert Bear annuals to the cottage,' Michael said.

'I want to keep the one I read to you in hospital.'

'Have you remembered anything about the accident yet?' Chris asked.

'No, probably never will.'

Later Chris suggested a quick walk to the pub.

'Why don't you come with us Aileen?' Lamorna asked.

'You go,' Sam urged. 'Give them something to talk about that will. Both of us down there in one day.'

'I will then. Haven't been for years.'

The Ship was quiet, and they pulled together two tables so that they could sit by the open fire. Aileen had a look around, noticing some new photographs on the wall.

'Torrey Canyon. What a mess that was. Not seen this picture before.'

A few people came over to congratulate Mary and Chris, and Mary showed off her ring. The landlord gave them all a drink on the house. Michael and Lamorna were sticking to ginger beer.

'Too much alcohol yesterday and I've got the drive to do tomorrow,' Michael said.

Chapter 4

At the end of November Michael and Lamorna drove down to Cornwall again. They had been invited to the official opening of Heather and Martyn's Gallery. Phil was there, recording the event.

The Gallery's first exhibition was an eclectic mix of Cornish landscapes by local artists. There were canapés and champagne flowed. Heather and her parents were thrilled when they managed to sell five paintings. Afterwards Michael and Lamorna stayed to help clear up.

'Phil suggested that we could show your Cornish photographs,' Martyn said. 'We saw some of your pictures of the standing stones in his studio window. What do you think?'

'I don't think they would be good enough,' she protested.

'That's not what Phil says, and I'd trust his judgement. We thought about your Commune photos too.'

'I'm not sure what I think about all the locals viewing them, especially where we're all naked on the beach,' Heather said.

'Lamorna might be getting them into a magazine,' Michael said.

'I forgot to tell you, it's going ahead. I took them over to show the editor last week. They're going to pay me hundreds. I don't know if I'd be allowed to exhibit them as well.'

'An exhibition could help promote the magazine, think about it,' Martyn said.

'My tutor did say I'd keep the copyright, so perhaps I will. It would be fun. You can have the pictures of stones. They're all mounted or framed from my course exhibition.'

'Shall we open with them in the New Year? We might sell some too. Then we could show your others when the magazine is out.'

'I think they'll be in the April issue.'

'Perfect timing, the place will be getting busy with tourists then, it should attract a lot of attention.'

Back at the hotel that evening Michael proudly told everyone about Lamorna's success, much to her embarrassment.

'I'll open a bottle of champagne to celebrate,' Sam said.

Michael groaned, 'Not for me, we had two glasses at the Gallery.'

'I don't need any thank you, just some dinner,' Lamorna said.

'Hint taken,' Aileen said, smiling, and headed off to the kitchen.

'We forgot to show you the brochures you designed last time you were here,' Sam said. 'We were so busy with the wedding that it slipped my mind.'

He went off to his office, coming back with one of each.

'They look miles better than I imagined, she said, looking through them. 'Oh, they've got my name on too.'

'Of course, you should get credit for all your work.'

'May I keep these two for my portfolio?'

'Yes, they're yours.'

'There's an invitation for you behind the clock,' Sam said.

Michael went over and opened the envelope.

'It's from Mary and Chris, they're inviting us for Sunday lunch at the cottage tomorrow.'

He handed it to Lamorna, and she read it through.

'That's lovely, but will we have time?'

'If we leave straight afterwards we should get to your place my mid evening and I don't have to be at college until three o'clock next day. Let's do it.'

'It'll be great to see the cottage again, and Mary and Chris of course,' she said.

*

Just before noon on Sunday morning they walked together through the village and around the harbour to the little cottage that Michael had renovated and where they had made a home together for a while in the summer. They called in at the newsagents to buy some chocolates. Sam had given them some wine to take.

'They've been married a month now. I wonder how it's going,' Lamorna said, as they reached the familiar blue door. 'It feels funny knocking on the door that used to be ours. I'm not sure how I'll feel about this.'

Mary opened the door and immediately gave her a big hug.

'We're looking after your cottage for you,' she said. And that made her feel better.

Indoors it was very much as it had always been. There were a few new knick knacks here and there, but the vases were full of flowers and the lovely cushions and rugs looked just the same.

'Married life suits you Mary, you look really happy,' Lamorna said when they were alone in the kitchen together.

'I am. I can recommend it. You should try it some time. Dinner's ready, will you help me serve?'

Chris opened the wine and they toasted the cottage and the couple's one month anniversary.

'Well, a month this Thursday, ' Mary said. 'I love it here. It'll be hard to move when we find our own place. I think the cottage should have a name though.'

'Never thought of that,' Michael said. 'Bit late for the brochure though. What do you suggest?'

'Fisherman's Haunt?'

'Sounds a bit spooky.'

'How about Husband's Trap,' laughed Chris, and received a crumpled tea towel on his head.

'Only joking. Seriously though, you did a proper job on this place. We love being here.'

Mary had made roast beef dinner and they all enjoyed it. Chris and Michael talked about fishing and Rugby football. Lamorna and Mary talked about the cottage, and Mary's plans for their eventual house. After dinner they looked at the wedding photographs.

'Phil did a great job,' Lamorna said.

There was a second album of the informal shots that Jude had taken, which Lamorna had seen at college.

'In a way I prefer these,' Mary said. They're more real somehow. Look at this one Michael.'

It was a photograph of he and Lamorna kissing just before he'd set off to take Chris to church.

'Ah, I didn't know she'd taken that.'

'We're all waiting for you two to get hitched,' Chris said.

'Might be Ian and Maureen next,' Mary said.

'Joy says we can have all the dresses back soon. Her exhibition was brilliant, and she got the highest grade in her year. We'll bring them all down for you at Christmas.'

'That's great, the little ones are always asking about them.'

'We'd better get going, it's two o'clock and I've got a long drive ahead.'

'Thank you for the lovely dinner,' Lamorna said. 'We'll see you when we come down for Christmas. Don't forget you're always welcome to come up and stay with us if you fancy some city lights.'

'Thanks, but we probably won't,' Mary replied.

Chapter 5

Lamorna spent the Saturday before Christmas with her family, swapping presents and catching up on news. Michael picked her up on the Sunday morning. It was the first time he'd met her family. There was a slightly awkward atmosphere Lamorna thought. Michael was an instant hit with her brothers, helping them to sort out a problem with an Airfix model they were struggling to put together.

'He seems nice, and he's Cornish,' her mother said rather oddly.

It was a relief to get going.

'Sorry Michael, they're a strange bunch.'

'Not strange, just a bit constrained. I don't know why your mother was asking me all those questions about my name, and where we lived.'

'They're not used to visitors, and I've never taken a boyfriend home before. I wonder what they've given me.'

She shook the parcel, and heard a rattling sound. They were tired when they arrived in Cornwall and the supper was most welcome. The traffic had been dreadful with a huge tailback following an accident at Indian Queens. So it was gone midnight when they eventually got to bed.

On Monday it was 'Tom Bawcock's Eve,' a quirky village event celebrated every year. Sam and Aileen went down with them to the pub for the evening, leaving Ellen and Klaus in charge of the hotel. There were a few guests staying over the holiday. Mary and Chris were already ensconced in their favourite seats, and had saved spaces for them.

'I'm thinking of making a study of Cornish Customs my theme for the year,' she told them, 'then I have an excuse to come down often. I'll get some shots tonight.'

'You don't need an excuse to come and stay, you're welcome any time,' Aileen said. She and Sam went over to join some friends.

Lamorna took photographs of the locals crowded round the bar; some of a group of older fishermen seated near the fire, and then captured the moment when the Stargazey pie was brought out.

'What's in the pie?' she asked.

'Pilchards and potato mainly,' Michael told her. 'It's the pilchards that are gazing up at the stars.'

'Where's Jude?' Mary asked.

'She's coming down tomorrow. She's at her parents. She's got her own car now.'

'I'll never want to drive,' Mary said. 'What about you?'

'It would be useful, but I can't afford the lessons.'

'I thought I'd teach you, Mary' Chris said. 'You could help drive the camper van when we go off next summer. If that American keeps his promise and brings it back down.'

'I'd be too scared. A big thing like that.'

'You could use some of your money from the magazine to have lessons,' Michael said, 'and I'll take you out to practise.'

'Would you Michael? Wouldn't we argue though?'

'I'll never argue with you.'

'That's cloud cuckoo land,' Mary said, laughing. 'You should hear me and Chris sometimes. The best bit is making up again afterwards.'

'Yeah, you wait until you're married, you'll always be in trouble. "You've left your clothes on the floor, Look at the mud on the kitchen floor from your boots. What's all this stuff in the kitchen?'

'Well you do those things Chris!'

'See what I mean,' he said. 'But I wouldn't swap my Mary for anything.'

Michael and Lamorna lingered by the harbour railings on their way home, admiring the Christmas lights. Lamorna took some photographs, fascinated by the reflections rippling in the water.

'It's lovely. I love the wriggly patterns of light.'

Later they had cocoa in the hotel kitchen with Aileen and Sam. Klaus and Ellen had gone off to their new flat in Penzance.

'I'm glad you could come down and spend Christmas with us Lamorna,' Aileen said. 'But won't your parents be missing you?'

'No, not really, I don't see them that often now, and there's nowhere for me to sleep. I had to take a sleeping bag and curl up on the sofa the night before we came down here.'

'That's a pity, but their loss is our gain. Just remember though, you two are on holiday, so don't go thinking you've got to work in the hotel.'

On Christmas Eve they went shopping for presents. They decided to get a cinema voucher for Aileen and Sam.

'They never go out, and they should now that Ellen is in charge,' Michael said. Pleased with all their purchases they caught the bus back home, and sneaked upstairs for some furtive wrapping.

'This is the best bit of Christmas,' Lamorna said, 'I love getting presents for people.'

Michael disappeared for a moment, and then came back into the room with a smile on his face.

'Do you want to know what my favourite Christmas thing is?' he asked.

'Yes, what is it? Is it Christmas pudding?'

'No, it's this.'

He held a piece of mistletoe over her and kissed her.

'Trouble is,' he said after a while, 'I need more practise. It's only once a year.' She laughed.

'When we've finished the parcels we could have a practice session couldn't we?'

'Think so, there's an hour before dinner.'

*

Lamorna was the first to wake on Christmas morning, feeling something heavy at the end of the bed. Michael seemed to be sleeping still. She shuffled her feet, and heard the crackling of paper. She sat up and saw a long red sock, bulging with lumpy packages.

'Oh, it's a stocking.'

'What did you say?' Michael murmured sleepily.

'I said I've got a stocking, a woolly red sock. Happy Christmas Michael.'

She leaned over and kissed him.

'Thought I heard something in the night. Santa must have visited. You'd better look. I'll go and make us some tea.'

He pulled on jeans and a sweat shirt and set off for the kitchen. When he reappeared with a tray she had already opened the parcels. There was a brush for cleaning her camera lens, some chocolate, a little notebook and pencils, massage oil and some packets of flower seeds.

'Michael, you shouldn't have. You're lovely. Everything is perfect. I love this necklace.'

She was wearing a necklace threaded with small sea shells.

'I made it for you with all the shells you stuffed in my pockets when we were on the beach at St Mary's.'

'It's beautiful, thank you.' I don't know what this is.' She held up a 45 rpm single record. 'It doesn't say who the artist is. What is it?'

She read the label. 'The first Time ever.' Turned it over and read the other side. 'Love me Tender.'

'Tell me about it Michael.'

He smiled shyly.

'Take it home and play it, and then you'll know.'

Chapter 6

A new term began. Lamorna received her money for the commune photographs from the magazine, and they were interested in looking at her pictures of Cornish customs. She showed them the photographs of Tom Bawcock's Eve, and as a result she was commissioned. It meant more visits to Cornwall during the year to document a variety of events. She passed her driving test first time, and was able to share the driving when she and Michael went down to Cornwall to attend the opening of an exhibition of her photographs in Heather and Martyn's gallery.

Mary and Chris moved out of the cottage and into a house near to her Mum and Dad. The cottage had the first of many holiday bookings at Easter, and so Lamorna and Michael always stayed in his room at the hotel when they visited. Sam and Aileen had bought a second cottage for renovation.

Rosa and Ced came back from their travels at the beginning of July, and handed the camper van over to Chris. They had caught up with Laura and Jean in Spain, and it seemed that they were intending to stay over there indefinitely. Ced took Rosa and Dylan back home with him to the States.

Their college years ended in July, and Michael and Lamorna had both done well. Even Jude had worked hard and improved her grades. After a brief visit to Cornwall Michael and Lamorna set off for their trip to Europe. They stayed with Klaus' parents, Hilda and Hans for a while in Amsterdam. Michael celebrated his birthday there. Lamorna sent a postcard to Jude and Phil;

We've explored the canals and hired bikes. There's this amazing park. All over the grass there are 'hippies' in sleeping bags, just waking up after a night. Nobody minds at all. And you can smoke pot here too and not be arrested. Michael was tempted, but I wouldn't let him, even if it is his birthday.

They hitch hiked their way down to Yugoslavia. Lamorna wrote to Aileen and Sam;

'We've travelled down south of Dubrovnik and found a quiet place to stay. We've been here for two weeks now. Washed my knickers and left them to rinse at the water's edge, weighed down with stones. Michael says there are no tides. But there must be, because they all got washed away. Only got one pair now!

And I can swim!! We've practised for days and I can swim on my own. I'm best at the crawl. Getting better every day and I love it! Spent more money than we should celebrating my success at a little bar down the beach. Ate some fried fish and potatoes. Michael has spent a lot of time looking at fishing boats!! We've tried some pastry and meat pies, a bit like Cornish Pasties'

There was a note from Michael here, *No they're not!!*

******

The next year flew by. Lamorna and Jude finished their course at the end of the summer term. Lamorna succeeded in getting a first. She and Michael went to Ireland for a few weeks in the summer. Lamorna had her camera, and she took a series of photographs of the barbed wire across streets and the political graffiti in Belfast. They were nearly in trouble when someone saw her photographing armed soldiers, and decided to leave the city very quickly.

At the end of their holiday they spent a couple of weeks with Aileen's parents at their farm in Sligo. Michael had only visited a few times, the last occasion when he'd been a boy of fifteen, and they were delighted to have his company again. His Grandfather, also Michael, was pleased he was interested in farming, and they were both drawn into helping out with the animals and vegetable plot. Lamorna renewed her acquaintance with chickens, and enjoyed baking soda bread with Michael's grandmother. She took lots of photographs.
'I'm going to make an album for your Mum Michael.'

On the way home they came across a market near Cork, and there were ponies and donkeys for sale. Lamorna fell in love with a donkey foal, and would have bought it if Michael hadn't intervened.
'One day you shall have one, when we get some land. But where would you keep it now? How would we get it home?'

At the end of summer Michael began his final year at college, and Lamorna and Jude went off together for a holiday in Greece. They set off in September, travelling by train through France to Venice, where they spent a wonderful day exploring the city.
'I'll have to come back some time and get some more photographs,' Lamorna said. 'It's amazing.'
From Venice they travelled deck class on the ferry. There were a couple of friendly Americans on board, and they spent time with them, improvising games of deck quoits and playing cards into the early hours. Jude started a relationship with Jed, sleeping with him on deck each night behind a lifeboat. It was difficult for Lamorna. She liked Dan, but had to explain to him that she had a boyfriend and wanted to stay faithful to him. Jude was cross.
'You're no fun Lamorna. Why don't you try, you might like it. It's harmless.'
Luckily Dan understood. He had a girl back home, and was content to sit and chat with her. They talked about life in the States, and she told him about her time in Cornwall and meeting Ced.

They arrived in Rhodes early one morning. The sun just rising over a liquid gold sea. Lamorna took so many photographs.
'It's so beautiful. Look at the colour of the walls Jude, and all those purple flowers.'
There were yet more strained moments between the two women. They had found a friendly pension and met up with a group of other young travellers. Jude started a fling with an Australian, and tried to put pressure on Lamorna to go with his friend. Lamorna once again found herself explaining that she was otherwise 'engaged.' They were hanging out with a larger group this time, and not everyone was pairing up, so it made things easier for her. But she felt that her friendship with Jude was tested to the limit.

After visiting a few other islands, they returned to the mainland, intending to visit Delphi and then head for Crete. Ellen had given them some ideas about where to stay and the location of the 'hippy' caves.

Back in Athens Lamorna called into the Post Office and found she had two letters from Michael. She read and re-read them. And then they set off for Delphi. They stayed a night in a hostel there, and next day climbed Parnassus. Lamorna was thinking about Michael the whole time. It had been six weeks since she had seen him, and she missed him.

'Jude, I'm going to ask the Oracle what to do,' she said. 'I want to be here, but I want to go home and see Michael too. I miss him so much.'

'You'd be crazy to go back, Jude said, 'It's lovely here, and we'll have a great time on Crete.'

'I know, but when I read his letters it made me pine for him.'

She lay back on the warm hillside and asked the question in her head as she drifted into sleep. Waking a while later, she knew what she must do. She felt the pull of thread that joined her to Michael, and her heart flooded with joy when she thought of seeing him again.

'I'm sorry Jude, I have to go.'

'Please yourself. I'm staying.'

So they hitch-hiked back to Athens. Lamorna put up a sign in the youth hostel asking for a partner to travel back to England with, and was immediately in luck. A young English student was heading home, and pleased to have an attractive woman for company.

'It'll help me get lifts,' he said. 'People don't stop for men.'

She felt awful leaving Jude, but her friend seemed unconcerned, planning to leave for Crete the next day.

Lamorna found her travelling companion Rick a little difficult. He was eager to accept every lift, and she had to argue with him.

'We can't take a lift to some village a few miles away, we could get stuck there for ages,' she insisted, 'We're better to stay here where people are coming off the boat and may be going further.'

He begrudgingly agreed, and she was proved right when a friendly Italian stopped for them and said he was heading for Rome. They arrived in the city at mid-day and Giovanni took them to a restaurant where he ordered lunch for them. Lamorna was worried. She had very little money. A huge plateful of spaghetti was plonked in front of her, and she ate it eagerly. It was very different from the spaghetti she and Michael had made. She politely accepted seconds, and was pleased when their host seemed delighted, but was then dismayed when more food was brought out, a huge platter of fish and potatoes and other vegetables. It was a struggle to keep eating.

Lamorna relaxed a little more after a few glasses of wine. She had been thinking about how much time she was wasting when she could be on the road, heading for home and Michael. But the company was pleasant, and the food and wine had a soporific effect.

'I can't believe how kind people are,' she thought, 'taking pity on scruffy travellers, wining and dining them in the most amazing places.'

She thought back to her adventures with Jude, how they had always managed to get good lifts, and how they had been invited for meals with families, given fruit for their journeys, how people had gone out of their way to show them interesting sites, or deliver them to a place where they could stay.

'I should stop fretting, I'll be home soon enough, and anyway Giovanni says he can take us further tomorrow. We might save more time than if we try to go now.'

Lamorna pulled out her purse when the bill arrived, noticing that Rick did not follow suit. But Giovanni waved it away and paid for it all. She tried to protest, but he wouldn't hear of it. He looked at his watch then, and managed to tell them in fairly good English that they should go with him to a small hotel, where they could book a room for the night, and enjoy a short siesta. He said he had business in the evening, and reminded them that he would be travelling north to Padua in the morning and would take them on their way. Rick thanked him effusively. Lamorna was not so sure. She managed to tell Giovanni that she and Rick were not partners, but it seemed that they would share a twin room.

Luckily Rick showed no interest in her, and she was grateful when he went out to explore, leaving her to rest in the room. It was hot, and she had drunk more wine than usual, so couldn't face trudging round the City. She lay on the cool sheets, reading Michael's letters again.

After an hour or so she was feeling better, and decided she might venture out for a while now that the afternoon was cooling. She crossed the landing to the bathroom, and enjoyed a refreshing shower, singing joyfully. She thought about Michael again, and how she would soon be with him. She thought about their time in Ireland, remembering how they had worked together on his grandparent's small farm, helping with the harvest, learning how to milk the goat. It seemed far away from the bustle of Rome. Wrapping a towel around her she opened a window to let out steam, and looked out over the red terracotta rooftops. There were doves preening themselves on a nearby ridge, and several scrawny cats lay sprawled below on a flat roof. A woman was hanging out washing in a courtyard, singing to herself. Somewhere there were church bells ringing. A clamorous clanging, very different from the church bells back home.

The door swung open. Giovanni walked in. Shut and bolted the door.

Chapter 7

He grabbed her and pulled her to him. Dragged off her towel.

'No, no, don't. Please don't.'

He pushed her against the door of a cupboard. His hands were all over her. She fought against him. But he was too strong. He pulled her down onto the floor.

She struggled, writhing against him to free herself. He gripped her more fiercely, his nails digging into her arms. She knew she should scream. But she couldn't. He pushed into her. She was shoved towards the toilet. Her head hit the pedestal. A smell of urine on the mat. She clenched herself against him. Inside her head she was screaming stop stop. She tried to focus on the sounds from outside; the gentle cooing of the doves, the clamour of car horns. But it was impossible to ignore the grunting, ignore his body heavy on her, crushing her. It went on and on.

He groaned. Slumped over her. She kept her eyes closed tight. His breath in her face. Stale alcohol-stinking gasps. She felt him move away after a while. Heard the sounds of a zip being fastened, a splash of water in the basin. She curled herself into a ball, arms protectively around her body.

He spoke again, something about going out. Back later. Shopping. Enjoying herself. Then it went quiet. She waited a few moments. Crawled to the door, pulled herself up and leaned against it. Pushed the bolt into place. She saw that there was blood on the mat. Sobbing now she dropped the plug into the bath, and ran the water. She lowered herself into the comforting warmth.

'What have I done wrong, why does this keep happening to me? Why can't I stop it? What's wrong with me? Michael, Michael I need you. Please come and help me.'

And then she was suddenly alert.

'I've got to get out of here before he comes back.'

She clambered out of the bath, picked up her towel from the floor and quickly rubbed herself dry. She tried to scrub the stain from the mat, but the traces were there still, a smear of pale red spreading through the tufts. There was a pile of bank notes on top of her clothes. She picked them up with a shudder of disgust. Went to throw them down the toilet, only at the last minute changing her mind. She pulled her clothes on, pushing the notes into her pocket, and cautiously opening the door, looked quickly each way along the corridor.

There was no-one. No sound. She crept quietly into her room. No sign of Rick. Good. She didn't want to have to explain. She stuffed her belongings into her rucksack. A sudden scrape of a chair on the floor above startled her. She felt her heart beating wildly. Taking a deep breath she slung the bag on her shoulder. Tiptoed from the room.

There was only a woman on reception downstairs, busy in animated conversation on the telephone. Lamorna stepped swiftly out into the late afternoon light, and walked away. After half an hour she felt safe enough to stop, and looked around for some kind of signpost, some way of showing where she was, and where the station might be. She saw a familiar landmark, the Coliseum, and taking her life in her hands she zigzagged across the highway, dodging the seething traffic, trying to ignore the outrage of car horns, to see if there might be a tourist guide. Someone who could help. A group of people were standing, taking photos. She went up to them.

'Excuse me, can you tell me the way to the station please?'

'Sure honey.' A friendly man in peaked cap and shades smiled at her. He opened a map and pointed out the route to her. She took out her notebook, and quickly wrote down the directions.

'Someone's raped me. Can you tell? Someone's just raped me.' The words pounded in her head. She just thanked them and went on her way.

Once at the station she scanned the departure board. A train was leaving for Milan in ten minutes. She bought a ticket, pushed a wad of notes over the counter. Grateful when some notes were passed back. And then she was on board, watching the sites of Rome slip away as the train glided smoothly out of the station. Only then did she relax.

They were travelling through countryside now, golden in the light from a sinking sun. She stared unseeing out of the window. All she could think about was what had happened. She couldn't get it out of her mind. It was as though a film was playing and replaying in her head. The pictures distorted and sounds blurred as she struggled to think about something else, anything.

The train pulled into the station at Milan at last, and she climbed down onto the bustling platform, not sure what to do. It was too late for further travel. She spotted a tourist office and went in for help. There was a hostel nearby, so she trudged the few streets and was relieved to find they had a bed for her. No-one else seemed to speak English, so after a few attempts at politeness she was left in peace. She climbed into her bunk, and burrowed down under the blankets. She thought about Michael.

'I'll see him soon. Maybe I can get to England by the day after tomorrow. And he will be there. He'll help me.'

She lay, crying quietly, hugging herself trying to blot out the horror. She was alert to every sound: doors opening and closing, the squeak of shoes on the tiled floors. Voices echoing in the corridor and bed springs squealing.

In the morning she bought toast for breakfast, and then checked her funds. She'd left most of her money with Jude, thinking her friend's need was greater, and she was realising now that she might be in some difficulty. There was no choice but to try and hitch hike again. She walked to the edge of town, and set her bag down at the roadside.

'Please God, let me be safe. Let me be safe.'

A car drew up, and she was so relieved to see a young woman driver.

'I'm going to Munich, any good for you?'

'Yes, yes please.'

Marguerite was Swiss, and spoke excellent English. She was on her way home after a visit with friends.

'I'm glad of company on the drive, what about you, where are you heading?'

'I'm going home too, to England.'

'You have been away alone?'

Lamorna had to explain then about her trip with Jude, and her decision to get home to see Michael.

'Ah, love, it can do such strange things to us! But you should not be travelling alone.'

'I did have a hitch hiking partner to Rome, but then, well things went wrong.' Her voice faltered.

'Do you want to tell me?'

She hesitated and then the words came blurting out. She would never see this woman again. She could tell her. It was a relief to tell someone.

'That's bad. Very bad. You should have called the police.'

'I thought it was my fault, he must have got the wrong idea about me. He must have thought I was okay with it.'

Her voice dwindled away as tears began to fall.

'I think we need coffee, and then we have to decide what to do. You can't travel alone.'

Marguerite pulled into a lay-by, and Lamorna saw a small café just along the road. She wiped away tears on her sleeve.

'Come on, bring your bag.'

They were directed to a seat by the window, and served with fresh coffee and pastries. Lamorna pulled her purse out, but Marguerite shushed her.

'No, no, I will buy this.'

They talked some more, and then Marguerite said,

'How much money do you have?'

Lamorna took out her purse again, and tipped the contents out onto the table. There were a few of the lire left, some drachma and a few pounds in sterling.

'You won't get far with that. You must come home with me, and I will ring my friends in Paris. They will help. You could get there tomorrow night.'

And so it was that Lamorna found herself in a pleasant house somewhere in the suburbs of Munich, a light airy house, filled with colour. Lamorna browsed the shelves, admiring a collection of bright ceramic cockerels. There were beautiful bowls, hand painted and on the walls etching of mountain scenes, some reminding her of her travels with Michael, when they had slept in just such a barn on a mountain side. Marguerite was talking on her telephone.

'That's it,' she said. 'My friend Helga and her husband Maurice are in Paris. I think you should take a train in the morning. It will take around nine hours. They will meet you, and you can stay with them a night. Then you can go on the next day. That is best I think. Please, stay here with me tonight. You cannot be in Munich and not see something of the city.'

'Marguerite, you are very kind, but I can't impose on you, and I can't go by train, I don't have enough money. It's best if I set off again now. Please can you tell me the best road to take?'

'I cannot do that, you are my friend now. I can't let you go again into danger. No, this is the best plan. I will lend you the money. You can send it to me when you are home again. Please, I will enjoy your company.'
Lamorna's eyes filled with tears.

'You're so kind. I was afraid to travel alone.'

Marguerite took Lamorna on a tour of the city, they went to see the site where the Olympics would be held in a couple of years, they strolled around the Hofgarten, and then met up with some of Marguerite's friends for a meal in the evening. Lamorna took photographs of the group, promising to post them to Marguerite when she was home.

'I didn't know you were an artist, we should have gone to an exhibition, maybe the Neue Pinakothek would have been interesting for you, and there are many famous paintings. You must come and stay again with me again. Bring your boyfriend too.'

'I would love to, it's a beautiful city.'

During the night Lamorna woke to the sound of her own voice crying out. Marguerite came to her.

'What's wrong? Are you okay?'

'Bad dream,' she said. 'I'm sorry. I didn't want to wake you.'

'That's okay, as long as you're alright.'
Marguerite tiptoed out, and she turned over to try and sleep again, but it was impossible. The events of the previous day were vivid in her mind. She relived her ordeal over and over again.

They drove to the station in the morning. She had a phone number for Helga in Paris jotted in her notebook, but she didn't need it, because Marguerite had phoned her friend with a description of Lamorna. She and Maurice were waiting for her at the Gare de Lyon, and approached her as she came through from the platform. Helga and Maurice also spoke good English and made Lamorna feel really welcome. Maurice cooked a fish supper for them, and Helga talked to her about her ordeal. She worked as a counsellor, and she tried to impress on Lamorna that the incident was in no way her fault. But Lamorna was too upset still to take in what she was saying.

***

In the morning Helga took her to yet another station, and in just a few hours she was back on English soil. She phoned Joy, and set off for her friend's flat overlooking Clapham Common. She had decided to stay for the night, and head off again to see Michael early the next morning. Joy was pleased to see her, showing her proudly around her new home, but she was going out for the evening, so there was no time to talk. Lamorna felt relieved. Somehow she couldn't face telling her story to a friend. It had been easier to confide in strangers. There was only Michael now who could help her and comfort her.

'I can't wait to see him,' she thought as she lay in bed that night. She pictured him sleeping in his bed. His dark hair on the pillow. She would creep in and wake him with a kiss. And then he would take her into his arms.

She slept a little better, only waking once after a disturbing dream. Up very early before Joy had woken, she scribbled a quick thank you note and quietly left the flat.

The journey passed quickly, and it was an excited Lamorna who walked up the street to Michael's student house. It was only six thirty and he would not yet be up. There was a bottle of milk on the step. She searched for the door key in its hiding place behind a loose brick in the garden wall. Quietly opened the door and tiptoed in. She stowed the milk in the fridge, and then crept upstairs, hardly daring to breathe, wondering what Michael would say when she slipped into bed with him.

The door to his room was closed, so she turned the handle slowly and stepped through, placing her bags down carefully on the threshold. She paused whilst her eyes adjusted to the gloom. A shaft of sunlight suddenly pierced the shadows and lit up the bed. Lamorna took a step forward, and then stopped. Michael was lying face down, sprawled in sleep, a sheet loosely spread over his legs. His arm was resting across the breasts of a girl. The sunlight gleamed on her golden hair. Long tresses spread across the pillow. Lamorna looked at the pale skin of the girl's breasts and her body. The sheet was no longer covering her, and she lay like an angel in repose.
'Rosa. No, no.'

She stumbled out of the room, snatching up her bags. Eyes blurred with tears. Her rucksack crashed against the banister. She fled down the stairs, reached the front door and flung it open. Struggled down the steps, bags smashing against her legs. Heavy clunk of camera banging the wall. She heard Michael's voice as she ran.
'Wait Lamorna, wait. Don't go.'
She turned the corner. A bus was just pulling away. She jumped on board, breathless from running and crying. Climbed the stairs. She saw Michael reach the bus shelter and stop dead in his tracks.

She didn't know where she was going. The bus stopped at last and the conductor told her they were at the terminus. She saw the railway station. It was barely half an hour since she'd walked out of that entrance. She went back through the portal and scanned the departure board. Penzance. A train in twelve minutes. In a daze she boarded and found a seat. Once again she was staring from a train window. Staring without seeing. Numb with shock.

***

The town was shrouded in grey mizzle. She stepped down onto the platform, went into the refreshment room and bought a cup of coffee. Sat for an hour. Thinking.
'What shall I do? I could go to Mary. No. Not Mary.' And then she thought of Phil.
'I can't go and see him at work. Have to wait.'

She crossed the rail tracks and went onto the beach. Walked on and on and back again. Sat shivering in a shelter until the watery sun was sinking to the horizon. In some sort of automatic state she walked to Phil's flat. He opened the door to her and she collapsed into a heap, at last able to release her pent up tears. He lifted her onto her feet and led her into his lounge. He made her a cup of tea, and she gulped it down.

'Be careful, it's hot. Whatever's the matter Lamorna? Is it Jude? Has something happened to Jude?'
She shook her head, but couldn't speak.

'I've made some pasta,' he said. 'We'll share it.'
But Lamorna couldn't eat. She was convulsed with crying, and he couldn't get any sense out of her. He ate her helping in the end.

'Would you like to stay the night, and we can talk in the morning?'
She nodded. Taking her hand he took her into his spare room.

'The bathroom is just through here, you probably remember. Have a bath if you'd like to.'
She nodded, and then curled up on the bed, still dressed.

***

Something woke her. She opened her eyes. There was someone lying beside her. She felt a wave of terror spread through her. Her heart beat wildly. She quietly pulled herself up, and saw that it was Michael. He was sleeping still, his clothes rumpled. Odd socks on his feet.

'I love you so much. I needed you Michael. Why did you do this to me? Why?' she whispered.
She shuffled to the end of the bed and rummaged in her bag, pulling out a pair of nail scissors. She bent over him and snipped off a lock of his hair, stuffed it into an envelope she found in the bin, and put it into her pocket. Through a blur of tears she picked up her bags and began to creep away. She saw some keys and a few coins on the floor beside the bed, and bent down. The keys to Michael's car. She picked them up and left the flat.

The car was outside in the street. She opened the door, flung her bags in the back and then drove away. At first she had no destination in mind. She drove blindly through the town. She saw the signs for the A30. At last she realised where she was heading, and a new purpose formed in her mind.

She parked by the familiar pathway, and leaving her bags in the car she set off down the rocky valley. She reached the bottom, and sat down on the turfy patch, the place that had once been so significant. The place where she and Michael had first made love. And she gave way. Let the tears stream down her face, hot, scalding, as her body was racked with sobs.
She watched as the foam was flung high and then sucked back down as each wave ebbed away. Luring her in. Inviting her to follow them. To be carried away.

'I'll wait until the tide's going out. Then I'll do it,' she thought.

After what seemed a lifetime she heard a voice and turning saw Michael hurrying towards her, calling her. He sat down beside her, trying to take her hand, but she pulled it away.

'Lamorna, please listen to me, please talk to me.'

'No no, not here,' she said.

'Shall we go back to Phil's flat? He'll be at work now.'

'Alright.'

She climbed quickly back up the valley, Michael almost struggling to keep up with her. She reached his car and clambered in. He held onto the door for a moment.

'You lead, and I'll follow.'

She nodded and started the engine. He had Phil's car, and set off after her. He was keeping up with her until a tractor suddenly turned out of a gateway in front of him. Lamorna saw the tractor in her mirror. A crossroads lay ahead, and she took a left turn, reversed into a gateway, and watched as first the tractor, and then Michael's car passed the end of the lane. After a time she set off again, retraced her journey, and headed for St Erth. She parked the car at the station, and bought a ticket with the last of her money. Ten minutes before the Plymouth train was due to leave she rang Phil's number and was glad when the answer machine clicked on.

'Sorry Phil. Tell Michael I left his car at St Erth station. The station master's got the keys. I'm sorry. I'm sorry.'

She boarded the train and it took her away from the places and the person she loved most in the world.

Chapter 8

The sun was low in the sky when Lamorna reached the house she had shared for two years with Jude and Joy. She opened the door, and a pile of post and papers avalanched on the floor.

She stood listening. Absolute silence. Dust motes danced in the shafts of light. There was a stale smell, a faint greasy hint of long ago cooking, and a sweaty odour that she realised was her own body. She pulled her jacket off and hung it over the wooden hat stand. She dragged her bag up the stairs and into her room. And then she lay down on the bed, pulled the duvet over herself and wept.

It was dark when she woke, and fumbling her way to the door she crossed to the bathroom. She sat desolately on the toilet for a while. Then washed her hands and face. The water was cold. She saw herself in the mirror; a pale face, dull, dark-ringed eyes staring blankly back at her, a tangle of uncombed hair. Not her. Some other ghost of a person.

She went slowly downstairs and into the kitchen. The fridge was empty. In the cupboards were a few packs of dry pasta and rice, and a tin of baked beans. She opened the beans and spooned some into her mouth, gagging on the cold slimy lumps, but then forcing herself to eat another mouthful.

She drank some water from the tap, letting it flow over her hands. Then she went back to her bedroom. She turned a light on, looked around. Saw the photograph of herself with Michael. A sob rose in her throat. She pulled the picture off the hook and laid it face down on the cupboard by her bed. She saw the photo Phil had taken. There she was smiling, her arms around Rosa. She wrenched it down and flung it at the wall, sending glass splintering over the carpet. She kicked off her shoes and crawled into bed.

Later she woke and crept downstairs again. The tin of beans was there still. A trail of ants led from its rim, over the work top and down to the floor. Suddenly there was a sound. She froze. Someone was knocking on the door. She heard the letter box rattle. A voice calling.

'Michael.' She stood, frozen. Her heart thumping in her chest.

'Lamorna, it's me. Please let me in if you're there, please. I need to talk to you. Please.'

More knocking. Then nothing. She stood for a long time. There was no more sound. She went back up to the bedroom.

She stirred, hearing a voice beside her. A flash of bright light as curtains were pulled open.

'Lamorna, it's me, I'm back. What's wrong? Why are you in bed at this time? What's the matter, what's happened?'

'Oh Jude.'

Jude reached out for her, and hugged her.

'What is it? What's wrong?'

There was no reply. Lamorna shook with sobs in her arms. After a while the crying subsided a little, and Jude wrapped a bath robe around her.

'I'm going to make us a drink, come on, come down with me.'

Lamorna allowed herself to be led downstairs and sat down on the sofa.

'Stay there. I got some milk and stuff, and some biscuits at the corner shop.'

She reappeared with a mug of tea for each of them.

'I'm just going to phone Phil, ask him if he'll pick me up this weekend, then we'll talk.'

'I saw Phil.'

'What do you mean? When did you see him?'

'I ran away. I didn't know where else to go.'

'What happened? What's gone wrong? Where's Michael Lorna?'

Lamorna started crying again when she heard his name. Between the sobs she blurted out a few words.

'Everything's gone wrong. Everything.'

Jude hugged her again.

'Can you tell me?'

'I went to see Michael. I was going to surprise him. He was in bed with Rosa.' Her voice was bleak, and the words tailed away as her whole body was shaken with dry racking sobs.

'Oh no, poor Lamorna, poor Lamorna. He didn't know you were coming? You didn't phone him?'

'It was a surprise. I wanted to surprise him.'

'What happened?'

'I went to the station. A train was going to Penzance. I got on it. I went to Phil. I didn't know what to do. And when I woke up Michael was there. I'm such a bad person. I'm so bad Jude.'

And she was sobbing again.

'Lamorna, you haven't done anything wrong. You're just upset. Anyone would be.'

'No. I left you all on your own. I shouldn't have left you.'

'I was fine, I had a good time. I understood you needed to be with Michael.'

'We got a lift. He seemed a nice man. He showed us somewhere to stay. He bought us lunch in Rome. But then I was having a shower. And he came in. He came in ....and he, he forced me....I couldn't shout. I was so scared. And it was all my fault. I let him buy lunch.'

'Lamorna, are you telling me this man raped you?'

She nodded.

'It was all my fault.'

'It was not your fault, listen Lamorna, it was not your fault. Did you call the police?'

'I wanted to see Michael so much. I got there early. And Jude, oh Jude, I couldn't bear it Jude. I couldn't bear it.'

'Oh Lorna, I'm so sorry. I can't believe Michael would do that. I thought Rosa was in the States.'

'It was Rosa. She looked so beautiful. I hate her. I hate her. I thought she was my friend.'

'When did you last eat anything?'

'I don't know. I'm not hungry.'

'I'm going to cook us something. You stay here.'

Jude tucked a blanket around her and turned the TV on. There was some children's programme. A cartoon. Lamorna was still huddled under the blanket when Jude reappeared with a tray.

'Dinner is ready, come and join me.'

Lamorna shuffled over to the table. She accepted a plate of food. Jude opened some wine and poured her a glass. Lamorna stared at her plate, then picked up a fork and scooped some spaghetti into her mouth. She took a mouthful of wine.

'Come on, try and eat some more, I made it especially for you. Then I'll tell you what I did after you left.'

'I believed him. I believed what he said in the letters. He said he loved me. He wrote it seven times. He said he missed me, but it wasn't true. It wasn't true.'

She let her fork drop onto the table, and she was crying again.

'It is true. Michael does love you, you know he does.'

'He doesn't. He was with her, with Rosa'

'It doesn't mean anything. I keep telling you it's the sixties...well seventies. He still loves you.'

'Michael's not like that. He used to love her, and now he's found her again. He won't want me now. Why would he?'

'Oh Lamorna, please try to eat, I know you're wrong. I spoke to Phil just now. He says Michael is desperate to find you. He's so worried. He came here, but he couldn't get in.'

'Don't tell him I'm here, I can't see him. I don't want him to see me.'

'Don't worry.'

'I can't eat. I'm sorry Jude. I'm just so tired.'

'That's alright. Will you help me wash up? Then I'll tell you about my travels.'

She persuaded Lamorna to join her in the kitchen, and they washed up together. Lamorna was silent. Twenty minutes later they were back in the living room, with mugs of coffee.

'When you left I met up with this great guy. We went over to Crete and hired a motorbike. We went all around the island, and then we stayed for a few days in the caves where Ellen met Klaus. It was fantastic, the people were great. And there's a place called Mermaid Café, a sort of taverna. John wanted to go over to Africa, but you know what, I was bored of travelling, and I decided to fly back.'

'I should have stayed with you. Then all the bad things wouldn't have happened. I thought Rosa was my friend.'

'I'm sure she is. She's a hippy, remember. It's all about free love. You should try and talk to Michael. He cares about you. There must be some reason, some ordinary explanation.'

'I can't talk to him. I never want to see him again. I'll go to bed now. Thanks for the dinner.'

'Why don't you have a nice bath first?'

'Why?'

'It will help you to sleep. I'll put some clean sheets on your bed.'

'Alright.'

Jude led her into the bathroom, and ran a bath for her, pouring in some relaxing bath oil. Lamorna was already in bed when Jude came back up with two mugs. She was reading a letter from Michael, her eyes wet with tears.

'Drink this Lamorna, it's cocoa.'

'Did you put something in it?'

'Like what?'

'Drugs.'

'No, of course not. It's just cocoa. Do you need something to help you sleep?'

'No, all I do is sleep now. I can forget then.'

'Okay, goodnight then, I'll see you in the morning. Everything will be alright, you'll see.'

Chapter 9

Lamorna woke when it was still quite dark. She felt a warm shape beside her.

'Jude, wake up, you've fallen asleep on my bed.'

The shape beside her stirred. She rolled over to see if Jude was awake. And saw Michael. She lay for a moment looking at him in the half light. He was fully dressed on top of the duvet. She gazed at him for a few minutes and then she started to slide quietly down the bed. The letter she had been reading was still lying crumpled beside her. She picked it up and folded it into her hand, hiding it. She was still watching him, holding her breath, willing him to stay asleep. But his eyes opened and met her gaze. She looked away. He sat up, reached out and took her hand.

'Phil phoned me. Jude told him you were here. I came straight away. I don't know what to.say. There aren't any words to tell you how sorry I am. To tell you how much I love you. I can't bear it that I hurt you. I love you so much Lamorna. I want to make time go backwards, make it all not happen.'

She was holding herself together tightly so that she would not give herself away, give herself up to him. She was still trying to get to the door, to get away. She couldn't look at him. Scrunched the letter in her hand.

'I came home to you. You sent me letters. You said you loved me. You wrote it seven times. I left Jude to come home to you.'

'I do love you Lamorna. Nothing else matters, no-one else matters. I love you with all of my heart. Please believe me.'

'I don't believe you.'

Tears spilled down her cheeks now, and she turned away from him so that he wouldn't see.

'I was stupid, please listen. It didn't mean anything. She'd just come back from the States. She was upset. Ced has been sent to Vietnam. She was devastated, needed someone to talk to. I took her out to eat. We both drank too much. I don't know how it happened. I don't love her. I thought I did once. But I know it means nothing now. I never imagined you would walk in on us. Rosa is upset too.'

'I don't care what she thinks.'

'I'm sorry, of course you don't. I love you Lamorna, you're the person I want to be with.'

'I needed you. I needed you so much.' She was sobbing now, her whole body shaking. 'I didn't have anyone else. I needed you.'

He drew her into his arms and held her close, kissing her hair, stroking her face. She clung to him, and there were tears in his eyes now as he gently lowered her down, and lay beside her. He kissed her again, and she began to respond and move closer to him. They lay like this for half an hour or more. He was just stroking her and kissing her, murmuring words of love to her. After a while he spoke again.

'Lamorna, Jude told me you'd been attacked. Do you want to tell me about it? I want to help you.'

She buried her face against his shoulder. Her voice was indistinct and muffled when at last she spoke.

'He gave me a lift, gave us a lift. I thought he was just being kind.'

Her words broke off, and she was crying onto his shoulder again. He soothed her, kissed her hair, and stroked her.

'Don't talk if it's difficult. You don't have to tell me.'

'I'm such a bad person, I'm no good. It's always happening to me.'

'Lamorna, you are not a bad person. None of it is your fault, none of it. It's because you're so lovely, so innocent.'

'I was in the shower. He came in. I was stupid, I didn't think. I didn't bolt the door.'

'My love, my love, I'm so sorry, I'm so sorry.'

He cradled her in his arms as she cried, and he kissed her wet cheeks, kissed away her tears.

'I came to you. I came to find you. But she was there.'

She couldn't find any more words, just hid her face against him and sobbed. They lay together, his arms around her tightly until at last she was calm.

'I want to look after you now,' he said. 'I want you to be with me, to be there all the time, to be safe with me. I never want to be away from you again. Come and live with me. Say you will, please. I do love you.'

He was stroking her hair, her face, gently kissing her nose, her mouth.

'I want you to love me now. I want to blot it out.'

She started to undo the zip on his jeans.

'Not like this Lamorna, not like this.' He took hold of her hand to stop her.

'You don't want me. You don't want me.'

'I do want you. I want you more than anything, more than anyone in the world, but not like this. It might hurt you.'

'If you loved me you would do it.'

'Lamorna, believe me, I love you, I adore you, but I can't do it like this. I want to make love to you. I'm longing to make love to you, but we have to do it with love, not like this.'

'Please, make love to me,' she whispered, tears slipping down her face again, as she relinquished her grip on him.

'Oh Lamorna, my love, my love.'

'Please Michael.'

'Have you seen a Doctor?'

'No, I can't, I can't.'

Her body stiffened beside him.

'Shall I look at you, shall I see if you're hurt?'

She nodded through her tears.

'I need to undress you, and then I will make love to you. You have to stop me if you don't like anything. Okay?'

She nodded again, and he stood up to open the curtains and let the sunlight into the room.

'You're so beautiful,' he said, as he kissed her mouth and then gently caressed her neck with his lips.

'I'm going to undo your top, is that okay?'
She just looked at him, so very slowly and carefully he unfastened her buttons, kissing her bare skin, and after a while she was lying naked on the sheet. She gazed up at him. She felt numb, as if she had no real feelings. He kissed her eyes closed then.

'I'm going to kiss my way down your body and then I'll look at you,' he murmured.

At first she was stiff, tensing herself against his touch, but as he kissed her softly she slowly relaxed and she reached out to touch him, to run her fingers through his hair, slip her hand under his shirt.

'I'm going to see if you are hurt now,' he said, and she tightened her grip in his hair. 'Tell me to stop if you don't like it.'
He gently touched her, and then kissed and stroked her until she relaxed and let herself open for him.

'What is it?' she said, as he stopped and looked at her, a shadow of concern flickering across his face.

'There's a small tear, it's just beginning to heal. We should be careful, I'll just kiss you.'

'No, no, you must do it. I need you. I need to forget.'

'Hush, hush, I will if you want me too.'

'Please Michael.'
He took off his clothes, and then lay down beside her. She was fierce in her passion now. She gripped him hard and kissed him with such ferocity. She was clenching him to her.

'Be careful, you'll get hurt, let's be gentle, not like this,' he said.
But she wouldn't listen, and when she came it was with a wild anguished cry.

'Please, again Michael, please.' Tears streamed down her face.

'I can't, not yet, and I need to see if it hurt you first.'
She rolled onto him.

'Please Lamorna, not like this.'
He couldn't make her stop, so he came into her again, and within seconds they both reached a climax and lay together, spent.

'I'm going to look at you again, make sure you're not hurt,' he said after a while.
She was just staring at him. After a few minutes he gathered her into his arms.

'I think you're alright. Didn't seem to do any harm.'
She took his face into her hands and kissed him. And it was Michael now who had tears welling up in his eyes.

'Don't cry, don't cry,' she said.
They lay together all morning, and she let him kiss her and stroke her. She was peaceful and relaxed in his arms at last.

Chapter 10

Jude knocked on the door.

'I've made you some food. I'm just going out for a couple of hours.'

'Thanks Jude,' Michael replied.

They heard the front door slam.

'Come on, let's go and eat, I'm starving.'

He dressed quickly and then lifted her up and wrapping her robe around her, carried her down the stairs. He sat her at the table, and then brought in the pots from the stove.

'It's a Jude special, Chilli and rice.'

He sat beside her, and fed her spoonfuls of the food, alternating with mouthfuls for himself.

'What shall I do with you now?' he said. 'Will you come home with me? I've moved to the top of the house.' An awkward pause. 'A different room.'

'Yes. I'll come with you.'

They washed up together, and then Lamorna showered and dressed. They were busy packing her belongings when Jude came back. She made them mugs of tea, and they sat together talking. Phil arrived to pick Jude up.

'I'm glad to see you two together again,' he said. 'You're looking a bit more alive Lamorna.'

'I'm going down to stay with Phil for a couple of months,' Jude said. 'If it works out I'll come back and get the rest of my stuff and move down permanently. My parents will keep the house on and let it again. You can stay here until then if you want to.'

'It's okay. I'm going to stay with Michael. I might leave a few things here if that's alright. We can pick them up in a couple of weeks.'

'Sure, no problem. '

Michael went out to help Phil load Jude's stuff into his car.

'Are you alright now?'

'Yes. But I can't stop thinking. I thought Rosa was my friend. How could she do that to me? She knew how important Michael is to me.'

'She has a different attitude; it doesn't mean anything to her. You let it get to you too much. It's not good for you. I keep telling you, loosen up.'

'I can't do that, it's not me. I don't want to be eaten up with jealousy but I don't know how to stop.'

Michael came in.

'I'm just telling Lamorna she should live a bit. She's made herself ill over what you did. You know what Lamorna? It was a bit of a relief when you left me in Athens. You were really cramping my style. All those dishy young men chatting us up and you wouldn't play the game.'

'It's hardly the right time to talk about other men. I'm glad that's how Lamorna is, I respect her.'

'Ha, you're a fine one to say that. Sauce for the goose.'

'Jude, I'm ashamed of what I did. I don't know how I'll ever make it up to Lamorna.'

'Well you shouldn't be. This is the twentieth century, the Age of Aquarius. Things are different, we're meant to be free. And you Lorna, you're an Aquarian; you should be up for it. You should be having fun.'

'None of what's happened to us is fun,' Michael said. 'Some of us are different.'

'Well as far as I'm concerned I'm going to enjoy life. I want the same freedom men have. There's no risk now with the Pill. What's the harm in it?'

'The harm is when it hurts someone. What about Phil?'

'He doesn't mind, he knows me. I expect he's had a fling or two while I've been away.'

'I don't think he has.'

'Well more fool him.' She flounced out with her bags.

She and Phil reappeared after a while, the car was loaded and ready, and they all talked about what to do for the evening.

'Let's go and see a film,' Jude suggested.

Michael looked at Lamorna,

'Would you like to?'

She nodded.

Jude scanned a local paper.

'Butch Cassidy's on, let's go to that. I missed it first time around.'

Phil rang for a Chinese take-away, and after they'd eaten and cleared away they set off to walk into town. Lamorna sat through the film holding onto Michael's arm, leaning against his shoulder. She had no idea what the film had been about when it ended.

Jude and Phil were up early in the morning for the drive down to Cornwall.

'I'll keep in touch and let you know what's happening.'

With that they were gone, and the house slipped back into quietness, almost sighing with relief at the sudden peace. Lamorna packed essential things, including her camera. They cleared up the kitchen, emptying bins, clearing out the fridge. They loaded her things into his car, finding space for a box of left-over food. Michael did a quick check to make sure the house was secure, and they set off.

He had moved into a different room at the top of his house, just as he'd told her, so she didn't have to overcome any physical reminders of Rosa in his bed. They had their own bathroom on that floor. She settled in quickly and seemed content, cooking for everyone, washing hers and Michael's clothes. There were nights when she had nightmares still. When she lay awake reliving the ordeal in Rome. It was always there in the back of her mind. But she didn't talk about it. She forced herself to focus on making a home for them in the flat, pushing the memories out of her head. And she was determined to find work as soon as she could, sending off applications for several posts. She was thrilled to be asked for interview with a journal based in Birmingham.

'It's not my dream job, but it's a start,' she said, setting off to catch a train.

'I'll make a special celebration dinner for you,' Michael said, kissing her goodbye.

'I've not got the job yet.'

But she was offered the post, and couldn't wait to get home and tell Michael. She called into an off licence and bought a bottle of sparkling wine for the celebration. She stowed the bottle in the fridge before running up the stairs.

Chapter 11

'What's wrong? What is it, what's happened?'
Michael was sitting on the edge of the bed, his head in his hands. After a few moments he turned to her, and she saw the stricken expression on his face.

'I don't know how to tell you Lamorna. Rosa was here just now. She came to tell me that she's pregnant. She says the baby must be mine.'

'No, no, it can't be. It can't be.'

'I don't know what to do, it's a mess.'

'Do you believe her?'

'I don't know what to think.'

'She's making it up. She wants you. It's a trap. I hate it. I can't bear her to have your baby.
I want to be the one to have your babies.'

'She came to see me because she thought I should know. She said I have rights as the baby's father. She's come up with a plan.'

'What plan? You don't have to be involved. You don't have to get mixed up with her again.'

'She says we could all live together at her Aunt's smallholding. Her Aunt wants to give it up. She thinks it could be a kind of commune. I could farm, and we could all share and live together. She says Laura and Jean might come.'

'Why? Why does she want that? She was never bothered about Paul. He disappeared out of Dylan's life. It's because she wants you Michael. She wants you.' Lamorna was shouting through tears at him. 'I don't want to live with her. I couldn't bear it.'

'I have to help her support the baby Lamorna. I have a responsibility. I'm not like Paul. I can't just walk away. But I don't want to be involved with her. Please believe me, you're the person I love. I want to be with you. This just sounds like a reasonable solution.'

'It's not reasonable. It's not. What if we tell her I'm pregnant too? It's not fair. I could have had your baby.'
She was pacing around the room.

'Lamorna, you're not being sensible. You aren't pregnant, it wouldn't be right to say that. You know it wouldn't.'

'I know it's not right but I don't care. I can't share you with her. I can't. What if I really was pregnant? What would you do then?'

'That's not a fair question Lamorna. You're not pregnant.'

'But what if I was?'

'You know that you're the person I love. I want to be with you. It doesn't matter whether you're pregnant or not. I will always want to live with you. I don't want a relationship with Rosa. But I have to take some responsibility for the baby, offer some support.'

'If that's what you must do then you do it. But I won't come. I never want to see Rosa again.'

'Lamorna, please, calm down. You're getting hysterical.'

'I'm not hysterical. I'm upset. I'm angry. She's ruined my life.'

'It's not just Rosa's fault. I'm just as much to blame for what happened.'

'You're on her side now. You're standing up for her.'

'That's not fair. It is my fault too.'

Lamorna stamped her feet.

'Why, why did this happen when everything was starting to go right again?'
She was still wearing her coat. She flung herself onto the bed crying. He reached
over and lifted her into his arms.

'Lamorna, please believe me, I love you so much. I never wanted this. I didn't
want to hurt you. We can be married. I wanted you to marry me. I will marry you
tomorrow if that's what you want.'

She lay stiffly against him, unresponsive. She heard him sigh.

'I didn't ask you about the interview, what happened?'

'I got the job.'

Her sobs increased.

'I knew you would, well done.'

He tried to kiss her, but she pushed him away.

'Please don't do this to me. I need you,' he said. 'I need you to help me get
through this. I was supposed to be cooking you a meal, and then this happened.
Let me take you out for a celebration dinner.'

She stood up and went to the bathroom to wash her face. They walked in
silence to a local pub. She allowed him to hold her hand, but she couldn't respond
to his touch. She couldn't let herself feel or the tears would start again. She kept
her coat on in the pub. She picked at her food. She wouldn't look at him. The meal
was like a torture to her. It was a relief to get back to the house.

Pete was in the kitchen when they walked in. Michael went to put the kettle on.

'What's this then?' Pete asked, holding up the bottle of wine.

'I bought it. I thought we could celebrate my new job.'

She walked out of the room quickly; before he could see her eyes fill with tears.
When Michael came in with mugs of coffee for them she was already in bed,
curled up tightly at the edge. He showered and climbed in beside her. He tried to
hold her but her back stayed turned against him. He stroked her arm, kissed her
shoulder.

'Please let me hold you. Please, tell me what to say, what to do. I can't bear you
to turn away from me like this. Please Lamorna, please.'

She couldn't speak to him. She was afraid to let herself go. She lay listening to
a rushing of blood in her ears, her heart beating, thumping in her chest. She felt it
was broken now beyond repair.

'I should have known this couldn't last. I didn't deserve it,' she thought.
She drifted into sleep, Michael's arm around her still.

***

She woke to find him crouching at the bedside.

'I've brought you some tea. I have to go into College. I've got an important
tutorial. I don't want to leave you like this. I don't know what to do.'

'I'll be alright.'

'I'll be back around four o'clock, and then we can talk. We'll talk properly then, decide what to do. Are you sure you'll be alright?'

She nodded. He kissed her forehead, her nose, and then her mouth. She responded to him then, taking his face in her hands, and looking hard at him before kissing him.

'I love you Lamorna. Please believe me. We can work this out.'

She watched him walk away, and tears rolled down her face again. She listened to the sounds of coming and going, doors opening, air in the pipes, the noise of water filling a tank, someone calling, until gradually the house was silent.

She got up, dressed and caught a bus into town. Walked to a garage near the station and hired a car. Back at the house she packed her few belongings and loaded them into the boot. Then she went back upstairs to their room, to Michael's room. She tore a sheet of paper from a notepad and sat down to write.

'I've gone to find somewhere to live. I hope it all works out for you. Please don't look for me. I will always love you.'

She picked the paper up and kissed it, and watched as a tear dropped onto the paper and smudged the words 'love you.'

Then she drove out of his life.

Chapter 12

The tower blocks of Birmingham came into view. She saw a sign 'Homeleigh House, Bed and Breakfast', and decided to see if they had a vacancy. Twenty minutes later she was sitting on the edge of a strange bed in a chintzy room, staring bleakly at the flowery wallpaper. She thought about how she used to scare herself as a child imagining monster faces in the patterns of her bedroom wallpaper. A Westminster clock chimed the hours away, two o'clock, three o'clock. And she just lay there on the bed, eyes closed, but awake. Waiting for that moment when Michael would come home and find her gone. Listening to the anxious buzz of a fly trapped on the window pane. A distant rumble of traffic from the road. Somewhere a solitary blackbird sang. The clock chimed four. She pictured him coming home. Rushing up the stairs two at a time, coming into their bedroom, speaking her name. Finding her gone, finding her note. She rummaged in her bag and pulled out the envelope with the lock of his hair. She took out the hair, smelled it and kissed it, and then holding it tightly in her fist she gave herself up to crying again.

Different pictures invaded her head now. The moment when she'd found them together. Rosa so beautiful, like an angel in his bed. His arm stretched across her naked breasts. She relived the moment when she'd cried out and then turned to run. His words went round and round in her head. He'd talked about responsibility for the baby. Rosa's baby…his baby. About how they could all live together at the smallholding her aunt had left her. 'He said he loves me…but I can't share him. I can't be there with them when the baby is born. It will change everything.'

The room grew dark and she slept for a while, waking when the clock chimed six. She sighed, and replacing the lock of hair in the envelope she sealed it and returned it to her bag. There was a wash basin in the room. She splashed cold water on her face. Peered at herself in the cracked mirror. Decided she looked normal enough and headed off downstairs.

The landlady directed her to a nearby pub where she could get a meal. She walked down the road, trying at first not to step on the cracks in the pavement. Just like when she was a child and she'd really believed the bears would eat her up. 'They can come and eat me now,' she thought. 'I don't care.' It was strangely liberating. Breaking a rule that had been a habit all her life. A stupid rule. It felt as though she was suddenly learning to grow up. 'Learning to be alone…fend for myself…' she thought. 'I don't need any man. I've got my new job. That's everything to me now.' But she had to swallow a sob that she felt rising in her throat.

The street lamps were wreathed in an ethereal orange glow. A few people were hurrying by. A group huddled at a bus stop. Young lads swigging beer from cans. A couple were having a heated row on the pub doorstep. She pushed her way past them and went into the lounge. A wall of sticky heat laced with greasy cooking smells assaulted her senses. Her feet seemed to stick to the carpet. Brown swirls against orange, looking like woven in stains. Like splodges where drinks had spilled. The pub was busy and nobody took any interest in her. She found a table in a quieter corner, and picked up a discarded evening paper. Despite their greasiness she managed to eat all of the fish and chips she'd ordered. She flicked through the paper and found two adverts for letting agencies. She tore that section of the page out and folded it into her bag. She ordered Spotted Dick pudding, but when it came she couldn't eat it. It was a lump of grey stodge, smothered in a bright yellow congealed mess of custard.

In the morning she made herself eat the full English breakfast, thinking she wouldn't need lunch then. She didn't have a lot of money left. The landlady was suffocatingly cheerful, chatting about the weather, asking her if she was on holiday. Lamorna was the only guest, so she was obliged to make polite conversation.

'I'm just about to start a new job. I'm looking for a flat somewhere in town. Do you have a phone I could use please? I've got a couple of agency phone numbers to try?'

'Of course. Just give me a couple of shillings.'

Lamorna was in luck. The first agent had a flat that had become available that week. If she liked it she could move in straight away. She didn't know the city, but the flat seemed to be in a nice area, and even better it was just up the road from the offices where she would be based. She arranged a viewing at eleven thirty.

The building was a three storey mock Tudor house on a quiet tree-lined street. She felt that it would be just right straight away. The landlord was there to greet her, a small dapper man with dark hair and glasses. He led her up to the top floor, passing first along a mosaic tiled hallway, up a wide flight of stairs onto a landing, and then on up a narrower twisting staircase.

'Just here on the left is a useful storage cupboard,' he said, opening a door. 'Hobbit hole,' she thought.

'It's a small flat, but would be fine for just one. I take it there is just one of you?'

'Yes, just me,' she said, and her heart lurched.

'This is the bed sitting room, it's at the front of the house, but you won't hear any noise up here, and it's a quiet neighbourhood.'

She saw a spacious room with a many-paned bay window. It was sparsely furnished, but adequate for her needs. A floor to ceiling bookcase divided the main living area and behind it was a smaller space where there was just room for a single bed and a chest of drawers. She followed him along the landing.

'Here's the kitchen.'

She liked the room; a square space with a big scrubbed pine table in its centre. Along the opposite wall was a range of yellow painted cupboards, a fridge, cooker and sink unit. The walls were a pale cream brightened by a wash of sunlight streaming in from a wide window. She walked over to the window and looked out. There was a view across to the neighbouring house and along the street to the busy road further down. A wide low sill would make a great perch for morning coffee. Next to the kitchen was a small bathroom.

'There's a family on the ground floor, and just below you are two women. They're out at work every day. It's a quiet house, no wild parties, no students allowed,' he told her. 'I'll need two week's rent now, and I'll call in once a month on Friday evenings for the rent and to empty the electricity meter. It's just here,' he added, pointing to a strange old-fashioned black box with a slot next to the hobbit-hole door.

'I'm afraid it only takes old pennies and they're not so easy to come by now, so it's best if you buy them back off me.'

She wrote him a cheque, grateful that she still had money from selling her photographs. She asked a few questions, and then he was gone. She wandered around the rooms again and then went down to the hire car to collect her few belongings.

She decided on a shopping trip next, and set off for the parade of shops she had seen earlier. It was only a few minutes' walk, and she saw that there was a good range of businesses, two pubs and a launderette. There was also a coffee shop with an array of luscious cream cakes on display. On impulse she went in and ordered coffee and a vanilla slice.

She gazed out of the window, wondering what Michael was doing now. It was Friday, so he would be busy at college all day. There was a regular folk club on Friday evenings, and they'd usually gone along, Michael always being persuaded to sing.

'There will be no-one else in my life now,' she thought. 'No-one could be like Michael.'
She shopped for food, forcing her thoughts to dwell on the mundane tasks, trying to blank out images of Michael from her mind.

On her way back upstairs she realised that someone was home now in the flat below. She could hear voices from behind a door. She decided to knock and say hello. A young woman with dark wavy hair and glasses opened the door and smiled at her.

'Hello, I'm your new neighbour, I've just moved in upstairs. I'm Lamorna, Lamorna West.'

'Hi, pleased to meet you. I'm glad to see you're a friendly sort. The last one was very grumpy. I'm Janet, there's just me and Fiona. Why don't you dump your shopping and come and join us, we've just got in and put the kettle on.'
'Thanks that would be great.'

Five minutes later she was sitting with a mug of coffee in her hand at a large kitchen table.

'We're both teachers,' Fiona told her. 'This is our second year here. We like the house, it's peaceful. There's a family downstairs, Clive and Pam. We don't see much of them. They've got a toddler and a young baby. They're very tolerant, didn't mind when we had a party for Janet's birthday.'

'We all share the garden, but to be honest we don't use it much. Clive and Pam look after it. They were okay about some of our friends camping out there in the summer though,' Janet explained. 'What do you do? Are you a student? And how did you get that amazing name? It's so unusual.'

'Oh, my Mum named me for her favourite place in Cornwall. We used to always go down there for holidays. I'm a photographer,' she said, and realised it was the first time she'd described herself in that way. 'I'm just about to start a new job a couple of miles down the road. I'll be working for a magazine.'

'That sounds exciting!'

'It sounds glamorous, but I'm sure it won't be. I'll be starting right at the bottom, doing all the work no-one else wants to do. This is a perfect flat. It's only a short bus ride away. Tomorrow I've got to go and get some more of the stuff from a house I shared with friends at college. Then I'll have to give up the hire car.'

'Haven't you just come from there?'

'No, I'd been staying with another friend for a while.'

If they noticed the slight hesitation and the shadow that clouded her face then they were too polite to mention it.

'Why don't you come for dinner with us tomorrow night? You'll be tired from travelling,' Janet suggested.

'Thank you, that's really kind. I'd love to.'

'We always go down to the pub on Friday nights to celebrate surviving another week in the classroom, come and join us if you like,' Fiona added.

'Thanks, I don't know anyone here, so it will be a good start to my new life.'

'Where have all your college friends gone?'

'Jude's gone down to Cornwall, she's going to work in her boyfriend's photography business, and Joy is in London. Some people have stayed around near college.'

'You've drawn the short straw then,' Fiona said, laughing.

***

Later she joined them in the local pub. It was difficult, because there was a folk night, and she had to try and ignore the familiar songs that reminded her of Michael. Someone got up to sing some Paul Simon, and this time she had to make a hasty retreat to the toilet to recover her composure. She stood in the cubicle for some minutes, wiping away the hot tears that threatened to engulf her. Then someone banged on the door, so she had to flush the loo and come out. Splashed her face in cold water, Checked in the mirror. A pale face stared out at her, but she'd managed to wipe away all trace of tears. She watched herself make some sort of half smile, decided she'd do, and hurried back to her new friends.

'Are you okay?' Janet asked.

'Yes, well, sort of. It's just the memories stirred up by those songs. I let them get to me. I'll be alright. I saw a poster in the loo. Something about a meeting in your flat next Saturday.'

'Yeah, Fiona and I have set up a women's group. We meet in our flat once a month. We're thinking of trying to set up some kind of women's centre in town.'

'That's great, I'd love to join. We all got a bit interested in our last year at college, after the women at the Ford factory went on strike, but we didn't do much. Too busy with final year work.'

***

She set off the next morning for her student house.

'I wonder if Michael has told Jude what's happened, I suppose I must write to her.'

As she turned into the street she saw a familiar car parked in the road.

'Michael.'

She drove quickly past. The hedges were high, and she couldn't see a sign of him. She parked a bit further up.

'I suppose I could just walk down and find him. I could tell him I want to see him again. I could tell him how much I miss him.'

She saw his car moving then, turning in the road, and disappearing around the corner. She waited twenty minutes, and turned her car around, parking in the space he'd left. The moment was lost. She locked the car and set off up the path. 'If he comes back he won't know it's me, my car.'

The house seemed forlorn, neglected. Rubbish had blown against the step. Old chip papers. A can.

'Last time I opened this door we were together and everything was alright.'

There was a pile of post on the mat. She carried it into the kitchen and flicked through. Mostly advertising stuff. A letter for Joy, something for Jude. And then an envelope bearing her name, written in Michael's hand. She stuffed it unopened into her bag.

'He must have just pushed it through the door. He probably thinks I'm staying here.'

She went up to her room and began to load her belongings into the boxes she'd brought with her. An hour later they were piled in the hallway. She took a last look around, and then cautiously opened the door, stepping quietly to the gate and looking up and down the road. She wondered what she would do, what she would say if Michael did suddenly appear. Would everything be alright again? She picked up the rubbish and stuffed it into a bag.

'I'll have to take it. No-one's here to put the dustbin out.'

She loaded the car and drove back to her new home. Janet and Fiona helped her to carry everything up to her flat. It was a long trip up all the stairs. After they had gone downstairs again to prepare a meal Lamorna opened the boxes and began to unpack. Some things were too painful to have around. She wrapped the photograph of herself and Michael in newspaper and put it into her small trunk, along with the little carved mermaid he'd given her and her photography journals from the summer of 1968, the summer when she had fallen in love with him. She put the envelope with the lock of his hair in with the other things, and then the recording he'd made for her.

It was at that moment that Janet appeared.

'Are you alright Lamorna? What is it?'

'I'm okay. Well, no. I'm not a bit okay. I just split up with someone.'

'Oh, that's hard. Do you want to talk about it?'

'I don't think I can, not yet. I walked out on him. Something happened.'

'Well if you feel you need a shoulder to cry on you only have to say.'

'Thanks Janet, I'll be fine, honestly.'

'We'll see you in a few minutes shall we? Dinner's almost ready.'

'Yes, thank you.'

She retrieved the letter she'd found on the doormat from her bag, and turning it over in her hands felt its weight. It seemed like a long letter. She looked at his writing, and held it against her face for a moment, as though drawing something of his essence into her. Then sighing she placed the letter in the trunk. Once all memories of him had been packed she locked the trunk and pushed it into the hobbit hole. Grabbing the bottle of wine and flowers she'd bought earlier she went off downstairs.

Chapter 13

Lamorna started her new job on the Monday morning and knew straight away that she was going to love it. She felt immediately at home with the small team she was to be based with, and the work seemed varied and interesting. There were just four of them, the team manager Greg, Alice, another photographer, and Joe, who seemed to do admin, finance and anything else that was needed. The week seemed to whiz by, and suddenly it was Friday evening again. She met Janet on the landing as she climbed wearily up the stairs, wondering what she might cook for dinner. Her funds were running low.

'Hi Lamorna, fancy a Chinese take away? I'm just ordering.'

'I can't really Janet. To be honest I'm broke. I don't get paid for a month.'

'Why didn't you say? I can lend you some money if you like. Please, come and join us. We can get more variety with three of us eating.'

'You have to be the kindest neighbours in the world. Are you serious? I really could use a loan. I need to get some food in, and visit the launderette. I can't ask my family, they're not so well off.'

'Of course, how much do you need?'

'About £10?'

'No problem. Come and look at the menu.'

Fiona was reading the take away leaflet.

'How was your first week?'

'Great, I really love the job. Thanks for inviting me to join you. When I get my first wages I'll cook for you two.'

They chose various dishes, and Janet rang them through.

'It'll be half an hour.'

'How did your weeks go?'

'Well I managed to solve a mystery that's been bugging me,' Janet said.' I couldn't understand where all the class pencils and rubbers were going. We seemed to be getting through them so quickly. And old grouchy Clark, the Deputy Head wouldn't let me have any more. He said I'd practically cleaned out the stock room. Then I caught the twins smuggling them out. One of them had made a hole in the lining of his coat, and they were dropping pencils into it. Ingenious. They'll go far those two.'

'You'd never imagine children could think of it,' Lamorna said. 'Well, maybe I can when I remember things we used to get up to at school.'

'And I'm completely exhausted,' Fiona told her. 'It's our school hundred year birthday next week and we all have to produce a special class performance. It's a nightmare. Rehearsals every lunch time and after school. The only consolation is we get a day off afterwards to recover.'

'You work hard. I don't know how you two do it.'

'I suppose we just love children. We want the best for them. That's what made me go into teaching anyway.'

The doorbell rang. The food had arrived. Janet organised the table and they sat around to eat. Lamorna told them about her college course and the projects she'd done.

'I want to get into the kind of photography that can change things for the better,' she said. 'Photography that raises awareness of issues and makes things happen.'

'That's good, but it sounds a bit dangerous. Do you mean war zones and stuff like that?'

'I don't know yet. I probably have to find the right job first.'

Later they went off down to the pub. Janet told Fiona about Lamorna's financial situation, and they agreed that the drinks were on them.

'When I get paid the drinks will all be on me,' she said.

It was over a week now since she'd left Michael. She sat listening to the music, a folk rock band. She thought about the folk club on St Mary's. The way he'd sung for her. How Ellen said he'd left some broken hearts there. 'I should have known it wouldn't last. I'm not good enough for Michael. For someone so special.'

On Saturday morning she walked down to the launderette. She loaded her stuff into a machine, and then decided she could just about afford to treat herself to a coffee. She chose a seat by the window, and sipped her coffee slowly, making it last, watching the passers-by.

There was an old woman shuffling along, stockings wrinkled around her ankles. A solitary long-haired young man in a grey air force style coat. A couple of young women dressed in hippy style, strings of beads around their necks, wandered past, feet in leather sandals despite the autumn chill.

It made her think of her time in the commune again, her friendship with Rosa. She thought about Rosa and Michael. 'They would make a perfect couple. They're both so good looking. I suppose he will live with her now. I wonder when the baby will be born.' She pulled a menu over and taking a pen from her bag scribbled a few calculations in the margin. 'July. Around Michael's birthday. I wonder if I'll find out any more. Suppose Jude will get to hear. Mary and Chris will. I wonder if Michael has told anyone what happened. Do Aileen and Sam know? If I ring Jude she may have heard.' She fought off tears, and sighing paid for her coffee and went to retrieve her laundry and load it into the dryer. She had thought about Michael every day. 'It will always be the same. I'll never be able to forget him. There won't be anyone else.'

***

After a quick lunch she hurried downstairs to join Janet and Fiona's Women's meeting. She was surprised at how many women were gathered around their big kitchen table as she sat down to become the ninth member of the group. Fiona poured her a coffee, and then introductions were made. There were a couple of other teachers, Jenny and Jacqueline, a Social Worker, Marjory, the oldest woman in the group, Pat, who worked for a local environmental charity, Paula, an accountant, and Diane, a musician. Lamorna introduced herself and had to explain the origin of her name as usual. There were apologies from Esther and Caroline.

'Why are you interested in joining us?' Pat asked.

'I'm new to Women's Group work, but I got interested last term at college. I was reading about the Women's Conference in May. I want to see how I can help because I know that a lot of women live difficult lives.'

Janet handed around a short agenda. The main item was to be a discussion on a proposal to set up a Women's Centre.

'We've only just formed,' Fiona said for Lamorna's benefit. This is our third meeting. We don't want to just sit around talking. We want to take action.'

'Let's get everyone's ideas down about what the centre could do,' Janet said, opening a pad of paper. 'We'll go round the table.'

There were a variety of suggestions ranging from a meeting venue and café exclusive to women, a haven for victims of domestic violence and a proposal for a women-only magazine.

'I've heard that abuse of women in the home is on the increase,' Lamorna said. 'A safe place to go for help and advice would be good.'

'My brother's in the police,' Paula said. 'They're getting a lot of calls from people complaining about noisy neighbours, and they increasingly turn out to be women screaming whilst they're being beaten up. He would come and talk to us.'

'We don't want any men in the group,' Jacqueline said. 'I don't want anything to do with them, they're all rapists.'

'That's a bit harsh,' Paula protested.

'Well, the police don't get my respect, the way they treat women victims sometimes,' Marjory added.

'I don't agree that all men are rapists, some of them could be helpful to us,' Lamorna said.

'Yes,' Janet said, 'we can't turn down useful offers of help.'

'Women who've been raped need support as well,' Lamorna said.

'What would you know,' Jacqueline challenged her.

'I've got a friend who was raped,' she replied quietly.

'Sorry, I didn't think.'

'It shows we shouldn't jump to conclusions, make assumptions,' Janet said calmly.

'We should have some ground rules for the group,' Marjory said. 'If we can't treat each other with respect then no-one else will.'

They discussed ideas for a few minutes and came up with statements that they could all agree on, and the meeting moved on.

'I wanted to follow up what Lamorna was talking about,' Pat said. 'Women who have been raped need help as much as women abused at home.'

'My friend didn't know where to go for help,' Lamorna said. 'She couldn't talk to her Doctor.'

'I think that's the best idea,' Marjory said. 'We get so many women referred to us who have suffered abuse, and we can't offer them what they need. And Lamorna's right, there's nowhere for women to get help if they've been raped.'

'It would have to be staffed by women, even if we had a doctor,' Jenny said.

'Here here,' Jacqueline agreed.

'We could involve men behind the scenes, fund raising, that kind of thing,' Janet suggested. 'Paula's brother could help us to get information, statistics.'

'I agree, if we are ever going to change society we have to make men aware, help them to understand what's wrong,' Lamorna said.

'I don't know about the police,' Jacqueline said.

'I don't usually talk about this, but I was assaulted a couple of years ago. My boyfriend made me go to the police and they wouldn't take me seriously. They listened to him though when he said he was a witness, and they were most interested when I said he'd also stolen my camera. We need to change the police attitude, and if there's a helpful one amongst them I say let's get him involved.'

'I agree Lamorna,' Diane said. 'I got interrogated by the Police when I missed a bus and had to walk home early in the morning. They seemed to be suggesting I was some kind of prostitute.'

'Maybe we should be collecting information like that as evidence,' Janet said.

'If we get women coming in for help we'll have plenty of evidence,' Jenny said.

'Yeah, of course. I mean before we open a centre. Evidence to help with fund raising.'

'I agree,' Marjory said. 'I can't give names but I can log numbers of women I see in trouble.'

'We can't be everything to everyone,' Fiona said.

After more discussion it was agreed that a women's centre should be set up to offer advice, support and information. An action plan was made, and everyone went away with a job to do. Lamorna had offered to research what was happening elsewhere, using her journalist contacts. There was a feeling of enthusiasm, a sense that something might be set up by the next summer. Lamorna stayed for tea after everyone had left.

'You sound as if you've had a tough time recently Lamorna,' Janet said.

'Sometimes I feel I'm a born victim.'

'You can't think like that. That's half the problem. Women always believe they're to blame, that it was somehow their fault.'

'It's not surprising when the police seem to think it is your fault.'

'Did the bloke who attacked you get convicted? Can you talk about it?'

'That was a couple of years ago now. We don't know what happened to him. I feel guilty that I didn't report him sooner. He could be out there somewhere abusing women.'

'One of many,' Fiona sighed.

'The thing is; it was obvious he had problems. I'm not making excuses for him, but it makes me realise nothing is black and white. The perpetrators need help too. It won't change anything if they just get locked up for a couple of years.'

'Well, you may be right, but we want to focus on women, the victims in all of this.'

'I agree,' Lamorna said. 'But I don't want us to have anti-men attitudes.'

'I think Jacqueline is a minority of one. Maybe she has an axe to grind.'

'What about your friend. Is she okay now?' Janet asked.

Lamorna hesitated.

'I didn't want to say in the meeting. It was me. It was only a month ago. I was in Rome. It made me realise that there's nowhere to go for help. The only people who know are the women who helped me to get home, and my friend, and Michael. He was my boyfriend then.'

'Did you break up with him because of what happened? Did it affect your view of men?'

'Not really. He was really understanding and loving. It's too difficult to talk about at the moment.'

Her eyes pricked with tears.

'Are you sure that being raped didn't have consequences that you haven't realised? Maybe you wouldn't have split up if it hadn't happened.'

'I don't know. It's all muddled up together in my head, in my feelings. I can't talk about it. This is the first time I've had courage to use the word rape.'

'I'm sorry, I shouldn't have asked.'

'It's alright.'

'You know where we are if you need to talk, or just fancy a cup of tea.'

'Thanks, I know. I'd better get moving. See you later.'

She climbed back up to her flat and sat on the broad kitchen window sill for a while, watching people making their way home laden with shopping. The sky was turning a deep blue grey in the twilight. 'I wonder if Janet and Fiona will let me borrow their phone. I ought to phone Mum and let her know what I'm doing, where I am.'

She went downstairs again. Only Janet was there.

'Sorry to disturb you again.

'Stop apologising for your existence Lamorna. I'm glad of the company. Fancy a coffee?'

'Thanks that would be great. I was wondering if I could borrow your phone. I ought to call my Mum. I was thinking of ringing from work, but they said personal calls weren't allowed.'

'Of course, help yourself. It's in the lounge. I'll get the kettle on.'

Lamorna delved into her diary, flicking to the address pages at the back. She dialled the number.

'Hello Mum, it's only me. Just ringing to say I've moved into a new flat. How is everyone?

'Can't grumble. Tom's had a bit of a cold. How are you?'

'That's good. I'm fine.'

'Are you down in Cornwall?'

' No, no, I'm in Birmingham. It's all been such a rush, haven't had chance to speak to you. I started a new job last week.'

'New job?'

'Yes, it's great, I love it. I'm doing photos for a magazine. I may see you at Christmas, not sure yet.'

'That lad of your'n rang. Michael. Wanting to know if you was here. Sounded a bit upset, but he wouldn't say owt to me. Just said he were a bit worried.'

'Did he? When was that?'

'Only the other day…You've not told him your whereabouts then?'

'No, he doesn't know. Can't really tell you on the phone.'

'You alright in yourself?'

'Yes, I'm fine. I'll see you. Love to Tom and the boys.'

She replaced the receiver just as Janet came in with two mugs of coffee.

'Has something upset you?'

'I'm just being silly,' she said, wiping her eyes. 'My Mum told me Michael rang her to ask for my address. She's been worrying. I haven't told anyone where I am. I suppose I just ran away.'

Janet sat down beside her, and sipped her coffee.

'Mum said Michael sounded really worried and upset. I feel awful. I didn't want him to worry.'

'Surely he's bound to? He must be wondering if you're safe. Can you find some way to get a message to him?'

'I didn't think. I just left whilst he was in college. He went off in the morning and I ran away. I left a note, I said don't try to find me.'

'That sounds a bit drastic. Couldn't you talk to him?'

'I don't know. I feel I'm in a messed up state. It's only my job and your friendship that keeps me going.' She sighed, and gulped her coffee.' We talked and talked. But it was impossible.'

Janet handed her a box of tissues.

'Shouldn't you at least let him know you're safe?'

'I can't, I can't talk to him.'

'What about your friend? She could pass on a message. She's probably really worried too.'

'Yes, I should phone her.'

'I'll go and wash up.'

Lamorna counted to ten and then taking a deep breath dialled Phil and Jude's number.

'Hello. Penzance Studios. Can I help you?'

'Hello Jude, it's me.'

'Where are you? We've been worried sick. Michael even phoned your mother.'

'I'm sorry. I didn't think. I'm in Birmingham. I started my new job.'

'I don't understand why you just went like that. Are you okay?'

'Yes, I found a flat, and I've made some good friends here.'

'I'll get a pen. You can give me your address and phone number.'

'I can't Jude. I can't risk Michael coming to find me.'

'Michael guessed you were in Birmingham. He's kicking himself that he didn't know what your job was. He's been up there twice, driving around, looking for you. You've really upset him.'

'Jude, he upset me. I couldn't cope with it any more. I thought it was best if I just got out of his way.'

'You're being silly again. You know you're the person he wants to be with.'

'I don't know anything anymore.'

'Don't you trust me with your address?'

'I trust you, but I can't risk it just now. I couldn't cope if Michael came. I need time. I'd better go. I'm using a friend's phone.'

'Come and stay with us at Christmas.'

'I couldn't, I can't see him.'

'What shall I tell Michael?'

'Just tell him I'm okay. Tell him I've found a place to live.'

'You don't sound okay.'

'I need to go. Bye Jude.'

Janet reappeared.

'Did you get through?'

'Yes, I just realised I didn't ask how she was. She bombarded me with questions. She says Michael is devastated. He's driven up to Birmingham twice to try and find me.'

'Didn't he know where your new job was?'

'No, everything happened on the day I came back from the interview. Everything went wrong then.'

'What did she say?'

'She's completely on Michael's side. I don't understand her. She was always trying to get me to sleep with other men, sleep around. She said I was too involved with him.'

'I suppose she's trying to help him, she's seen how upset he is.'

'She wants me to go and stay for Christmas, but I can't, I'd be bound to meet him.'

'What will you do, go home to your family?'

'No, there's no space for me. It's a small house, and there's my Step Dad and two brothers.'

'We could spend Christmas together if you like. Fiona will be with Mark, and my parents are going abroad to celebrate their anniversary.'

'I'd love to. We could go away somewhere perhaps.'

Chapter 14

Lamorna immersed herself in her work and the plans for the women's centre. Paula's brother was proving really helpful in getting evidence together for fund raising, and they all felt they were making progress. She was able to pay her friend's loan back when she received her first wages, and they slipped into a comfortable pattern of cooking for each other once a week, and sharing a take away before heading off for the folk club on Fridays. She was attracting some attention at work, and had been asked out already by Greg, her boss. She told him that she was already spoken for.

'It is true really, I just don't want anyone else,' she thought.

She wrote to Jude, sending her address but asking her to promise to keep it secret from Michael. A week later she received a reply.

'Michael was in Cornwall last weekend. He's so unhappy without you. He wants to know if you read the letter he pushed through our house door. He seems to have lost weight too. He's not in contact with Rosa. He asked me to tell you that he loves you, and please can he come and see you.'

It was another few days before she could write back to Jude. She wrote about her job, and then she tackled the difficult issues.

'I didn't read Michael's letter. I knew it would upset me too much. I've saved it. I can't throw it away. I didn't want to upset Michael. I love him, but I'm so hurt. I can't see how things can ever be right for us. I can't forgive Rosa, and I couldn't be part of the arrangement she suggested. It seemed the best thing for me and for them to get out of their way. There will be a baby. Michael feels responsible. I can't compete with Rosa and a baby.

I can't afford a phone yet. Will let you know if I do get one. I've made some good friends here. We're trying to set up a women's centre, it's really exciting. You could come up and stay sometime, I'd love to see you.'

*

At the beginning of December she was sent up to Yorkshire for her first big assignment, returning a week later. There was a chatty letter from Jude, telling her all about the studio and their plans for development of new projects.

'I told Michael what you said in your letter. He says he will write to you and ask me to post it for him. You should let him come and see you Lamorna. You're crazy. You know how he feels about you.'

'I don't know anything anymore,' she thought. 'I can't see him. I hope Jude keeps her promise.'

She went down for a meal with Janet and Fiona. They were completely absorbed with the Christmas plans in their schools.

'The children get so excited, it's exhausting,' Fiona said.

'Yeah, I've got a nativity play to organise, and a whole school assembly.' Over coffee Janet and Lamorna discussed their proposed trip.

'We could stay at my Aunt's cottage in Youlgrave if it's available,' Janet suggested.

'That's great, we could do some walking. I've not been up to the Peak District since I was a child.'

'I'm going skiing in Austria with Mark's family,' Fiona said. 'My first time, I'm terrified.'

'A perfect place for Christmas though, a real white Christmas,' Lamorna said.

A week later she received some cards, one from her parents, one from Joy in London, saying things were going great and she'd met a fabulous new man, and four with Penzance post marks. One of these was a card from Mary and Chris with a short letter from Mary enclosed.

'I'm sorry to hear about you and Michael. I can understand how you must have felt. We saw him a couple of weeks ago. He looked so miserable. He went to the pub with Chris and got very drunk. Never seen him like that. He just kept saying over and over how stupid he was, how one stupid moment has ruined his life. Can't you just see him again Lamorna? He's really sorry.'

Lamorna brushed away tears, and then opened the card which bore Jude's handwriting. The message read; 'Have a Merry Christmas.' There was a card from Aileen and Sam which just said 'Season's Greetings.' Aileen had written along the bottom;

'I'm so sorry to hear about you and Michael. I am so disappointed in him. I hope you can work it out between you both. Please feel that you can visit us any time. You will always be welcome. All our Love Aileen.'

'I can't, I don't want to risk seeing Michael. I couldn't talk to her. Wonder if she knows about the baby.'

She sighed and picked up the final card.

'Who could it be, don't recognise the writing.'

The card was a picture of Christmas lights around Mousehole harbour. Written inside were the words;

'To Lamorna, all my love, Michael.'

There was a folded piece of paper. She opened it.

'Lamorna, please don't go away from me. I love you so much. I can't bear to live without you. I'm so sorry for the mess I made of things. Please can't we try again? There will never be anyone else in my heart.'

At the bottom of the page he had written, *'Giving this to Phil to post. They still won't tell me where you are. I've been up there to try and find you.'*

She placed the cards on her mantelpiece and then holding Michael's letter she crawled into bed and gave herself up to sobbing.

*

In the week before Christmas her life was suddenly a social whirl. Janet and Fiona had organised a party and she met a whole new group of people, friends of theirs from college days and their work. Clive and Pam from the ground floor came too. Pam's mum was babysitting. Lamorna invited people from work, and Greg, her boss immediately homed in on Janet. It was the beginning of a whirlwind romance for her. One of Fiona's college friends took an interest in Lamorna and invited her out for a meal with him in a couple of days. She accepted graciously, but she knew that he would be nothing to her. They met in town and went to a small Chinese restaurant in an unpromising location behind the station, but it turned out to be very pleasant, and the food was great. John was good company and she enjoyed the evening. She allowed him to kiss her when he dropped her off. As soon as he'd gone she went into the house, closed the door behind her and leaned against it for a moment.

Janet was just coming out of her kitchen with a mug of cocoa as she climbed up the stairs.

'How did your evening go? Want some cocoa?'

'No, I'm alright thanks. I'll come and talk to you though. She followed Janet into the lounge and they sat together on the settee.

'No Greg tonight?'

'No, he's in Manchester. Fiona's out with Mark, so I've managed to get all my parcels wrapped while it's quiet. Well come on, tell me about your evening.'

'John is really nice, such fun to be with, but the trouble is he's not Michael. Seeing another man made me think about him even more. I don't know how I'm ever going to get him out of my mind.'

Janet handed her a box of tissues.

'Oh Lamorna, I don't know what to say. If he means so much to you can't you try to make it work?'

'I don't know. It's such a mess Janet. I've never told you the whole story. There was someone else.'

She went on to tell Janet everything that had happened.

'So you see there'll be a baby. He'll want to be with Rosa then.'

'You're right, it is a mess. But who is this Rosa?'

'When I first went down to Cornwall Michael had been in some kind of relationship with her, but she was already pregnant by someone else. She has a baby boy. They split up, and then I came along and got together with Michael. She came to see him while I was away with Jude. So he'll want to be with her. I was just something that happened in between.'

'It must have been terrible coming back and finding them after what had happened to you.'

'I'm sorry, I keep on crying.'

'Don't be sorry, you need to cry.'

'I ran away when I saw them. In the end Michael found me, and told me that he'd been stupid, that Rosa had come to see him because she was upset. A friend had been sent to Vietnam. He took her out for a meal, and they had too much to drink. That's how it happened. But he was so lovely then Janet. He listened to me when I told him about Rome, what happened. He was helping me to get over it. I trusted him then when he said she wasn't important. And just when it all seemed to be going right again, and I got my job, she turned up and told him she was pregnant.'

'He seems to be trying to do the right thing, but I can understand how you feel.'

'Rosa is beautiful Janet. When I saw her with him she was golden and lovely like an angel. I was all grubby and dishevelled from travelling, and I felt horrible, I felt so ashamed.'

'I think that's what's really wrong,' Janet said. 'I've been reading some women's stories because of our work with the women's group. Women who've been raped have no self-esteem, they feel worthless. That's how you must have been feeling. Did you go for counselling, for help?'

'No, I didn't know where to go.'

'That's why we need a women's centre. I don't know of anywhere either. But I'm serious, I think you need help. If that hadn't happened you would probably have coped, you could still be with Michael.'

'I don't know Janet, I'm not sure I could trust him. It's better like this. I must get to bed, early start tomorrow. Thank you for listening.'

'Any time. I'll ask around and see if there's anywhere you can go to talk.'

'Thank you, but I'm not sure it will make any difference.'

'Lamorna.'

'Yes?'

'Take a look in the mirror when you get upstairs. You are actually lovely. I can't believe Rosa is any more beautiful.'

'She is Janet. She is. She's perfect.'

With that she was gone.

Back in her kitchen Lamorna poured herself a glass of water and stepped over to the window to gaze up at the sky. She saw that it was filled with stars, and she thought about the stars in Cornwall, and the night when they'd slept in the hammock, and how she'd made it sway so it felt as though they were out on a boat, and the stars were tracing patterns over their ocean as they rocked. Tears rolled down her cheeks.

She walked into the bathroom to clean her teeth, and she did look in the mirror. She saw a pale, tear streaked face with the constellation of freckles that she hated. She turned the hot tap on and was relieved when the mirror steamed over and her image was lost.

Chapter 15

At the end of January Lamorna went off to Ireland to take photographs and report on a newly fledged Women's Peace movement.

'Might give us some inspiration,' she told Janet. 'I'll be gone for a couple of weeks. Will you have a key and look after the flat for me?'

She was bursting to tell her friends all about the women's movement when she got back, and knocked on their door as soon as she'd arrived.

'Hi, I'm back.'

'Tea?' Janet smiled. 'Have you eaten?'

'Yes thanks, but tea would be great. Women Together for Peace is an amazing thing. Monica and the others were wonderful. I think there are some lessons we can learn from them.'

She sat at the big table with Fiona and Janet and talked about her experiences in Ireland, showed them a few pictures that she'd had developed over there and then they gave her an update on the Women's Group plans.

'We've found a possible place for our Centre,' Fiona told her. It's a former grocery shop in a quiet area.'

They talked non-stop over tea, until at last Lamorna announced that she needed to get unpacked and have a shower.

'I'll help you carry your stuff upstairs,' Janet said, standing.

'No need,' Lamorna protested, 'I can manage.'

'Don't argue.'

'Okay, you win,' she laughed. 'It's good to be back.'

Janet opened her door for her, and they carried her bags in.

'Looks just the same, thanks for keeping an eye on the place Janet.'

'It's not quite the same. There's a letter for you. You had a visitor. You didn't tell us you were having a birthday in February.'

'Well, I was going to be away, no point. Who came? Was it Jude?'

'No, it was Michael.'

'Michael? How did he find me? Why?' Her bag slipped out of her hand and thumped onto the floor.

'He went to see your mother. She gave him your address.'

'I never thought he would do that.' She spoke quietly, her face drained of its glow now.

'He brought you a lovely bouquet of daffodils, Cornish daffodils. He's lovely Lamorna. I can see why you fell for him. I looked after the flowers, but they didn't last for you. He left you a note on your table. It's with all the post. He didn't think you would read it. But I hope you will. He at least deserves that. I'll get going now, dinner will be ready. Are you okay?'

'Yes, thank you.'

She walked into the kitchen, and saw the letter lying there. After a while she picked it up and opened it.

'Dear Lamorna,

This is a hard letter to write. I wanted to see you but you were away. Your mother told me your address. Jude wouldn't.

It's difficult to know how to put my feelings into just a few words on paper. I've wasted so much of Janet's note pad already.

I just want you to know that I will always be there for you. I will always love you. I won't try to contact you again, if that's what you want. I'll let you get on with your life. I know you are going to be really successful, and I will be so proud of you.

Mum's Dad has died in Ireland and I am going over there when I finish college to take on the farm for a while and help my Gran. You will know where to find me.

All my love,

Michael.

She read it through several times. And then she just sat and stared at the wall. That's how Janet found her when she came up.

'Are you okay?'

'Not really. I don't know what to do.'

'I came up to invite you down for coffee.'

'It's such a short letter. It seems so matter of fact. He seems to be telling me to get on with my life.'

'Isn't that what you want?'

'I suppose it is. What did he say when he was here?'

'He told me how much he missed you, that he was concerned about you. We talked for a long time. He wanted to know how you were, what you were doing. He said that he'd told Rosa he didn't want any future with her. He said he'd help financially with the baby when he could afford to, but that was all.'

'He didn't say any of that in the letter.'

'Perhaps he wants you to make your own decision without any sense of obligation to him.'

'That sounds like Michael. He wouldn't try to blackmail me.'

The next morning she had an intriguing letter. It was from the magazine that had bought her Cornish photographs. The editor was offering her a permanent job, on a salary that was twice what she currently earned. There would be lots of travel involved. It was an offer she couldn't refuse. That evening she shared the news with Janet and Fiona.

'I told Greg today,' she said. 'He thinks I should go for it. But I'll miss them all so much.'

She wrote to Jude and Mary to tell them the news.

'I'm going to keep the flat on here, so you can always contact me. I will probably be abroad a fair bit, but will keep in touch with you.'

Her last assignment for the magazine was to cover a new Women's Refuge that had just opened in Chiswick. It would be a great help to their group. She would get lots of information, ideas and photographs to share. 'I'll miss this work,' she thought, it's more focussed on the things I want to do, but I can't turn the international work down.'

*

By the end of the next month she was down in London, finding her feet in her new role, staying at her friend Joy's flat. Almost immediately she was sent on her first assignment, so that it was the middle of July before she managed to get back home. There was a letter waiting from Jude.

'Good luck with the new job you lucky thing, sounds exciting. The studio is doing well, I'm really enjoying being down here. Don't know whether you knew that Rosa's baby was born last week, he was black, so definitely not Michael's. We're all wondering who the father is, but apparently she hasn't said. Michael was there for the birth. He came down here after it all. You can't imagine how relieved he was. Phil took him out for a drink. Can't believe he wasn't angry with Rosa. Phil reckons she must be a bit of a slag. Why don't you go and see him Lorna? Now you know. Phil tried to persuade Michael to ring you.'

Lamorna put the letter down. She wondered what Michael was really thinking. What would he have said to Rosa? What would Rosa do now? She wondered why Michael had not been in touch to tell her himself. Maybe she should contact him, talk to him. If we'd known it wasn't his baby would we have split up? Would I have left him? She didn't know.

'Maybe everything is for the best. I've got a new job. I won't be around. Michael will be in Ireland. I can't get in the way of that. It's his dream.'
She read on.

'Ian married Maureen in May. Phil and I did the photographs. Nice wedding, not anywhere like as good as Mary and Chris's though. Rumour is that Maureen is pregnant, probably the only way she could tie him down. Mary and Chris are fine. They're expecting another baby.'

Janet called her down for coffee, and she was glad of the chance to stop thinking.

'Lamorna, are you alright? You haven't heard a word I was saying.'

'Sorry. I had a letter from Jude. Lots of news. My friend Mary is expecting a second baby. I was a godmother to her first daughter Emily.'

'Do you think she'll ask you again?'

'I don't know. It will be awkward because of Michael.'

'Oh, I see. Is that all you've got on your mind?'

'No. She also told me that Rosa's baby was born, and it was black. So not Michael's.'

'How do you feel about that?'

'Pleased I suppose. I know it's selfish of me, but I didn't want her to have his baby. And I'm sad. Sad that she caused a problem, a situation which made us split up, made me run away from it all. I'm wondering if she knew that it might not be his baby. It makes me feel sorry for her too. She won't have any help. I ran away for nothing I suppose.'

'You could contact him.'

'I don't know if I should. He didn't let me know.'

'But he told you that he wouldn't contact you again, that it would be up to you. He left it up to you. He tried hard to persuade you to come back to him.'

'I know. But he's got a chance to follow his dream now on the farm in Ireland. I miss him so much. I can't imagine ever finding anyone else I care about. But I don't know if the farm would work for me. And I feel I have to stay with my new job for a while, achieve something after my degree. It's what I've always wanted. I need to feel I can be independent.'

'You're lucky to have a choice.'

'I know. I'm being greedy. In a way I feel as though I met Michael at the wrong time. I want everything. I want to be with him and have a family. But I want my job too.'

'Surely you could have both? Couldn't you live in Ireland and still travel?'

'I don't know. It would be difficult. And he hasn't been in touch. Maybe he's trying to move on and forget me.'

'Well,' Janet said, 'it's your decision. But I can understand why you want to be independent.'

Later Lamorna was back in her flat, reading through the letter again.

'What shall I do? I love this job. I can't just walk out on them now. If Michael got in touch, maybe it would be different. I don't know. I've worked hard to get so far. I can't let this job go. What if I wrote to Michael, told him about my job, would he wait for me?'

Thoughts rambled around her head as she lay in bed that night. It was several hours before she eventually fell into an uneasy sleep.

***

A letter arrived from Mary the next day. It was full of news about Ian and Maureen, and the expected new baby.

We wondered if you would like to be a godmother again. Michael has already said he will. I know it's a bit early to ask but I know you're busy. I thought you might be able to take some holiday around the time the baby is due, come and stay with us. It seems so long since we saw you. I expect you heard about Rosa's baby. Michael told Chris he was so relieved the baby wasn't his. He was really worried. You could get back together with him now, couldn't you? I know he misses you. He was so miserable at Christmas. Aileen was really mad with him. I don't know if she knows the whole story. He told us what happened. I can understand why you left him. I would have done the same. But now things could be alright again couldn't they? You could live together on the farm. He says he's going out there as soon as his course finishes. Sorry, I'm rambling on. Mum sends love and a big kiss from Emily. She loves the little boats you sent her. Come and see us soon.'

It was over a week before she replied. She was struggling to write, unsure what to do. In the end she decided to apologise, and tell Mary that she couldn't be a godmother.

'I've started a new job which involves a lot of travel. I have to be available at a moment's notice, so it will be hard to commit the time. I'm sure you'll find someone more suitable. Jude told me about Rosa's baby. I've not heard from Michael. He's getting on with his life now. The farm is what he wanted. I'll keep in touch and try to get down and see you in the autumn.'

She sighed as she sealed the envelope. It seemed a lifetime since that summer when she had first met Mary, and fallen in love with Michael. She thought about Mary, how content she was with Chris. Her own life seemed empty without Michael. 'But I need to move on, I've got to make something of my life, nothing can really be the same between us again, after what happened. And I've got an opportunity I never dreamed of. I can't waste it.'

The next few months were a whirlwind for her, there was so much work, and she was rarely at home. Each time she returned from an assignment she would always look through her post as soon as she walked through the door. There was never a letter from Michael. She knew in her heart that there wouldn't be, and yet there was a part of her that hoped for something, some word from him. She imagined him working on the farm in the autumn, preparing for a busy season. Jude had mentioned in a letter that he was busy repairing and renovating neglected buildings, and turning a disused barn into a small cottage for himself. She pictured him, sleeves rolled up, brown skin, toiling about the place. She thought about the time they'd spent there together, the album of pictures she'd made for his Mum.

'I'm glad I did that,' she thought, 'it will be great for her to have photographs of her father just before he died.'

Chapter 16

There was barely time to think after the Women's Centre opened in 1972. Lamorna was busy with her career and whenever she could she was down there helping to support the women who sought sanctuary and advice. She was financially secure now, and her main contribution to the project was money that she set aside for it out of her salary. She made her flat available as a temporary refuge for women in need. She had stored her personal belongings in her 'hobbit hole' cupboard and invested in camp beds for the children. Fiona and Janet were happy to organise things in her absence. Luckily the landlord had updated the meter arrangements and now never visited the flat. She was not sure he would approve of the visitors. A number of battered women and occasional children were grateful for a place to stay whilst more permanent arrangements were made. Sometimes she had to camp out for a couple of nights with her friends if her flat was occupied when she arrived home after a trip.

'Sorry we can only offer a bed settee,' Janet had said.

'It's no hardship, not when you compare it to the lives of these women and children,' she'd replied. 'I wish I could do more.'

The Centre provided support and advice, and they had raised funds to enable the employment of a full time worker who could refer women for other appropriate advice and help. Eventually they hoped to have resident medical staff and counsellors.

Lamorna found time to see a counsellor who volunteered at the centre, and was able to talk over what had happened to her in Rome. She found it helpful, and each time she was home made a point of visiting for more support. The counsellor had asked her to keep a diary of her thoughts and dreams as part of the process of healing and this made her examine her feelings in ways she had never done before.

She'd been in Northern Ireland in February, covering the aftermath of the Bloody Sunday massacre, taking photographs for a feature on the impact of women affected by the incident. And she'd found the experience deeply moving. Her thoughts went back to the women time and again; their courage and bravery after what they had suffered.

'How can I be brooding about something as trivial as losing someone I loved when all of this is happening to other women?' she wrote in her journal. 'Why would I dwell on things that happened so long ago?'

And then inevitably she thought of Michael again.

'I could so easily have gone to see him. Taken some holiday and travelled down to Sligo.'

She had lain awake on the last night of her visit, wondering how it would be if she were to just turn up at the farm and walk into his life.

'It wouldn't be fair,' she'd decided then. 'He has his own life now. Maybe he's found someone new.'

She made a 'to do' list in her journal, to remind her to stay positive. It began with the words;

1 Think of three great things in my current life before I get up in the morning.
2 Write down the best thing that happened that day before I go to bed.
She still kept in contact every now and again by letter or postcard with Mary and Jude, but neither of them mentioned Michael these days.

At Easter she spent a few days with Jude and Phil, and plucked up courage to go and see Mary too, knowing that she would face some difficult questions. Despite Mary's support and understanding she knew that her friend thought she should be getting back with Michael. The latest addition to their family was named Catherine for Mary's Mum.

'Chris was convinced she would be a boy,' she said, laughing. 'He was going to be named Michael. But he loves her to bits. Michael always asks after you, I never know what to say.'

'Tell him I'm well, and I think of him.'

'You two are crazy. I don't understand you at all.'

'I don't understand myself. I'm just so involved with my work. Has Michael found someone new?'

'I don't think so. I'm sure he would tell Chris. He asked me the same thing when he came over for Catherine's Christening. But I don't suppose he'll wait for you forever.'

'I don't expect him to wait for me. How is he?'

'He's well enough, there's a lot to do on the farm. We saw him at Christmas too; he was over for a few days. He always seems lonely though. He told Chris he misses you. We might go over for a week, have a holiday with him in the summer.'
Lamorna's eyes filled with tears.

'Look at you. What's to be done with you? What's the matter with you both?'

'I don't know Mary, I don't know. But don't tell him you've seen me like this. Please.'

Chapter 17

Another year without Michael began. Another year when Lamorna immersed herself in her work. She went over to Florida to cover a Led Zeppelin tour. The publishing group she worked for had started up a cultural journal. A local music magazine writer took an interest in her, and liking his easy going personality and sense of humour she went out for an evening with him, and then found herself agreeing to a few days on the Gulf Coast before she returned to England. He was good company, and attractive, with dark blonde hair, and a short beard. She liked the way he held hands with her as they walked. He had friends who owned a condominium on an offshore island, and they enjoyed a relaxing break, swimming in the clear warm water, exploring the neighbouring islands and Cypress swamp.

She allowed herself to be seduced by him on the second night. He was an attentive lover and it wasn't an unpleasant experience, but her heart was not there. She lay awake afterwards, shifting uncomfortably under the weight of his arm flung over her, thinking about Michael; thinking about how he would have kissed her afterwards and held her in his arms. She felt herself ache with longing for him, tears running down her face.

She made more of an effort the next day.
'I've got to try, maybe one day it will work,' she thought. 'Spencer is nice enough.'
They spent another day on the beach. Lamorna was fascinated by the shells washed up on the shore line, and she wandered along, gathering up curious specimens she'd never seen before. Tiny urchin shells and spiral shapes in shades of white and cream and pink. Her thoughts drifted back to the time she had spent on the Isles of Scilly with Michael, how she had gathered small shells, and how he had surprised her by making them into a necklace for Christmas. 'I still have that necklace somewhere,' she thought. Suddenly she discarded the shells. 'I've got to stop this. I've got to stop dreaming about him.'

She walked back up the sand to the spot where Spencer was sprawled on his towel, lay down beside him and wrapped her arms around him.
'Hey, what's this all about?' he said, grinning.
'Must have sun stroke,' she answered.
They made love again after they'd showered for dinner. She had been determined to make a real effort, but somehow it didn't really work. He didn't seem to notice that she wasn't fully relaxed and that she'd managed to fake an orgasm.
Later they sat together on the verandah to eat. Spencer had made them a barbecue. He'd opened a bottle of red wine, and drank most of it, as well as a few cans of beer. Lamorna noticed that the alcohol made him more talkative.

'It's been great,' he said. 'Wish we could stay longer. I think we should get together. I gotta tell you. I'm married. It's been four years. But Claudia, well, she kinda doesn't get me, understand me. Not like you. We've got something special. You and me. We could make a go of it. I could help you find plenty of work over here. You'd love it. I'm based in LA. It's wild. So many opportunities. We could maybe live in London part time. I'd get work there for sure. I've made a name in the music scene....'

He talked on, only stopping now and again to take a swig from a can.

'I don't think so,' she said, when at last he stopped and turned to her. 'I wouldn't want to cause a break up in your marriage. Besides, there's someone else in my life.'

In a way he seemed a little relieved by her response, but later was displeased when she rejected his advances.

'You're a married man,' she said, brushing him off. 'I won't let you hurt your wife. I know how that feels.'

She moved into a separate room for their last night, and the whole trip ended with a cold atmosphere between them. He was courteous enough, dropping her at the airport for her plane. There was no talk about meeting up again.

*

The music theme continued in her work. In August she went to the Salzburg Festival to record the visit by the London Symphony Orchestra: the first time a British orchestra had played there. Afterwards she took a week off and spent time with Marguerite again. They travelled together to the French Riviera for a few days, and lay on the beach in Nice, soaking up the sun. She was amazed by the art deco buildings and clicked away with her camera.

Marguerite quizzed her about her love life.

'Oh, there's no-one at the moment. I'm just enjoying my work and independence. What about you?'

'I never feel the need for a man in my life. Not anymore. I love my freedom too much. I've had, how do you say it, a few flings. That's nice, but they always want to intrude on my privacy. I got very close to one guy. But he was just the same in the end. Talked about living together. He said I should sell up and move in with him. He was always wanting to change me, change everything. He moved books around on my shelves so that they were alphabetical. That's when I knew it wouldn't work out. Besides, I'm too old now and set in my ways.'

'Marguerite! You're only thirty seven.'

'Too old for babies maybe. So what's the point? Did you ever think of having children?'

Lamorna thought for a moment.

'We talked about it once when I was with Michael. But it seemed so far into the future. He would have made a good father.'

'You miss him still I think?'

'I do. I can't help it. I never meet anyone that can compare with him. I had one of those flings a couple of months ago. He was okay, but he was married. It was the first time I'd slept with anyone else.'

'Was Michael your first?'

'Yes. There was no-one else.'

'That's your problem. He was your first love. It's hard to forget them. You probably never will. But someday you will find someone. It was the same for me. Now Stefan is just a fond memory, special, yes, but it no longer hurts.'

'I suppose you're right. But I'm thinking now I'll stay as I am. I don't need a man around. I've got my work. I love it. I've loads of friends.'

'You are happy?'

'Yes, I think I am.'

In October she was in Australia, getting photographs of the Queen's visit to open the new Sydney Opera House.

Mary and Chris produced a third daughter, Jenny, in November, and she went down to see them for a weekend just before Christmas, bearing Australian themed gifts of toy koala bears and kangaroos. There was no conversation about Michael, although Mary talked about the hotel.

'Aileen says they are struggling a bit, so many folk are going abroad for holidays now. She always asks after you, you know.'

'I miss her,' Lamorna confessed. 'She and Sam were good to me. I'd hate to think of the hotel failing. They've worked so hard.'

'Ellen's talked about moving on, starting up in Spain or Greece.'

'Oh. Sam would be so disappointed. They've not started a family then?'

'No. Ellen's never been interested. Aileen's very disappointed. What with…' She broke off in mid-sentence. Lamorna guessed that she was about to mention Michael…maybe something about there being no grandchildren there either. She longed to ask about him but she couldn't. She was afraid he might have another woman in his life now. Bound to have.

Lamorna never seemed to find time for a proper holiday. She travelled so much for her work that it was almost a relief just to spend time at the flat. She was back there for a few days after her trip to Cornwall, enjoying decorating the kitchen. A woman victim of abuse and her young son had been staying for a couple of nights, and the walls were looking a bit grubby. Everyone else was out at work, so she had the whole house to herself. She was up a ladder listening to the radio when she thought she heard the doorbell ring.

'Who could that be at this time of day?'

She popped the paint roller into the tray and ran briskly down the stairs. Opening the door she was suddenly faced with a tall scruffy man.

'Where's Emma?' he said, leering at her, and pushing past her into the hallway. He was dressed in jeans and a sweatshirt with grease smeared over it, dirty trainers on his feet. Her heart skipped a beat when she glimpsed the flash of a knife blade in his hand.

'I don't know what you mean. I don't know anyone called Emma. You've no right to come barging into this house.'

'I've been told she was 'ere and I've come to get her. I want my kid back.' He strode off down the hall, pushing at the doors. All were locked.

'There's no one in, they're all at work. A family live here. There's no-one called Emma.'

She felt her heart thudding in her chest. 'I should run. Get out,' she thought. But fear paralysed her. He turned, the knife gleaming. Sharp blade catching a shaft of sun from the window.

'I don't believe you. She's here. I've been told. Let's go upstairs.'
He gestured to her to go ahead, and she did as she was bid.

'What's going to happen when he finds nothing?' she thought. 'What will he do? Maybe I should make a run for it.'
But something compelled her to walk on, to stay calm. She watched in silence as he tried all the doors to Janet and Fiona's rooms. They were all unlocked, and he pushed her in front of him into each room. She watched helplessly as he searched, turning cushions over, opening drawers and cupboards.

They went on up to her flat, and again he pushed her first into each room and searched around. She noticed a small toy car half hidden under her bed. She breathed in. He didn't notice it. He saw her suitcase in the corner and kicked it open. She hadn't finished unpacking, and her clothes were still jumbled inside. He tipped it over, and she felt herself reddening as he sneered at her underwear. Whilst he was preoccupied she pushed the toy further under the bed with her foot.

'She was here.' He said, turning and pointing the knife against her throat. 'Where is she now?'

'I don't know. You can see I've been away. I got back last night. I don't know any Emma. I've never seen her.'

He stared, motionless, for what seemed a lifetime, then turning on his heel he ran downstairs again. She followed him. He turned in the doorway.

'If I find you've lied to me....,'was all he said as he ran the blade across close to his own throat before walking out and away down the road to a waiting car. She made a mental note of the registration number as it pulled out, tyres screeching and sped away.

She closed and locked the door, then ran back up to her flat. She rang the police and told them what had happened, giving them the number of the car. She didn't feel confident about going out on her own as she'd planned that afternoon, despite needing a trip to buy food. Janet had some bread and cheese in their fridge, so she helped herself. It was a relief when her friends came back from work.

'I've raided your fridge,' she told them, 'I hope that's okay.'

'Of course, you know you're welcome, but why? What's happened? You look a bit pale. She put the kettle on and made them all tea.

'I had a visitor.'
She told them what had happened.

'Oh God, how terrible for you. I suppose it was bound to happen someday. But who could have told him? Emma was here last week with her little boy. We only found her a place to go yesterday. She was in a terrible state. He'd come in drunk and beaten her up. She came to the Centre and they had to take her to Casualty. Have you reported it?'

'Yes, I rang the police, and gave them the car registration number. I didn't get much sympathy. I felt there was an underlying feeling that I was a fool, that I should expect something like that to happen. Someone is coming to interview me.'

'We persuaded Emma to report him, so this should help to get him convicted if they can find him.'

'We really need that refuge,' Fiona added. 'It's too risky, he might have used the knife on you Lamorna.'

Chapter 18

The following year was just as busy. She went to China to cover the discovery of the Terracotta Army amongst many assignments. But she was beginning to feel weary of the work, wanting something different, missing the companionship and social life she had enjoyed in her first job with Greg. She was enjoying some fame, had been interviewed on Woman's Hour, and the magazine had actually done a feature about her, but she was restless. When Greg rang her up after a trip to Paris in the spring and told her he was setting up his own agency, wondering if she would work for him, she responded immediately without hesitation.

'That's great. No pressure,' he said. 'I can try and find a market for stuff you want to do, but I can't promise you a fortune.'

'The money doesn't matter,' she told him. 'I'd like to do something different, get back to the things I feel passionate about.'

That summer Fiona married Mark, and gave up her share of the flat. Lamorna spent a little more time there, getting to know Janet and Greg again. It was no surprise when they announced that they would be finding a place of their own.

'I'm not sure about marriage,' Janet told her over coffee one night, 'it never seems all that necessary to me. But I do love Greg; I want to live with him. What about you Lamorna, has there been anyone new in your life whilst you've been globe-trotting around?'

'No, not really. I met someone in the States last year, but he turned out to be married. I know it's crazy but I'm still hung up on Michael. I can't get him out of my head. It's actually his birthday tomorrow. I'm finding myself wondering what he'll be doing.'

'Oh Lamorna, it's not good. Why don't you just go and see him? Maybe you can make it work again.'

'I couldn't. I don't think I'd have the courage after all this time.'

She did phone Jude the next day though, telling her that she was now freelance, and may not be travelling around so much.

'We went over to Ireland at Easter,' Jude told her, stayed with Michael a few days. His Grandmother's died, so he's on his own there now. Seems to be making a go of the place. He has the loveliest little donkey foal, and he's got a small boat for fishing. He asked about you.'

'What did you say?'

'Told him we never see you. I told him about Woman's Hour. He didn't hear it. But he's got a folder of cuttings, all your work from magazines. Why don't you go and see him? He said he bought the donkey for you.'

'I don't know Jude. Scared I suppose. Scared there'll be nothing left, that we won't feel the same.'

'You won't find out, will you, if you don't take the risk? He's joined a group, a Celtic band, sort of folk rock. 'Celtic Wings,' they're called. We heard them when we were over there. Really good. Maybe you should do a feature on them.'

'Oh, I'm not doing that kind of stuff now Jude.'

'Just thought you might like to help a friend make it to the Big Time.'
'I don't think anything I did could have that effect.'

She felt uncomfortable after the call, sensing that her friend was increasingly exasperated by her, more firmly taking Michael's side of things. There had been no mention of any woman in his life though. She examined her feelings about that.

'He should have someone,' she thought. 'He's so lovely. But I couldn't bear it if he did. I know that's not fair of me, but I can't help it.'

***

Work took over again, and it was October before she felt there was a moment to spare.

'Get your jeans on and a warm woolly,' Janet said one Saturday afternoon. 'Greg's picking us up in ten minutes.'

'Where are we going?'

'Surprise!'

Just over an hour later they were riding together on a big wheel at the Nottingham Goose Fair.

'I can't believe I've never been before. I grew up about ten miles away. I suppose it's because my Mum wasn't keen on fairs. She had some strange idea I'd get stolen by gypsies I think.'

She was amazed at how enormous it was. She walked around, finding lots of subjects for her camera. She was fascinated by the people in the crowd, a woman with an amazing towering blonde beehive which looked exactly like the pink candy- floss she was holding in the red glow of fairground lights. Some children were feeding coins into amusement machines with feverish excitement, and a group of green-faced teenage girls staggered drunkenly in high heels from the waltzer.

'You can't give up working, can you?' Greg said, laughing.

'It's like my camera's a part of me, I have to take photographs. I seem to see everything as a photo.'

'Might be able to sell these though.'

'Greg! You two are as bad as each other,' Janet complained. 'Come on, let's go and find some stalls.'

'Look at that,' Lamorna said, pointing to an amazing 'steam yacht' swing boat ride.

'Michael would love that. I wish he was here,' she thought.

Janet looked at her.

'What are you thinking about now Lamorna?'

'I was remembering how I've always wanted to go to a fair with a boyfriend so that he could win me a fluffy teddy at the rifle range.'

'I'll win one for you,' Greg said, and he went over to the booth, straight away hitting every target and presenting her with her bear.

'Greg, that's amazing! How did you do that?'

'I grew up on a farm. I was shooting rabbits when I was eight, and they move fast. That was a piece of cake.'

'Come on Lamorna,' Janet shouted. 'Galloping horses.'

The carousel slowed to a stop, and they clambered on board. Lamorna rushed around, trying to find the right horse. She climbed up. Janet came and sat on the horse next to her. Lamorna saw her looking oddly over at her whilst they waited for the ride to start.

'Why did you choose that horse Lamorna?'

'I don't know. I liked the look of him I suppose. The red bridle and saddle I think. And a sort of look in his eye.' She glanced over at Janet, and suddenly saw the name 'Rosa' painted on Janet's horse's harness. She looked down at her own steed, and her heart stood still when she read 'Mike.'

But the carousel started to move then, and she brushed aside her silliness as she hung on, trying to photograph the whirling motion, as the horses swooped up and down and around and the organ music drowned out their voices.

They bought hot chestnuts, and burned their fingers and mouths trying to eat them too quickly. And then the others went off to find a pub. Lamorna stayed for a while longer, taking photographs of the crowd again. She got some good pictures of the dodgems, and spent a while focussing on the crowds gazing up at the big wheel, before deciding to head off and join them.

In November she worked for the Guardian, covering the aftermath of the pub bombings in the city, then finding herself agreeing to go over to Ireland with a journalist to get pictures for a feature on the families of the so-called Birmingham Six who'd been arrested for the bombing. The focus was to be on the women from the area, including those involved in peace initiatives, and to explore views of the men's relatives.

There was absolute conviction from everyone they spoke to that the men were innocent. It was the kind of work she enjoyed most. She travelled to Dublin for a couple of nights afterwards for another small piece of work for Greg. It was the first time in the city since her trip with Michael, and she found time to wander around, noticing familiar landmarks, reading a local paper, looking up timetables for travel to Sligo, and then deciding she couldn't go. She saw a poster for 'Celtic Wings.' There was a blurry picture, but she could identify Michael, looking serious, guitar in hand. She noticed an attractive dark haired woman by his side. It seemed the band had played in Dublin just a few days before.

She caught up with her family at Christmas, and then spent Boxing Day with Janet and Greg. It felt lonely when she arrived back at her little flat. The floor below was occupied by a young couple now, and she missed her friends.

She had given herself a couple of weeks off work and decided to go house hunting. She had considerable savings now, never getting round to spending her money. She travelled up to Derbyshire, thinking she could buy a cottage and work from there, feeling the need to go back to her roots. Most of her assignments involved travel, so it didn't seem to matter where her starting point was. She liked the idea of a place in the country, somewhere quiet, away from the hectic schedule of work. After a couple of days hunting she found a perfect cottage in a small village overlooking Lathkil Dale, made an offer and was accepted. The Peak District seemed a good location, not too far from Greg's office in Birmingham, close to Manchester airport and more or less in the centre of the country. Three months later she had moved.

Chapter 19

In the January of 1975 International Women's Year was launched in Britain, and the Women's Group organised a celebration event at the Centre. They were still busy fund raising, and on target to open a women's refuge in the near future. Greg used his contacts to get an article about their work into the national press, and Lamorna, of course, took the photographs.

At the end of September she was in New Zealand working on a feature about a Maori woman's protest march and efforts to claim back their lands. She was invited out by a local radio journalist. He was tall and dark haired, with brown eyes and dark skin. He claimed to have some Maori blood. He was actually called Mike, which she found a bit awkward, but then she had always called Michael by his full name. She was attracted to him, but after an evening out and too much wine she found herself in his bed, staring at a ceiling fan as he grunted over her, and then rolled away, leaving her lying awake and frustrated. She stayed another night, thinking they'd just drunk too much, and maybe she should make an effort, give it another try, but it was just the same.

'What happened to your leg?' he'd eventually asked.

'I was burned when I was a child.'

She noticed that he avoided touching the scars. Really he was not much into touching her at all, just eager to get on with the sex. Once he was satisfied he clambered off her and fell immediately asleep, snoring. She lay for a while watching again the interminable sweep of the ceiling fan's blades cutting though the dust motes in a shaft of moonlight, and then got up, dressed, and went back to her hotel. She didn't see him again, and flew home the next evening.

Back in the cottage she reflected on her experiences. 'Why doesn't it work? Is it me, or the situation? Jude always seemed to enjoy sex with all sorts of men, people she'd only just met. And me, I found it wanting.'

She lay in her bed that night with the curtains open so that she could see the stars in the dark sky, and the moon, almost full now, staring insolently at her through the glass. And she thought about Michael. She wondered if he could see the moon over on his farm. Thought about the way he made love to her, the way he talked to her when he caressed her, his concern that she should enjoy it. She remembered how their lovemaking was a long and loving joy, an exploration of each other's bodies. He would never have left her frustrated, always held her and kissed her afterwards, told her how much he loved her.

'I don't expect declarations of love, she thought. I don't love them. But it would be nice if they cared about me, about how it felt for me.'

Lamorna was in Birmingham again with the Women's group in spring 1976, celebrating the opening of the first women's refuge in the City, the refuge they had worked so hard to set up. Of course there was no publicity, the location had to be secret, but it was so exciting for them all. Lamorna still managed to give funds each month towards the Women's Group, and they had also secured grant aid from several local charities. She still thought about the rape, but felt the memory no longer had the power to distress her.

'What if the centre had been open then,' she thought. 'If I'd had help then maybe Janet is right, perhaps it would have made things so different. I was so down, so devastated by it. And I really thought it was my fault.'

She thought about the counsellor she had seen, what she had said about guilt and shame, how women feel they are to blame, and how that can impact on their lives, their relationships.

'Is that what's wrong with me still, even after all these years? Do I still feel that I'm not good enough? Is that why I drive myself so hard, why I have to do everything to perfection? I have to do well, I have to for Dad. He had such confidence in me, wanted so much for me. I wish he could be here to see what I've done with my life. Would he be proud? What would he say? I could have talked to him about Michael. Do I still feel I'm not good enough for Michael?'

Her thoughts meandered on. She wondered where Rosa was, the baby boy would be five years old now. 'Must ask Jude if she's heard anything. Wonder what happened to Ced in Vietnam, and where Laura and Jean are now. So many people, and I don't know where they are, what they're doing.'

Chapter 20

A month later she was on her way to Venice. Greg had succeeded in getting her a commission from The British Council to photograph the work of British Artist Richard Long at the Venice Biennale. In particular she was there to capture the response of visitors, the ordinary people in the crowds.

She spent the first morning wandering around the British Pavilion, getting the feel of the exhibition, following the spiral of stones the artist had arranged to lead visitors through a series of rooms. She unobtrusively photographed a range of people as they stood and looked, sometimes poring over their catalogues, sometimes approaching the stones for a closer view. She captured some lively children trying to balance on the stones, and the gallery staff remonstrating with them.

'I'm on the children's side,' she thought, 'they're just the thing to climb on. Wonder what the artist would think.'

She found a trattoria in a small sunny campo to eat some lunch, and she relaxed and let her mind wander.

'Maybe I should have a proper holiday, take a couple of weeks here, and then spend some time at the cottage.'

A voice cut into her thoughts.

'Would you mind if I shared your table?'

She looked up and saw a well-dressed older man smiling down at her.

'Please do,' she said, sliding her camera across to leave space for him.

'Can I get you anything?' he asked, summoning a waiter.

'That's very kind, perhaps a coffee? How did you know I spoke English?'

'I don't know. I'm pretty good at guessing nationalities. I watched you taking pictures of the stones and the people, but you seem far away now, lost in thought.'

'I was. I was thinking how I've come full circle, or possibly spiral. She laughed. I started with pictures of stones, and here I am again. Although these are a little different, and I'm more interested in the people. That's why I'm here.'

'You are a professional photographer? What were your first stones?'

'Oh, it was long ago, 1968. I was just a student then. I was taking pictures of standing stones in Cornwall, that's in the south west, and they were exhibited at a friend's gallery in Newquay. It was my first success. I even sold some.'

'That's extraordinary, I saw that exhibition. I was working in London then. My wife and I were in Cornwall for a break that winter. I bought one of your pictures for her.'

'That's an amazing coincidence!'

'Yes, but don't you find life is full of such moments?'

'I'm not sure,' she replied, 'but I'm pleased to meet my first client. I'm Lamorna, Lamorna West.' She held out her hand to him, and he took it, and kissed it, much to her surprise.

'The feeling is mutual. I'm Roberto Loredan. I own a small photographer's gallery here in Venice. I wondered if you might like to exhibit some of the photographs.'

'I would love to, but I'm not sure it's possible. It's a special commission and I probably won't own the copyright.'

'I could commission you to work for me.'

'You could, but I may not have time. I'm thinking of taking a holiday. And I think perhaps my lunch break is over,' she said, smiling again, and standing up. 'Thank you for the coffee, I enjoyed talking to you.' She was suddenly worried. Not sure what his motive might be.

'Lamorna, would you have dinner with me tonight? I would appreciate your company, and we could talk about your work, the photographs. Don't worry, my wife died several years ago, and I meant strictly as a business meeting. Don't believe all you hear about Italian men.'

She studied his face for a moment. Thoughts whirling around in her head. What harm could come of just a dinner?

'Thank you, that's very kind."

'Good. Where is your hotel, I can meet you there?'

'I'm only staying at the hostel, I always do when I'm travelling, it's cheaper and you can meet so many friendly people.'

'Well then that is where I shall meet you.'

At seven thirty that evening she was waiting a little nervously. She had brought very little luggage with her for a stay of one or two days, and had difficulty deciding whether to wear her trouser suit or long dress and jacket. In the end she chose the dress.

'What am I doing, going out for dinner with a complete stranger,' she thought. 'Jude would be proud of me. But what if it all goes wrong…what if…? No. I can't believe he would be like that.'

Roberto was suddenly at her side, lifting her hand to kiss it.

'You're looking lovely,' he said. 'Smiling so serenely.'

'I was just thinking about when I was here with a friend, just after we finished college. We sailed from here to Greece, and I always said I must come back to Venice. So here I am.'

'Well, we are embarking on a short voyage now. We are going to my favourite restaurant.'

He led her down some steps and they climbed on board a water taxi to cross the canal to Giudecca. Half an hour later they were sitting on a flower filled balcony overlooking a canal. Lamorna ordered crab linguini, and thought about when she had first eaten crab. She wondered if Michael went fishing for crabs in Ireland.

'You are lost in thought again,' Roberto said quietly.

'I'm sorry, I was just thinking how beautiful it is, the golden light on the water, on the buildings. I'm always thinking of subjects to photograph I suppose.'

She found Roberto to be good company, and they talked all evening. He had changed the smart grey suit he'd been wearing earlier for casual trousers, shirt and jacket, but he still looked suave; 'a typical Italian,' she thought.

'Would you like to come and see the gallery tomorrow?'

'I could. I'll be finished by around twelve o'clock.'

'I will take you for lunch and then we can see the exhibition.'

'Oh no, I couldn't let you buy me lunch.'

'Why couldn't you? It would be my pleasure. And it may encourage you to let me have your work.'

'You're very persuasive,' she said, laughing. 'It would be nice to have some company. It can get lonely, this work. I'm always living out of a suitcase. Hardly have time for a social life.'

'Perhaps you should stay here for your holiday, see more of Italy.'

'Perhaps I should. I have an open ticket. I was intending to have a couple of weeks and then spend some days at home. I bought a small cottage last year, and I've probably only spent about fifteen days there since. Have you always lived in Venice?'

'Yes, I was born here, but I have travelled, worked abroad. In London as I mentioned. My wife loved England.'

'Do you mind if I ask about your wife? You must miss her.'

'I do. She was diagnosed with Leukaemia, and it was only a few months later when she died. It was as though she gave up.'

'I'm sorry. Do you have children?'

'Yes, I have two daughters, perhaps just a little younger than you?'

'Oh.'

'You're thinking 'how old could this guy be.'

'Yes, I was. You don't seem old enough to have children my age.'

'Well I am fifty two.'

'You surprise me, I thought ten years younger.'

'You flatter me. Would you like coffee?'

'No thank you, it will keep me awake. I need to be up early for my last session tomorrow. I'm hoping there will be some interesting visitors.'

'I could arrange for some eccentric locals to come around the exhibition.'

She laughed. 'I don't think it will be necessary. They seem to arrive of their own accord if yesterday is anything to go by.'

'Shall we still meet for lunch?'

'Of course. Why not?'

'Well you know my age now.'

'Roberto, that really doesn't matter, I'm enjoying your company.'

'Thank you, the feeling is mutual.'

The return trip was lovely. It was a warm night, and the sky was full of stars. A full moon shining over the water.

'You speak excellent English,' Lamorna said. 'I feel ashamed of my poor language skills.'

They had arrived at the hostel now, and she reached up impulsively and kissed him on his cheek.

'Thank you for a lovely evening.'

Later she lay in bed watching the curtains blowing gently in the breeze through the shutters, listening to the gentle lapping of water on the walls below her window.

'A different sound from the wild Cornish sea,' she thought, remembering how she had been lulled to sleep in Michael's arms, listening to the distant waves crashing onto the rocky shore. And then she sighed, and turned her thoughts to the evening.

'Roberto is lovely, so kind, and Venice too, it's dreamlike, so peaceful and romantic despite the crowds.'

She found herself looking forward to lunch the next day. She busied herself with her camera all morning, pleased that a school group had arrived, giving her some new and fascinating responses to the stone spiral to record. Some children looked bored, shuffling along behind their teacher, whispering in a huddle. Others seemed intrigued and were punished for daring to touch a stone, or get too close. One girl reminded her of her childhood self, a dreamy child, lingering alone at the back of the straggle, gazing wide-eyed at the sculpture, bending to run her hand over the stones when no-one was watching. She took a sequence of pictures of her, feeling that the artist would enjoy her quiet response to his work.

'It lends them a magic,' she thought, as she watched the girl's expressions. She wanted to intervene when a teacher suddenly turned, and seeing the girl drifting and unattached, went over to pull her into the group, shouting at her.

She returned to her hostel towards the end of the morning and packaged the photographic reels for Greg, intending to post them later in the day. He would organise the processing. She phoned him to say that she had completed the assignment, telling him something of the exhibition, and then informing him that she was planning a short break before returning home again.

'I've been talking to a local gallery owner, he would be interested in showing my photographs, but I'm not sure we can let him have them.'

'What did you say to him? Would you like to do it?'

'I didn't promise, but yes, I would like to if possible. I'm meeting him for lunch. Perhaps if we can't use the photos I'm sending you I could take some different images for him.'

'Don't see why he can't have these. I'll check. Sounds like you might have someone new in your life.'

'No Greg, nothing like that,' she said, laughing. 'Sorry to disappoint you. He's old enough to be my father. I'll let you know. I'll ring in a week or so to hear what you thought of the pictures.'

'Okay, we'll be in touch. Watch out for those amorous Italian men. Enjoy your break.'

'Thanks, I will. Love to Janet.'

'Greg has no idea about my past experience with Italian men,' she thought wryly. 'And why do people always assume there's a romance when women go for dinner with a man?'

She took a shower, and changed into a summery dress and her leather sandals, her straw sun hat. She took her package to the post, and then returned to the exhibition to wait for Roberto.

He arrived promptly, and took her through quiet back streets, and narrow canal sides, away from the crowds swarming around San Marco. They sat down at a table beneath a graceful tree outside a small trattoria, and ordered lunch. Roberto talked to her about Venice, telling her something about the city's history.

'It's so beautiful, but so crowded around the main tourist areas.'

'Yes, it's changing year on year, more and more visitors, and more houses becoming holiday properties. Local people forced to move out because of the expense.'

'It's the same everywhere people want to spend their holidays. In Cornwall the local people are moving away from the loveliest places, renting out the old cottages for holidaymakers, so that the villages are no longer real, just empty shells most of the year. It defeats the purpose somehow. People come to see the quaint old places, but they're not authentic anymore.'

They enjoyed a pleasant lunch, and then coffee. Roberto looked quizzically at her, and ventured to ask,

'Now tell me why such a lovely young woman has no ring on her finger.'
She gave the answer that she always did when questioned about her love life.

'Oh, I'm so engrossed in my work, always travelling, never spending enough time anywhere. It's impossible to meet anyone, and difficult to develop a social life. Some of my friends have tried to match make when I'm at home for a while, but they've given up now.' She laughed. 'Come on, let's go and see your gallery.'

'Should alarm bells be ringing?' she thought to herself. 'All those questions. No. He seems genuine. He's kind, courteous. I've got nothing to fear.'

He led her back towards the touristy areas, and then onward and across a bridge to a different part of Venice she had not yet seen. A small building came into view beside the bridge. He unlocked a sturdy wooden door and led her into a cool interior.

'We are closed for lunch until 2 pm,' he told her.

It was a small gallery, specialising in photography. The current exhibition was focussed around Italian landscapes, all in colour, atmospheric scenes, some of them almost abstract. Something about them made her think of Jean's paintings of Cornish landscapes that had decorated the walls in the commune house.

'They're lovely, I really like them,' she said.

'But very different from your current work?'

'Yes, I'm fascinated by people, street scenes, observing people's everyday lives, or recording particular events, that kind of thing.'

Afterwards they went for coffee in St Mark's Square.

'It's outrageously expensive, but everyone must do it once in their lives,' Roberto told her.
She watched the crowds wandering by, the pigeons wheeling around with a flurry of wings

'And what has suddenly made you smile?' Roberto asked.

'I was thinking it's funny that I'm the opposite of all the tourists. They're busy taking pictures of everything, and I'm sitting here on the first day of my holiday with no camera, and no intention of taking any photographs. And I'm also thinking how I've eaten more since I met you than I have during all my days here, and probably a week before that too.'

'You don't look after yourself, you need to eat well. It's one of life's pleasures.'

'I know. I'm always resolving to be more organised, and then I slip back into buying a sandwich somewhere, or a takeaway pizza. I'll make an effort now I'm officially on holiday.'

'What are you planning to do?'

'I don't know, I'd like to see more of Italy, but I just want to do something different, forget about work for a while. I've not had a real holiday for ages.'

'Perhaps you might like to join me. I have a small yacht. I like to go sailing every summer. I would enjoy some company.'

She thought for a moment, looking down at her coffee cup, stirring the cream around.

'No strings, only ropes,' he said, 'just as a friend.'
She laughed.

'It sounds interesting, but I don't know anything about sailing.'

'You don't need to. I'm used to sailing single handed. I'm thinking of going down the Dalmatian coast, visiting islands, swimming off the boat.'

'It sounds wonderful. I'm not sure I have any suitable clothing with me though.'

'Why don't you stay at my apartment tonight, my daughters' rooms are free, and then you can come with me to the boat tomorrow, we could take her out and then you will know if it is for you.'

'Will your daughter mind if I use her room?' She hoped he wouldn't see that she was playing for time, asking herself whether this was a risk. What his intentions were.

'Of course not, they are both away. Chiara is in Milan, she rarely visits. Francesca is married with two children, in Genoa. There may be clothes of theirs you can borrow, Chiara is much the same size and build as you. She never touches her clothes here now, they are no longer fashionable.'

'I see you've noticed I'm not a slave to fashion.'

'Yes, and it's very refreshing. Some women here in Italy are always striving for perfection, it can be stressful.'

He walked back with her to the hostel and she packed her few belongings, collected her camera from the secure safe in the office, and joined Roberto outside again. They caught a vaporetto, disembarking at a small quay, and he led her across to a historic building on the canal side.

'My apartment is on the top floor, that's how I keep fit.'

Chapter 21

She followed him up the spiralling staircase, admiring the beautiful tiles and stone carvings on the way. At last they were at the top, and Roberto crossed to a heavy carved wooden door. He held it open for her, and she found herself in a cool entrance area, the floor tiled in marble, and walls covered in framed photographs. She immediately noticed her own photograph of Men an Tol.

'Yes, he said, that's the one I bought for Isabella. It seems strange that you are here to see it. I remember the Gallery owner told me you were a student, and a friend of hers. I had quite a chat with them. It was a new venture, wasn't it?'

'I think my photographs were their second show. I remember now Heather telling me some Italians had bought a picture. I was really surprised.'

They went through a second door into a spacious living area. She saw that it was furnished simply with a mix of antique and modern items, all working harmoniously together. In the centre of the room were two long sofas, piled with glorious rich coloured cushions, a coffee table laden with books was set between them on a woven wool rug. There were small tables with modern sculpture pieces, and on the walls in here were paintings of landscapes, and also portraits that she guessed were family members. She noticed a family group that was obviously Roberto and Isabella with their children.

He crossed the room and opened shutters at two tall windows, letting in sunlight through delicate lace curtains. She heard the sounds of the outside world suddenly impose themselves into the tranquil room, a flurry of pigeon wings, a distant sound of voices and the buzz of a water taxi on the canal below. It was just possible to hear the sound of waves caused by the wake as they slapped against the walls of the building.

'This is my family home,' he told her. I grew up here. I couldn't afford to buy such an apartment today. I'll show you around.'
He led her back out into the entrance hall and through a second heavy wooden door.

'In here is the kitchen.'
Another spacious room, with an attached dining area through an arch in the wall. The surfaces were smooth marble, with only a bowl of fruit and basket of vegetables for decoration. Very different from the muddle of stuff scattered around her kitchen back home. There were pots of herbs on a window sill, and through the glass she could see the roof of a neighbouring building, and above that the blue of the sky. They returned to the entrance area, and he picked up her bags and led her across the cool marble floor.

They walked on down the corridor, and turned right into a bedroom. He opened shutters again and in the flood of light she saw a lovely room, its walls painted in pale creams and grey, the floor covered in islands of bright woven rugs and durries.

'I thought you might like this room, it's my daughter Francesca's space. She was a bit of a collector.'

'Me too,' Lamorna said. 'It's lovely.' She was picking up and examining shells that were lying on a small table. Every surface seemed to be adorned with all manner of interesting objects, pieces of driftwood, old toys, and glass vases in rainbow colours.

'Are you sure this is okay? Will she mind very much if I use her room?'

'No, she is rarely here now, so busy with her children and marriage. They come and visit once or twice a year. She would be pleased that you are enjoying it.'

He watched as she lifted up shells and stones, holding them against her face, looking at the colours and patterns.

'Settle in, and I'll make us a cool drink on the balcony. You have your own bathroom through here.'

He indicated a second door that she hadn't noticed, and then was gone. She unpacked her bags and headed into the bathroom. Like every room it was wonderful. She opened the shutter, and saw that this room looked out over a garden at the side of the building. She could see the tops of flowering trees, and a green oasis of shrubs and plants below. She washed and then changed into a wraparound skirt and white linen top.

Back in the bedroom she went over to the window and looked out. Down below was the canal, busy with boats coming and going, a gondola decorated with flowers, and opposite another pink building with stone carvings and balconies. Away over the rooftops was the deep blue cloudless sky.

'What am I doing here? Why has Roberto invited me? He seems kind. Maybe he's just lonely. What if he wants more? What will I do? He seems to be making it clear he's just a friend. I'll have to be vigilant though. Am I crazy, coming here with a seemingly kind Italian.....after Rome, what happened to me there?' Deciding once again that this felt very different and that she was a stronger woman now she padded barefoot back to the living area. Roberto was already seated on the balcony. He stood up to greet her as she came through.

'Thank you, I feel better now,'

'You're looking very summery, have a seat. There's sparkling water, is that okay for you?'

'Perfect. Thank you.'

She sat down on the cane chair, leaning back on the cushion. The view was similar to that from her bedroom.

'It's strange,' she said. 'This is my second visit here, and yet I haven't really seen the city, not even one single tourist sight. I always seem to be put off by the crowds.'

'It's better to wait until autumn when most of the crowds are gone. When we come back from our voyage I would be happy to show you around.'

'Autumn? Would we be gone so long?'

'Only if you wish. You may not want to come sailing at all when you have seen my boat. Does a long trip with me worry you?'

She saw the look of concern in his eyes.

'Not at all,' she said, realising that she meant it. 'You will more than likely want to throw me overboard after a few days.'

'I don't think so. I managed to survive with my daughters on board, and they were never easy passengers, but I will keep it in mind as an option. We'll visit the boat later. Take her out for a sail. You can decide then how it feels.'

She laughed.

'I do love boats, but I've never sailed. I've canoed, and been in small motor boats in various countries.'

'You have done a lot of travelling for your work?'

'Yes, especially in the last five years. My first job was based in Birmingham. That was mainly work in the UK.'

'Ah yes, Birmingham. The city that has more canals than Venice.'

'It may have, but you wouldn't really notice them, and it can't compete for beauty and atmosphere.'

'I was once in Birmingham to see the Pre-Raphaelite paintings. There is something about you that reminds me of them. Perhaps Rossetti's Beatrix?'

'People often say that, it's because of my hair.'

'More than just your hair I would say, an ethereal beauty.'

'I'm tired of travelling now,' she said, changing the subject quickly. I bought a cottage in Derbyshire last year. I was heading there for a while after a few days here.'

'And I am enticing you to travel with me.'

'That's different. I won't be working, and I'll see more of the country.'

'Well, it depends where we choose to journey. We can look at some charts after the trip tomorrow if you are still wanting to come. Are you ready for some lunch?'

'Yes please, can I help?'

They walked through into the kitchen. Lamorna made a salad whilst Roberto expertly cooked chicken breasts in a sauce and served them up with rice. There was fresh crusty bread which he said he had made that morning. There were fresh figs too. He suggested they eat on the balcony, and loaded the tray again. It was idyllic, drinking white wine and watching the world hurrying by below them.

'This is perfect, it's enchanting,' she said.

Roberto suggested an afternoon siesta.

'It is so hot now in the afternoons.'

'I love the idea of siesta,' she said, but I seem to have always worked through it.'

She went back into her bedroom, closed the shutters on the glorious view and then stripped off her clothes, leaving them draped on a chair, before slipping between the cool sheets. She lay for a while, looking at the stripes of brightness made by the sunlight filtering through the shutters. The curtains blew gently, and she was reminded of the little cottage in Cornwall where she'd stayed with Michael. She imagined how it would feel if he were here now beside her, his arms around her, kissing her softly. It was always the same, every day she found herself thinking of him, remembering the way he kissed her, the way he made love to her. She missed it so much.

The sound of shutters creaking open woke her, and a paler light spread into the room. She pulled the sheet around her and sat up. Roberto was there, a mug in his hand.

'I thought maybe I should wake you, I hope that's okay. It's four o'clock. I've made tea.'

'Thank you, I had no idea it was so late. I was sleeping too long.'

'Not a problem, but if we want to sail today we should set off soon. Do you have jeans and a sweatshirt? It will feel cooler on the open water of the lagoon.'

Twenty minutes later she was up, washed and dressed, in her one pair of jeans and a light sweater, leather sandals on her feet, sunglasses perched in her hair.

'Will I do?' she asked, finding him in the kitchen.

'Yes, unless you have better shoes.'

'I only have these and some flip flops.'

'It may be wise to buy some deck shoes. We can check Francesca and Chiara's wardrobes. There may be something to fit.'

The phone rang. He spoke in Italian, but she guessed from his tone of voice that it was family or friend.

'That was Chiara. She is calling in to see me in the morning on the way to a business conference. She was a little shocked to learn that you are here. My daughters have not known me to have any female friend since their mother died. I think she will be even more surprised when she meets you.' He smiled.

'Perhaps it's better if I go out while she is here?'

'No, of course not. My daughters have their own lives now. They need to understand that I can enjoy friendship with women too, have a life of my own. Come, let's go.'

He had called a water taxi, and they sped across the water to San Giorgio Maggiore, where his yacht was moored. It was a white painted boat, named 'Isabella' for his wife.

'She looks lovely.'

'Not so beautiful as her namesake.'

'Did Isabella sail with you?'

'Yes, we spent a week or two sailing every year. After she died I had some modifications made so that I can sail single handed. So you see you will not have to do anything, just talk to me and keep me company.'

'Oh, I think I should like to learn.'

'Well if you feel like this after our short trip now, then you shall.'

They clambered on board and explored the boat. There was a small galley and living area, an even smaller bathroom, a bed in the fore-peak, and a cabin with a little more space in the stern.

'This would be your quarters if you choose to come. There is more room.'

'Oh, I couldn't take the best room.'

'Why not? You are my guest. In any case I usually sleep in the bows. It feels a little lonely down here.'

She saw a double sized bunk with drawers below, and a shelf above. Pinned to the wall were some family snaps.

'Did your daughter's enjoy sailing?'

'Not really, they were both sea sick, and it wasn't their thing.'

He prepared the boat for sailing, talking her through the various actions, and then giving her a run down on safety issues.

'Can you swim?'

'Yes, I'm a good swimmer.'

'That's very good; we should get some swimming off the boat.'

He handed her the tiller to hold steady whilst he jumped ashore to release the mooring ropes, then deftly stepping back aboard, placed his hand over hers.

'I'll guide your hand so that you can get the feel of it.'

She liked the warm protective touch of his hand enclosing hers. The motor chugged and they moved away from the berth and out into the wide canal. He turned the boat so that she was into the wind, explaining that this was the right position for hoisting the sails. She held the boat steady as he went up to raise the fore sail, and then he showed her how to raise the mainsail. She could feel the tug of the wind as the sail rose white against the blue of the sky. The sails flapped, and he guided her hand to turn so that they could go with the wind, and suddenly they were away, sailing lightly over the water like a great white bird. He talked to her about the sails, showing her how to hold the main sheet so that the sail did not flap or luff, spilling the wind, but neither was too taut.

'It's wonderful, the way you can feel the wind taking us.' Her eyes were bright with excitement. He talked her through 'going about,' and they sailed back the way they had come, tacking to and fro against the wind.

Two hours went quickly by, and he sailed them up to a small quay.

'We'll stop for supper here. You're a natural sailor. You stayed calm and didn't panic. Do you feel okay, not sea sick?'

They were ashore now, walking through a small canal- side street.

'No, but I feel a bit wobbly now we're on land.'

They ate a simple but delicious meal in a small family run trattoria, and then sailed and motored back to Isabella's berth.

Later they enjoyed coffee on the balcony, watching the sunset spread like a red flame over the rooftops.

'That was lovely.'

'So do you think you might come with me on an expedition?'

'I think it's just what I'd love to do, thank you.'

'Good. Chiara will be here in the morning. We'll find some more clothing for you. Perhaps you may want to do some washing. Then in the afternoon we'll get the boat ready, organise provisions and be ready to set off the next day.'

Lamorna lay in the luxurious bed, watching the billowing curtains once more, thinking this time they were like the white sails of a boat, luffing in the wind. And then her thoughts turned to Michael again. She wondered what he might think of Roberto.

'I think they would get on well, they're both passionate about boats, about the sea.' She thought about the last time she had seen Michael, when he had bent to kiss her goodbye, held her face in his hands, told her he would be back at four o'clock.

'But I was gone. I wasn't there.' And she felt tears run down her face again. She rolled over and held a pillow close to her, hugging it tightly until she fell asleep.

Chapter 22

Chiara arrived just as they were finishing breakfast on the balcony. Her eyes sparked with a sort of shock and fury, and she launched a tirade of words at her father. Lamorna couldn't understand a word, but she could guess what she was saying. Roberto replied calmly, and then turned to Lamorna,

'Chiara is understandably shocked that I have a friend no older than she. I have told her that we will speak only in English now, and that she has been impolite and discourteous. She has allowed her imagination to run away.'

Chiara looked suddenly sheepish. Lamorna stood, and took a step towards her to take her hand, and was surprised when the girl kissed her cheeks.

'Forgive me please, I was wrong to behave so badly to my father's guest.'

'There is nothing to forgive. I understand how you must have felt. I am not here to replace your mother in any way.'

'Lamorna lost her own father when she was very young,' Roberto said.

'I was a horrible beast when my mother met someone and married again, so I know how you must feel. But please, I am here as a friend. I am going to be a crew on your father's next trip, and perhaps learn how to sail.'

'I suppose if I had been a better daughter, and enjoyed the boat this would not happen,' Chiara said, smiling now. She went into her own room to collect some belongings.

'If there is anything of mine that you might need to borrow, please do,' she said on her return. 'I don't suppose you have any sailing clothing.'

'No, that would be very helpful, thank you.'

Over coffee they talked about work. Chiara telling her of her lawyer's practice. She was amazed to discover that it was Lamorna who had taken the photograph hanging in the hallway.

'I loved those stones, so mysterious, although I was a little afraid of them too, they seem, how do you say, a little weird in the dusk.'

'Yes, at twilight when the shadows reach out towards you they can seem really sinister.'

'We all loved Cornwall. Are you from that area?'

'No, I was just working down there one summer.' There was a slight catch in her voice, and she was aware that Roberto had noticed. He had glanced briefly at her with a concerned expression.

After Chiara had left they packed a few belongings for the trip. She had laid out her clothes for Roberto to inspect.

'Will this be enough?'

He was surprised at how little she had.

'You should have seen what the girls always wanted to take when we went away.'

He led her to inspect Chiara's and Francesca's wardrobes, and they selected some shorts, a waterproof coat and a pair of deck shoes. Francesca was pretty much the same size. She also picked a warmer sweater in case the evenings turned cool. Then Roberto produced a life jacket.

'In case we have a storm.'
She found some underwear and a few of her clothes to wash, and he showed her where to hang them out in the courtyard below.

'While you're busy washing I'll go and buy basic provisions,' he said, 'then we'll be ready to go.'

Later they were back on board Isabella. Lamorna stowed away the food supplies and other items whilst Roberto completed a few repairs and maintenance tasks. She came up on deck after a while, and watched him working. He told her the names of the various parts of the boat.

'I don't know the English,' he apologised. 'I had no need to learn these words when we were in London.'

'Will you teach me some Italian? I'd like to learn.'

'Of course, I will speak to you only in Italian whilst we are sailing, unless it is an emergency! You will learn quickly.'

'That sounds challenging, but let's try.'

In the evening he cooked for them again.

'I feel so guilty letting you do all of this for me.'

'Don't be guilty, it is my pleasure.'
He told her the names of ingredients as they worked, and she repeated them, soon discovering that she could remember them well. He was pleased,

'Very good!'

'Grazie.'

'Prego.'

***

They rose early the next morning to make a start on their voyage before the midday heat.

'Even when there is a breeze the sun is hot and you could get badly burned,' he said. He had found her a peaked cap that had belonged to his wife, and insisted that she brought her straw hat too.

They sailed north east around the coast, making for Trieste, and he suggested that they should aim to sail down the Dalmatian coast, exploring the islands and villages en route. It was a leisurely voyage, Lamorna learning how to sail, becoming confident about jumping ashore to tie them up, getting the feel of the ropes, managing the sails, and even starting to take the helm. Their days fell into a relaxed pattern. They were up early every day, breakfasting on deck. Just before lunch they would drop anchor in a peaceful cove and swim off the boat. Lamorna would then put together a simple lunch whilst Roberto checked the boat and surveyed the charts, listened to weather reports on the radio. They ate crusty bread, cheese, salad and olives with a glass of wine most days. Sometimes there was fish, grilled sardines or shellfish if they'd been ashore. Afterwards they would have a siesta, before setting off again in the late afternoon. Sometimes they tied up on shore, and dined in a local taverna in the evening, sometimes they dropped anchor and Roberto would cook for them.

She thought about Michael sometimes. 'He would love this. Jude said he had a boat. Maybe he's out now shutting up the chickens for the night, listening to the sea.'

They came to a small town, Trogir, and Roberto suggested that they should stay for a couple of days.

'We can stock up on provisions, and I can do a couple of jobs on the boat. If you would prefer we could book into a hotel.'

'Oh no, I love being on board, I sleep so well with the rocking motion. It's so peaceful. I can do a bit of cleaning too.'

They went ashore and explored. Trogir was a medieval town, with cobbled streets and little hidden squares. They bought postcards, Lamorna persuading Roberto to send one to his daughters. She posted cards to Mary, Jude, and her family, and another to Janet and Greg. They drank iced tea on the quayside in a small café, and visited an ancient monastery. There was a busy market, and they bought vegetables, fruit and meat, cheese and fish. Back on board they ate a salad lunch. They were the only yacht moored at the quay.

'It's idyllic,' she said.

'One day it will be discovered and the hordes will come. We should enjoy it whilst it is still unspoilt.'

'It's hard to imagine, it feels so far away from everywhere, but I suppose you're right.'

She found herself looking at Roberto whilst he was washing up. She was drying the dishes and stacking them in their locker.

'He is lovely,' she was thinking, and then blushed with embarrassment when he turned and caught her gaze. He just smiled.

'Siesta now, and then shall we go ashore and explore again, find a restaurant for dinner?'

Back in her cabin she stripped off and slid between the sheets. She lay watching the sun scribbling patterns of light on the cabin wall.

'I would like to make love to Roberto. I'm lonely. Maybe he is too. What harm would it do? What would he think if I suggested it? There's Michael. He will never know. I've lost him now forever.' She thought again about the last time she had seen him. 'If I could go back in time I wouldn't run away. I would wait for him. It would have been alright.' It was a discussion she often had with herself. A pointless debate. 'I have to move on. I can't run away all my life. He probably has someone new, forgotten me now. But I love him so much; he's in my heart, in my blood.'

She felt the familiar ache of longing, and she pulled the pillow into her arms again and hugged it as she drifted into sleep. It was dusk when Roberto woke her with tea.

'You were sleeping so deeply, I couldn't disturb you.'

'Oh, thank you,' she yawned, pulling the sheet over her naked body, suddenly embarrassed, but he had already gone.

'He's such a gentleman. He's never tried to proposition me. Maybe he just doesn't feel that way about me.'

As the sun glowed red in the sky they were sitting together in a small restaurant courtyard. Candles flickered on the table and peaceful music wafted around them in a warm breeze. She found herself flirting with Roberto, but he seemed careful to remain impervious to her comments, shrugging off her mischievous remarks. Afterwards they walked around the town again before returning to the quay.

'Let's sit for a while on the wall,' she suggested.

There was a huge round moon spilling its light over the sea.

'When I see the full moon I always think about my friends far away, and I wonder if they're looking up at the same moon.'

'It's the same for me. When I was away from Isabella I would phone her and ask if she could see the moon. I would say that the moon was there to tell her I loved her.'

Lamorna turned to look at him then. 'How could it be that he was saying the same things, the things that were in her thoughts?'

'I hated it when they landed on the moon. It felt like a violation to me,' she told him. She thought about how she and Michael had gone out to look up at the moon that night. 'We were in Amsterdam,' she remembered. 'Watching the moon landing on TV with Klaus' parents.' It seemed a lifetime ago. I wonder if Klaus and Ellen are still at the hotel. Perhaps they have a family now. I must ask Mary when I see her.'

'Yes, it is as though some of her magic is lost,' he said.

They sat for a while longer, listening to the sea lapping quietly against the wall, the sound of the yacht's shrouds clinking against the mast and a distant murmur of voices from the taverna.

'I'm so tired of D.I.Y. sex,' she thought. It's getting so hard to fantasise about Michael, to remember how it felt when he made love to me.'

She reached over and took his hand in hers, not looking at him, and he responded with a gentle squeeze of her fingers. After a while she broke the silence.

'Roberto, would you think I was a terrible person if I asked you to make love to me?'

'I wouldn't think that of you. I would be honoured.'

'Then please will you? I would like it very much.'

He turned to her and gently touched her face, turning her towards him, and then leaning over to kiss her softly on her mouth. She wrapped her arms around him, sinking into his embrace. He kissed her with a warmth and passion that she could not resist.

At last he spoke.

'Are you sure about this?'

'Yes, but I don't have any contraception,' she whispered.

'You don't need to worry. Isabella was told she must not have more children, so I went to England for an operation, a vasectomy. It was not possible in Italy. I wanted to be sure there was no risk for her.'

'What would Isabella think about us now?'

'She would be happy. When she was very ill she told me that I must find someone to love, she did not want me to be alone. And what about you, is there anyone to be hurt?'

'No, there is no-one.' Felt the lump in her throat, the held back almost sob.

'Then come, let's go below.'

They clambered back on board the yacht and went hand in hand into her cabin, and he sat with her on the bed, talking to her in Italian, telling her that she was beautiful, that it was special that she should want to be with him. He stroked her hair, her face, talking softly to her. He kissed her, and caressed her. She felt herself yielding to him, and let him slip her dress over her head, laying her down beside him. He nuzzled her neck, her breasts.

'This may not be so wonderful for you,' he whispered. 'I am out of practice.'

'That goes for me too,' she murmured.

But he was wrong. He was a gentle lover, holding her close to him afterwards as she wept silently onto his shoulder. He murmured sleepily in Italian.

'Michael, forgive me, I'm unfaithful to you, but I'm so lonely, and you are so far away,' she whispered inside her head.

Chapter 23

Lamorna woke in the morning to find that Roberto was already up. She slipped her robe on and padded barefoot up onto the deck. Roberto was in the cockpit, drinking from a mug of coffee. She thought he looked a little anxious. She took the mug from his hand and slid onto his knee.

'Buon Giorno mi amore,' she said, and kissed him.

'Lamorna, you are bringing me joy, but is this what you really want?'

'Yes, I do, let's be happy together for a while, please Roberto.'

'How can I resist you,' he laughed. 'But Lamorna, I know there is someone in your heart, and it will be hard for me because I am falling in love with you.'

'What do you mean?'

'You have a faraway look in your eyes, and there is sadness there too. There is something you keep locked away, something you don't want to talk about.'
She sighed.

'There was someone. Someone I cared about, but it was a long time ago, years ago. I want us to be together for a while Roberto, I want us to love each other.'

'Then we shall,' he said, kissing her, 'but now we shall have breakfast.'

They stayed for another day and night in Trogir, exploring more of the town, discovering a beautiful little church, watching boats come and go in the harbour, watching the fishermen unloading their catch. They bought some fresh fish from one of the boats, and cooked it on a driftwood fire on the stony beach, eating it with fresh bread. There was local cheese and wine too, a perfect picnic meal.

Lamorna's thoughts wandered back to the camp fire on the beach at St Ives, when Ced had cooked mackerel. It had been the day she and Michael had got together. The day they'd made love for the first time.

'Will there ever be a day when nothing reminds me of Michael?' she thought. 'Does a new memory of a similar occasion blot out the past one?'
As the fire died down they sat together with their arms around each other watching a golden moon rise above them.

The next morning they sailed on down the coast, stopping now and again to explore an island, or a little cove. They were swimming off the boat every day and making love most afternoons, sharing a bed at night.

'I learned to swim in this country,' she told Roberto as she dried herself after they'd bathed in a peaceful bay. 'It seems ages ago now.'

'And now you are learning to sail here,' he said.

They stayed two nights in Split. She thought about her holiday here with Michael. They had explored the old walled town together, and he had bought her a new straw hat because hers had blown away. 'We got a lift with that crazy American, and I thought we'd drive off the road into the sea.'

She was wandering, hand in hand in the town with Roberto now. They found new things she had not seen before: a statue with a lucky toe, worn shiny and polished by the many hands that had stroked it, that you had to touch and wish for good fortune. Lamorna touched the toe. But she struggled for the right wish. 'I wish that I will be truly happy one day. And Michael too.' They explored some little stalls down in a basement area. They ate grilled fish and fried potatoes in a small café by the market, and watched as the stall holders washed down the street with hoses. Later they found a table overlooking the harbour for tea and cake.

'This is lovely, she said, 'the best holiday I could have had. Except that it's not Italy! I was supposed to be discovering Italy.'

'Well maybe we should do that next year,' he said. 'In spring I can have Isabella taken by truck to Liguria. We can sail around the Italian Riviera, or we can go to the Bay of Naples and Sorrento, be bewitched by the sirens. I thought perhaps we could sail from Athens then in the summer, explore the Greek islands, if you would like to.'

'Roberto, I couldn't take over your life like that. And I should go back to work I suppose. I was only thinking I would have a few weeks away.'

'It would not be taking over my life. I would enjoy spending time with you. I find myself always lonely on board now. I've done all the voyages so often. With you each moment is a new adventure, discovering places all over again. But you don't have to decide now. We can talk when we are back in Venice. You may be tired of sailing, tired of my company by then.'

At last they reached Dubrovnik. It was just as beautiful as she remembered.

'I've been to so many places around the world, but I still think this is the loveliest town. Sorry Roberto, I do like it more than Venice.'

'I can see what you mean, he said, 'it seems to be full of light.'
They ate a wonderful meal at a seafood restaurant near the marina, and sat watching the light dancing over the water, listening to music from a nearby café, before heading back to Isabella to read and listen to music. Roberto had bought an Italian paper, and she suddenly noticed the date; July 19th, Michael's birthday.

'Do you mind if I sleep alone tonight Roberto?

'Of course, I will miss you, but perhaps it's a good idea sometimes. We don't want to take anything for granted.'
But she knew he was wondering, perhaps guessing she was dwelling in the past. And she struggled to sleep, wallowing sadly in her memories, trying to imagine where Michael was for his birthday, what he was doing.

Chapter 24

It was the end of September when they sailed into Venice again. They cleaned the boat, stowed all the gear away and prepared her for the winter, and then returned to Roberto's apartment. Lamorna phoned Greg, and was updated on all that had happened with her photographs.

'The British Council were pleased with your work, and I think they might commission us again. What are your plans now?

'I'd like to stay here a little longer. I haven't explored Venice yet. I think I'll be here for Christmas.'

'Sounds good. I'll miss you, but it's an opportunity for you. To be honest there's not much work in your field at the moment anyway. I can get some of your Biennale pics framed up and ship them over. Your friend could have them for his gallery. He'd only need to pay the framing and shipping costs.'

'Oh, hang on Greg, I'll ask him.'

She went off into the kitchen. Roberto was cooking their meal, and she asked him what he thought.

'That would be great, I've got a new exhibition scheduled for the next three weeks, and then we could run with your work. I'd love that.'

'But you haven't seen the photographs Roberto'

'Don't need to.'

So it was all agreed, and Greg said he would be in touch as plans progressed.

'I'm thinking of bringing Janet over to Venice for a few days over the New Year, we could meet up if you're around.'

'You could stay with us, I'm sure. I'll ask Roberto.'

'Oh, we couldn't intrude.'

'You wouldn't be.'

Roberto was busy again with his gallery, and Lamorna found herself helping out. There were a few hectic weeks of a busy social whirl. Lamorna attracted a lot of attention and speculation. Roberto seemed to take it in his stride, and soon she was as relaxed as he was, forgetting her initial nervousness. Whenever they had a few hours spare he delighted in showing her around his city, and she declared that it was the most enchanting and romantic place she had ever visited.

'Even Dubrovnic?'

'Equal, but there is more happening here perhaps.'

'I ought to go home and get some winter clothes, it's getting cool now,' she said one morning.

'No need, I'm sure we can find you some here, I will take you shopping.'

'No Roberto, you can't do that. I have money. I can't be so dependent on you. It just seems so extravagant when I have things at home.'

He laughed then.

'I don't think you'll ever be an Italian with that reluctance to shop.'

He took her to Milan, and insisted on helping her choose some new clothes, and she found that she enjoyed the experience, managing to acquire several dresses, some new leather boots and shoes, and a stylish yet comfortable woollen coat that she felt at home in. She gulped a little when she received the bills. Roberto had accounts with the fashion houses, and the invoices were sent some weeks later. He repeated his offer of paying for them, and she refused again.

'After all, she thought, I never spend money on myself, and I'm saving so much over here.'

In mid-October she curated the exhibition of her photographs in the gallery, and presided over a grand champagne opening. She was awed by the positive response from the critics, and she cut out several reviews recommending the exhibition.

'I can't believe how much they all liked my photographs,' she said.

'It's because they are different, they tell us something about ordinary people, the way they respond to art.'

***

Chiara and Francesca and her family came for Christmas, and Lamorna plucked up courage to cook them a traditional English dinner, evening managing to provide a pudding. They declared that it was 'estupendo.'

Janet and Greg came over for a few days and Roberto hosted a party for them on New Year's Eve. Lamorna managed to spend an afternoon later that week with Janet whilst Greg was visiting the gallery again with Roberto. They had planned to loan Lamorna's work to a place in Milan afterwards where Roberto had contacts. The two women relaxed over coffee in a canal side café.

'What are you planning next Lamorna? Roberto is lovely, isn't he?'

'Yes, he is. We get on so well, and I'm really enjoying life here. But I don't know what next. I have to get back to work eventually.'

'Has Roberto said anything? Do you think he will ask you to marry him? He seems to be very fond of you.'

'I honestly don't know.'

'What if he did ask you?'

Lamorna thought for a while, scraping the cream from the rim of her cup and licking it from the spoon.

'I don't know Janet, I really don't. I love it here, I'm fond of Roberto. But I don't know. I suppose I'm tired of being alone, but it's not a good reason for a permanent relationship, is it? I don't think he will. He once asked me if there was someone in my heart, and I said there had been someone. I think he knows it's hard for me to make any commitment.'

'Oh Lamorna, it's Michael isn't it?'

'I can't ever forget him. That's just how it is.'

'Well you're crazy, you should go and find him, find out where he is. He may be married. He may have forgotten you and moved on. You can't let this destroy your future.'

'I know. I know you're right. I think I'll stay here a little longer, and then I'll do that. I'll go and look for him.'

'Lamorna, you're not convincing me. I have a good mind to go and find him myself; tell him you're pining for him.'

'No, no, you can't do that.'

'Why not? Are you scared to know the truth? You're living in a fantasy world. It's not good for you. It's not healthy. Let's have some more coffee.'

She ordered, and they sat in silence for a while. Lamorna was fighting off tears.

'I'm sorry, I was too brutal.'

'No, no, you're right. I am being stupid. I can't go on like this. Perhaps I just need to move on and forget him.'

'But how will you do that? He'll go on creeping into your thoughts won't he? No-one will compare with him. How can that work? You need to know about him. If you can't go and find him at least talk to your friends, ask them what he's doing now.'

'I've tried not to do that for a while now.'

'And why have you?'

'I suppose it's because I'm afraid of hearing that he's found someone.'

'Exactly. You need to know. If he has then you have to try and forget him. If he hasn't, then you have a choice. Try and forget, or go and find him.'
She sighed.

'You're right Janet.'

'I'm not going to let you off this hook. I will expect you to have taken some action by mid-summer's day this year. And I'm going to come and find you, and ask you.'
Lamorna laughed.

'I never realised how bossy you could be Janet! But it's a deal.'

'I've given you too much time, but you seem to want to do some more travelling with Roberto. The longer you leave it of course, the more chance there is that you will lose him. Have you told your friends about Roberto?'

'Yes, I did tell Jude.'

'Well then, I'm sure she has mentioned it to Michael, and if it were me I would have resolved to forget you and find someone new, you can't expect him to wait forever. Come on, we need to get back and meet up with the men.'

On Janet and Greg's last evening they all went out for a meal, catching a water taxi to Roberto and Lamorna's favourite restaurant. They enjoyed the evening, although Lamorna was a little quiet after her conversation with Janet.

'So, when will I get my favourite photographer back again?' Greg asked.

'I don't know, I don't feel the need to work at the moment, I'm getting used to a life of leisure.'

Later in bed, Roberto scrutinised her carefully.

'Something has upset you.'

'Oh, it's nothing, just something Janet said, and then Greg asking me when I'd get back to work.'

'Do you miss your work?'

'Not really, not at the moment, I'm enjoying it here.'
He drew her into his arms then and she resolved to put it all out of her mind.

Chapter 25

Lamorna did stay with Roberto. She helped with the gallery and the transfer of her work to Milan, and then in spring they went off to hire a boat and sail along the Italian Riviera and down the Liguria coast where they explored the beautiful harbours of the Cinque Terre. Lamorna found it fascinating.

'Look at the little terraces on the hillside, how do they work those? And the houses, all jumbled up the hills, ice cream colours. They're so lovely.'

They had a few weeks back in Venice whilst Roberto was busy with a new exhibition, before setting off for a voyage around Greece. In July they were sailing around Skopelos, finding a mooring in the harbour at the old town.

'Why don't we stay for a few days, maybe a week?' Roberto suggested. 'I like this island, although it is more beautiful in spring when all the wild flowers are in bloom.'

'I'd like to explore a little,' she agreed, 'I'm beginning to lose the use of my legs on shore.'

'Good, that's what we'll do, and perhaps we could stay in the town, rent a house?'

'We could if you'd like to, but you know I love being on the boat.'

'Well, let's go exploring, have a meal somewhere, and then we can decide later, have a look at some possibilities.'

So they changed and set off into town, wandering around the narrow streets, stopping for a lemon tea at a harbour-side taverna, and then browsing in the little shops. Roberto presented her with a small parcel.

'Oh, you shouldn't Roberto,' she protested as she opened the little bag. She drew out a small carved wooden mermaid, and at once she was back in St Ives, remembering the mermaid Michael had given her.

'She is a little mermaid, a gorgona they call her here. She reminds me of you.'

'Thank you, she's lovely.'

They strolled to a bar at the far end of the harbour, and relaxed with a glass of local beer. Roberto had bought an Italian paper, and was engrossed in news of home. Lamorna was lost in thought. 'It's gone mid-summer. I haven't honoured my promise to Janet. How can I do it? Perhaps I could phone Jude from a call box here.'

She glanced over at a television screen. A football match was showing. She suddenly saw a date on the screen.

'What is it?' Roberto asked, concerned.

'Oh it's nothing, I just saw the date, and I remembered I should be phoning Greg about work.'

Her heart thumped because she was lying to Roberto, and because she had seen the date. July 19th: Michael's birthday again. Another year had gone.

Later they were getting ready for bed, and Roberto took her face in his hands, looked at her gently, concerned.

'Lamorna, would you like to be alone tonight?'

'No, please Roberto, I would like to be with you. I'm sorry. I just felt a sudden sadness. I can't explain.'

She was not really there with him when he made love to her, and she was aware that he seemed to have sensed her mood. He was especially tender with her.

In the morning they ate breakfast up on deck. When they had finished eating, and were sitting quietly finishing their coffee Roberto took her hands in his.

'Lamorna I know now who it is who holds your heart. It is Michael. I want us to talk about this.'

She looked down at her cup, blushing, blinking away tears.

'How do you know that,' she whispered. She couldn't look at him.

'You were talking in your sleep last night. You called out his name.'

'I'm sorry Roberto. It's just that I noticed the date yesterday, it was his birthday. It made me think of him.'

'And it has made you sad.'

'Please can we go below, and I will try to tell you?'

'Yes, come.'

They went into the cabin and she asked him to lie down with her and hold her. And then she talked. She told him about how she had first met Michael, and how their lives together had been, their time at college. And then she was quiet. He stroked her hair, murmuring to her.

'If it is too hard you don't need to tell me all.'

'No, I want to.' There was a long pause whilst she gathered herself, and then she told him about her trip to Greece, faltering again when she came to the memory of what had happened in Rome. Roberto soothed her as she cried against him.

'I don't want to think that such a thing could happen here in Italy, that one of my countrymen could do such a thing to you. I am amazed you would ever want to set foot on this soil again.'

'You have redeemed all Italians Roberto,' she told him, holding him closer to her.

She sighed, and struggled on with the story. She heard her own voice, sounding calmer now, and yet detached as she described what happened when she found Michael with Rosa, and confessed to him how she had tried to push him out of her thoughts, bury herself in her work.

'I heard that Rosa's baby was not Michael's, but it seemed too late to go and find him then. He didn't contact me to tell me himself. I tried to convince myself that it was for the best that we were not meant to be together.'

'And yet he is still in your heart.'

'Yes.'

They lay together for a while, rocked by the quiet motion of the boat as it rose and fell on the wake of other boats coming and going. And then Roberto spoke again.

'I think you need to go and find Michael. You need to know his situation, to know if this love still is there for you both.'

'I can't do that Roberto.'

'You are scared of what you might find I think, afraid that he no longer feels the same. You feel safe believing that he is there for you. Because of him you won't risk losing your heart again. This is bad for you. You need to resolve this, and then you can move on. Perhaps you will have a happy future with him, or perhaps that is not to be, and in time your heart will heal and there will be someone else to hold it for you.'

Chapter 26

Three days later she arrived in London, bereft and afraid. Roberto had insisted on flying her back to Venice, booking her flight to London.

'You must promise to follow this through. When you are ready you may come back to me if that is what you want. I will be here for you,' he said, as he left her at the airport.

She had argued and protested but it was all to no avail. Here she was trying to find the courage to take what seemed an impossible step. She stayed a night with Joy and her new husband in London, and then set off for her cottage in Derbyshire. She phoned Roberto to tell him she'd arrived safely.

'Don't forget, you are doing this for me too,' he told her. 'If you come back to me it will be to bring me your heart. I couldn't be with you any other way.'

'Thank you, Roberto. I know you're right, but I'm still afraid.'

'You will find the courage,' he said quietly, then after a brief farewell he was gone.

She busied herself around the cottage for the next two days, washing her clothes, taking her neighbour Ann out for a meal, and then beginning to unpack other boxes that had remained untouched since she had first bought the cottage. She found the mermaid that Michael had given her, and placed it next to the one Roberto had bought in Greece.

'They could almost be twins,' she thought.

That evening she sat down with her address book and the phone. She began to dial Jude's number, her heart thumping, wondering what she might hear about Michael. Halfway through she stopped dialling.

'Better phone my mother first, let her know I'm here.'

It was her stepfather Tom who answered.

'I'm glad you've rung, I were looking for your number. Your mother's poorly. She's only got a few weeks to live mebbe.'

'Oh. What is it Tom? What's wrong?'

'It's cancer.'

They talked for a while, Tom filling her in on the details, and she arranged to travel down the next day. She called Roberto and told him the news.

'I made a promise to you. I will do it when this is over.'

In the morning she packed a few things in an overnight bag and popped next door.

'Whatever's the matter?' Ann asked 'You're white as a sheet.'

Lamorna told her the news, explaining that she would be spending time with her Mum, and was not sure when she would be back.

'Tom seems lost. I don't think he's coping. I'll try and get home some weekends though for a break.'

Her brothers were away at College, so Tom gave her the largest bedroom, a room dominated by posters of pop stars that she didn't recognise and piles of super hero comics.

'Your Mum'll be glad to see you. And I'm grateful, I need to work. You'll be better company for her in the day,' he said awkwardly. 'I'll make us some tea.' She unpacked and stood for a moment looking out of the window at the familiar scene, the garden sloping up to a small gate and a field beyond, the pasture grass long now and bright with buttercups. She thought about when they had first moved here, and how she would go through into that field and pick cowslips for her Mum. The bouquet she had bought from a garage on her way today seemed lacking somehow. She hung her clothes in the wardrobe, next to the discarded glam rock outfits and flowered shirts. The room smelt of pungent socks and stagnant air. She opened a window and then went out again onto the landing. Tom was emerging from the main bedroom, fingers on his lips.

'She's sleeping; let's take our tea into the garden.'

There were a few flower beds now, and the grass was no longer worn from football boots. A few petunias and salvia straggled together in a haphazard display. Tom was no gardener.

'When did Mum get ill?'

'She'd been ailing for a while. We found out in May, but she wouldn't let me call you, she didn't want me to tell you, spoil your trip.'

'How is she?'

'Not so good. There's nowt to be done, they can't operate.'

'Is she having any medical care?'

'A nurse pops in, and the Doctor calls in every week. I'm trying to keep her at home as long as I can. She hates the hospital.'

'Poor Mum, it must be terrible for her.'

'Yes, she never complains though. Only about my cooking. She's not eating much now.'

She went up to see her Mum. Gently eased open the door. The room was in semi darkness, a narrow shaft of sunlight lit the candlewick bedspread, highlighting the ridge and furrow pattern over the slight hummock that was her mother.

'Is that you Tom?'

'No, it's me Mum, it's me, Lamorna.'

She sat down on the edge of the bed and took her mother's thin pale hand in her own. A bony hand, skin translucent and ridged with blue veins, like worms twisting over the surface.

'Lorna? What you here for?'

'I came to see you Mum.'

'Didn't need to bother.'

'I wanted to see you.'

'Thought you was away.'

'I was. I was in Italy, but I came back.'

'No need on my account.'

'I didn't know you were ill until I rang Tom yesterday.'

'Aye well. I'm badly Lorna.'

'I know, I'm sorry Mum. I'm so sorry.'

'Pull curtains back, let me look at you.'

She went over to the window and tugged the curtains aside. The summer curtains, cream with green stripes. Her mother wouldn't be around to change them for the winter ones. She turned and saw her more clearly now. A thin pale face, sunken cheeks. Wisps of white hair. Watery grey eyes gazed unblinking at her.

'You'll do. Shall you tell Tom I need that tea?'

Tom was already in the kitchen, filling the kettle.

'Thought you'd be wanting tea. How did you find her?'

'She's so thin and frail.'

'Aye, she's not good. She's on morphine. Nowt else to be done. Sleeps most of the time. Sometimes she'll wake in the night and want to talk.'

'I'll take her tea up,' Lamorna said.

Her mother was sleeping again. She tiptoed back downstairs.

'I'll cook for us tonight Tom if you'd like.'

'That'd be good.'

'I'll have to do some shopping,' she thought. There were no fresh vegetables. She walked to the corner shop and bought a limp lettuce, some cucumber, mushrooms and an onion. She had found a packet of unopened macaroni in the cupboard. It was past its sell by date but would have to do. She managed to make something resembling a pasta meal.

'Roberto would be horrified,' she thought.

'Would you like me to do the shopping for you?' Lamorna asked.

'It'd be good. Molly next door's been a great help, but she's away at her sisters this week. I can't keep asking. Are you over for long?'

'No plans at the moment. I could stay and help out until....'

'I won't say it wouldn't be handy. I need to get back to work. Mortgage to pay. I'm not much of a cook. Not that yer Mam's eating owt. She managed two spoonfuls just now when I said you'd cooked it.'

'I could stay in the week and go home for weekends.'

'If you want. The boys take turns to come on Friday nights. You'll need a break any road.'

They washed up, and then Tom went upstairs again.

'Sleeping,' he said, coming back and turning on the television, slumping into a chair. Lamorna stared unseeing at the screen.

Tom went off to work at seven thirty next morning. Lamorna began to get the house into some sort of order, clearing out mouldy food from the fridge, cleaning and tidying. She made some soup, but her Mum could only manage a few mouthfuls.

As the days passed her mother was sleeping more, and Lamorna had time to get the house organised, finish the cleaning and get some shopping for them whilst the neighbour popped in. She washed and ironed, and sowed some late salads in the garden. She thought about Michael, the day they'd spent in the hotel garden all those years ago, sowing salads for the kitchen. 'I miss Aileen,' she thought.

She prepared breakfasts, made a pack up lunch for Tom each day, and cooked for them in the evening, finding herself quite enjoying the very English domestic life again. Sometimes her mother ate a good meal, sometimes she wanted nothing. A nurse called in every day, and together they changed the sheets and washed her Mum.

Chapter 27

She hired a small car so that she could more easily shop for them and travel home on Saturday mornings for the weekend. She enjoyed seeing her brothers again on the Friday evenings, but the weekends were an essential breathing space, away from the house and all the sadness. She and Ann took turns to cook on Saturday evenings, and they had lunch together at the pub on Sundays before Lamorna set off once more. She phoned Roberto on Sunday mornings and it helped her get through it all. He offered to come and be with her, but she refused.

'I can only cope with one emotion at once,' she told him. 'I don't think I'd be much company.'

She liked to walk in the dale on Saturday afternoons, noticing the changes as summer began to slip into autumn, following the river as it cascaded over its rocky weirs, watching for the white throats of dippers bobbing on mossy rocks at the water's edge. The birch trees were beautiful now, a pale tracery of branches against straighter, darker trees. On distant hills tree branches were etched into the sky. Sometimes it was drizzly in the morning, and the flowers of cow parsley were a delicate white lace in a shawl of mist along the river's edge. The pale browns and oranges of the dogwoods stood out like a child's crayon scribble on the deep green surface of the river.

She loved to look out for the river birds. There were two coots that she always saw. She watched them as they busied about on the river, one this way, one that, sometimes calling to each other, then drifting apart as one was taken by the current. And she loved best a lone swan, and looked out for it as it sailed along with the river's flow. The walks filled her with peace, a haven of solitude in the midst of all the stress and worry.

The drive back on Sundays was hard, she wondered what to expect, how her mother would be. She always phoned ahead to say she was on the way, and cut flowers from her garden, shopped for special things, some local honey, meat from a farm shop, a Bakewell pudding and always a bottle of beer for Tom.

'That's good of you mi duck,' Tom said when she came back with the treats after the first weekend away. 'We've missed you. Me and the lads are not up to much in kitchen.'

So she started to prepare meals for them to heat up whilst she was away, stocking up with bread, fruit and cans of baked beans and soups for simple lunches.

Sometimes she sat and read from magazines for her Mum, other times they talked. Once she asked about Michael.

'What happened to that Cornish lad you brought home? Christmas it were.'

'Oh we split up a long time ago.'

'He were a nice lookin' lad. I thought you might've had that dark hair. But you're yer Granny's girl. '

'Why Mum, why would I have had dark hair?'

But she had closed her eyes and drifted into sleep.

One afternoon her mother was particularly lucid.

'I weren't much of a Mam.'

'Don't say that Mum.' She picked up her mother's hand in hers and held it. 'It was hard when Dad died.'

'No, hark to me. When your Dad died I pushed you away. I couldn't cope without him. I couldn't cope with the grief, and I blocked you out. In a way I blamed you.'

'You didn't Mum. I knew you were unhappy without Dad.'

'We rowed over you. Over the money he'd got for you. I thought at first he'd killed hisself. They said it were an accident. But it were my fault. I told him it were wrong to save for you, for college. It preyed on his mind. He weren't thinkin' that day.'

'Mum, don't get upset. It was a long time ago. You don't have to say sorry; you don't need to talk about it. It wasn't your fault.'

'No. Hear me out. Then I can go in peace.'

'Don't say that Mum.'

'It were my fault, what happened to yer Dad. And I mixed you up in the blame. I thought he'd killed hisself because of what I did. I knew he were upset. They said he was talking about taking us away. He must have made up his mind to spend the money. He weren't thinkin' and that's why he died, didn't see the wagons. So it were my fault. It weren't even a lot of money.'

'It was Mum, it was a help. I bought the camera for my course.'

'You were such a good little girl, you loved your Dad. But you were lonely. I weren't a good mother. I pushed you away. When you was only a slip of a thing I lost those babies. One were born dead. The other. He were blue. I warmed him by the fire, but he went. Your Dad didn't know I was expecting. He never knew.'

'I thought you'd had miscarriages, I didn't know the babies were born.'

'You were always one for burying yourself in books. He were trying to be a Mam and a Dad to you. And coping with me. My depressions.'

'I used to have a little case under my bed. I thought I might run away.'

'I know. Yer teddy and a jam tart. You've done well. Your Dad would be proud. I'm tired now.'

She closed her eyes, and Lamorna tiptoed away, her eyes full of tears.

Lamorna lay in the narrow bed that night, remembering her childhood. She thought she could recall the days before her Dad had died. A tension in the house. 'I used to play with my doll's house behind the settee. Away from the shouting. Trying to make it go away.'

For the rest of that week her Mum slipped into quietness again, hardly eating, just lying in bed, seeming to watch the streaks of sunlight move across the wall as the shadows lengthened into evening. Her fingers moved over the sheet, trying to pick up something that no-one else could see. Grasping like pincers, plucking and pulling at the bedspread.

'The spiders are mitherin me again.'

'There aren't any spiders Mum.'

'It's the morphine,' Tom said later. 'The Doctor says it makes her imagine it.'

'When are you getting wed?' her Mum suddenly asked the next day 'That boy, the one you brought home.'

'We're not Mum, I told you, we're not together now.'

'He's so like him, so like him. He came lookin' for yer.'

'Like who Mum, who's he like?'

No response. Lamorna sat and watched the hands on the bedside clock move on around the dial. After a while her mother suddenly spoke once more.

'I'm tired of this. How long is it goin' on?'

Some moments later she drifted into sleep again. And that was the routine of each day. Sometimes she talked. Often it was about her own childhood. But each day the periods of sleep lengthened.

When Lamorna took her tea one morning she suddenly grasped hold of the gold locket chain around her neck, tried to undo it. Lamorna reached round and unfastened it for her.

'Open it.'

Lamorna opened the locket. There was a photograph of her Dad's smiling face. She showed it to her mother, and watched as she looked at it and sighed.

'I meant to put his hair in there, but I never did. I want you to have it.'

'I couldn't Mum.'

'It's no use to me where I'm going. I want you to have it. Your Dad gave it to me when we were courting. It's Welsh gold.'

'Thank you Mum, I'll treasure it.'

But her Mum was asleep.

Later that evening she struggled to speak again.

'I want you to take my ashes to the cove.'

'Won't Tom want to be involved?'

'No, I told him what I want. He knows I'm askin. You must take yer Dad's too.'

'Oh Mum, what do you mean 'Dad's?'

'I've got his ashes. They're in a trunk. In wardrobe. Kept them. Couldn't get down there.'

She paused, and Lamorna helped her to sit up a little so that she could sip from a glass of water held to her lips. She was so light, so frail, her eyes sunk further into the dark rings like bruises under her brow. It was an effort for her to move.

'Tom don't know. Don't tell him about your Dad's ashes. He's been good to me.'

She struggled to sit up higher, reaching out a hand. She scrabbled towards the cupboard.

'Can't do it. Look in the drawer. There's a key. In my bag.'

Lamorna opened the bedside drawer, pulled out a bag, and opened it.

'There's a pocket.'

She looked and found a small key.

'That's it. Fer the trunk. After I'm gone you tek it. It's fer you.'

'But Mum…'

She had lain back and closed her eyes. Lamorna waited for a few moments, listened to her breathing. She seemed to be sleeping. She opened the wardrobe and peered in. There was a small metal trunk tucked in under some shoes and bags. Her eyes filled with tears, and she turned to look at her mother.

'Oh Mum, how did we lose each other, how did it happen?'

As the week passed her mother was sleeping most of the time, so Lamorna was surprised when she suddenly opened her eyes and spoke lucidly again.

'There's my wedding ring in the trunk. The one your Dad put on my hand. It's for you. When you marry that boy. I loved your Dad. But I couldn't help it. He was so handsome. So handsome.'
The words dwindled as she closed her eyes again.

'What do you mean Mum? What do you mean?' she whispered.

The following evening they had eaten dinner, and Tom was washing up. She went up to her Mum, and found her lying with her eyes wide open. She reached for Lamorna's hand. She tried to speak, but it was just a faint whisper, a rasping sound.

'I'll get him for you,' she said, suddenly feeling that her Mum wanted Tom. She ran back downstairs.'

'Mum wants you, I'll finish this.' She took the towel from him and dried up the pans.

A few minutes later he was back, his eyes filling up

'She's gone.'

Chapter 28

After the funeral she helped Tom to clear away her Mum's things. They packed her clothes and other items and took them to a charity shop. Lamorna stayed until the next Friday evening, when the boys were due home again.

'Thanks for everything you've done love,' Tom said, after dinner. 'I couldn't have managed without you.'

'I'm glad I was here, glad I could see Mum before, before she went.'

'She was pleased you came. She said she'd made amends. It weren't easy for you, were it, your Dad, and then a new family. We didn't do enough for you, but you seemed a steady 'un.'

'I was, it was fine,' she said as convincingly as she could.

'You know you're always welcome here. The boys are fond of you.'

'Yes, thank you, I will make time to come and see you all.'

She had placed the trunk in her car that afternoon when Tom was busy, thinking it was easier if he didn't see it, ask questions. She drove home late, after dinner, and so it was almost midnight when she unlocked the trunk and looked inside. There was a cloth bag, and inside the urn containing her Dad's ashes. She opened it, just grey powder, like her Mum's ashes.

'I'll drive down to Cornwall tomorrow, and then I'll go and see Mary.'

There was a bundle of letters, tied up with ribbon. She unfastened it, and opened one. It was a letter from her Mum from hospital, the day after she'd been born.

'Oh Will,' she read, 'she's not really ugly; it's just the way her face was squeezed with the birth.'

She laughed and put the letters to one side to read another day. There was an envelope with a lock of her own baby hair. And then she reached for the locket around her neck. 'I will put Michael's hair in here,' she thought. She opened a small box and found some silver cardboard horseshoes edged with the remains of white icing, a few cards congratulating 'Myra and Will on your wedding.' There was a gold wedding band. She slipped it onto her finger. It was a perfect fit. Replacing it in the box she wiped her eyes on her sleeve, and then opened a second box. Here were relics of Cornwall, a black and white postcard picture of Lamorna Cove, a silver Cornish Pisky charm, a few sea shells, and some faded dried flowers pressed between tissue paper, brown and crumbling with age. There were photograph albums, pictures of their wedding, of her as a young child. And an envelope with 'Lamorna' scrawled on it.

'For another day,' she thought.

The following morning she drove down to Cornwall, arriving in Penzance at six in the evening, and booked into a Guest House near Morrab Gardens. It was a beautiful autumn morning when she set off next day for Lamorna Cove. She parked by the harbour, and walked up the cliff path until she reached a place where the little cove was still visible, but there were also views of the wide sea. She left the track and climbed up to some gorse bushes, where she sat for a while, thinking about her parents, her childhood, and the days they had spent down here in Cornwall. She reached into her bag and pulled out the two urns, then opening the lids one by one she tipped out the ashes, and with her hands mixed them all up together under a flowering gorse.

'Goodbye Mum, goodbye Dad, you're together now.'

She walked slowly back down to the harbour, calling into a public toilet to wash away her tears, run a comb through her hair.

'I'll go and find Mary now. She'll know how it is with him.' Suddenly the world seemed a brighter place. On the way up the hill she saw that 'The Lamorna Wink' was open. She parked and went in for a sandwich. And then she drove on to Mousehole. It was quiet in the village out of season, and she easily found a parking space by the harbour. Some of the boats had already been pulled out for winter, and lay jostling together behind the little beach. She looked for 'Merry Maid' but couldn't see it.

Mary was there with her daughters, the two youngest. She watched as they worked together to fill buckets and tip the sand out onto a large heap, and then one of them began to shape a doorway in the castle, poking holes for windows, smoothing sand away for a roadway. She stepped onto the sand.

'Mary, it's me.'

'Lamorna, I can't believe it! What are you doing here?' She stood up to greet her friend with a warm hug. The girls put down their spades and stared at the stranger.

'I came to scatter my Mother's ashes. She's just died. She asked me to bring them to Lamorna Cove, and my Dad's too. She kept his all these years. That's where I've come from.'

She smiled down at the two children, who were now holding onto their mother's skirt. She crouched down.

'Hello, I'm a friend of your Mum. I haven't seen her for a long time.'

'Say hello to Aunty Lamorna,' Mary told them, and obediently they did. 'This is Jenny, she's four now, this is Lamorna, she's two.'

'They're lovely; can I help build your castle?'

They nodded shyly, and she followed them over and scooped sand up to make a wall and a moat. Jenny passed her a spade, and she went on digging. Mary joined in now, and they soon had the moat finished and went on to create a garden. Lamorna went paddling and found seaweed trees and sticks for fences.

'Come for tea with us.'

'I'd love to. I'd like to see Chris.'

'Oh, he's out on the boat, won't be back for a couple of days.'

'Do you miss him?'

'Yes, but I'm used to it now. It's the way it is. He's skipper on one of the big trawlers now. The money's better.'

They watched as the two girls smoothed the walls of their castle and added small stones to make a door.

'Come on girls, time we got going.'

They walked up the hill, past the little cottage where she had stayed with Michael, and where Mary and Chris had spent the first months of their marriage. It looked closed up now, shutters across the windows, sand blown onto the doorstep.

'You've called your youngest Lamorna.'

'It was Chris's idea. She has an auburn streak in her hair, just like yours.'

'So she does. I hope she doesn't share my awkward streaks of temperament.'

'I would be proud if she turned out like you, so successful, travelling the world.'

'Success isn't everything.'

They reached Mary's home now, and went inside, leaving a pile of buckets and spades on the step. Lamorna was reminded of the photographs she had taken for the cottage brochure, how she and Michael had placed a similar bucket and spade by the cottage door.

Mary got drinks for the children, and then put the kettle on for tea. She and Lamorna sat around the kitchen table whilst the girls played with their toys on the rug. Little Lamorna carried small toy animals over and dropped them into her new Auntie's lap.

'My Mum's picking the others up from school today. I'll go up for them at six. Come with me, she'd love to see you again.'

'I'd like that. I always loved your Mum.'

'I wish you'd been here to be Godmother to the youngest girls, especially Lamorna.'

'I would have liked that, but I'm away so often, I don't feel I'd be much of a God parent to them.'

'Michael is Godfather to them all, and both of you for Emily of course. Thank you for all the lovely things you've sent them. They're so proud of the toys from around the world. No-one else around here has them.'

'Mary, I'm thinking of going over to Ireland to see Michael.'

'Oh.'

'What is it? What's wrong Mary?'

'I don't know what to say. He's living with a woman now.'

'Oh, then I won't go.' Her eyes filled with tears, and she was suddenly glad to be distracted by Jenny bringing her a pretend cup of tea.

'Why now, after all this time? I heard you were happy in Venice, that you'd found someone.'

'I was, but he knew I wasn't committed to him, he found out about Michael, what happened. I had to tell him. He made me come over, told me I had to find him. And then I heard my mother was ill, so I've been with her until she died. And now it's too late. It's my own fault.'

'I don't know what to say. Michael was so unhappy when you left him, he was always asking for news of you. And when he told us he'd met a girl we thought it was what he needed. It was for the best. When we found out the baby wasn't Michael's, well, we thought you'd get back together then.'

'I was so happy the baby wasn't his. It's mean, but I didn't want Rosa to have his baby. I don't know what was wrong with me though. I was so hurt, and I thought in some way I wasn't good enough for him. I thought he'd chosen Rosa. I couldn't go and find him then. I didn't have the courage. He didn't try to contact me. I thought he wouldn't want me.'

'What a pair you are. Michael said he couldn't get in touch with you. He said he'd told you that he would leave you to make up your own mind. But he never stopped thinking about you. He saved articles with your photographs in.'

Jenny came over then, and climbed onto Lamorna's knee, plonking her book down.

'Read it to me.'

'Manners Jenny.' Mary spoke sternly.

'Please Aunty Lamorna.'

So Lamorna read her a story about a little lost teddy, and suddenly found she had two children on her knee. Mary put the kettle on again, and found a tin of biscuits. She poured drinks for the girls and placed them on a small table for them. They scrambled down and sat on their little chairs.

'Aileen was furious with Michael that first Christmas after you split up. She told him you were a vulnerable young woman and he'd broken your heart. Until now he's never shown any interest in anyone else, and it's not for want of opportunities. Half the girls around here are in love with him.'

'I'm glad he's found some happiness then. He shouldn't be alone.'

'It was only after I told him you were in Italy with a man. I'm sorry Lamorna. He gave up hope then I think. What will you do now? Were you thinking you'd get back together?'

'I don't think I dared to hope. It's been so long. I don't deserve him. I'm tired of all the travelling though. I've bought a cottage in Derbyshire. I'll go back up there and make it my home. I'll write you the address and phone number. You could all come up and stay with me.'

She fished around in her bag for a paper and pen.

'You're not going back to Italy then?'

'No, I couldn't. Roberto is a lovely person, but it's not fair to stay with him when I can't be committed in the way he'd like.' Her eyes filled with tears again. Jenny appeared at her side, a tissue in her hand, and a solemn expression on her face.

"I'm sorry Jenny. I'm not a good visitor am I? Thank you.' She smiled, and took the tissue.

'Aunty Lamorna is sad because her mummy has died,' Mary explained.

'Yes, she was very poorly, and very old,' Lamorna added when she saw a look of concern cloud the girl's face as she turned to look at her mother.

'Look at the time, it's nearly six, come on girls, we need to go. Granny will be wondering where we've got to.'

They walked together up the hill, Lamorna giving the girls piggy back rides until they reached the house that was still so familiar to her after all the years away. Emily and Catherine remembered her and clamoured for attention. Kate was delighted to see her too.

'Let me look at you. What's this sad look, you such a lovely maid and no ring on your finger yet.'

'My mother just died Kate. I came to scatter her ashes at Lamorna Cove.'

'I'm sorry to hear that. Won't you have some dinner with us?'

'Oh, I couldn't impose. You didn't know I was coming.'

'You won't be imposing my lover. One more won't make a difference. We'd love to have you. And the men are all at sea.'

'Even Frank?'

'Yes, he can't give up the habit. There's no need for him to go out, but it's in his blood I reckon.'

They sat around the table with the four girls. After dinner she read them a story, and then they were bundled off to bed in Mary and Ian's old rooms. Kate made them all tea.

'You're so lucky with these lovely children,' she told Mary.

'We were hoping for a boy, but I think I've persuaded Chris to stop trying now,' Mary laughed.

'I always thought you and Michael Tremayne would be the next ones to wed after our Mary,'

'Mum.'

'It's alright Mary. I was stupid Kate, I threw it all away.'

'Well I daresay there's some cause, but I won't say I'm not sorry. You'd have made a good couple.

'Well it's too late now, he's found someone new. I haven't seen him or spoken to him for nearly seven years.'

'But you still care for him, don't you?' Kate said then, giving her a searching look.

'Yes. I can't imagine feeling the same for anyone else. But that's enough about me. Tell me all your news.'

'Our Ian and Maureen are expecting their second child. They've got a boy, Peter, named for her Dad.'

'Remember my sister Tamzin? Mary said. 'She married a Londoner, lives in Walthamstow now. What happened to your friend Joy? I've still got the wedding dress she made, can't get into it now.'

'She's in London too. I stayed with her for a night when I got back from Italy. She's doing well, and married a photographer she met through work.'

They talked for a while longer, Lamorna telling them something of her travels, and hearing more of the local gossip. At ten o'clock she was ready to leave, noticing the two women seemed tired.

'I'd better get off or I'll be locked out of the Guest House.'

'Don't leave it so long until you come again, you're always welcome. No need to book a hotel, you can always stay with us.'

'Thank you. I'll come down again soon. I have to get home tomorrow though, I've arranged for a builder to call and I can't leave it all to my neighbour.'

She drove back to Penzance, and an hour later was in bed, lying awake, a great emptiness engulfing her.

'What shall I do now? What next?'

Chapter 29

The builders arrived to finish the bathroom refurbishment the following morning and she began to unpack more of the belongings she'd left stored soon after moving in, starting again with the trunk her mother had left for her. She found the letter addressed to her, slit open the envelope and began to read.

Dear Lamorna,

This is a hard letter to write. I shouldn't have left it so late. When they told me I'd got cancer I got to thinking. I knew I had to tell you. You'd found that young man in Cornwall. You need to know. Just in case.

You see love your Dad was not your real dad. He never knew. Not til the day he died. Then it all came out. When we had that row about you. That's when I told him. I never meant to. It just came out.

I met your real Dad in Cornwall. I knew him before me and your Dad were wed. He was a handsome man. But he was married see. I loved him. When your Dad went off fishing I met up with him. It went on for a good few years. That's how I got you. You see your dad couldn't seem to give me babies. We tried. The other babies, the ones I lost, they weren't your Dad's neither. I can't tell you who he is. He's married see. I promised I would never tell you. He saw you. He said he could see you was his. It was the hair. It's in his family. I told your Dad you took after my Mam. You know I loved your Dad. And he loved you.

I'll be gone when you read this. I did it for you. I wanted a baby and I loved him. But he wasn't free. Don't try and find him. He has family. He wouldn't want that. I never saw him after Will died.

Mam.

The letter fell into her lap, and she sat, numb, unable to think. Unable to take it in. The phone rang. She picked it up.

'Yes.'

It was Greg.

'Hi Lamorna. Heard from Roberto you were back in the country. Sorry to hear about your Mum. Did the funeral go well?'

'Yes. I've just got back from Cornwall, scattering Mum's ashes.'

'I wondered if you were up for a job. I'm desperate. Dan Spinks has let me down again. Janet seemed to think you might be otherwise engaged though.'

'What is the job?'

'It's short notice, you'd have to leave tomorrow. It's a project documenting a film crew in South America. They're filming some threatened tribal people. You'd have to be away until early next summer probably. Your inoculations will still be valid from your last trip. Can you do it?'

'Why not? What are the arrangements?'

They discussed the organisational detail, and then Lamorna asked to speak to Janet.

'Lamorna, I thought you weren't going abroad again!'

'Yes, I must be mad. I just agreed to go off for half a year.'

'Have you kept that promise to me yet? Surely that's something to keep you here?'

'I was in Cornwall Janet. I found out that Michael has a woman living with him.'

'Who is she, how did he meet her?'

'I don't know any more. Mary told me he's in Ireland still, and she's Irish. I didn't want to ask any more questions.'

'How do you feel?'

'I feel devastated to be honest. I was stupid, I didn't expect it. In a way some work in another country is just what I need. I can throw myself into it and not have to think.'

'Will you go back to Roberto?'

'I can't talk about it on the phone. I'll catch up with you when I get back. See you Janet.'

She put the phone down, sighing. 'Another job, another country. I've nothing else.'

She packed her bag and gathered her photography equipment together, then went next door to talk to Ann.

'Sorry Ann, I was looking forward to being here, spending some time with you, getting the cottage sorted. I've just said I'll go to South America.'

'You could have turned it down.'

'I could, but I don't like to let Greg down, he's given me great jobs and this was an important contract. But it will definitely be my last.'

'Stay for dinner with me tonight. It's only cottage pie.'

'Thank you, I'd like that. Will you keep a key for me again? The builders have finished, so there shouldn't be anything else. I'll leave you with some leftovers as usual!'

She couldn't believe how normal she was, how calm she could be, when all the time her heart was broken and all she could think about was the letter.

A taxi arrived for her at eight thirty the next morning. She locked her door as the driver loaded her bags into the boot. And then the phone rang.

'Hold on, I'll just take this call.'

She unlocked the door again, but as she stepped inside the ringing stopped.

Chapter 30

It was the end of June the following year when she stepped through the door of her cottage again. She unpacked, opened windows, groaned when she saw the pile of post on the window sill. Decided to leave it all until the next day. There was no sign of Ann, so she walked down to the local pub for dinner. She sat by the window, looking out over the dale, watching the sheep browsing in the field below, sparrows busy bathing in a gravel patch on the lane, a group of walkers striding up the footpath, hurrying for a welcome drink.

Later she noticed Ann's lights were on, so she knocked to let her know she was back.

'Oh, I'm so glad to see you, come in, come in, and have a coffee with me.'
They sat together in Ann's sun lounge, and Lamorna told her about the latest trip.

'It was amazing, I've been to so many different countries, met so many people, but I'm really happy to be home again. It all gets so exhausting after a while, living out of a rucksack, never knowing where I'll be sleeping next.'

'I can't imagine it. I've never been further than Scotland.'

'The world is full of beautiful places, but you know I think I love the view from my window here most of all. And I intend to stay now and really get to know it. Thank you for looking after the place for me. I hope it's all been okay.'

'Some tiles blew off your roof. I asked John to fix them. We had some bad weather over the winter. I've kept low heating on for you, so there were no problems, and your handyman came regularly to do the garden. Everything's been fine.'

'Thanks Ann, will you come round for dinner with me tomorrow night?'

'That would be lovely.'

The next morning, a Saturday, she shopped in Bakewell, and then washed some clothes, before starting on the mound of post. In the afternoon she pottered in the garden for a while, deciding where she would create a vegetable patch for next year, thinking she might even plant some salads now.

Ann came round for dinner later and they spent a pleasant evening chatting. Ann wanted to hear more about Italy and her travels, and Lamorna found one or two photographs of the sailing trips to show her.

'It's a funny thing, but I don't usually have any pictures of my own trips, or my own life. I only seem to use the camera for work.'

On Sunday morning she just couldn't face the pile of letters and bills again, so she pulled out the trunk that was still unexplored from her college days. She didn't want to investigate her Mother's trunk just yet. Or read that letter again. She lifted out the throws and cushions she'd bought for her room in the shared student house, thinking she would take them to a charity shop. Underneath were some photographs wrapped in newspaper. The photographs she'd taken in Cornwall, the picture Phil had taken on the beach. There she was, leaning on Michael's shoulder, looking up at him. She touched his face with her fingertip.

'Oh Michael, I thought then we would be together forever. And now I've lost you.'

She opened a small box, and found the necklace of sea shells he'd made for her. She hung it around her neck, feeling the familiar cool touch of the small shells against her skin, remembering how he had fastened it around her neck that long ago Christmas. There was a bundle of letters he'd sent her. The ones she had read in Greece, the letters telling her how much he loved her, missed her. The letters that had made her come home early.

'I wonder what might have happened if I hadn't come home then. If I'd stayed in Greece with Jude as we'd planned. I wouldn't have been in Rome. I wouldn't have found Michael with Rosa. I probably would never have known he'd slept with her. But then there was the baby.' She sighed. 'What's the use of 'what if'?' She put the letters to one side. She found the lock of his hair, wrapped in crumpled tissue, a curl of dark brown, still smelling slightly of him she thought. She went into her bedroom to find the locket her mother had given her, and opening it placed the hair inside. Her Dad smiled up at her. Not her Dad. 'But he was my Dad. I believed he was. He loved me.'

Here was her journal from the summer in Cornwall. She looked through at all the meticulously recorded technical details of each photograph. She saw the date next to information about the photograph she'd taken when she first arrived in Penzance. July 4th. 'That's tomorrow,' she thought. 'Ten years since the day I first saw Michael. That would have been the 5th, the day I came to the hotel.' And then she found the record he'd made for her. She knew it was probably a mistake, but she wanted to hear his voice again. There was no record player now, she'd never owned one of her own since giving up her flat in Birmingham. One of the women victims of abuse who had stayed in her flat had stolen it. She carried it next door.

'Ann, do you have a record player?'
'Yes, why?'
'Do you mind if I just play this?'
'Of course not, come in. What is it?'
Lamorna handed it to her. She read the label.
'Who is the artist? It doesn't say.' She looked at Lamorna. Placed it on the turntable.
Michael's voice filled the room, singing 'The first Time ever.' Tears rolled down Lamorna's cheeks. Ann went out to make tea, reappearing just as Michael finished 'Love me Tender' on the other side. Lamorna was drying her eyes now. She drank gratefully when tea was passed to her.
'That was lovely.'

'He was someone I used to know. I haven't heard that for so many years, eight years I suppose. He made it for me, it was a Christmas present.'

'Oh, I see. He has a lovely voice.'

'Yes, he's a lovely person.'

Tears welled up in her eyes again.

'I'm sorry, I shouldn't be crying like this. It was all so long ago. I shouldn't have listened to it. I have to put it all behind me now. I'm being silly.'

'Lamorna, what does he look like?'

'He's a bit taller than me. He has dark hair that curls into his neck. And the bluest eyes. Why do you ask?'

'It's just that a man came looking for you a few days after you went away. I'd completely forgotten. I found him knocking on your door. I told him you'd be away for a year. He didn't want to leave a message. But I remember he looked so disappointed, so sad.'

'But who was he?'

'He didn't say, but he had dark hair, and I'm sure his eyes were blue.' She blushed then. 'I thought he was very handsome. I wish I'd had the nerve to invite him in. He had a lovely accent too. I couldn't place it.'

Lamorna smiled.

'That sounds like him. He is gorgeous. And he's Cornish, that's the accent. Did you tell him where I'd gone?'

'I can't remember. I think I just said you were away. I don't think I said where.'

Lamorna walked back round to her cottage.

'Why would he have come? Mary must have given him my address. If only I hadn't gone away.'

She pulled open the journal again, flicking through the pages. At the back were some numbers, Phil's Studio, the hotel. On an impulse she went over to the phone and dialled the hotel number. A voice answered. Aileen's voice. She took a deep breath.

'Hello, I'm wondering if you have a room available from tomorrow night.'

'Yes, we have just one double, how long will you be wanting to stay?'

'A week?'

'Yes, I can do that. How many of you?'

'Oh, just one. Just me. Does it have a view of the sea?'

'That room does. It overlooks the garden to the side, and there is a glimpse of the sea.'

'That's lovely, thank you.'

'Could I have your name please?'

'Oh. Yes, Lorna, Lorna Roberts.'

'Would you like to book a meal for the evening?'

'Ummm, yes please. I'm coming down by train. I'll arrive about six o'clock I think.'

She put the phone down, and was surprised to find that she was trembling.

'What have I done? I must be crazy. I'll try and find out who my father is. I want to know. Mum said I shouldn't. But I have to. I have to.'

She stuffed everything back into the trunk, except for the photograph, which she placed on the mantel piece. She went into the kitchen, packed all the left-over food into a carrier bag and took it round to Ann.

'It's me again Ann. I'm sorry. I have to go down to Cornwall tomorrow. I may be mad, but I have to go. Can you use this stuff?'

'You're going to find him aren't you?'

'I don't think he'll be there. I know he won't. He lives in Ireland now. It's exactly ten years since I first met him. I'm going down to lay a few ghosts. I have to do it. Then I can move on.'

'I hope you're right.'

'Will you let me buy you a meal tonight? I can't face the torture of waiting alone. I need distractions or I might be tempted not to go through with it.'

'I'd love to.'

Later they walked home together from the pub, and Lamorna invited Ann for coffee. She saw the photograph on the mantel piece straight away, picked it up and scrutinised it.

'This is the man who came to call for you last year.'

Chapter 31

The train was on time, and she was waiting by the door as it snaked around the curve of Mounts Bay. She could make out every detail of St Michael's Mount, the steps, carved stonework and the windows gleaming where sunlight caught them. They pulled into the station, and she stepped out onto the platform. A clamour of gulls assaulted her ears once again, just as she remembered on that day ten years ago. She stood for a while as she had done then, looking out across the bay.

'I came down here to escape, I was running away, and I didn't know how those few weeks would change my life,' she thought. 'And then I suppose I ran away again. I'm not sure why I'm here now. Am I a different person? Am I strong enough now for this, to face up to the past, to move on?'

She walked around to the bus stop. The bus pulled up, and she clambered on board. The journey was so familiar: the hill up past the lane to Youth Hostel where she'd stayed that first night, the busy harbour at Newlyn with trawlers moored along the quay, lobster pots piled up amongst nets and ropes, the cries of gulls as they swept in a white cloud over the decks. And then up along the cliff, around a bend, past the lifeboat house, all closed up today, and her stop. The hotel looked much the same. There were tubs of bright petunias and a newly painted sign swinging in the breeze. She took a deep breath, hoisted her bag higher on her shoulder and climbed the steps, pushing open the door before her courage failed her.

She was surprised to see Aileen on the reception desk, peering at a register. A rush of emotion swept through her, a feeling of joy at seeing this woman she had cared so much for mixed with a sudden doubt. 'What would she think? Would she welcome me?'

Aileen looked up and her anxiety dissolved as she saw a broad smile.

'Hello Lamorna, I was hoping it would be you. Come in won't you?'
She stepped forward as Aileen came round from behind the desk and opened her arms to her.

'It's so good to see you. You're looking well and so lovely.'

'How did you guess?'

'I recognised your voice, and you hesitated when you gave your name. You said you were Lorna. I remembered that it was how you were known sometimes. And I dared to hope. But why did you just book a room like that? You're always welcome here; you've no need to book like any other guest.'

'I wasn't sure. I didn't know how you would feel after what happened, after all these years.'

'We've thought of you often, and we're all so proud of you, what you've achieved.'

'I'm just back from a job in South America. I didn't want to go away again, but Greg, my agent was desperate. Someone let him down. And well, I had no other plans.'
There was a catch in her voice as she thought about Michael, about the woman he was with now.

'Come and have tea with me in the kitchen.'
'I'd love to, but could I have a quick bath first, I feel so grubby after the journey?'
Aileen took her up to her room, showing her a new shower in the bathroom.
'Ellen's doing,' she said, 'and it is popular with guests. Come down to the kitchen and find me when you're done.'

She slipped off her jacket and stepped over to the window for a moment. The gardens had changed. No sign of the chickens or the vegetable plot. Instead she saw a larger sweep of lawn dotted with tables and chairs spreading down towards the wall and the dazzling sea beyond. She thought about her first glimpse of that view. An image of Michael, in a turquoise shirt, crossing the garden. Sighing she stepped out of her clothes, pulled on a bathrobe she found hung on the door and padded across for her shower.

Feeling fresh and invigorated afterwards she dressed in a long skirt and pale green silk top she'd bought in Italy, fastened the shell necklace around her neck, put on a pair of Italian leather sandals and set off to find the kitchen. The door squeaked open as it always had, and she found Aileen pouring water into a teapot. They sat down together at the big old table. She noticed the small scribbled marks that Michael had once shown her, marks he'd made when he was a little boy.
'It's exactly ten years tomorrow that I first drank tea with you here.'
'I thought it might be something like that. What made you come after all this time?'
'I found my photography journal from that summer. I saw the date. And I suddenly knew I had to come. An impulse.' She sipped her tea. 'Just what I needed after the journey.'
'I would have thought the journey here was nothing compared to the travelling you've done. You seem to have been everywhere in the world.'
'Yes, I suppose I have. How is the hotel doing now?'
'Keeping things going is hard. So many people are taking holidays abroad now. The cottages have done well. We still use the brochures you designed, but I think they're maybe due for an update. Ellen and Klaus have made changes we need to include. They're really in charge now. I'm trying to persuade Sam to retire. Michael sold the farm in Ireland, and he shared the money with us. Ellen is planning some more refurbishing to bring the hotel up to date.'

Lamorna drank some more tea. 'Sold the farm?' she thought. 'Why, what's happened?'
'How is Michael?'
'Why don't you ask him yourself?'
'What do you mean?' she whispered, as her heart lurched.

'I mean you can ask him. He's here in the hotel. He rang me about five minutes after you'd booked a room. I told him I had a hunch it might be you. So he came over today. He's in the bar now, helping Sam restock. I've told him you've arrived.'

'He might not want to see me.'

'He does want to see you. That's why he's here. But he told me to say that he will understand if you don't want to talk to him. He'll go away.'

'I would like to see him.'

'Perhaps you'd like to meet up with him in the garden. Ellen's created a pretty seating area.'

'That sounds lovely.'

'Take some tea with you, you'll find the arbour at the top of the lawn. I'll go and tell him.' She stood up, and then turned to Lamorna again.

'Lamorna, please don't hurt Michael. He's had a bad time of it recently.'

'I won't hurt him. I've never wanted to hurt him.'

'I'm sorry, I know you haven't. I shouldn't have said that. It's just that I worry about him.'

'It's alright. I understand. Do you know everything that happened, what happened between us?'

She fought back the tears that threatened to fall.

'Yes, at least I know what Michael told me. I can understand why you walked away.' She sighed. 'He made a bit of a mess of things.'

'I was to blame too. I couldn't believe him, I wouldn't see him, wouldn't open his letters.'

'Will you be alright?'

'Yes, please tell him I'm waiting for him.'

She poured some more tea and carried her mug up the path to the arbour. It was roughly where the vegetables used to be. She sat down on the painted bench, under the fragrant pink roses. Her heart was beating wildly. She drew her legs up, resting her feet on the bench, and her chin on her knees, and waited.

'What if there's nothing, no feeling between us now? What if he's like a stranger, and I don't love him anymore? What if I do love him, and he's still with her, the Irish girl?'

And then she was aware that he was beside her. Her heart missed a beat.

'Hello Lamorna, it's good to see you.'

She smiled up at him. He hesitated for a moment, and then sat down, leaving a space between them.

'You look well. I thought you looked like a Cornish Pisky, perched like that on the bench. You've cut your hair.'

'Yes,' she said, putting her feet back on the ground, and turning towards him. 'I've just come back from Ecuador. It was so hot. They were making a film. I got one of the camera crew to hack it all off. Should have done it years ago.' She faltered. 'I'm babbling,' she thought.

'It suits you. You've made a success of your life, your work. I've seen your photographs.'

'I suppose it's what I wanted to do. Thank you for teaching me to swim. You won't believe all the times I've needed it. I've just been swimming with pink dolphins.'

'Where will you be heading off to next?'

'I haven't got any plans. I'm not keen to do any more travelling. It gets so tiring in the end. Hark at me, I sound like a ninety year old. What about you? Your Mum said you've sold the farm.'

'Yes, I had an offer I couldn't refuse. Someone wanted the land for a holiday resort. I've bought a boat. I'm aiming to sail around the world.'

'That's amazing. Explains your piratical appearance. You just need some gold hoops in your ears and a parrot.'

'I'll probably get my hair cut and shave the beard off, just haven't had chance recently.'

'Don't, it looks right.'

'Would you like to come over and see the boat tomorrow? I bought her in Bristol a few months ago, had some work done and sailed her down to Padstow yesterday. I rang Mum last night. She said you might be here. I thought I'd come over and see.'

Aileen called.

'Mum thought you might like to eat with the family.'

'Are you sure? I don't want to impose.'

'Everyone will be pleased to see you.'

'Then I'd love to. Thank you. I was going to call in on Mary and Chris tomorrow, but it can wait. I'd like to see your boat.'

'That's good.'

She walked with him back up the garden, wishing she had the courage to reach for his hand.

Lamorna sat next to Michael at the table, and just as she always had she felt his presence with her whole being, longed to touch him. Klaus and Ellen were opposite, and they dominated the conversation, plying her with questions about her work. And all the while she talked she thought about Michael beside her. He was quiet, hardly speaking. She turned the discussion to the hotel.

'Aileen says you have exciting plans.'

'We've got lots of ideas. Klaus and I think we need to go up market, appeal to people with a bit more money. The cottages are great for families, they're always booked. The brochure needs re-doing though; we don't have one for the second cottage yet. Any chance of an update?'

'Ellie,' Sam scolded her, 'Lamorna's on holiday.'

'I'd love to help, but I haven't brought a camera with me. I'll do it sometime if you'd like, if Phil could do the printing again.'

'Great,' Ellen said. 'People notice your name in the brochure; they always ask if you're the famous photographer.'

'We want to build on the back of the hotel, create a new restaurant, hire a chef,' Klaus added. 'We could open to outsiders for meals then, try to get a good reputation. It's the only way we'll keep going now people can go abroad so cheaply.'

'Michael's money will really help. We want to introduce a special package for honeymooners, more wedding receptions, that kind of thing. We can offer extras such as massage, special diets,' Ellen said.

'It sounds amazing, what do you think Aileen, you'll lose your kitchen?'

'I can't wait. I'd love to move into a little bungalow. Maybe go abroad for a holiday, and see what all the fuss is about.'

They talked more about the hotel, and local tourism in general, and then Aileen said,

'I'm sorry to hear your mother passed away last year Lamorna. Was it unexpected? Mary told us.'

'Yes, it was a bit sudden. Luckily I had just come home from Italy, and I was there to help nurse her before she died. She had cancer. She asked me to bring her ashes to Lamorna Cove. That's why I came down here.'

'You should have come to see us then,' Sam said.

'I couldn't stay. I've bought a cottage in Derbyshire, and builders were coming in to do the bathroom. It wouldn't have been fair to leave it all for my neighbour to sort out.'

'No of course not.'

There was an awkward pause then. Lamorna broke the silence. She turned to Michael.

'When are you off on your world trip?'

'Oh, there's more work to do on the boat first. Maybe in a month. I'll have to get around to the Mediterranean before winter sets in.'

'He got his way in the end,' Sam said, laughing. 'It's maybe not a fishing boat, but it'll worry us just the same.'

'Dad, I'm thirty four years old for goodness sake.'

'I know, I know, but we're parents. We're bound to worry. Look how we fretted when Ellie was in Greece.'

'Don't get started on that again,' Ellen protested.

'Well, Lamorna said, getting to her feet. 'Thank you for the lovely dinner Aileen. I think I'll go up to bed now. I'm not completely over the jet lag. What time are you heading over to Padstow tomorrow Michael?'

'There's no hurry. Shall we say nine o'clock?'

'Okay, I'll see you then. Goodnight everyone.'

She struggled to get to sleep. Her head was in turmoil. 'What is Michael thinking? Why did he come to see me? Why is he so quiet? He asked me to come and see the boat. Does he want to be with me? What about the woman he lived with? Where is she now? Why did he come to Derbyshire to find me? Why hasn't he mentioned that? Please God, let it work out. I love him. I want to be with him.'

She pulled a pillow against her body and held it tightly, curling herself around it.

'Oh Michael, please, please want me.'

Chapter 32

The sun woke her at seven thirty. She went over to the window and drew the curtains back. Another beautiful day. Sunlight dancing over the sea. Two fishing boats were heading out. She showered, and dressed in jeans and a linen shirt, pulling on the deck shoes she'd worn on Roberto's yacht. Reaching the bottom of the stairs she paused, unsure of where to go next. And then Michael appeared.

'You'll come and have breakfast with us in the kitchen?'

'Can I?'

'Of course, unless you'd prefer to eat in the dining room.'

'I'd rather eat with you.'

'Come on then.'

He led her through into the kitchen, and they sat together at the table, just as they had the night before. Aileen was busy cooking. And then Mary appeared.

'Lamorna, what are you doing here?'

'I could ask you the same question. I didn't know you were working here still.'

'Yes, I'm here some days. Mum has the girls for me. When did you get here? Michael too. What's going on?'

'I just decided to come down yesterday. Can I come and visit you?'

'Of course. Come on Saturday, Chris will be back then. He was sorry he missed you when you were down last year. How long are you staying?'

'I booked a week. It feels strange just sitting here, I ought to be helping.'

'You shouldn't, you're not staff now,' Mary said.

'I don't feel like a hotel guest,' she said, laughing.

'You're family, that's how it feels,' Aileen said.

She felt herself blush.

'What are you doing here Michael, you didn't say?' Mary went on as she tied her apron around her and started to load the dishwasher.

'I didn't say. You ask too many questions.'

She threw a dish cloth at him and somehow everyone relaxed then, and the strange tension that had been in the room dissolved.

'Come on Lamorna,' Michael said. 'We'd better get going.'

'I'll just clean my teeth and get my bag and a sweater. It might be cooler on the north coast.'

Michael had borrowed Ellen's car to drive them over to Padstow.

'I've got some stuff to take over. It's easier than by train. I sold my car.'

'It's great to be in Cornwall again, I love being here. I don't know why people want to go to all those resorts in Spain. It's so beautiful here.'

'People go for the weather. It's unreliable down here.'

'I suppose so.'

She leaned back in the seat as he drove out of the village and onwards. Michael was quiet again. She risked looking at him, noticing how his longer hair curled right over his collar now. She wondered if he'd ever realised that she had cut a lock of his hair. She reached up and touched the locket around her neck. Her mother's locket. She had put it on this morning, somehow feeling it was a good luck talisman. She looked at his tanned arms, remembering that journey with him along this same road all those years ago. Remembering how she had wanted to reach over and stroke his arm.

'It's feels just the same now. I don't know where I stand. I don't know what he's thinking. I can't touch him. But it's different now,' her thoughts rambled. 'I know how it feels to have that arm around me. And I'm a different person now. I've known other men, I've grown up. But I still don't know what to do, what to say.'

She sighed.

'Are you alright?'

'Yes, I'm fine.

The journey continued in silence, and at last they reached Padstow. He found a place to park near the harbour and she helped him to carry a few boxes.

'It's bits for the boat, I got them at the chandlers in Penzance yesterday morning. She's moored on the quay.'

'I've still got the boots I bought there,' she said. 'For cleaning the chicken shed.'

He stopped halfway down the quay.

'Here we are. Can you manage this ladder?'

She looked over and saw the metal harbour ladder leading down to a wooden deck.

'Is this your boat?'

'Yes, you can't really see her from up here. Will you come on board?'

'Try and stop me!'

He smiled, and climbed down. She passed him the boxes and followed him. She took his hand as she jumped the last two steps. And she felt the shock of his touch, just as she had that first time. She didn't know if he felt it too.

'We'll get this stuff away, and then I'll show you around. Can you pass it down to me again? Just the two smaller boxes, the others can be stowed up there.'

He climbed down into the galley, and she handed him the boxes before following him.

'It's lovely,' she said, gazing around the compact galley area.

'I'll make us some coffee,' he said, filling a kettle and placing it on a small stove.

'Yes please. Can we look around on deck?'

They went back up and forward to the bows. A wooden mast towered over them, and she saw a canvas cover enclosing the sails that would be furled along the boom. Michael was talking about the boat, showing her various features. She ran her hands along the sleek wooden surfaces. Noticed a shiny new white and red lifebelt, and felt a jolt when she saw the name LAMORNA in black letters around its rim. The kettle began a piercing whistle, and he ran lightly back to the galley. Lamorna looked again at the lifebelt, before going below. Over coffee he talked to her enthusiastically about the jobs he needed to do on board, and she was half listening as she sipped from the enamel beaker. He was standing, leaning against the companionway, looking down at her.

'Michael,' she said at last. 'Is this boat called Lamorna? I saw the lifebelt.'
He seemed embarrassed.

'Yes. I named her after my first boat.'
There was a pause before he spoke again.

'Do you remember that boat?'

'How could I forget it? But Michael, she wasn't called Lamorna. She was Merry Maiden. Merry Maiden of Lamorna.'

'You're right. She was Merry Maid.'
He looked uncomfortable. Embarrassed. She smiled at him.

'I think it's dangerous to call a boat Lamorna. She's probably not going to be very seaworthy.'
She gazed steadily into his eyes.

'I think she's able to weather most storms.'

'Maybe she's a little battered and broken.'
He hesitated a moment.

'Perhaps that can be sorted with a bit of careening and caulking.'

'What are careening and caulking?'

'Would you like me to show you?'

'Yes, I would like that.' She felt a lump in her throat.

He stepped over to her and took her hands in his, raising her from the bench, and leading her into a cabin area.

'First you take the boat out of the water, like this.'
He lifted her into his arms. She felt her heart thudding as he held her close, his breath warm on her hair. And then he was laying her on the bunk.

'Then you must lay her on her side to check her over and prepare her for the caulking.'
He sat down beside her.

'What's caulking?'

'That comes later, there's a lot of preparation, careening first. Shall I show you?'

'Yes.' Her voice sounded strange and remote to her.

'You must check the hull for any damage, and then clear away the barnacles and limpets.'

He stroked her arm, and then she felt his hand move down gently over her body, her waist, hips and then legs. And she was longing for him. Her whole body came alive to his touch and she felt a deep stirring, an aching within her.

'This boat has beautiful curving lines,' he said. 'There doesn't seem to be any damage, but it's hard to say with all the barnacles.'

She smiled up at him.

'Must be neglected. What do you do about them?'

'It can be a long job, getting them all off,' he said. 'Shall I try?'

She nodded, and then felt his hand caress her as he gently undid the buttons of her shirt, then lifted her up, cradling her in his arms as he slipped first one sleeve, and then the other skilfully over her arms and hands.

She began to speak.

'I....'

But he interrupted. Kissed her lightly on her mouth, a soft tender kiss. She felt a wave of desire run through her. A feeling of joy overwhelmed her. He was stroking her shoulders now, and then moving his hands over her breasts.

'These are a different kind of barnacle. Never seen them on this hull before. Bra-nacles I think they're called. Very pretty, but they'll have to go.'

He lifted her again to unfasten her bra and slip it off. And then he laid her down again, and she closed her eyes and gave herself up to the sensations as he stroked and caressed her. The boat was rocking gently below them now.

'The tide is coming in,' he murmured.

He unlaced her shoes and took them off and then carefully unzipped her jeans before easing them over her legs, gently peeling off her socks and knickers. He was touching her softly over her body now, and she felt herself trembling as he lay down beside her. She turned to face him and he kissed her again. She tried to wrap her arms around him, but he moved them carefully away.

'You're to lie still for the careening.'

He was kissing her as his hand moved over her, easing her legs apart and curling around her, stroking her. She felt herself shuddering with desire for him. 'The limpets take a while,' he whispered, as he caressed her, his mouth moving over her breasts now and down, his breath warm on her skin. She gave herself up to him with a cry of ecstasy, almost agony. Her hands reached out to him, and she twisted her fingers in his hair. Wanting more of him, longing for him, wanting to feel his skin against hers, his mouth on hers, to hold him. He moved up to lie beside her again, and folded her into his arms, kissing her neck, her mouth, his skin warm against her, their bodies trembling.

'I think the hull's ready for caulking now. Shall I show you?' he said quietly.

'Mmmmm.'

'I'll need to get ready, it can be messy.'

He drew the duvet over her. And she lay and gazed at him as he took off his clothes, modestly turning away from her. He was just as she remembered, maybe a little thinner. His skin brown where it had been in the sun. There was a new scar on his back. And then she noticed a pattern of waves rippling in reflected sunlight on the cabin ceiling.

'I'm like a pool, waiting for him to enter me.'

He pulled off his jeans, and something fell out of the pocket, rolled onto the floor. It was a small grey pebble. He picked it up and placed it reverently on the shelf. 'I know that stone,' she thought. She noticed a small photograph pinned beside the bed. A picture that was ragged at the edges, had been torn into pieces but stuck together again with tape. The picture Phil had taken of her on the rock at St Michael's Mount.

He lay down beside her now, kissing and caressing her again.

'Caulking is when you fill up all the seams on the hull with oakum, and it makes the boat water tight and sea worthy. I'm out of practice, so it may not be a good job.'

And she felt him enter her gently then, heard him whispering, 'so soft, so lovely.' A rippling ran through her and then wave after wave as they clung together until she felt herself swept away with him. He was murmuring 'my love, my love.' And he gathered her into his arms then as he had always done, and he was talking softly to her. 'I've missed you so much, I've longed for you.'

She moved so that she could be closer to him, feel more of his body against hers. She kissed his neck, breathed in the scent of him, kissed his mouth. She was overwhelmed with joy, and tears rolled down her cheeks which Michael kissed away. And they lay still together, listening as the waves thumped against the boat. She felt his heart beating close to hers. And it seemed to her that their hearts were thudding together with the rhythm of the tide as it rose and fell.

They slept for a while. Michael was the first to rouse.

'Are you hungry? We should go and get some lunch.'

She couldn't speak yet. She pulled him closer, and kissed his neck, stroked his hair. And he kissed her mouth, then at last lifted her so that her feet could reach the floor. They dressed quietly.

Lamorna was ready first. She picked up the little pebble that had fallen from his pocket.

'I gave this to you.'

'You did. I've kept it always. But the words you wrote got worn away. Mum washed my jeans. She found the stone in a pocket and threw it into the garden. It took me hours to find it, and the words were gone.'

She reached into her bag and found a pen. Wrote 'I love you' around the white band that circled the stone. She held it out to him.

He took the stone and read what she had written.

'Do you mean it?'

'I will always love you. I've never stopped loving you. There has never been a single day when I haven't thought about you, wondered where you are, what you are doing.'

'It's the same for me.'

Chapter 33

After a while they went up and into the village.

'Let's buy pasties and eat them on the beach,' she said.

So they sat together, eating their pasties from paper bags, drinking lemonade from cans, and watching boats go by.

'I never imagined I'd be doing this again, I'm more used to coffee and pastries in Italian trattoria But I like this better, it's more real.'

'Why did you leave Venice, come back? Mary told me you'd found someone. You were living with him.'

'I was. He was, is, a lovely person. But he isn't you.' She took his hand in hers. 'I went over to Venice for a commission. I met Roberto. He was so kind and charming. He asked me to show my work in his gallery, and took me for dinner. He's more than twenty years older than me. His wife died some years ago. He has daughters my age. I grew fond of him, and I stayed. I was tired of all the travelling. Venice is lovely. It seemed a good idea to stay for a while. We got on well. Maybe we consoled each other. He made me feel good about myself again, after everything that had happened. Then last summer he sent me away to find you.'

'Why did he do that? I could never send you away.'

'He said he knew I was only on loan, I belonged to someone else. He heard me call your name in my sleep. He told me I needed someone young, someone who could give me children. It was hard to leave. I'd begun to grow dependent on him. He was right; it wasn't good for me really. And then I found out that my mother was dying, so I stayed and nursed her. I came down last year to bring her ashes. I was resolved to come and find you in Ireland. Then Mary told me you were living with someone and I didn't know what to do. I couldn't go back to Venice. Greg rang me about a job, so I went off again.'

'Mary rang me soon after you came down. Chris came back from sea and she told him you'd been, asked about me. He said I should know. She gave me your number and address. I rang you, but there was no answer. So I just went up there to find you. The woman next door told me you'd gone away. I thought you'd gone back to Venice.'

'Oh. I heard the phone just as I was leaving. I went back in, but I was too late. It stopped ringing.'

'If only I'd rung for longer.'

'There are too many 'if onlys' Michael.'

'I didn't know what to do then. When I got back to Ireland Aisling had left me. Packed her bags and gone. I don't blame her. She guessed it was something to do with you when I went off to England.'

'How did you meet her?'

'She sang in the band I got involved with.'

'I saw a poster for your band. I was in Dublin, working. I looked up timetables for Sligo, thinking I might come and find you, but then I didn't have the courage. I just went home.'

'When was that?'

'I can't remember exactly. It was after the Birmingham pub bombings I think. I was in Belfast for an article about it.'

'I hadn't got together with Aisling then.'

'What happened between you?'

'I was just one more bloke in the band that she got involved with. At first it seemed good, but she knew I was never really hers, that there was someone else. She found all the articles and photographs I'd saved about you. She ripped them up and burned them.'

'Sounds like something I'd do.'

'We got on at first, tried to make it work. Then I discovered that she'd slept with all the men in the band, and still was every now and again. We argued a lot. We both started drinking too much. There was a drinking culture in the band, too much Guinness and whisky flowing. It was easy to slip into the habit. I began to neglect the farm. It was a relief really when she left. We were bad for each other. She went back to the drummer, and I think they'll make a go of it. I tried to get my life back in order, stopped drinking, and worked all hours to get the farm back into shape.'

'How did you come to sell it?'

'I had a great offer. Someone wanting to develop a tourist place. Phoned Mum. By rights the farm is hers. She said 'sell it' so I did. I was pretty low. I felt I'd driven away two women in my life and I may as well give up. I decided to get a boat and go to sea. I didn't really care what happened to me. Then Mum told me about your phone call, said she thought it might be you. So I had to come, take a chance. What made you come down?'

'I found my old photography journal from 1968, and realised it was exactly ten years ago, so I just felt I wanted to come. I don't know why. It's how it was. I felt I must be here.'

'All the years we've wasted. Every day I've asked myself why I slept with her, with Rosa, why I was so stupid.'

'I remember saying to you once that I thought I was like my Dad. But I realise now that I'm far more like my mother. I never really knew her when I was a child so I'm glad I was there before she died. We talked a lot. I'm my mother's child, too jealous. I get too emotional. I have to have all or nothing. I was so jealous of Rosa.'

'But I love your passion, the way you feel about things, see things. The way you are.'

'It scared me sometimes. I really meant to throw myself in the sea that day. If you hadn't found me I would have done I'm sure.'

'You wouldn't talk to me, or look at me.'

'I know. I thought it was all my fault. I thought I didn't deserve you. I was so insecure then. And when I was a child, growing up. Mum always seemed distant. I couldn't talk to her like I could my Dad. I didn't understand what had happened in my family, what had happened to my Dad. My Mum talked to me a lot before she died. She told me she'd been depressed after I was born, and then she'd lost two babies. She felt she'd pushed me away, was never there for me. I didn't know that then, but I knew I was lonely, and I felt I was to blame for Dad's death somehow.'

'You were just a child. How could it have been your fault?'

'I know that now. She told me that she blamed me, that they'd had an argument about me the day he died. So she believed it was her fault and mine too, what happened. She said she was a bad mother, and that she knew I was insecure and unhappy, but she didn't know how to help me. I've thought about it a lot since she died. I did hate myself. I had the horrible scars. The children at school had all teased me, called me names. I felt no-one would ever want me.'

She didn't feel she could tell Michael about her father yet. That he wasn't even her real dad.

'It must have been so hard for you.'

'I met you, and everything was so wonderful, I couldn't believe that you could want to be with me. So when I came back from Greece it was terrible. It confirmed all my fears. It seemed that you'd chosen Rosa, it felt like you'd betrayed me, rejected me. You were the first person to make me feel good about myself. And then that happened. I can understand it now, but I was irrational then. I couldn't think. I just ran away. I drove myself to do well in my work. It was all I had.'

'Oh Lamorna, my love, I'm so sorry. Janet told me that you were affected by what happened in Rome too. Do you mind if I mention that?'

'No, it's okay. I went for counselling in the end. I learned that rape can make you feel ashamed, guilty and humiliated. I did feel worthless, that it was all my fault. It's taken me a long time to get over that attack, I had nightmares for ages. I needed you so much then. Finding you with Rosa was more than I could bear. But then you were so lovely when you found me again, when we started to live together. I thought it would all be okay.'

'And then I had the crazy idea we could all be together, support Rosa's baby. I'm so sorry. How could I have been so insensitive?'

'She looked so perfect when I saw you together that morning. She was lying there in your arms, her beautiful blonde hair, like an angel, a Greek Goddess, and I was scruffy from travelling, disgusting and degraded.'

'She was never an angel. I didn't tell you this at the time, but I caught crabs from her. She slept with hippies in California and picked them up. And she doesn't even know who the father of her baby is. She had sex with several guys. I realised that night with her that I'd never really loved Rosa, it was just an infatuation.'

'Why didn't you tell me?'

'I don't know. There was so much going on I suppose, and I'd got rid of the lice before you moved in with me, before I came to see you in Jude's house. Now I feel I have so much to make up for. I feel unworthy of you. You're so successful, so lovely.'

'Don't say that, you're not unworthy. I have been successful, but it's not what really matters. I'm still so unsure about myself, about whether I could begin to trust again. I think Roberto was like a father to me, a calm in the centre of my life. I didn't have to think. I was afraid of coming to find you. I still have to fight my jealousy demon, the fear of losing you.'

'How can I make you believe in me, trust me?'

'I don't know. We both have to try. I can't believe I'm here now, that this is happening. It seems like a dream.'

'It's real Lamorna, and it's made me so happy. I've longed for you, for this moment. I want to be with you so much.'

Chapter 34

They sat together quietly, holding hands, watching the world go by, not needing to talk. And then it was Michael who spoke first.

'What shall we do?'

'Do you mean right now, or the rest of our lives?'

'Just for now, but we can talk about forever if you want to.'

'Let's go swimming.'

'I never thought I'd hear you say that. There's a small cove near here, it's great.'

They walked back to the boat and Michael rummaged in a locker, pulling out a couple of towels.

'These are old, from the hotel, but they'll do. Not the luxury you're used to.'

'I don't know what you're imagining about my life, but it's never been about luxury. I've slept in all sorts of disgusting places, woken up with leeches on my arms and legs, gone days without being able to wash.'

'It always looks glamorous, exciting in your photographs.'

'It's all an illusion, come on, let's go.'

'There's a village just across the estuary, but no-one will see us from there,' he said as they walked down onto a beach.

'No coastguards with binoculars I hope.'

He laughed, 'No, not here.'

'I'm not sure I'd be bothered now, I've swum naked with tribal people, in the Amazon. They have a much more enlightened attitude to their bodies. They often took an interest in my scars. I've been given all sorts of weird stuff to put on them.'

'They're much better now.'

'Yes, swimming helps too, strengthens the muscles in my leg.'

She stripped off quickly and ran down the beach.

'Race you to the buoy,' she called.

The tide was high, and the swimming good. Lamorna was noticed by a couple of passing yachtsmen and whistled at, but she was oblivious.

'I can't believe it. You beat me, ' Michael said, laughing they towelled themselves dry.

'Lots of practice, swimming every day in Italy.' She shivered. 'I'd forgotten how cold the Atlantic is down here.'

He stepped over to her and wrapped her in his arms, using his towel to dry her hair, and then they ran back into the dunes to warm up in the sun.

'Lamorna, will you stay with me on the boat tonight?'

'Of course.' She rolled over and hugged him.

'I'll need to phone Ellen and check if we can keep the car though.'

'Let's go and find a cream tea, swimming has made me hungry.'

'I've noticed you're more curvy now, I like it.'

'It's all the food in Italy; they feed you up over there.'

They strolled hand in hand down to the harbour and found a small café with an empty table by the window. Sat watching the rest of the world go by.

'What's this,' she cried, as the tea arrived. 'Where are the splits? It's not a proper cream tea.'

'They don't bother with splits so much now, scones are quicker to make. Even Mum makes scones. The guests expect them. But she'll make some splits for you.'

Michael went to phone Ellen from a call box, and Lamorna wandered into a gift shop and bought several bunches of sand castle flags and a pirate flag.

'This is for your boat, as you're a pirate now. People need warning.'

'Thank you. What are the other flags for?'

'Castles. I thought Mary's girls would like them.'

'Ellen's fine about the car. They're all bursting to know what's happening, but I wouldn't say.'

'What is happening?'

'I'm falling madly in love with you all over again.'

'Isn't that what pirates always say when they capture women?'

'I don't think so, usually they just ravish them.'

'Oh, sounds interesting. I can't wait!'

The tide was still high and the harbour gates open for boats to come and go.

'You have to time it well to get in and out of here,' he told her. 'The gates are only open for two hours either side of the high tide. If you miss them you have to drop anchor in the channel. And there's the Doom Bar to get across. It can be tricky.'

'What's Doom Bar? It sounds like something out of Treasure Island.'

'It's just a sand bank.'

'I never did finish reading that book.'

They stepped on board and hung their towels over the boom to dry in the last of the sun, and Lamorna went below to make them more tea. They sat in the cockpit area for a while, watching holidaymakers wander by.

'What's your next voyage?'

'I was planning to take her down to St Ives, then round Land's End to the south coast. I've booked her in at Fowey for careening. I've rented a cottage there.'

'What about caulking?'

'Doesn't need it, she's clinker built, no seams between the planks, they overlap.'

'Can I come with you?'

'It won't be easy. It can be rough around Land's End.'

'I've learned how to crew. Roberto has a yacht. I've sailed with him around the Mediterranean.'

'Oh, you're probably more experienced than me.' He looked crestfallen.

'No, I only crewed. I can't read charts and do all that stuff. But I don't get sea sick.'

'I'd love you to come. Are you sure? It's not like the Med, the tides and currents are tricky.'

'I've been in some difficult situations around Greece, sudden strong winds.'

'I don't need to press gang you then.'

'No, you won't keep me off this boat now Michael.'

'Lamorna, will you stay and be with me now? I'll go wherever you want to be.'

'What about your round the world voyage?'

'It's not important now. You're what matters to me.'

'Can I come with you around the world?'

'It'll be hard.'

'If I pass the test on this trip can I come? I'll learn to read the maps and things.'

'There isn't a test.'

'I wouldn't want to be a liability.'

'You would never be that. But if you're serious you could do a short course for crew, learn some navigation in case I went overboard.'

'That doesn't sound much fun.'

'No, but it's reality. You would need to know how to manage.' He drew her into his arms and kissed her. 'You are the most amazing person.'

She nuzzled his neck, licking his skin.

'Mmmm, lovely salty taste.'

A family were just walking by. They heard a child's voice.

'Dad, why is that lady licking the man?'

'Perhaps he's spilt some ice cream. Don't stare, it's rude.'

'But he hasn't got an ice cream.'

'We'd better go below before we get arrested,' she said, laughing.

'You don't get arrested for kissing.'

'No, but you do for what we're going to do now.'

They went below and she pulled him into her arms.

'You're shaking. The swimming must have given you a chill.'

'No, it's my timbers shivering. I need some more caulking.'

Chapter 35

Later they reluctantly rose and dressed, and went ashore to find a restaurant.

'What about fish and chips?' she said.

'It's not up to your Italian standards.'

'Michael, stop it. I'm just plain old Lamorna West. I ate fish and chips in Venice. It's just called something different. I've eaten barbecued guinea pigs and cows head cooked in a pit. I love fish and chips in Padstow.'

'Sorry, it's just that your life seems to have been so exciting compared to mine. And you're not plain or old.'

'Michael, I won't tell you again. I've spent so many days stuck in airports, sitting about in dreary run down hotel rooms waiting for the rain to stop, queued for buses. It was never glamorous. It was just a job. Yes, it was sometimes exciting. But you know what, I'm longing for ordinariness, sitting with you in a garden, watching cricket even.'

'Cricket is never ordinary,' he protested.

'Come on, we're getting fish and chips in this café, and we'll have a glass of wine to liven it up.'

'I don't drink alcohol now,' he said, quietly.

'Oh, I'm sorry, I didn't think.'

'It wasn't that bad, but I just don't want to drink again.'

'Do you know what,' she said, as they finished their meal. 'The most exciting times I've had were down here with you. Everything has been a piece of cake since. And that reminds me, I've not had any saffron cake yet!'

He laughed.

'Mum's baking most days; we'll ask her to make one for you. Let's go back to the boat. We'll have to get the car back fairly early tomorrow.'

She insisted on making them coffee when they were back on board.

'I need to get to know this galley before the voyage. And I need to know all the English words. I learned to sail in Italian. You don't think women crew are bad luck?'

'No, that's just superstition.'

'I never heard anything like it in Italy.'

It was still warm, so they sat up on deck, looking at the stars and watching the passers-by. The moon was rising. She thought about Roberto, wondered if he was watching the moon too, remembering their conversation. 'I must phone him soon.'

Later they made love again, and afterwards lay wrapped in each other's arms. Lamorna felt a sudden tugging sensation. 'It's an egg. It's popping out.' She thought about it travelling down….what might happen next. She lay quietly as if waiting for something else, some other sign. But there was nothing. 'I want it to happen, to be our baby. Mine and Michael's. I'll know in a few days…if I miss my period. I won't tell him just yet…wait and see.'

Chapter 36

Michael made their breakfast in the morning and they ate up on deck again. Lamorna was thinking about babies. Wondering.

'You're quiet. What is it?'

'I was just thinking about Rosa again. Wondering what she's doing now. Wondering if she ever got back with Ced.'

'I went to see her on my way to Bristol. She's set up a sort of commune with a new man. They're living on her aunt's smallholding. She's got four children now.'

'Oh. What made you go?'

'Don't be upset, it was just a friendly visit. I knew she was happy in a relationship.'

'Sorry Michael, it's my nasty jealous mind again.'

'No, you've every right to question me.'

'Did you hear what happened to her sister Marie?'

'Yes, she went to University, she's training to be a vet. There was some bad news too. Ced never made it back from Vietnam.'

'Oh no. That's terrible. I really liked him. So many people died over there, and what for?'

'I know. It doesn't make any sense. Come on, we should get going.'

They packed everything away and walked over to the car. Crowds of tourists were already flooding into the harbour. Michael drove out of the village, and then turned left onto the main road.

'You've gone the wrong way!'

'No I haven't, wait and see.'

After a short while he parked in a small gravel area, and she knew at once where they were.

'For old time's sake,' he said.

They walked hand in hand down to the turfy patch where they had made love that first time. It looked just the same. The grass was studded with flowers still, and above them gulls wheeled, crying, and the waves groaned and splashed against the rocks below just as they had that first time.

'Do you believe in destiny, in fate?' she asked. 'It seems strange that something made me come down here to Cornwall at just the same time you were arriving. I didn't know you would be here. I thought you were in Ireland.'

'Perhaps something is trying to tell us this is the right moment.'

'The right moment for what?'

'The right moment for me to ask you to marry me.' He knelt down in front of her,

'Please will you marry me Lamorna?'

'Yes, I would love to marry you Michael.'

He kissed her, holding her face in his hands.

'Thank you.'

He pulled a small box out of his pocket, taking out a ring. It was a simple silver band, with words inscribed around it.

'This was my Grandmother's engagement ring. She wanted me to have it just before she died. I had to give her wedding ring to Ellen, although I doubt she'll need it. She says she doesn't believe in weddings. Do you mind if it's not new? I could buy you one.'

'I don't need a ring Michael, but if I'm going to have one then this is lovely. It's special because it's got family history.'

He took her hand then and slipped it onto her finger. It was a perfect fit.

'What do the words mean?'

'They're Gaelic. It means I am my beloveds and my beloved is mine.'

'That's lovely.'

'When should we marry?' he asked. 'I'd like it to be soon.'

'Can it be just a small wedding? I don't want a big fuss, not like Mary and Chris.'

'We could elope to Gretna Green.'

'No, I think that would be wrong. Your Mum would like it to be here. Let's talk about it later.'

'Shouldn't we go up to your home for it, that's the tradition?'

'Mum and Dad aren't there. Tom wouldn't be bothered, or my brothers.'

'Okay, shall we tell everyone when we get back?'

'I think we'll have to, they're bound to notice the ring. Of course we should. What will they think? I feel a bit shy.'

'They'll be so thrilled. Mum was so angry with me for what I did. She always wanted you for a daughter. Don't cry Lamorna, what is it?'

He enfolded her in his arms, and she cried on his shoulder. After a while she managed to speak.

'I'm sorry. I'm crying because I'm happy. And because I'm sad that my Mum and Dad aren't here to celebrate with me. My Mum told me I had to find you again. She thought you were special. And I love your Mum; she's been so good to me.'

'I'm sorry about your parents too. They should be here.'

'This is my Dad,' she said, opening the locket.

Michael looked at the photograph.

'I can see a little bit of you in him. He looks like a good sort of bloke. Is this his hair?'

'No, it isn't.'

'Is it your Mums then?'

'It's your hair Michael.'

'My hair? What do you mean?'

'I stole it. I cut it when I found you asleep next to me in Phil's flat. I'm sorry. I wanted a bit of you to keep forever.'

'Oh Lamorna. I'm so sorry for what I did to you. How can I make it up to you?'

'You already have, you came to find me. Michael, there's something I have to tell you. It's important. It's just that after my Mother died I found this letter. I want to tell you. I couldn't think how to. Please will you read it?'

She opened her bag and pulled out the crumpled envelope. Handed it to him.

He scanned it quickly.

'Oh Lamorna.'

'Poor Dad. To find out like that. And he died. He died that day. Michael, who is my Dad, my real father?'

'I don't know Lamorna. Don't suppose we could ever find out.'

'I suppose it would be better not to, just to try and forget. He was never part of my life. Do you still want to be with me? You don't have to marry me.'

'Lamorna. Don't say that. I want to be with you forever. None of this matters. It doesn't change the way I feel about you.'

They sat for a while longer, and then Michael took her hand and led her back up the valley.

'I'm not letting go of you,' he said.

'I won't run away, I promise. But don't let go of my hand please.'

Chapter 37

It was almost lunch time when they drew up outside the hotel and climbed out of the car.

'Don't worry. I told you, they'll be really pleased.'

He wrapped his arms around her and kissed her.

'Anyway they'll guess. I've just seen Mum looking out of the window.'

Taking her hand again he set off for the kitchen door. The very same door he had emerged from the moment she first saw him. The whole family were in the kitchen, about to sit down and eat.

'Hello,' Michael said. 'I've got something to tell you. Lamorna has agreed to marry me.' He was smiling broadly. Lamorna stood quietly beside him, squeezing his hand tightly.

'Isn't that just the most wonderful thing, I'm so pleased,' Aileen said, crossing the floor and immediately giving Lamorna a big hug. 'I didn't dare to hope.'

'It calls for a celebration. Shall I open a bottle of champagne?' Sam said, shaking Michael's hand, and then kissing Lamorna on her cheek.

'No, please, not just now, can we just have lunch?' Lamorna said.

Aileen laughed.

'That sounds like the Lamorna we know and love. Of course, come and sit down won't you. I'm just about to serve it out.'

'When will you marry, have you thought of a date?' Ellen asked. 'I hope you'll have the reception here.'

'Ellen!' Michael protested.

'Sorry, but I'd love to make it special for you.'

'We haven't really decided, but we want it to be a small occasion, nothing too big. And I think it would be perfect to hold it here,' Lamorna said.

They all sat down, and Aileen served out the meal.

'We're going to sail the boat round to Fowey together, and then while she's being refitted there'll be time to plan.'

'I want to join Michael on his round the world voyage. So maybe we'll get married before we go.'

In the afternoon they sat together under the rose arbour and made some plans for the next few weeks.

'I will have to go up to Derbyshire before we set off on the voyage. I'll need more clothes, and I'll have to sort out arrangements with Ann. I suppose I'll have to decide what to do about the cottage too. I won't need it now.'

'You could keep it. I thought it was a lovely place when I went up to find you.'

'I'm not sure why I'd keep it. We won't be living there, will we?'

'Won't we? I will go with you wherever you want to be. It's your decision.'

'No Michael, it's our decision. We will plan together. That's how it should be. But I'd like to spend a little time with you there before we set off.'

Michael scrutinised the calendar.

'I've booked the boat in for some work in Fowey, and she won't be finished too soon. We'll need a few days to sail her round from Padstow, maybe we need to plan for a week or more, no need to rush, and the weather is always a factor.'

'Do you think we could go over to St Marys and see your Aunt Ellen? I'd love to sail there.'

'It's not easy, and it all depends on the weather, but yes, let's try. Then we could come in to Newlyn for a day or two before we head off down to Fowey. Mum would like it. She worries about me sailing. She'd see that we've survived then.'

'Can we sort the wedding out now? And I promised to go and visit Mary on Saturday. We need to tell them our news, and Jude and Phil too. It's a shame Mary's not at work for the rest of the week. I can't wait to tell her.'

They pencilled in plans on the calendar, and decided that Saturday August 5th was a potential date for the wedding. It would be in the church up the hill where Mary and Chris had wed. They spoke to Ellen about a small reception afterwards in the hotel.

'We can do that day. I could book a marquee for the garden if you like.'
A menu was decided on, and Ellen said she would arrange a cake.

'No need for special decorations,' Lamorna said, 'we'll be spilling out into the garden if the weather is good.'

'What about your dress and bouquet?' Michael asked.

'I'll make a bouquet with flowers from the garden, just a small one. And you and the other men could have button holes from the garden too. I don't know about a dress. I'll have to think. And we need to decide about bridesmaids. I'd like to ask Mary and all her girls, they'd love it. Every little girl wants to be a bridesmaid.'

'I'd like Chris for best man. Let's ask them on Saturday. My grey suit I wore for their wedding probably still fits. And we'll get Phil and Jude to take some photos shall we?'

'Yes, I suppose so. It's getting bigger than I imagined all of a sudden. But we don't have to invite many people.'

'I suppose I'm thinking of Mum. She'd love it. What about Tom, will he come and give you away? What about your family?'

'I'll ask Tom and the boys, but there's no-one else. I'd like to invite my neighbour Ann, and Janet and Greg. And there's my friend Marguerite in Germany, she's been so good to me.'

'What's the matter?' he said then. 'You suddenly look worried.'

'Oh Michael, I need to tell Roberto. It's going to be so hard. I must phone him today. Will you come with me?' She reached out for his hand.

'You can phone from here.'

'No, I mean will you be with me when I ring him?'

'Of course, if that's what you want.'
Aileen called them for tea, and there was a saffron cake especially for Lamorna.

In the afternoon they went to arrange the wedding ceremony and then Michael borrowed Sam's car and drove to Porthcurno so that they could go swimming. They lay together on the warm sand to dry out in the sun. Lamorna was thinking about her previous visits to this same beach. The time she had been cut off by the tide, and Michael had come and rescued her. And then the day of the terrible accident. 'I hope it's not an unlucky place for us,' she thought. 'At least if we get cut off I could swim around that headland now.'

After dinner Lamorna and Michael went into the hotel office to make some calls. It was Klaus and Ellen's domain now, but they were busy in the dining room poring over plans for hotel extensions. Lamorna rang Tom first.

'He's happy to come for the wedding, but my brothers are away at Camp America.'
She turned a page in her diary and found Roberto's number. She dialled. Roberto answered immediately. She spoke a few words in Italian.

'Roberto, we need to speak in English now, Michael is here with me.' She squeezed Michael's hand tightly.

'You have found him.'

'Yes. He has asked me to marry him Roberto.'

'And you have agreed.'

'Yes.'

'I am so happy for you. It is right that this should happen.'

'Roberto…'

'No, you are not to say any more. I mean it. It's what I want for you. But I would like to speak with him please.'

'He wants to talk to you Michael.'
Michael looked apprehensive, but he took the phone.

'Hello, yes, thank you. Thank you for looking after Lamorna and for sending her to find me.'
There was a pause whilst he listened.

'I would never be so stupid again. Thank you, yes I will.'

He handed the phone back to her. She spoke to Roberto for a few more moments, and then there were some more words in Italian, and she was crying as she replaced the receiver. Michael took her into his arms and held her as tears rolled down her cheeks.

'I'm sorry,' she said at last, taking his handkerchief and drying her eyes. 'He said he won't come to the wedding. I asked him. But he said I mustn't buy a dress. He made me give him the address of the hotel.'

'I wouldn't come to watch you marrying someone else if I were him,' Michael said. 'I couldn't bear it.'

'What did he say to you Michael?'

'He told me I was very fortunate, and he asked me to promise never to hurt you again. He sounded like he would come over and sort me out if I ever did that.'

'That would be his Mafia connections.'
Michael looked horrified.

'I'm only joking Michael. He's the kindest person. He wants me to take you to meet him.'

'I'm not sure.'

'Michael, you'd like each other, you have so much in common, sailing, loving the sea.'

'And you.'

That set her off crying again.

They took the bus into Penzance on Friday morning and walked together unannounced through the door of the Studio. Phil was behind the counter talking on the phone. He smiled widely when he saw them.

'Well, I never thought I'd see you two walk together through that door again.'

'Where's Jude?' Lamorna asked.

'In the dark room, I'll call her.'

Two minutes later Jude bounced into the room.

'What's happening? You're together.'

'Yes, we know,' Lamorna said, smiling. 'We're going to be married. We came to tell you.'

There were lots of hugs, and Lamorna was astonished to see tears in Jude's eyes.

'I hope you'll let us take the photos,' Phil said. 'It could be our present to you.'

'That would be perfect.'

'When is it?' Jude asked. 'I hope we're free.'

'August 5th, at 3 o'clock.'

Phil consulted the dairy.

'Phew, we've got a ten o'clock wedding that morning in Penzance, but we can do it.'

'We only want a few pictures, it's a small thing,' Lamorna said.

'Let's have lunch together, you can tell us what's been going on,' Jude said.

'Okay, is that alright with you Lamorna?'

'Of course. Meet you in the coffee bar at twelve.'

'If you mean the usual one we can't, it's closed down.'

'Oh no. That place had such memories for me.'

They made alternative arrangements and then she and Michael went out into the sunshine.

'What shall we do now?' Lamorna asked.

'I thought we should go and choose a wedding ring for you.'

'We don't need to. My mother gave me hers when I was with her. She insisted I should have it for when I married you. I told her we weren't together, but she wouldn't listen.'

'I wanted to buy you a ring, do something special for you.'

'I'm sorry, do you really mind? I don't need you to do anything for me, it's enough that you want to be with me.'

'Shall we go and look at dresses for the bridesmaids then?'

'Michael! I can't believe you said that. Men aren't supposed to be interested.'

'I thought you'd like to.'

'No, I was thinking I'd come in with Mary and the girls tomorrow. You wouldn't need to be there. You could spend some time with Chris. Let's go round the harbour and have a walk on the beach.'

'Michael,' Lamorna said, as they sat on the beach together with ice creams, 'I've been thinking I'd like to find out who my real father was.'

'Are you sure? Your Dad was the one who brought you up. You loved him. Wouldn't it just cause an upset? Whoever he was he didn't want to know you.'

'I feel I ought to. I could try and find out without him knowing.'

'I don't see how.'

'We could go out looking for likely men.'

'And what would a likely man be?'

'Well Mum said he was handsome and he had dark hair.'

'That narrows it down then,' he said, laughing. 'We could talk to Mum and Dad. See if they've got any ideas. See what they think.'

'I don't know. What would they think of me? My family. They might worry I'd be like my Mum.'

'They would never think that.'

She thought for a few minutes.

'Okay. Let's ask them.'

***

Back at the hotel later that afternoon they joined Sam and Aileen for tea in the garden. Lamorna fidgeted with her spoon.

'Mum, Dad, we want to talk to you,' Michael began. 'Lamorna's Mum left her a letter. It says that her Dad was not her real father. It seems he was a man from round here that she met up with. She said not to look for him, but Lamorna wants to try. We thought you might have some ideas.'

There was a long silence. Aileen sipped her tea. Sam put his mug down at last. He wiped his face on a crumpled handkerchief.

'Thought this'd come up sooner or later. I knew your Dad Lamorna. He was a mate of mine since school. He told me years ago when you were born. Swore me to secrecy. He wanted to help with you, but your mother wouldn't let him. He only saw you for a few years when you were just a little child. Then suddenly your Mum stopped coming down in the summer. He never saw her again. He didn't know how to get in touch. In the end he decided it was for the best. I knew you were his lass when you told me your name that first day. That and your hair.'

'Can you tell me?' she whispered.

He looked at Aileen. She shrugged her shoulders.

'Don't suppose it would harm. He's been gone years now.'

'Gone?'

'Yeah. Fisherman. Drowned. His missus died a couple of years ago. There's the girls, but I reckon they'd be alright with it.'

'Who is it Sam?' Aileen asked.

'Jack. Dolly's man.'

'I can't believe you never felt you could tell me,' Aileen said.

'I promised.'

'That means Chris is my cousin,' Lamorna said quietly. 'Nora and the others are my sisters.'

'Reckon so.'

'Did Dolly ever know?'

'She never knew exactly about your mum, or you. But she knew he'd had other women. Pretty much everyone did. But he said it was different with your mum. He would have stayed with her if she'd have had him. That's what he said.'

'Is that why you gave me the job?'

'I suppose it was. Felt I should keep an eye on you, help you. For Jack's sake. He chose your name, thought it would always be a connection like.'

'What will you do Lamorna? Will you tell them? Chris, Nora,' Michael asked.

'I don't know. I need to think. I talked to Nora about her Dad. She said they always thought there'd be other children around. She wondered if she might have a brother somewhere. But she never tried to find out.'

Chapter 38

'I've been so desperate to know what's happening,' Mary said as soon as she opened the door to them next morning. 'I keep thinking I'm imagining it all. I never thought I'd see you together again.'

'Me too, I keep thinking it's all a dream and I'll wake up and things will be the same as they were,' Lamorna said, her eyes filling with tears again. 'Chris is my cousin,' she thought. 'This is my family.'

There was a sudden clamour of voices, and four young faces peered around Mary's skirt.

'Aunty Lamorna. Aunty Lamorna! Michael.'

'Come in,' Mary said. 'Move away girls, let them get in.'

They managed to get into the hallway and then both of them were besieged by children. Lifting them up they carried two girls each and followed Mary into the kitchen. Chris was there cutting bread.

'Took you long enough,' was all he said, but he was grinning from ear to ear. 'Girls, let them go. Get off and get the garden table set.'

Three girls obediently ran out through the door, but the youngest, Lamorna still clung to her namesake, twirling her fingers into her hair and gazing at her with wide brown eyes. They all helped carry the food out, and sat down around the table under an apple tree, Lamorna with the little girl on her knee.

'We've come to ask a favour,' Michael said. 'Chris, will you be my best man?'

'Oh! You are getting married,' Mary said. 'Aileen hinted a bit.'

'Yes, and we want you and the girls for bridesmaids.'

The girls all started talking at once.

'Can we, can we, oh please.'

'I don't know as you can,' Chris said. 'You make too much racket.'

There was an instant silence.

'Your Dad's only joking,' Mary said. 'But you are too noisy. Sit quietly whilst we talk.'

Lamorna found herself looking at Chris, searching for some sort of resemblance. She wanted to tell him. See what his reaction was. But she couldn't. It didn't seem the right moment.

'I've still got my wedding suit, that'll do,' Chris said.

'I've got the dress Joy made, but I can't get into it now.'

'Well I thought we could go into town this afternoon and look for dresses for you.'

'We could, but these girls are a handful,' Mary said doubtfully.

'I think they'll be very good, especially if we have ice creams afterwards.'

'We will all be very good,' Emily said.

'We will be so goodest ever,' Jenny said.

So the women and girls set off into town on the bus, and the men went down to the harbour to mess about in Chris's boat.

Mary and Lamorna found some perfect dresses, and they were July sale bargains. Mary was to wear a deep pink dress with lace bodice, and the girls loved their long dresses. They chose a small basket for little Lamorna to carry.

'We can put some flowers in it,' Mary said.

'No, teddy, put teddy in it,' she said, clutching it tightly in her hand.

'Of course. Is he a little teddy?'

'He's a horrid grubby little thing she found on the beach,' Catherine said.

'Well, we could give him a bath, and then I'd love to have him at the wedding.'

They were all invited up to the hotel for dinner in the evening. It was a special treat for the girls, who rarely ate out. Michael and Chris had been to The Ship and appeared sheepishly just in time for the meal.

'Chris, you're getting him into bad ways!' Mary scolded.

'No, it was my idea Mary. We went to talk to your uncle about an evening party for the wedding. We booked the room, and he's let us have it for free. I thought we could invite a few more friends to join us then.'

'Michael's too good to be true, 'Chris said. 'Couldn't even persuade him to have more than a half. And your cousin was there. Says he'll get the band to come and play.'

'Oh Michael, this was supposed to be a small wedding.'

'I want everyone to know how happy I am. I'm sorry, do you mind?'

'No, I don't mind.' She embarrassed him by kissing him.

The little girls all giggled, and Emily decided to kiss Michael too.

'I wanted to marry Michael,' she said.

'I'm sorry Emily, but I can't let him marry you. I'm sure you'll find someone special when you're grown up.'

'I won't. But when you get fed up you can send him to me.'

They all laughed.

Chris took the children home to put them to bed and give Mary a chance to spend some time with Lamorna. Michael had volunteered to help Sam with a cottage he'd bought. They went off to look at it and plan what work needed doing.

'Well,' Mary said, when they sat together in the garden, 'tell me all. What's been happening?'

'There's not much to tell. I came back from the job I'd been doing in South America, and I decided to finish unpacking the trunks I'd moved in with. Never got around to it before. I found my old journal, with the details of the photographs I'd taken down here that first summer. And I realised that it was exactly ten years since. I don't know why, but I just had to come down. And then my neighbour told me that a man had come to see me whilst I was away. She saw Michael's photo and said it was him. I didn't know why. I didn't dare to hope.'

'It's because I phoned him and told him you'd asked about him. I said I thought you wanted to see him.'

'Yes. But then I wasn't there. If only I hadn't gone away. I didn't want to go away again. But when you told me he had someone new, that he was living with an Irish girl I didn't think I'd ever see him again. There was nothing else.'

'I thought you seemed really upset. I didn't know what to say. I wasn't sure I should have told you.'

'You did the right thing. It would have been worse if I'd gone to Ireland and found her there. I couldn't bear that. Did you meet her?'

'No, she wasn't around when we went over.'

'Well, I rang the hotel and gave a false name. I lost courage Mary. It was such a relief when Aileen knew it was me. She made me feel so welcome. She guessed it was me when I rang. And she told Michael. The amazing thing was that he'd just arrived in Padstow, and he rang her a few minutes after I did. So he came over. And you know the rest. I went to see his boat. And then he asked me to marry him.'

'I'm so happy for you. I'd given up on you both.'

'I know. I was such a fool. I convinced myself he wouldn't want me. I made myself work all the time.'

'You've done so well.'

'I know. I can't say I'm sorry, because I loved my work. But I could have found a way to be with Michael too.'

'What was it like when you were first together again? It seemed a bit strange when you were in the kitchen that morning. None of you would tell me a thing.'

'I know Mary. I think we were both scared, afraid that it wouldn't work out. I was thinking 'what if he doesn't care about me anymore?' I didn't dare to assume anything. We were both being so polite and distant. At least until we got on the boat. And then, well, it was alright.'

'What will you do after the wedding?'

'We're thinking of sailing around the world. That was Michael's plan. But it depends....'

'Depends on what?'

'Oh, all sorts of things.'

'Are you pregnant Lamorna?'

'Why do you say that?'

'You are aren't you? I could tell. There's something about you.'

'Mary, I might be. I don't know for sure. I haven't told anyone yet. Not even Michael. It's only a few days. But I just knew I was straight away. I want it to happen so much. Please don't say anything, not even to Chris.'

'Of course I won't. I hope you come and live down here. Will you?'

'I don't know yet. It depends on Michael. He might want to farm again. We haven't got that far with planning. But I'd love to.'

'What are you two talking about with such serious faces?'
Michael appeared beside them, mug of coffee in hand.

'Oh you know, weddings,' Mary said. 'I'd best be off, see if the girls have all settled. 'I'm so glad for you both Michael.'
She stood up and kissed him on the cheek.

'Ooooh, tickly beard.'

'I'm going to shave it all off.'

'Don't, what's the point if we're going sailing?' Lamorna said.

'Suppose so. See you Mary. We should be back here before the wedding at the beginning of August, we'll see you then.'

'Aren't you bringing your boat round here?'

'Yes, but only for a couple of days.'

Michael sat down and wrapped his arms around Lamorna.

'I was missing you.'

She laughed. 'It's only been an hour.'

'Did you say anything to Mary about your father?'

'No. I need more time to think.'

'Dad's been grilling me about how I'm going to keep you!'

'Oh, what did you say?'

'I said I'd keep you locked up in a trunk.'

'Michael!'

'Only joking. But he's got a point. I don't have a job. I think he was worried that I'd want the hotel to support us too, so I reassured him that we weren't planning that. I said I'd got savings, and I would look for something.'

'I've got savings too, and a house to sell.'

'That's yours. I want to be responsible for you now.'

'No Michael. I told you long ago that I wanted to be independent, that I didn't want to be beholden to you. Whatever I have is yours too. And I can look for work as well.'

'You said you were tired of travelling.'

'I don't want to travel. I could get some free-lance work down here. Maybe I could work for Phil and Jude! And I thought you'd want to find a farm again.'

'Would you want that?'

She thought for a moment.

'Yes. It would be great. I'd want it to be down here, near the village. We could get some ducks.'

'And you could have your donkey. We'll look around and see what's available after the wedding. I was thinking just a small place, a smallholding, a few chickens to start with. We could supply hotels with fresh stuff. Something like the place Rosa has would be ideal. She offered for me to come and join them, said my knowledge would be useful. But I couldn't do that.'

'I don't think I'd want that Michael.'

'I know. But shall we call in on our way north? I know she'd love to see you.'

There was a long silence.

'Lamorna? What do you think?'

'I don't know. I'm not sure if I could go and see her. I'm not brave enough.'

'Lamorna, you are just about the bravest person I know. And Rosa would want to make her peace with you. She feels terrible about what happened.'

'Alright, I'll think about it.'

Chapter 39

They were up early next morning, eager to set sail and be alone together. Sam offered to drive them to Padstow so that he could have a look at the boat, and Aileen came to see them off, bringing a huge box of provisions for their trip. Soon they were slipping out of the harbour and into the mouth of the Camel.

'I thought we could sail to St Ives today. If the weather's good we could make it over to Scilly from there.'

'That will give me chance to find my way around and learn how to sail her.'

The entire trip went well, and they were fortunate in having good weather, especially on the crossing to Scilly. Lamorna had a great surprise in store for her. Michael phoned ahead, and they were met at the quay in Hugh Town, St Marys by Aunt Ellen and none other than Doctor Davy who had looked after them following their accident all those years ago.

'When I heard that Ellen was here running a Bed and Breakfast place I decided to book for a long weekend,' Douglas told Lamorna.

'And then he kept coming over, and we got married in 1972.'

They were delighted to accept an invitation to the latest wedding.

Lamorna and Michael stayed a couple of nights before setting sail again ahead of a change in the weather. They put into the harbour at Newlyn, taking the opportunity to get some washing done at the hotel and spend a bit more time with Aileen and Sam. They slept in Michael's old room again.

'A parcel has come for you Lamorna,' Aileen said next morning.

It was a large parcel, postmarked Venice. Heart in mouth she opened it. A beautiful dress emerged from layers of tissue paper, a silk wedding gown in cream, with delicate lace and embroidery. There was a headdress and veil too.

'Oh,' Lamorna said. 'It's from Roberto. There's a letter.'

My dear Lamorna and Michael,

I hope you will accept this gift from me. This is the dress worn by Isabella for our marriage. I am sure that it will be a good fit for you Lamorna, and I am equally sure that it will suit you very well. I have no doubt that you will look beautiful, and I am sorry that I cannot be there to see you marry. I will understand if you would prefer to have your own new dress, and in that case hope you will forgive me for this intrusion. If you choose to wear this dress then I may hope that it will bless your marriage and bring you the happiness that Isabella and I enjoyed. Chiara and Francesca share with me in sending our love and best wishes to you both. I remind you that you would be most welcome to come and stay here on your voyage.

Roberto

'Oh Michael, it was Isabella's dress, his wife. He wants me to have it. Read the letter.'

Lamorna was sorting out the brown paper.

'There's something for you Michael.'

She handed him a small package. He opened it, and held up two silk ties. There was a note telling him that they were for him and the best man to wear on the day.

'That's really kind of him, they're great. Are you going to try the dress on?'

'Yes, but I can't let you see. Aileen, will you come with me?'

The two women went upstairs to Aileen's room, and Lamorna slipped into the dress. It was a perfect fit. It was full length, slim and figure hugging.

'You look really beautiful Lamorna,' Aileen said with a catch in her voice.

'Not as lovely as Isabella, I saw a photograph of her. She was gorgeous.'

'He seems like a kind fella, this Roberto. How did you meet him?'

'He saw me taking photos at the Biennale. He asked if I would exhibit them in his gallery. We just got talking, and then he invited me to go sailing with him. He really is the kindest person. I did grow very fond of him Aileen. But I couldn't forget Michael.'

'I'm glad it's working out for you. You've made him so happy.'

Lamorna twirled in front of the mirror.

'I love it. It feels so wonderful. And it's so long, it covers my scars.'

'Lamorna, you worry too much about them.'

'I know, but I don't want them to show on my special day. You were right though Aileen, when you told me I would meet someone who accepted me how I am. We didn't know then it would be Michael.'

'I hoped it might be. I had an inkling he was falling for you because he was suddenly behaving oddly and trying to avoid you.'

'It seems so long ago. So much wasted time. I never thought this day would happen Aileen, I'm so happy.'

'Well you know that Sam and I are happy for you too.'

'Even though you know about my father, what happened?'

'Of course. It really doesn't matter.'

'Thank you Aileen. I was worried you'd think…I don't know. Think badly of my family.'

'What happened is not of your making.'

'I know that's true. But I worry that people will think I'll turn out like her. I know I won't. I will never betray Michael.'

'You know,' Aileen said then. 'It may have been the best thing for you to go off into the world and do what you did, build your career. You were so young, so inexperienced when you and Michael first met. Now you have grown up into a successful, self-assured young woman, more certain of what you want.'

'Yes. I think you're right. I loved my work. I'm proud of what I achieved. I had to prove I could. But it would have been unbearable if I'd never had this chance of happiness with Michael. I can't believe how lucky I am.'

'Perhaps. But if Michael had been spoken for you would have reconciled yourself and met someone eventually, put it all behind you. Maybe you would have gone back to Venice.'

'I don't know. It's hard to imagine. I don't even want to think about it.'

Lamorna smiled, looked at herself in the mirror again.

'Another great thing, I can just wear comfy flat shoes underneath the dress.'

'Oh Lamorna, you should treat yourself to some new shoes, at least some underwear.'

'I don't need them Aileen, I'm happy with what I've got. I bought new underwear in Italy that I've never worn. I just need something blue to follow the rhyme.'

'Well, you could have blue flowers from the garden; there are larkspur and delphinium that are in the shadier area of the garden that may still be in flower. The dress is something old.'

'No, it's something new, because it's new to me. I was going to wear my mother's locket for the old thing.'

'Then what could I lend you? You need something borrowed.'
She rummaged in a drawer.

'Here you are. It's a garter I wore for my wedding. It was made for me by my grandmother in Ireland.'

'Thank you, it's perfect. I'd better get out of this dress now. Will it be alright to leave it in your room Aileen? I want it to be a bit of a surprise for Michael.'

'Yes, you could get ready in here on the day. Shall I reserve you a room in the hotel for the night before?'

'Oh no, I'll sleep with Michael. We talked about that after Mary's wedding.'

'It might help you to sleep if you had your own room.'

'I won't sleep anyway, I'll be so excited.'
Aileen hung the dress up in her wardrobe.

'I expect Roberto would like to know if the dress arrived safely.'

'Yes, you're right. May I phone him now?'

'Of course, you don't need to ask.'

'Thank you Aileen. You're the best mother in the world.' She gave her a big hug, and they went together downstairs.

'What did it look like Mum?' Michael asked.

'That would be telling. Lamorna is going to phone Roberto now, perhaps you could thank him for the ties?'

Chapter 40

On Sunday they set sail again, spending Michael's birthday in Falmouth. By the 21st they were in Fowey, unloading the boat and stowing everything in the cottage Michael had rented. Lamorna had never been here before, so after he'd been up to the boatyard and discussed the work to be done they set off to explore the town. It was bigger than she'd imagined. A long sprawling street with little alleyways and lanes leading upwards, and glimpses of the river between the buildings jostled together along the shore. They made a simple meal together that evening to use up supplies, and talked about the plan for the next week.

'Have you made up your mind about calling in on Rosa?'

'I hadn't thought any more about it to be honest, but I will. She was my friend, and I'm a different person now, I'm not hysterical anymore.'

'You were never hysterical.'

'You accused me of it once Michael.'

'I'm sorry. I was wrong to say that. I was wrong about everything then. Will you forgive me?'

'I forgave you a long time ago. When I knew why I behaved like that. The counselling helped. I didn't tell you that I talked to the counsellor about my childhood too. It helped me to understand why I was such a difficult child, why I always thought about running away. I know now that running away doesn't solve anything. I ran away from the situation with Gary, I ran away from you. I had a little case packed to run away from home when my Mum married again. I won't be running now. I'll talk to Rosa.'

'I'm glad you ran away from Gary. I would never have met you if you hadn't. You wouldn't have come down to Cornwall that summer.'

'I'm glad too. But it would have been better if I'd stayed and faced it out. She shuddered.

'What's wrong?'

'I had a sudden thought that I might have married him. I couldn't bear it. I wonder where he is now.'

'I would rather not know. The way he treated you. And that goes for Paul too.'

'I seem to have attracted the wrong sort, before I met you. Did Rosa ever hear from Paul again?'

'She never mentioned it. Don't suppose so. We'll go up to Rosa's place tomorrow. I think we'll go into St Austell to hire a car. We should be with them by lunch time. We could stay a night.'

'No, I don't want to do that. Let's go up to see Janet and Greg, stay with them. I need to tell them what's happened. I didn't tell you this, but they came over to Venice and stayed with us for New Year. Greg was sorting out an exhibition of my photographs with Roberto. Janet told me that I had to come and find you that summer. She dragged it out of me that I couldn't stop thinking about you. She was right. It was something I had to do. But I put it off. I was scared to find out that you were happily married. Not knowing was a kind of comfort blanket. It meant I didn't commit myself to anyone, just in case you were still there.'

'It was the same for me. After Rosa's baby was born I thought of calling you, but I couldn't. It was easier to just keep hoping you'd come back to me someday. Everyone told me I should go and see you. But I'd written that letter, I convinced myself it was all up to you. I didn't want to hear that you didn't want me anymore. I thought you were wanting to be independent, what with your success. That's how I felt when I came to see you in the hotel. I couldn't believe that you would want to speak to me.'

'Is that why you were so quiet?'

'Yes. Even after Mum told me you were in the garden and you wanted to see me. I thought maybe you were going to tell me you were heading back to Italy. That you despised me for what I did.'

'I was worried that there would be nothing there anymore, that we wouldn't love each other. Even worse I thought you wouldn't love me, and I would still be in love with you. Your Mum asked me not to hurt you. She said you'd been having a bad time.'

'She shouldn't have said that.'

'She did apologise. But Michael, I can understand her, she loves you, she wants you to be happy.'

'You wouldn't have thought that if you'd heard her after we split up. She was so angry with me. I thought she didn't care about me at all. I didn't go home for a whole term after that Christmas. Couldn't face her. Couldn't face everyone, Mary, Chris, Phil, asking me about you.'

'If I was me now I would stay and be with you, I wouldn't run away. I'd fight the Rosa's of the world for you.'

'You won't have to. There won't be anyone else ever again.'

In the morning they caught the bus to St Austell to pick up a hire car. They reached Rosa's place just before noon. Lamorna leaned back in the seat. Michael came round and opened her door. He took her hand.

'Come on,' he said softly, 'you'll be fine.'

She clambered out, and he folded her in his arms and kissed her.

They walked hand in hand up the stone flagged pathway. She could hear the sound of children playing and laughing. The door was wide open, so they bobbed their heads under the blowsy yellow roses that hung over the porch roof and stepped inside. Michael called,

'Hello, anyone at home?'

And suddenly Rosa was there, looking just the same as ever, dressed in an ankle length mirror work batik skirt and short sleeved blouse. Her long hair was tied back, and rows of beads spilled over her top and floury apron. A small child with brown skin, shining black hair and big brown eyes was clinging onto her skirt.

'How lovely to see you both. I'm glad you've come Lamorna.'

She bent down to lift the child into her arms.

'This is Sireena, she's my baby. You won't recognise Dylan, he's so grown up.'

'She's lovely, how old is she?' Lamorna asked.

'Just three, she's very shy.'

Sireena clung around Rosa's neck, but she stared interestedly, and Lamorna smiled at her. Rosa led them down the hallway into a bright kitchen. The big square room was full of the smells of baking and food being cooked. It reminded Lamorna very much of the kitchen at the commune house as it had been in 1968. There was a cork board covered with children's drawings and paintings, a rack of herbs hung from the ceiling to dry and a huge table filled the centre of the room.

She heard a rumbling sound, and noticed a basket of kittens by the range. Sireena wriggled out of Rosa's arms, and trotted over to the basket. Picking up a tabby kitten, and holding it dangling from its tummy, she thrust it towards Lamorna. She released her hand from Michael's and stooped down to take the little cat.

'It's lovely. Is this one your favourite?'

Sireena nodded and stepped closer to lean against Lamorna, reaching up to touch her hair. Then she grasped the locket around her neck and tugged. Lamorna lifted it over her head and gave it to her. She watched as Sireena handled it, turning it over in her hands, and then trying to prise it open.

'Be warned, she'll want to keep it,' Rosa said.

But the child looked solemnly up at Lamorna and handed her the necklace. Lamorna opened it for her. Sireena looked, and then turned to Michael.

'It's not a picture of Michael, it's my Daddy.'

Sireena picked up the kitten and returned it to the basket, causing all the kittens to meow together. A cat appeared and jumped in to suckle them. There was a sudden thud as a ball flew through the open window and hit the wall, startling them all.

'Ranjit's playing cricket with the others, 'Rosa said.

A tall boy holding a bat appeared in the doorway, an apprehensive look on his face.

'It's okay Dylan, no damage done,' Michael said, tossing the ball to him.

'Michael! Come and play.'

'Games over. I need Michael to help me,' someone called from outside.

They all followed Dylan into the garden. A tall man strode over to greet them, holding out his hand and smiling.

'Ranjit, this is Lamorna,' Rosa said, 'you've heard me mention her. Lamorna, meet Nina, and this is Ced.'

Nina was dark like her father and Sireena, and she ran to Michael and tugged at him until he picked her up. Ced was much darker, with tight black curls. Lamorna felt a sticky little hand in hers, and saw Sireena looking up at her. There were lots of warm greetings. A reluctant and sulking Dylan was persuaded to join them.

'You've grown so much Dylan,' Lamorna said.

'I don't remember you.'

'No, I only knew you for a short time.'

'Did you know my Dad?'

Lamorna looked at Rosa, who nodded, and then went off into the kitchen.

'Yes, I did meet him. In Cornwall when you were just a baby.'

He seemed satisfied.

'Michael, are you playing with us?'

'Yes, I'll play when we've done what Ranjit needs to do.'

'I want everyone sitting down for a drink before we do anything,' Rosa said, coming out of the kitchen with a large jug full of home-made lemonade.

They sat around a big table under the trees.

'Did you live with Rosa for long?' Ranjit asked.

'No, just a few weeks that summer. I was suddenly homeless and Rosa and her friends rescued me. This is a lovely place you have here. Is it the farm Marie was so reluctant to be sent to?'

'Yes, it was my Aunt's. The place was fine. It's just that my aunt is formidable. She would have made Marie work hard.'

'What happened to your aunt?'

'She married again and went to live in Denmark. She just decided to give me the place.'

'That's amazing. Michael told me that Marie is studying to be a vet.'
The children wandered off to play, all except Sireena, who had clambered onto Lamorna's knee.

'Will you come and take a look at the meadow with me Michael?' Ranjit asked. 'I need advice on where to build the chicken run. Come on kids, come with us. Let's leave the women to chat.'

'Then can we play cricket?' Dylan asked.

'After lunch.'

'I was winning,' he told Michael.
The children obediently followed, except Sireena.

'Come on, Michael said to her, I'll carry you.'
She reached up her arms to him and he lifted her up and strode off with her, after kissing Lamorna on her cheek. Nina ran to him, wanting to be carried too, but had to make do with holding his hand.

'He's so popular with them all,' Rosa said. 'They don't take to everyone like that. He stayed with us for a few days on the way to pick up a boat in Bristol.'

'Yes, he told me.'

'And Sireena has decided she likes you too.'

'Maybe it's because we like them,' Lamorna said. 'They are all lovely.'

'Thank you, I think so too, but I'm biased. Let's go to the orchard, we've made swings.'

Lamorna followed her into the trees. There was a huge old ash tree on the far side of the orchard, and two rope swings with wooden plank seats hung from a branch. They each took one and swung side by side for a while. Lamorna felt the cool swoosh of the breeze as her swing swept forwards, and then a calm as she slipped back again. Rosa was the first to speak.

'I'm glad you came. You're looking so happy. You've done well Lamorna. I've seen lots of your photographs.'

'I suppose I've done well in my work. It's just my personal life that was a mess.'

'I'm sorry. I didn't help did I?'

'No, you didn't help. But I don't suppose you thought I would turn up like that out of the blue and find you both.'

'No, Michael said you were away with Jude. I wouldn't have hurt you for the world. It's just that I'd come back from The States. Ced was sent to Vietnam. I was so upset. I'd been to my aunts. Left Dylan with her. I knew Michael was at the college. It's not far. So I went to see him. I didn't mean anything to happen. We both got a bit drunk.'

'I managed to cope with that, but I couldn't bear to think you were having a baby. I don't suppose you know what happened to me before I turned up and found you both.'

'No, he's never said.'

She swung backwards and forwards for a few moments before she spoke again.

'I missed Michael, so I left Jude and hitch hiked back to England. I managed to get raped in a bathroom in Rome. So you see I was in a pretty bad state when I turned up that morning.'

'God, Lamorna, I'm so sorry. It must have been awful.'

'It was. I needed Michael so much. And then you were there with him. I wanted to die. I know now that the rape had a really bad effect on me, on the way I behaved over the whole thing. The way I walked out on Michael. I decided I wasn't good enough for him, that I couldn't compete with you. Even after I heard the baby wasn't his, I couldn't go and find him again.'

'But you've found him again now.'

'Yes, I can't believe it.'

'You are lucky to have him. When I found out I was pregnant I wanted the baby to be Michael's. I knew he'd be a good father. I wished I'd known it that summer of 68. I wished I hadn't pushed him away then. He was there for me when Ced was born, and he stayed around to help with Dylan for a few days. He didn't have to. It was obvious then that the baby, Ced, wasn't his. I really believed he was Michael's. I hope you'll understand. I felt so lost and alone. I wanted him to stay, but he had his farm. He made it clear to me that he cared about me, but he didn't love me. Didn't want to be with me.'

'I am lucky that I've found him again. We're going to be married Rosa.'

'I saw you had a ring. Why do you need to marry?'

'I don't need to. No, maybe I do. Michael asked me, and I said yes.'

'Perhaps Michael needs the security of marriage too.'

'I don't know. What about you? And Ranjit? You've got children now. This is not a hippy commune is it? What makes it different from marriage?'

'We won't get married. I'm still a hippy at heart. I'm not interested in other men now, but I don't want to go through all that ritual, all that stuff about owning and obeying.'

'It doesn't have to be like that. You don't have to promise to honour and obey.'

'I suppose so, but I still think there are men who want to believe in those words.'

'Michael is not one of them. He respects my independence. He knows that I have a career I can return to.'

'You're completely free and independent I suppose, whereas I have no way of earning money if you look at it like that. I need Ranjit, or someone like him to help me. And children have a way of tying you down too. But I don't want to conform to society's arbitrary rules, to be approved.'

'I think of it more as a celebration that everyone can share with us.'

'Will you keep your own name?'

'I don't think so; after all it's just another man's name, my Dad's, and his father's before that. They're all men's names. My mother's maiden name was her father's name, and so it goes back and back. A name means nothing to me. I'm going to be Mrs Tremayne instead of plain old West. I wouldn't change my name if I married someone called Bottom though.'
They laughed and swung together quietly for a while.

'How did you meet Ranjit?'
'At a festival. He was a roadie for one of the bands.'
'He seems really nice.'
'He is. I'm so lucky. Will you forgive me Lamorna? For what happened? For wanting Michael?'
'Yes, of course I will. I couldn't blame you for wanting him, anyone would. I was just as much to blame in my screwed up way, so possessive and jealous. I didn't deserve him because I didn't believe in him. Trust him. I'd like us to be friends again.'
'I'm glad, thank you.'
'I've learned a lot since then. I made some new friends, and we set up a women's centre and refuge in Birmingham. That's how I came to get counselling help. We're going to see Janet, one of the women tonight.'
'I feel we ought to be doing something good for people here on the farm. I don't know what, but we could help, there's so much space here, and we've got a little cottage too. It must seem very selfish to you, having all of this just for ourselves.'
'I wasn't thinking that, but you could help. You could provide holidays for people from the city, people who can't afford it. You could offer them to the women we help at the refuge and their kids.'
'That would be great, but we couldn't afford to feed them.'
'You could get grants. The Women's Group could help with that. Shall I talk to Janet? They could come down and see you. I used to give money to the group when I was working. I'll have to stop now because I've got no income, but I've got a cottage to sell, I could use some of that money to help here.'
'Would you do that Lamorna, for us?'
'It's not really for you. It's for those women, women who've been abused, victims of domestic violence. And for their children too. Let's make it happen.'
'It would be brilliant. Ranjit could do yoga with them. I could do massage. Would they be okay with a man around, after what they've been through?'
'I think so. We have male trustees now and they help at the advice centre sometimes. I'll talk to Janet tonight.'
'Shall we go and find the family and get lunch organised?'

They worked together in the kitchen to prepare the lunch. It only needed serving out, a salad making. Rosa had been busy all morning.
'Do you do all the cooking?'
'No, Ranjit makes great curries. We take turns. Dylan and Nina are getting interested too. We try to involve the kids in everything. Nina wants to be in charge of the chickens. I think it's because Michael told her he used to keep them. She hopes he might stay and help her.'

The others reappeared and went to wash their hands at the outside tap. Lamorna noticed that Nina was hanging on to Michael's shirt and when they sat down to eat she wriggled her way between them so that she could be next to him.

'Nina,' Rosa said, 'come and sit with me.'

'It's okay, let her stay,' Lamorna said.

Sireena was back at Lamorna's side too, pushing her hand into hers.

'Lamorna has come up with an amazing plan,' Rosa said, and proceeded to tell them what they'd discussed. Ranjit was just as excited.

'It'll be good for the kids too, meeting new people. We're a bit isolated here,' he said.

There was time for a quick game of cricket after lunch, and everyone joined in.

'I'm glad Dylan's found himself through sport,' Rosa said as they waited for their turn to bat. 'I worry about him. Sometimes I see Paul in him, an insecurity, and uncertainty. It's hard for him because he never really knew Paul, and then he grew fond of Ced, and lost him. It took him a while to warm to Ranjit, and he was jealous of the other children, but I think he's over that now. Ranjit works hard with him. The enthusiasm for cricket helps.'

Lamorna surprised herself by hitting a six. Dylan made the best score and was really pleased with himself. At the end of the match there was more lemonade, and they sat together on rugs under the trees to drink it.

'I keep wondering if all the commune stuff is still stored somewhere at Heather's parent's place. Laura told me that's where it went when we saw her in Spain.'

'Must be,' Lamorna said. 'I'll find out for you when we're in Cornwall again. Are you thinking you could have it all here?'

'Yeah, I don't think Laura and Jean will mind. I'd love the paintings and stuff like cushions and throws.'

'It doesn't seem as if they're coming back home in a hurry.'

'No, they've got a great place down there. Ced and I spent a couple of weeks with them. They're way out in the countryside. They keep goats and chickens, and they've got vines and olive trees. What are your plans?'

'We're going on a 'round the world' voyage. Then we'll find somewhere to live, we're not sure yet. Maybe a little farm. A smallholding.'

'Come here, come here, this is a little farm,' Nina shouted.

'That's really kind, and we'll come and see you again. But I think maybe we will want to be in Cornwall. I hope you'll come and stay with us when we find somewhere.'

'Can I come? Can I come on my own?' Nina asked.

'Of course,' Michael said, and she almost seemed to burst with happiness.

They eventually managed to tear themselves away with promises of a return visit very soon.

'I'll drive now, shall I? I can find Janet's place.'

So Michael climbed into the passenger seat and they set off back down the bumpy track.

'How did it feel?'

'I'm glad we came. I had a good talk with Rosa. I really like her. I'm happy we can be friends again.'

Chapter 41

It was Michael's turn to feel apprehensive when they pulled up outside Janet and Greg's home a few minutes away from the house Lamorna had shared with her.

'I'm feeling a bit odd,' he said. 'They spent New Year with you and Roberto. And they know about what happened, the thing with Rosa.'

'Michael, don't be silly. Janet knew I was never intending to stay in Venice. She was the one who made me promise to come looking for you remember.'

'You're right, I'm being stupid. Let's go.'

Janet opened the door to them,

'Lamorna, it's great to see you. She hugged her friend and then turned to Michael. 'Hello Michael, it's good to meet you again too. I can't tell you how happy I am to see you both. Come in. Greg's cooking.'

'Hi Greg. This is Michael.'

Greg wiped his hands on a tea towel, gave Lamorna a swift hug and shook hands with Michael.

'So you're the one who's stolen my best photographer away. Pleased to meet you.'

'I've heard a lot about you,' Michael said. 'Can I help?'

'Let's leave these two to get acquainted. Come and talk to me.' She led Lamorna into the spacious lounge. The French doors were open onto the garden, and they wandered through after pouring themselves glasses of wine.

'We'll sit here,' she said, plonking herself down on a hammock seat. 'Now, tell please. All you said on the phone was you were bringing Michael. I want to know what's going on! And you're wearing a ring.'

'Oh Janet, I can't believe how wonderful everything is. There's so much to tell you.'

Half an hour later, every detail shared and discussed, they were summoned to eat. A table had been set in a light and airy conservatory. Greg served, and they began the meal.

'Michael's been telling me you're planning a sea voyage Lamorna.'

'Yes, we're heading off after the wedding. Will you both come? We're getting married on August fifth.'

'I hope you can make it,' Michael added. 'I have a debt to repay to you Janet for convincing Lamorna she had to come and find me. And for your kindness that February back in 1971.'

'You don't owe me a thing, that's what friends are for.'

'If you get some good photos of the trip I could try and sell them for you Lamorna.'

She laughed.

'I'm not sure about that. It will be our honeymoon Greg.'

The evening went well, and there was a good discussion about Lamorna's idea for refuge holidays at Rosa's smallholding. That was the only awkward moment, when Lamorna mentioned Rosa, and Janet couldn't hide her look of concern.

'We've just come from there,' Lamorna told her. 'I've made peace with her, and I'd like to see us develop the work with them, it would be so good for the families.'

'It's a fabulous idea. We were just saying the other day that these women and kids never get a holiday. I'll bring it up at the next meeting in September. Pity you can't be here though.'

Michael and Lamorna were staying the night, and later they lay snuggled together in a huge four poster bed at the top of the house.

'They're really nice people aren't they?' Michael said. 'I liked Greg. Did you know we're only a few minutes from the Edgbaston Cricket ground?'
Lamorna hit him with her pillow.

'Cricket! Is that all you men can talk about?'

'No. Actually we talked about you. Greg told me about your first job up here. He said he really fancied you, but you told him there was someone else.'

'There was, it was you. What else did he say?'

'He said what a brilliant photographer you are, and he talked about your loyalty, how you never let him down.'

She thought for a while. Remembered that first real job. How kind Greg had been to her.

'Lamorna.'

'What?'

'We could go and see Derbyshire play Hampshire at Derby on July 26th. I was looking at Greg's fixture's list. You said you'd like to.'

'Yes, I said I wanted to do 'ordinary' things. But there's one condition.'

'What's that?'

'You have to make mad passionate love to me now.'

Chapter 42

'I want to finish looking through the things my Mum left me. Will you help me Michael?

He carried the trunk through into the little sun room she'd had built. From the windows there was a glorious view across the dale. They worked together sorting through photographs.

'You look very cute in your little plaits. Is this your Dad?'

It was a photograph of a man with a fishing rod, on the deck of a boat in what looked like Newlyn Harbour.

'Yes. I'd forgotten he used to go fishing when we came down. Always went for a day trip. Once he went shark fishing at Looe. I remember watching when they came back in with all the dead sharks hanging. It was really horrible.'

'What did you and your Mum do when he was off at sea?'

'I can't really remember. We used to stay on a farm near Lamorna at first. Someone from the farm gave him a lift I think. Mum and I used to stay at home. I remember I didn't like those days. It was always in the middle of the holiday, and Mum used to make me go for a sleep in the afternoon. She said it was good for me.'

'How do you feel now, about Jack being your real father?'

'I've been thinking about it a lot. I feel better now I know he did care about me, want to help. And I'm pleased that he chose my name too. It shows he wanted some connection. It's hard to think of him as my Dad though. I never even met him.'

'Will you tell everyone?'

'I think I'd like to tell Chris and Mary after the wedding. See what they think. I hope Nora and her sisters won't mind too much.'

'Sounds like a good plan.'

'I like the idea of having Cornish blood. Must be why I love it down there so much. There are some photos of me there on holiday. This is a picture of me on the beach at Mousehole. I'm making a sandcastle. Look at my little metal bucket. I loved Muffin the Mule. You can just see his head on this side.'

She passed it over to Michael.

'Lamorna, that's me and Chris in the background. We're messing about in his Dad's dinghy.'

She took the picture and looked closely at it.

'That's amazing! Just a few feet away. I probably never even noticed you.'

'Same here, we never took any notice of emmets and little kids. Let's get it blown up and framed. Our first time together!'

Lamorna started looking through the letters next, opening some and reading them.

'This one's funny,' she said, handing it to Michael. 'I read it before. Mum wrote it from hospital when I was born.'

Michael read the letter. Laughed.

'You could never have looked ugly.'
Lamorna put down the papers she was holding, and took his hands in hers.

'Michael. I've got something to tell you. I think I'm pregnant. I'm sure I am. We're going to have a baby.'

'Oh Lamorna. That's wonderful.'

'We might not be able to go on that voyage just yet.'

'I don't need to,' he said, gathering her into his arms. 'You are all the world to me.'

Thank you for reading 'Lamorna.' If you have enjoyed it please submit a review so that I can sell more copies for charity. Check out my facebook page for updates on charity giving.

https://www.facebook.co/susannalambertauthor

or contact me at;

susannalambert22@gmail.com

Printed in Great Britain
by Amazon